LEGEND *of the* WHITE WOLF

TERRY SPEAR

sourcebooks
casablanca

Published by Sourcebooks Casablanca, an imprint of Sourcebooks, Inc.
P.O. Box 4410, Naperville, Illinois 60567-4410
(630) 961-3900
FAX: (630) 961-2168
www.sourcebooks.com

Printed and bound in the United States of America
QW 10 9 8 7 6 5 4 3 2 1

I dedicate *Legend of the White Wolf* to my mother, who lost the fight with breast cancer, and to all those who have gone before her or who are facing the same insidious disease. I wish you all my love, Mom, for always being there when I needed you, who even to the end listened to my revisions and offered suggestions. You will be in my heart and memories always.

Prologue

THE BLACK BEAR WAS RUNNING AWAY A HELL OF A LOT FASTER than Owen Nottingham and his P.I. partner David Davis thought capable. Their hunting guide, Trevor Hodges, yelled at them to keep up, but at the rate the bear was going, Owen and David would never last. Already Owen had shin splints, and his side was aching something fierce. Damn, here he thought he was in good shape.

They couldn't use dogs on the bear this late in the year in Maine, but the owner of Back Country Tours, Kintail Silverman, got around that by sending his pet wolves on the hunt. The sleek white-furred creatures made Owen feel like he was part of a wolf pack, hunting for survival, diving around snow-laden firs, blending in, exhilarated, hunting together as a cooperative team. The experience would have been more pleasurable if his other partners were with them—Cameron MacPherson, who wouldn't hunt for anything other than criminals, and Gavin Summerfield, who'd rather stay in Seattle and work than fly anywhere. But the four of them were like a wolf pack, solving crimes together as a collective unit and socializing as the best of friends throughout the good times and bad.

So Owen wished they could share hunting excursions together, too.

He noticed then that there were only snowy woods in front of them. The wolves and the bear were lost in the forest ahead as the chilly wind howled through the trees. Trevor was still keeping a good pace in the distance. For a white-haired old guy, he was lean and in incredibly great shape.

David had dropped way behind, but Owen was too busy trying to keep up the chase to wait for him to catch up. One last day before their hunt ended. And, hell, they'd tried to bag a bear for the last four years without any luck. The way the bear was outdistancing them in a hurry in the Maine wilderness; Owen was beginning to lose hope they'd make it this time either. But it was the closest they'd come.

When Owen didn't hear David's heavy breathing behind him, or his size ten boots trudging through the deep snow, he turned and looked to see how far behind he was. David was holding his thighs, leaning over, gasping for breath.

"David, you all right?" Owen asked, knowing it was a dumb question, when he figured David was trying to catch his second wind and couldn't answer anyway.

David motioned him on, wheezing, his face red and pinched with pain. "Get the bear! I'm fine. Go. I'll catch up."

But it wasn't like David not to keep up on a hunt and Owen ran back to check on him. "What's wrong?" Owen asked, grabbing his arm to steady him.

"Go. You'll… never… forgive… me… if… we…" David clutched his chest.

The wolves and Trevor circled back and joined them. The old man shook his head. "Chest pains?"

Through clenched teeth, David growled, "From… running… damn it."

David was the oldest of the four partners in their private investigator practice, but at thirty-five, David couldn't be having a heart attack.

With millions of acres of forest land all around them, they were too deep into the wilderness to get help. Cell phones wouldn't work out here. Owen knew CPR, but…

He helped David to sit. "What are you feeling?" he asked, trying to disguise the anxiety in his voice, although he couldn't hide a deepening frown, and David noticed.

"Don't be a… worry…" David clutched his chest even harder, his face sweating in the frigid air.

"We can't get any help to him way out here," Trevor said quietly. "If he's having a heart attack, it's not a bad way to go. Quick, no lingering illness."

"No!" Owen snapped. "Do you have any aspirin?" How could he let his friend from childhood and one of the best partners he'd had in law enforcement before they'd left the force die on him? He couldn't. "I know CPR."

"It won't be enough." Trevor sounded like the voice of reason, but Owen didn't want to hear it.

The image of David lunging in front of him, taking a bullet in the shoulder two years ago, flashed across Owen's mind. He wouldn't let him go. He couldn't.

The wolves watched silently, almost sympathetically as if one of their pack members was in trouble, their ears perked, their tongues hanging out, panting after the long run.

His hand clutching David's shoulder, Owen clenched his teeth to bite back the overwhelming feeling of hopelessness. "Can't we do something? Anything?"

"Possibly," Trevor said, "but it will change his life and yours, forever."

"I'd do anything to save my friend's life," Owen said, figuring Trevor was thinking in terms of if he had enough money, they could air-evac him out somewhere, maybe in a clearing where the loggers had been.

Trevor put a hand on Owen's shoulder. "You sure?"

"Anything, damn it. However much it costs, it's worth it."

Trevor looked back at the wolves. The biggest one bowed its head slightly, then bared his teeth and lunged.

Before Owen could fathom what was happening, the wolf bit David in the arm. He cried out in pain.

As Owen swung his rifle to his shoulder to shoot the beast, he caught a blur of white fur in his peripheral vision, right before one of the other wolves pounced on him.

Chapter 1

In the dark of night, the roads slushy, the snow plowed in dirty heaps beyond the shoulders, Faith O'Malley drove her rented SUV from Maine's Bangor International Airport to Millinocket, a prickle of awareness making her uneasy. She glanced at the rearview mirror, sure the headlights had been tailing her all the way. Which made her wonder again if her father's concern that he'd been followed for some time before her boyfriend had stolen his research paper was based on reality.

On the other hand, maybe believing someone was now stalking her had all to do with the kind of work she did as a forensic scientist solving crimes and being way too suspicious of everyone and everything. *Normally.* When it came to Hilson Snowdon, she hadn't been suspicious enough.

A mile from the turnoff for the hotel, she heard a tremendous boom. Gunfire?

Her rental swerved toward the shoulder as if a ghostly force had taken control. Adrenaline flooded her as she twisted the steering wheel to the left, veering away from a speed limit sign. The back end of the vehicle on the right side felt like it was listing. A blow-out, not gunfire. A smidgen of relief washed over her. She eased onto the shoulder and pulled the vehicle to a stop, but didn't cut the engine. What next?

The truck she thought had been following her pulled up behind her, the lights shining in her rearview mirror. The pickup idled, waiting.

Her heartbeat sped up again. Not about to hang around for the truck driver's help, in case he was bad news, she fumbled in her purse for her cell phone, yanked it out, then punched in the number for roadside service.

When the operator asked her location, Faith gave her the exit number off the highway.

"It'll be about an hour, ma'am," the woman said.

"Thanks, I'll be here." *Unfortunately*. Faith hung up when she saw movement near the right back door. She jerked her head around. In the dark of night, looking through tinted windows, Faith couldn't see who the person was who had come up behind her vehicle, but she heard the click as the individual yanked on the door handle. *Locked*.

Something pounced against the door. Her heart gave a little start. Large almond-shaped eyes, shining an eerie greenish orange color, peered in through the window.

Steeling her nerves, she made sure all the doors were locked again, and considered driving the mile into town on the bad tire.

What looked like a big white Samoyed, but not half as fuzzy, raced around the front of the car, her headlights illuminating him as he headed for the driver's side. She wondered if the dog was half Arctic wolf. His long muzzle was not Samoyed in appearance, but more wolflike. The person who'd tried the door handle wasn't in sight as the dog jumped against her door. Reflexively, she jerked away from it. The animal peered in at her with its shining eyes, its huge front paws resting on her window.

A key clicked in the front door lock on the passenger's side. Without a second's hesitation, she jammed her foot on the gas pedal and sped off.

Bad tire or no.

Her skin crawling from the experience, she slowed up ahead, figuring it would take the dog and his owner a little while to follow her, and she didn't want to make more of a mess of the tire than she had to. She crept toward the off-ramp, hazard lights flashing, then headed for a lighted service station on the corner. The truck's lights had vanished. Either he continued on past the exit, or he was driving without lights.

She parked at the service station where, inside, she found two middle-aged men drinking coffee who offered to help her change the tire, so she cancelled the road side service. The whole time the men changed the tire, they asked her where she was from, what she was doing here, genuinely friendly, idle talk, while she watched for the pickup that had parked behind her on the road. Either he was afraid she'd tell on him and he was waiting for her to leave the well-lit service station, or she'd somehow missed seeing him drive on by when she was getting help to change the tire.

Thanking the men, she offered to pay them. They gave her small smiles and declined, the one saying he had a daughter who he hoped someone would help out if she was ever in need. Faith thanked them again, hoping she wouldn't encounter the pickup driver again, left, and a few minutes later arrived at the Woodlands Travel Lodge.

Glancing up at the rearview mirror, she swore the streetlights illuminated the same gray pickup truck that had been following her, but the tinted windows hid the driver as he drove past. *Slowly*. Didn't matter that the speed limit was thirty here or that the road was perfectly drivable, salted or sanded. She still thought he was going much slower than necessary. As if he was checking her out. But maybe it wasn't the same vehicle at all.

Yep, shades of her father. Although after her boyfriend stole her father's research paper, she could see how Dad would be somewhat paranoid.

Faith sighed. She fully intended to get his flash drive back from Hilson, one way or another. Yet as much as her father wanted it returned, he still wouldn't tell her what information it held. She'd find out soon enough, just as she had told him. It would be just like any other mystery-solving mission she did. Well, maybe not just like any other. This time it was personal.

She grabbed her suitcase and headed inside the blue lodge, her overnight stop before she trekked into the remoter part of Maine and the cabins where she'd stay during her dealing-with-Hilson mission, when her cell phone jingled. She stopped midstream in the lobby, fumbled around in her oversized leather purse, then finally fished the phone out. She kept telling herself she was going to wear it around her neck for easier access as many times as her father had called her since she'd left her apartment in Portland, Oregon.

"Yes, I'm finally, finally here, Dad."

"Any sign of Hilson?"

"He's not here. I have to stay at a lodge for the night in Millinocket since it's too late to navigate the wilderness in the dark. At least that's what the owners of the cabins said. He's supposed to be at a cabin resort about two miles or more from mine, only accessible by snowmobile. I'll confront him as soon as I can, return to Millinocket, and call you."

"You don't need to read my research paper, Faith. Just bring it back home safe and sound."

She couldn't understand why he was so secretive about the research he'd done. But now, just as he was going to reveal it at an upcoming conference, voila! Hilson steals his flash drive as well as his hard drive. "I'll bring it home, Dad. I promise." At least she prayed she wouldn't fail him. He hadn't worked on anything else beyond teaching at the local community college in years and this was so important to him. She kept wondering if Hilson had put the moves on her just so he could get to her father and his research. "Got to check in at the lodge. Call you later."

"Night, Faith. And Faith?"

"Yes, Dad?"

"I hope you dump the guy."

"Consider him dumped." Although it appeared Hilson had already dumped her. "No way would I trust him again. Love you and good night, Dad."

Everything that had gone on between her and Hilson kept running through her mind like a continuous computer loop. How he'd wined and dined her, bought her gifts, but always held back. As if there was someone else in his life. Maybe someone he was still married to? She'd joked about it, but he'd smiled coolly and made love to her as if to prove to her no one else existed. And yet, something had been missing.

Then again, maybe it was all her fault. She'd been looking for love, but hadn't really felt it for him either. She'd needed the intimacy, but somewhere along the line, it hadn't felt real. Now all she felt toward him was anger, betrayal, hurt, and every other negative emotion in the book—but it all had to do with his stealing her father's research and nothing to do with the end of her relationship with Hilson. That's what worried her the most. What was wrong with her?

When she reached the front desk, the clerk said to someone on the phone, "Just a minute, honey. Got another customer."

"Faith O'Malley," Faith said, leaning against the counter, ready for a room-service meal, a hot shower, and a good night's sleep, after missing one connecting flight due to engine trouble, being delayed three hours because of a snowstorm en route, and problems getting her assigned rental car. Not to mention the flat tire. What should have taken only a few hours—if everything had gone smoothly—ended up being an all-day string of disasters.

"Room 318, miss," the clerk said, handing her the card key, nodding as she listened to someone on the phone. She raised her brows at Faith. "Need a wake-up call in the morning?"

"No, thanks." If that was one thing Faith didn't need was a wake-up call. Sleeping in was just something she couldn't get her body to agree with. "Do you know where the Back Country Tours office is?"

"Down the street about a half mile. Can't miss it." The clerk smiled. "Sign out front has a carved white wolf on it. And the owners, Lila Grayson and Kintail Silverman, can be seen around town with a couple of pet wolves in tow when they're not guiding hunting tours in the way back country."

"Wolves."

"Yep. Tame, sweetest-natured old things, just like big beautiful huskies, only pure white."

"Arctic wolves." She thought back to the animal that had pounced on her rental vehicle. It wasn't a Samoyed, but a real wolf? Then it had to belong to the same people she needed to get in touch with. She'd report the man with the wolf who was following her, whoever he was, to the owner of Back Country Tours.

"Guess they would be Arctic wolves. The couple is from the Canadian Arctic up around Yellowknife. Return there in the summers. Real cold weather folks. Although they like hunting different animals here, black bear, bobcat, moose, rather than caribou and whatever else they go after up there. Pretty neat, huh? Winter home here and summer home there? They don't like the summer heat at all, although it's nothing like living in some hot weather places like Florida. When I lived there—"

A man jingled his keys behind Faith, and she glanced back. He frowned at her.

"Thanks, I'll be checking out early in the morning," Faith said to the clerk and grabbed her suitcase, then headed for the elevator, looking forward to dinner and a hot shower without any more delays.

Once she reached her room, she slid the key card in. *Green light*. She twisted the handle and pushed. The door didn't budge. She tried again. Same thing. She hated key cards. Why couldn't they just use regular old brass keys?

She tried a third time and this time she twisted the handle harder and shoved the door more firmly. And was rewarded. Lights were on in the room and the place was already toasty warm as if the welcoming mat had been set out for her. *Perfect*. She walked into the room and glanced at the two queen-sized beds, one with the chartreuse covers pulled back from the pillow, a chocolate wrapped in gold foil sitting on the center of it. She smiled and pulled off her parka, peeled off her boots, and reached for the phone to call room service when she saw a leather bucket filled with ice. Wow, they sure knew how to coddle their guests.

That's when the bathroom door opened. She whipped around and faced a naked man towel-drying his hair. Or at least until he saw her.

His mouth gaped. Her expression matched his, and he quickly wrapped the towel around his waist. "I didn't think room service would come this soon." He glanced down at her sock-covered feet, her boots lying beside them.

"I'm not... I'm... they gave me a key to your room by accident." Faith tried not to look at the man's physique—too much—but ripped abs, arms muscled just enough to give a woman a good hug, and toned legs that looked like they could run a marathon, were just too appealing.

And his eyes—blue like the ocean, dark, hiding a wealth of secrets, that held her gaze with way too much interest, as if she was the specialty of the house and just what he'd ordered from the menu. Light blond stubble covered his square jaw, making him appear a bit roguish and intriguing.

He folded his arms across his broad chest. A light smattering of blond hair trailed down to the towel slung low on his hips. Her gaze dropped lower. He cleared his throat to get her attention, making her skin heat in a flush of awareness, but he wasn't moving out of her path to the door. Just now she wished it were her room, and *he* were part of the amenities.

He inclined his head a little, a hint of a smile on his lips, his eyes sparkling with mischief. "Then I guess I'd better get dressed before—"

A knock rapped on the door.

"Too late." His deeply amused baritone sounded like he was enjoying this a little too much, as he turned, took a couple of steps, and opened the door.

Great. Faith hurried to pull on her boots, when the aroma of steak wafted into the room as a man brought in a tray. Faith's stomach growled. The room service guy glanced at her, green eyes smiling. She could just imagine what he was thinking, what with the room's occupant wearing a towel, and her pulling her boots on.

The toweled guy signed the bill, and the lodge employee grinned, dimples appearing in his ruddy cheeks. "Thanks so much, sir. If you need anything else, just ring." He glanced at Faith, smiled even more as if to say she could visit him next if she had a mind to, then left the room.

"Enough for two of us, if you want to split a medium-rare steak, baked potato, and salad," the sandy-haired hunk said.

"Thanks so much for the offer, but I'm returning to the front desk to get the right room key. Have a nice night." She brushed past the mostly naked man, smiled when he smiled, then hurried out of the room.

"The night could have been better," he murmured.

She glanced back at him, wishing he was the kind of man she had been dating, and could justify staying and splitting his dinner with him, then maybe share the chocolate treat resting on his pillow with him. And more. For the first time ever, she seriously wanted to flirt with a man. Something about him appealed to her, as if he were the real McCoy, spontaneous and fun-loving, and for an instant, she yearned for that. Wanted to feel that a man who looked like this guy with a hint of the devil in his expression and actions found her appealing, too.

The man lifted a brow and smiled again, his chiseled features and intensely intriguing gaze nearly irresistible. She faltered, but shook her head, and hurried for the elevator before she did anything she might regret in the morning. She didn't look back at him, although she wanted to see if he was still watching her. But she felt he was doing just that, observing her, maybe hoping she'd change her mind? Or maybe it was just wishful thinking on her part that someone was truly interested in her after Hilson ditched her. On further introspection, she realized she hadn't heard his door shut.

It wasn't until she returned to the front desk with her suitcase in tow that she realized she'd left her parka on the man's desk chair. She let out her breath in exasperation. Okay, so the day turned night wasn't going to get any better.

A line of five guests was waiting for rooms. The clerk still had the cell phone stuck to her ear as she nodded and chatted it up with the woman first in line.

Faith didn't hesitate to stalk up to the counter, pulling her bag with her. The woman who was being waited on looked at Faith as if she was ready to clobber her for trying to barge in.

"Excuse me," Faith said to the clerk and handed her the key card, "but someone else was already in Room 318."

The girl's eyes widened. Then she smiled. "Oh, my, you mean you got the key to Cameron MacPherson's room?" She put her hand to her breast. "If I'd made the mistake, I would have just stayed."

That's saying he wanted the clerk to stay. And jeesh, the clerk had made the mistake. No apology? "Another room, please?"

The clerk held out the new key card. "This one is for Room 317."

"Three-seventeen."

"Yep. The numbers were close. It's directly across the hall from Mr. MacPherson's." She winked. "Tell him if he needs anything, just to give me a holler."

Faith shook her head, grabbed the key card, and headed back to the elevator. At least with his room being across from hers, she could ask for her parka without having to traipse across the whole of the hotel and back.

As soon as she reached her room, she struggled to get the key card to work, then gave the door a shove. The room was dark and cold. She fumbled for the light switch, but when she turned on the lamps, the bedcover wasn't pulled back from the pillow, nor was a gold foil-covered chocolate waiting for her either. And of course the ice bucket was perfectly empty. She wondered if Cameron got the special treatment because he was a big tipper, or just an incredibly smooth-talking hunk.

She sighed and rolled her bag next to the bed, then headed back for the door. She might as well get this over with before she finally settled down for the night.

Glancing at her watch, she hadn't realized how late it was already. Probably too late to order anything from the kitchen. But if she ate at this hour, the food would most likely just sit like a lump in her stomach when she went to bed anyway. She knocked on Cameron MacPherson's door.

While waiting for him, she closed her eyes and yawned. Man, she was ready to skip the shower and just collapse in bed.

The door squeaked opened. Wearing only a pair of stone-washed jeans that looked incredibly soft, shirtless and barefoot, Cameron smiled, but he hadn't brought her parka to the door. He looked every bit as sexy as when he was wearing only a towel.

"Are you sure you don't want to have a bite with me?" He motioned to the tray on the table.

The old werewolf movie with Jack Nicholson was playing on the television, and by the sound of the growling, she envisioned he had shapeshifted and was fighting the bad wolf, if she recalled the movie correctly.

She gave Cameron a tired smile. "Under other circumstances, maybe. I left my parka here?"

"You look like you could use a meal and the kitchen's closed by now." His voice, deep and pleasing, sent little chills of expectation through her.

But she resisted the temptation and held out her hand for her coat. "Thanks, but I'm fine." He retrieved her coat and gave it to her, his hand brushing hers in a sensuous way, which made her skin heat again. She thought he looked a little wistful, hopeful that she'd stay and keep him company, but she figured if she did, she would melt under whatever spell he seemed to cast over her. It wasn't like her to be that attracted to a guy she'd just met. She glanced down at his hand, no wedding ring. When her gaze returned to his, he was smiling broadly.

Usually a lot less obvious than that when she was scrutinizing a man's marital status— although he might be married and just not wear a wedding ring—she felt her skin heat even more. "Thanks," she said quickly, turned around, and left his room before she made any more of a fool of herself. But as soon as she reached her door and slipped her hand in her jeans pocket, she realized she didn't have the key.

Cameron watched the petite blonde stand before her room, her parka draped over her arm, her hand shoved into her pocket, but she didn't make a motion to unlock her door.

She'd left the key in the room?

The poor woman. She looked like she was about to pass out from exhaustion. However, he'd seen the way she'd looked at him and checked to see if he was married, which meant only one thing. She'd been intrigued. Might have even stayed for dinner if she had been more impulsive. Probably a good thing she wasn't. At least, not the way she looked, wearing a sparkling white sweater that caressed nice-sized breasts and form-fitting black jeans that showed off lots of curves, conjuring up the image of *sexy,* soft, and cuddly. Gold curls swept over her shoulders, and she looked like she belonged on a beach in a bikini, soaking up the sun, a long way from here.

"Want me to call down and have the hotel staff bring you up another key?"

She hesitated, mulling over her options, he figured, not saying anything for a minute, just staring at the immovable door. Then she turned around and her lush lips, glossed with something shimmering, pink—and sensuous—curved up. Her stunning green eyes sparkled like emeralds in the bright hall lights, mesmerizing him. Hell, he was a sucker for green eyes.

She arched an eyebrow and gave a cute little snort. "Uhm, thanks, but I can manage." She straightened her shoulders and trudged down the hall toward the elevator.

She had spunk, he had to admit. And some damned nice curves. He watched her wiggle her tush all the way to the elevator, then waited until she was inside, just in case she changed her mind. She didn't. His loss.

He closed his door and padded back to the bed. But he couldn't put the woman out of his mind. Not that he needed any distractions for now while he was on his mission, but until tomorrow morning, he couldn't get much done anyway. He slipped out of his jeans and climbed into bed. Bright and early, he was going to check out Back Country Tours to learn why his friends hadn't arrived home on time, without any word of explanation.

But even so, Cameron couldn't help listening for the woman to return to her room, and when he heard the door click open and shut several minutes later, he relaxed a little. Then the door clicked open and shut again. He waited, listening. The ice maker down the hall ground, the ice clunking into the bucket. Then her door opened and shut again.

He tucked his arms behind his head and fantasized how he might have breakfast with the little lady before he took off for his next destination—cabins in the wilderness, no land phones, no cell phone service—he'd have to rely on his instincts more in this investigation. Cameron hoped his friends weren't in any real trouble, hoped they had just been unable to get in touch with him and their P.I. partner, Gavin Summerfield, who was still running their business back in Seattle in the meantime.

Cameron sighed. Seven days. That's how long the hunting trip was supposed to last. Add a couple of days travel time. Two weeks, max. They'd even had to turn down some lucrative jobs because they were so short-handed. But it beat the heck out of him how he got stuck leaving Seattle to land in this snow-filled landscape instead of Gavin.

Cameron's cell phone rang. Speak of the devil. *Gavin.* "Hey, no word yet, but I'll be going to the cabins tomorrow after I stop by Back Country Tours to see if anyone's in the office in the morning. We'll have a phone blackout for a while once I reach the resort."

"I received a garbled message. Sounded like Owen and he said something about being unable to get word to us. It sounded like he said he and David were all right. And quitting. Quitting the hunt? The static was too bad, and I couldn't make out any more before the phone line cut out completely."

"But he really sounded all right? Not under duress? Not in any kind of trouble or anything, were they?"

"I'd like to say no. But the connection was so bad, I couldn't really say."

Cameron opened his mouth to speak, when a woman screamed—from the room across the hall.

Chapter 2

THE GRAY-HAIRED MAN APOLOGIZED PROFUSELY AS FAITH pushed him out of her room, her towel clutched tightly around her torso, her wet hair wrapped in another. She'd kill the hotel clerk. Couldn't the woman give one customer a room that wasn't already occupied?

If that weren't enough of an embarrassment, here came her knight to the rescue, wearing a pair of vivid blue silky boxers—and nothing else—none other than Cameron MacPherson.

He raised his brows at her as the man hurried off with his bag, apologizing under his breath.

"Clerk gave him a key to your room?" Cameron asked, a wrinkle creasing his forehead.

Faith began shutting the door to hide her state of undress in case anyone else happened to walk down the hall. "Yes."

"I'll call down and complain to the manager. We haven't been properly introduced, though. I'm Cameron MacPherson. And you are?"

"Faith O'Malley." She pressed the door closed a little more.

"Want to have breakfast with me in the morning?"

She was so annoyed with the clerk, she hadn't planned to let the grudge go, until Cameron asked to have breakfast with her. He was just too cute. And persistent. Her stomach grumbled. Although initially she thought eating too late could keep her awake, now she reasoned she might sleep better if she had a bite to eat. Besides, Cameron could take her mind off Hilson, for a little while. It didn't mean she was going to stay the night or do anything she didn't want to do, she reminded herself.

"Still have some dinner left over?" she asked.

Cameron smiled, the skin beneath his eyes wrinkling, dimples appearing, his blue eyes gleaming with delight, the devilish look saying he knew he could break her down eventually if he tried long enough. "I'll even dress for dinner."

She wondered just what his definition of dressed would be. "Be right over. And thanks… for the rescue." She glanced at his boxers, the same blue as his eyes.

Grinning, he saluted her and stalked back to his room as if his mission was done.

———

As soon as Faith said she'd eat with Cameron, she'd surprised and pleased the hell out of him. He really figured he didn't have a chance to convince her he was one of the good guys and just wanted a little company. *Her* kind of company.

He couldn't get the image of her—standing half naked, wearing only a skimpy towel to cover herself—out of his mind. For certain, the gods had smiled on him tonight.

After hurrying back into his room, he jerked on his jeans and threw the rest of his scattered clothes into his suitcase. Then he moved one of the two pillows he'd been using over to *her* side of the bed. He glanced at the door. He hadn't heard her door opening yet, so he rushed into the bathroom to pick up the wet towel he'd thrown on the floor and hung it up on the towel bar. Afterward, he tossed his toothbrush and toothpaste and shaving gear back into his shaving kit.

Her door opened and closed. He rubbed his bare chest. Shirt? Or no?

He stalked out of the bathroom and grabbed his flannel shirt out of the suitcase, then yanked it on, just as she knocked. He returned to the door, opened it, and smiled at Faith. "Dinner's served."

Wearing emerald-green velour running clothes, she looked incredibly soft and touchable, her blond curls caressing her shoulders like he wanted to do.

She smiled a little to see his shirt hanging open. He supposed he should have buttoned it, but she didn't seem to mind.

She raised her brows at the bed where his tray of food was sitting, and he started his salesman's pitch. "I was watching the Jack Nicholson movie in bed. It's about over. Want to see what's coming up after that one?"

She hesitated, then took a deep breath and headed for the bed. "So what's on next?"

"Looks like werewolf movie night. Something called *The Howl of the Wolf*."

"Ah." She sat on the edge of the bed and slipped off a boot and already his thoughts were of seeing her take off more. But she yanked off the other boot, dropped it on the carpeted floor to join its mate, then climbed on top of the floral covers. "That's Julie Wildthorn's third book in her werewolf series. I'd heard the book was better so never went to see the movie version."

A woman after his own heart. "You like fantasy? Urban fantasy?"

"Both of the above." She took the lemon-lime soda he handed her, her legs stretched out on the bed, a whiff of her floral fragrance enticing him to take a deeper breath. "So is this a vacation or business trip for you?" she asked.

"A little of both." Although he hadn't planned on having any fun until she popped into his room and began stripping while he'd been in the shower. "And you?"

"Strictly business."

He smiled. Yeah, strictly business. That's why she was sitting on his bed, sharing dinner with him.

The movie version of *The Howl of the Wolf* began, and he couldn't help notice the way she smiled at the funny scenes, chuckling under her breath, but her cheeks grew a little flushed when the hero and heroine went beyond kissing, got naked, and ended up in bed together.

She cleared her throat and leaned back against the pillow. He thought she was going to say something. She didn't, and then she sank lower onto the mattress, her eyes half closed, her long lashes hiding them further, her hand still clasped around the soda can.

When her eyes closed, he reached over and slipped the drink from her hand so she wouldn't spill it, half hoping she'd spend the night. To his regret, her eyes popped open. "Oh…" She stared at the TV, then smiled. "I like the book version better. She ends up with the hunky werewolf, not the wimpy human in the story." A small wrinkle appeared on her forehead, then she turned to Cameron. "If I fall asleep again, wake me and send me home."

He shook his head. "I'm enjoying the company." And he was. The last girl he dated was only into chick flicks. Absolutely no fantasy, no sci-fi, no urban fantasy, no historical, westerns, war movies, nothing. He pulled the tray off the bed and settled back against the pillow like Faith had done, only he drew closer this time, enjoying the warmth from her body, her subtle fragrance, the companionship.

Before long, her eyes were shut again, only this time he slipped his arm under her head. When she smiled at him, her expression quizzical, he said, "I was getting a little chilly. Weren't you?"

She chuckled, the sound low and amused. But she played right along with him, and snuggled up nice and close. Too bad she was here strictly on business. He smiled at the notion, but it didn't take long before she closed her eyes again, and he nodded off also.

He hadn't even realized he'd done so until Faith pulled away from him, waking him, and gave him a weary smile. "Guess we missed the end of the movie. Just remember, the werewolf gets the girl in the correct version." Then she climbed off the bed and stretched like a sleek feline wrapped in green velvet-like duds.

He wanted her to stay the night, but he didn't figure she'd agree. Still… he had to make the offer. "Another werewolf tale coming up."

"I've seen *Underworld*." She checked her watch. "It's nearly one and I've got business to take care of early in the morning. Snowstorm's supposed to be coming now."

"Want to have breakfast with me tomorrow?"

She didn't hesitate to respond this time, and he knew he'd hooked her for a date. "I'm an early riser. Would six be too early for you?"

He frowned, but at the same time, he was glad she'd share another meal with him before he had to traipse off into the wilderness alone. "Uh. Sure. Pick you up at six."

But he could tell from her expression, she was already distancing herself from him.

"Or we could meet down in the restaurant," she said.

That clinched it. But he wasn't letting her go, just yet. He shook his head. "I'll knock on your door at six."

When she left his room, he waited at his open doorway while she unlocked her door, but then she just stared into the room. He hoped she was changing her mind about staying with him a little longer, and not that something more was wrong.

"Faith?"

"I think the clerk let someone else into my room." Her voice was a little shaky.

Cameron crossed the floor to check out her room when his door automatically shut behind him. He swore under his breath, realizing at once his room key was lying on the desk.

She raised her brows at him. "Did you leave your key—"

"Yeah."

"You could stay here and watch *Underworld* with me while you're waiting for another room key."

He chuckled and rubbed his hand over her back, but every muscle remained rigid with tension. "You've got a deal. How do you know someone came into your room?" He escorted her inside and shut the door.

"My suitcase was open. My bathroom door was closed. And my overnight bag is on its side now, not standing upright."

"Check and see if anything's missing." He stalked over to the phone and called the front desk and asked to speak with the manager.

"Nothing's missing that I can tell."

A businesslike male voice responded on the phone. "Yes, this is Mr. Dodson, the manager on duty. How may I help you?"

"The clerks on the front desk had given Ms. O'Malley the key to my room and twice, had given a key to her room to other customers."

"I'm so sorry for the trouble, Mister…"

"MacPherson."

"May I speak with Ms. O'Malley, Mr. MacPherson?"

Cameron handed the phone to Faith as she finished looking through her bags. "Yes, this is Faith O'Malley."

Cameron watched the expression on Faith's face change from annoyance to surprise as she glanced up at him. "A complimentary room for the night is fine. Thank you. And can someone send up a room key for Mr. MacPherson in Room 317? Thanks." She hung up the phone. "They'll be right up with your key." She motioned to the bed and turned on the TV. "Might as well get comfortable while we wait."

"No one stole anything, I take it?"

"No." But she was back to looking perturbed.

"If you want me to, I'll spend the night."

That got a big smile from her, which brightened her whole expression, her eyes beaming with amusement, her glossy lips turned up in a big way. He figured she wasn't buying it.

"I'll bolt my door after you leave. I should have done so when I was taking a shower."

He was glad *he* hadn't bolted his door when he was taking his shower.

He was quick to settle in the bed with her as she turned on the television and found the channel they'd been watching. He hoped the hotel staff would forget the key, but in short order someone knocked on the door, probably trying to accommodate them after all the fiascoes tonight.

He wanted to ignore whoever was at the door, but Faith gave him a little smile. He sighed. "We have a date for the morning," he reminded her.

"Six a.m. sharp."

He leaned over and kissed her lips, just a brush of flesh against flesh, her mouth soft, warm, sweetened with lemon-lime, and way too enticing.

Whoever was at the door knocked again. Faith almost looked hopeful the intruder would vanish as she leaned a little into the kiss, her eyes closing slightly, her breathing nearly nonexistent, her hand barely touching his thigh. But when Cameron went to do the kiss more justice, she pulled away. "Tomorrow, bright and early."

His hands cupped her face, brought her to him, and he pressed his lips harder against her mouth. He gave her something to remember him by, just like he'd be thinking about the enticing woman when he was alone in his room tonight, wishing for more. *Then* he left the bed.

When he answered the door, a man dressed in a suit apologized profusely.

Cameron glanced over his shoulder before he left Faith, and he thought she looked like she needed more of a kiss, her lips slightly parted, begging for more attention.

But she quickly said, "'Night," as if that would keep her out of trouble.

Smiling, he shook his head. "'Night, Faith. See you in the morning." He just hoped he could wake up in time. He had better arrange for a wakeup call and hope the staff would at least get that right or he'd have somebody's head.

Okay, so Cameron was really a dreamy hunk, but did that mean Faith was supposed to lie awake half the night thinking about his kisses? The first one as light and airy as it was promised so much more. And the second one, he was ready to stay the night for sure. She touched her lips again for the hundredth time, wondering how his kisses, as sweet as they were, made her whole body tingle, when she'd felt barely anything with Hilson's. Maybe because Cameron was new? Something unexpected?

That's what it had to be. An uncanny attraction that made her whole body heat up, again, with delicious anticipation.

Breakfast, that's all this was. And then she'd be on her way to find Hilson, and Cameron MacPherson would be on his way to whatever business he had to conduct. And regrettably, she'd never see him again.

With her bag packed and sitting next to the door, Faith glanced at her watch, and then the room clock one last time. Cameron MacPherson was twenty minutes late. She couldn't wait any longer, no matter how sexy or intriguing the guy was. She whipped out a note on the hotel stationery telling him to meet her if he made it in time and planned to slip it under Cameron's door when she saw the tip of a note under hers.

She opened her door and found a folded note. Inside, the message on hotel stationery said, "Sorry to have missed you. Had to leave earlier than expected. If I return before you have breakfast, I'll meet with you in the restaurant. Cameron."

She sighed, left her room, and closed her door, then headed for the elevator, rolling her suitcase along behind her. Probably for the best. Although self-doubt began to worm its way into her thoughts. Had she turned him off by one too many rejections? She groaned at herself, always overanalyzing everything.

After the hostess seated Faith in the mostly empty lodge restaurant, where the dark brown furniture and décor made her feel as if she were in a bear's den, she watched the entryway. Hoping for a glimpse of Cameron's sparkling eyes and his roguish smile that would brighten up the place considerably, she couldn't help wondering what he might be wearing this morning. From nothing, to a towel, to a pair of jeans and nothing else, to boxers, and jeans again with an open shirt, he seemed like the kind of guy better suited to a hot weather climate.

She delayed ordering her cinnamon roll for a good twenty more minutes. But he never showed. Trying not to feel any disappointment or think anything more about Cameron, she finally gave up, had her green tea and roll, then got into her rental vehicle and drove in the direction of Back Country Tours. She had business to take care of, after all, and Cameron wasn't part of the deal.

When she reached the office, Faith found that the hotel clerk was right. The carved white wolf sign hanging off the building couldn't be missed. Pictures

of snow-covered peaks hung in the windows and everything was white—the trim, the brick façade, even the
roof was nearly white, which made it blend in with the
snow accumulated against the buildings as if it were an
ice cave in the Antarctic.

A light was on inside and her spirits lifted.
According to Hilson's itinerary, he was coming here
first. And maybe she'd finally get some answers to
where the hunter guide, Trevor Hodges, was. The
man who had taken her father on the tour that changed
her father's life forever had to have seen something.
Or at least confirm that nothing extraordinary had
happened. But when her father had returned home, he
began writing the research paper with such zeal, she
suspected whatever had happened here had triggered
his need to write it. And, besides locating Hilson and
the flash drive, she wanted to know the story from
Trevor's point of view.

As soon as she walked into the office, she sensed
something wasn't right. The place was entirely too
quiet. A massive oak desk sat near the entrance, like
a fortified barrier to keep the riffraff from going any
further into the labyrinth of offices. Or at least that's the
way it appeared to Faith.

Then she heard a rustle of papers and a drawer sliding
open down the hall. "Hello?" she said, moving toward
the hallway leading to several rooms.

The noise instantly ceased. She really didn't have a
good feeling about this.

She backed up and turned around to leave the building
pronto, when she saw a man's shoe sticking out from
behind the massive desk near the entryway.

It's just a shoe, she told herself. A door somewhere else in the building opened, then closed. She hurried around the desk and started, seeing a white-haired old man lying still on the floor, clothed in a suit, missing one shoe, his face gray, his eyes staring at the ceiling, lifeless. She reached for his wrist, felt no pulse. His skin was cold. He'd been dead for a while.

She couldn't see any sign of a struggle, or foul play, but if someone had killed the man and was still in the building, she could be next. She headed for the door, jerked it open, and came face-to-face with Cameron MacPherson.

She gave a wispy gasp, threw her hand to her chest, and took a step back.

Tousled by the wind, sandy blond hair fell to the top of his plaid collar, softening his stern look a hint. His parka was open, a soft cabled sweater hugging his broad chest, the sky blue color electrifying his eyes even more. But his eyes widened at the sight of her, and he quickly reached out to steady her.

Her mouth dropped open and he stared at her with a look of disbelief.

"Faith O'Malley?" he said, as if he was so shocked to see her here, he had to confirm it really was she.

"I… there's…" She pushed against him to get out of the building. The killer, if there was one, could be inside, and might decide to finish them off next.

Cameron took hold of her arm and stopped her, the strength of his touch defeating her panic. "What's wrong? You look as white as this building."

"A dead man's in there. Not that I haven't seen a lot of them in the work I do, but the police always call me to the scene after they've dealt with it. I'm never the first one at the scene."

"The work you do?"

"I'm a forensic scientist."

His brows raised a little, but she swore a hint of admiration appeared in his expression.

"Did you touch anything?"

"Sure, the man's wrist. To make sure he's dead. Been that way for a while. Skin's cold."

"You're sure you're all right?"

"I'm fine. He's not, and if he was murdered, the guy might be still in the building. I heard noises in one of the offices off the hall."

Cameron reached under his jacket and drew out a gun, but he still hadn't released her, as if he feared she'd collapse or something. "Go outside and call 9-1-1."

Her lips parted, she stared at the weapon, then looked up at Cameron.

"Private Investigator. I have a permit to carry one. Former police officer, too." Cameron pulled out some ID to confirm it.

She closed her mouth, looked back at the other offices, then slipped her cell phone out of her purse. "Then I'm staying right here." She figured she was safer with him since he had the gun and credentials, than away from him.

"All right." However, instead of checking for the intruder, Cameron did a quick check of the body.

Faith got the 911 operator and said, "I'm Faith O'Malley and I'm at Back Country Tours where I found a dead man behind the receptionist's desk."

The operator asked a million questions, or at least it seemed like it, before Faith finally ended the conversation to see what Cameron had discovered about the victim. "Do you see any evidence of a crime?"

He pointed to the man's shirt. "Speck of blood on the front of his dress shirt. I don't see any evidence of any kind of trauma, blow to the head, strangulation, nothing. Looks like he might have been injected with something. No way to confirm my suspicions without stripping him down and looking for a needle mark, and then identifying something foreign in the body. Stay here, or go outside and wait for the police. I'll be right back."

Cameron strode off down the hallway.

"Wait! Don't you think that's a little dangerous?"

"That's why you're to wait here or outside for the police." He didn't say another word, but headed down the hall.

A cold breeze from the open doorway thoroughly chilled her, and she rubbed her arms, then leaned over the body again and opened the buttons on the man's shirt. Peeling the shirt away just a little, she examined his chest. Cameron was right. He'd been poked with a needle and the area had bled slightly before the man died. But what was really bizarre was a drip of shiny silver glistening at the point of entry.

A couple of sirens wailed down the road, and she quickly rebuttoned the man's shirt, then wiped the buttons clean with a tissue.

Before the police arrived, Cameron hurried back into the office, took hold of her arm as if he were her knight to the rescue, and led Faith out of the building. But even outside, he didn't loosen his grip on her. She could envision him as a former police officer rescuing women in distress and taking great pride in his work. "Did you see any sign of anyone?" she asked.

He looked a little blank.

"When you went into the back offices. Did you see anyone?"

"No. A door was wide open at the back of the building. He or she probably got out that way."

Instantly, Faith was suspicious. Not just of the person who had been in the building looking for something, who probably killed the old man, but of Cameron. Because she could swear he was holding out on her.

As soon as the police arrived, Faith and Cameron showed their credentials to the officers. She thought they acted oddly. She wasn't sure why. Maybe because they didn't seem too surprised. Or because they didn't appear very much concerned that Faith and Cameron might be the murderers. Which may have been because the police were dealing with a serial killer and they knew Faith and Cameron couldn't have been involved because they were out-of-towners and both worked or, in Cameron's case, had worked, with the police. Or maybe it was because the men were jaded—just another dead guy case.

The one had brownish butch hair, his light brown eyes glued to her, as if he was interested in more than her story in regard to her finding a dead body. As if he recognized her, or was intrigued with her, but not as a suspect or witness. Officer Mick Whitson. She couldn't figure out the mixed messages. The other, Bert Adams, moved around the room, his gaze darting about, taking everything in. Several times he sniffed the air. His hair was darker, his eyes hazel, and he had a heavier build. He was the one who asked the questions, as if he was in charge, while Whitson watched Faith's reactions. Not Cameron's, just Faith's.

Officer Adams finished his preliminary cursory examination of the room, then faced Cameron. "And why were you here?"

"Looking for friends of mine, fellow private investigators in a partnership, who haven't returned from a hunt."

"With Back Country Tours?"

"Yes. They made the arrangements with the staff here and are a week overdue back in Seattle. No word, except for a garbled call to our partner in Seattle, which isn't like them."

She was impressed. If she worked for an outfit like that, she'd never expect one of her partners would come looking for her. Just a few calls made, and wait it out a while longer to see if she was just delayed.

Neither of the officers commented concerning Cameron's story, though, which bothered her. She'd hoped they'd reassure him that his friends were okay. She truly thought they'd say something about a recent snowstorm that might have delayed them, or how bad communications were out in the wilderness, but they said nothing, both just seemed to stiffen a little.

Officer Adams shifted his attention to Faith. "And your business here?" Curt, abrupt, businesslike.

She hesitated. Everyone watched her, anticipating her answer. She was sure she'd alerted them something about her story wouldn't quite be on the up and up.

Well, she could say the same about Cameron. The part about looking for his friends was probably true, but he wasn't just checking for the killer in the building either when he went to investigate. And she felt something wasn't quite right about the two cops either.

"Can I see your ID again?" she asked the men.

From their non-reaction, she figured she'd stunned them. Although Cameron managed a small smile.

The officers exchanged glances, and then the one in charge, Officer Adams, pulled out his ID. After she looked at it, at him, and at the ID again, she nodded and handed it back. His face stern, he never broke a smile. But the other one, now he did. The smile showed dark amusement. He handed his ID over, made a point to touch her hand, and when she returned his ID, he managed to sweep his hand over hers, lingering a little longer, a little more invasive, as a prelude to something more.

Cameron looked miffed, even stepped closer to her, and glowered at Whitson as if to remind him to act professional and stay away from Faith.

Not needing the rescue, she tilted her chin up, gave Whitson a look like this was strictly business to her, when Officer Adams reminded her he was waiting for an answer.

"I'm searching for a tour guide who took my father on a hunt last year," she told the officer. "I wanted to take the same trip he'd taken. The guide worked for Back Country Tours." She spoke matter-of-factly, as if she told the whole truth and nothing but the truth, so help her God.

She thought about mentioning her father's research paper, that her former boyfriend had stolen it, and was in these parts close by, but she knew the police wouldn't be interested in any of it. But if they were, they'd ask what the paper was about, and she wouldn't be able to explain. How crazy would that sound? It was better not to bring it up.

More than that, and for whatever reason, she didn't want Cameron to know she had a boyfriend. Well, he was an ex, but she hadn't officially told Hilson that. Although she was pretty sure Hilson knew already. And had planned it that way. Unless he was dumb enough to think she couldn't figure out who stole her father's flash drive and hard drive and then intended to come back to her. She couldn't forgive him though.

Cameron's brows raised just a hint. And she was certain he didn't believe her.

The officers again exchanged glances and Officer Adams said under his breath to Whitson, "Kenneth O'Malley's daughter."

"You met my dad?" she asked, unable to contain her surprise.

"No," Adams quickly said. "It's a small town. He was asking a lot of questions, which caught the police department's attention. We discovered he was doing some kind of sociology study and that was the end of it."

But they seemed to have recognized she was related to her father even before she mentioned her name. Or maybe she was just making more of their reactions and wasn't correct in her assumptions. So much for keeping her father's business here secret. At least they probably didn't think she'd totally lied. She did want to see where he'd gone on his trip here.

But what really got to her more than anything, though, was neither asked who the guide was. Although maybe they'd talked to Trevor about him and already knew that he was her father's guide. Small town. Sure.

"If we have any more questions for either of you, where will you be staying for the next several days?" Officer Adams asked.

Cameron, being the gentleman he was, let Faith go first. She cleared her throat, dug around in her purse, then pulled out a piece of paper. Wrong one. List of what she wanted to do when she got here. She dug around a little more, found the slip of paper that she wrote Hilson's itinerary on—after having discovered the password on his computer, teach him to run off with her father's stuff—the receipt for breakfast, for the hotel, and yes! The information on her cabin rental at Nahamkanta Lake Rustic Resort.

She handed it to Officer Adams, who jotted down the information.

"No telephone service that far out. And cell phones won't work," he warned. "When you reach the trail-head, you have to ski in, get in by dogsled, or snow-mobiles. Snowshoes if you want to trek ten miles on the unplowed road."

"Yes, that's what the clerk said. But they're the only other cabins near Baxter Park that still had a vacancy and that's hopefully where Trevor Hodges is camping. At least the hotel clerk said she thought he was when I called earlier. But I dropped by here first to speak to the staff that employs him to learn more of his current whereabouts in the event he moved camp, if I could."

"You've made arrangements to get to the resort once you reach the trailhead?" Officer Adams asked.

"Yes. I'm renting a snowmobile."

Cameron smiled a little and she wondered if he thought she couldn't do this. Not that she was really a rustic type, but the place had two heated shower houses, flush toilets, and a hot tub. So it couldn't be all that rough. And she'd sledded before so no problem there.

Cameron handed Officer Adams a piece of paper and the guy looked at it, then back at Faith. "All right." He jotted the information down in his notebook. "If we need to get in touch, we will. Have a safe trip."

Officer Whitson gave her a slight nod of his head, as if sharing the other officer's sentiments. For her, not for Cameron. The officer didn't give him the time of day.

Cameron escorted Faith outside, but not before she overheard Officer Adams tell Whitson, "She's a wanted woman, and you don't stand a chance."

She wondered if the officer thought she and Cameron were already an item as Cameron walked her to her vehicle, which amused her and seemed to Cameron also.

"What's the name of your cabin?" he asked, as they crunched along the crusted snow on the walk, his body touching hers in a possessive and provocative way.

There was something about the way he moved beside her, as if she was truly with him, not like the way Hilson would have acted as though he just happened to be there walking in the same direction she was at the same time. She wondered if Cameron acted the same way with all women. Maybe he was a womanizer, well versed in how to make himself more attractive to the female sex. "Don't tell me you're staying at the same rustic resort."

She slipped a little on an icy patch on the snow-covered sidewalk, and Cameron's hand shot out to take hold of her arm. Hilson would have done the same, but then Cameron went a step further, pulled her in close to his body and wrapped his arm around her waist, making sure she didn't slide again. She hid a smile. If he slipped next, they'd probably both go down. But it was damned cold out, and she enjoyed the heat of his touch.

"Seems we're looking for clues in the same direction. I'm at White Wolf Den."

"The cabin I'm staying at is Black Bear Den. Are you using a snowmobile?" she asked.

"Yeah, from Skidoo Rentals."

"Guess we *are* headed in the same direction. Maybe we could have lunch together."

Cameron smiled and the expression was as if he'd found out *her* itinerary beforehand and had this whole thing planned from the beginning, from handing out keys to his and her rooms, to leaving his own key by accident in his room. "I thought you'd never ask."

"Yeah, well after you stood me up for breakfast…" She arched a brow at him.

He gave her a warm squeeze and chuckled. "I knew I'd never live it down if I saw you again. You want me to lead the way?"

"Sounds—" She spied a gray pickup sitting across the street at a barbershop. No driver in the vehicle, and it might not have been the one that she thought had been following her last night, but then again, maybe it was. She had the most awful urge to take a peek in the truck to see if the seats had white dog hair, or make that—white *wolf* hairs—on the seats.

Cameron looked over at the truck. "Something wrong?"

She took a deep breath. "No, no, lead the way." As tinted as the windows were, she didn't figure she could see inside all that well anyway.

Again he considered the pickup, then patted her SUV. "All right. Don't lose me."

"I don't intend to lose you." Flakes were already falling, and she was sure if they didn't hurry, they might be caught in the middle of the snowstorm. She definitely didn't want to be alone if that happened.

Once he made sure she got into her vehicle all right, with the pretense he didn't want her slipping again, which was fine by her, he climbed into his rental car. But as they drove off, he inched past the gray pickup as if the speed limit were five miles per hour. She swore he was writing down the license plate number—she had done that too.

When they reached the place for the snowmobile rentals an hour later, Faith and Cameron went inside a small grocery store next door to get provisions. Cameron was picking up a few items on another aisle, when Faith noticed how much the snow was falling. Too fast.

Last time she was in a snowstorm, she'd been visiting her dad at Portland Community College, taking in the hilltop view as she enjoyed a hot cocoa with him in between his classes. The falling snow looked majestic, blanketing everything in a fresh coat of white. Beautiful, until they tried to leave after his final class that day and were trapped with tons of other vehicles attempting to return home in the storm. Pile-ups. Stuck cars. While she and her father had struggled to get snow chains on the tires. What a mess.

"Hurry up, Cameron," she said, coming up behind him as he weighed the options of buying one package of tuna over another.

"I always bargain shop."

"That's great, but do it faster then. We've got to get out of here before we're stuck staying at the lodge in Millinocket for another night because of the storm. And who knows whose room we'll end up in this time if the same clerk is on the desk."

He chuckled and tugged gently on the tassel of her blue and red striped ski cap. "Would be all right if we ended up in the same room again." He eyed the prices again on the packages of tuna. "If I don't choose the right tuna, I could be broke before I return home."

She grabbed one of the packages from him. "Fine. I'll pay for it." Then she hurried to the checkout.

He soon caught up with her with a basket loaded with a week's worth of goodies, and she eyed the snack foods and a couple of salmon steaks in the mix. "If you're so broke, why did you have that gigantic steak for dinner? And room service at that? Plus salmon also now?"

He just winked at her. Yeah, he wasn't so broke. She thought it admirable that he bargain shopped, although about now, all that mattered was that they get on their way.

Then they were off, leaving their rented vehicles in a parking area behind the snowmobile rental shop, bags and sleeping bags loaded onto their snowmobiles, the snow falling way too rapidly. But Faith was sure they'd make the ten-mile trek in time before they lost their way.

She called her father, although she knew he'd still be sleeping at this hour and by the time she reached the cabins, he'd be in the middle of teaching Sociology 101 to a bunch of tired students in the early morning class, but she wanted to leave him one more message. "Dad, I'm off to the dead zone."

She didn't mention how she'd found a body, or a hunk, or how the police officers knew of her father.

She sighed and signed off with, "I love you. Call you later when I have a signal again. Don't work too hard.

I'll get the flash drive back. And I'll be home as soon as I can. Don't worry."

But now *she* was worried. She envisioned getting here, locating Hilson, having it out with him, and he'd have a conscience and give the research back to her. Now she was having doubts her plan would work. What if she couldn't find him? What if he refused to give the flash drive back? Or what if he got rid of it already?

What then?

And something she'd been avoiding considering— why did Hilson want the information so badly? And what had he planned to do with it? Plus, what was the research all about that made it so damned important in the first place?

Chapter 3

AFTER ALL-NIGHT SURVEILLANCE OF A RENT-A-COP ON THE graveyard shift at a warehouse, who was suspected of worker's comp fraud, Gavin Summerfield yanked his bedcovers to his chin at four in the morning in his tidy little condo in Seattle. He closed his eyes, wishing his P.I. partners would return to help run the business. Since Cameron had left, Gavin was being run ragged and he didn't think he could take much more of these kinds of hours.

But as soon as he shut his eyes, the phone rang. He ignored the first two rings as he stared at the red numbers on the digital clock. Then he growled and grabbed up the phone, ready to strangle the caller if it was a wrong number or overzealous telemarketer who didn't know what time it was in the Northwest. No phone number listed on the Caller ID.

"Hello!"

"Gavin?"

Gavin bolted upright. The voice sounded a million miles away and the phone crackled with static, but he'd recognize Owen's voice anywhere. "Owen? Owen, you all right?"

"We're quitting."

"The hunt? Are you and David okay? Coming home soon?"

"Quitting... partnership. Tell—"

The phone sputtered.

"Owen? You're breaking up badly."

"Tell Cameron don't come."

"He's there already. Where are you?"

"Dangerous."

"Owen, Cameron's there. I can't get word to him. What's dangerous?"

"… kill him. We're okay." Crackle. "… go."

"Owen—"

"No!" someone else yelled in the distance on the other end of the line. Then the phone crackled again and died.

"Owen!" Gavin stared at the phone. "Shit." He jerked his covers aside and sat on the edge of the bed, trying to regain his equilibrium. At thirty, he was getting way too old for all-night surveillances without a partner to back him up. But helping his friends if they needed him—and they better damn well need him—that, he would never be too old for.

He rubbed his tired eyes. If he had the time, he'd drive to Maine. It didn't matter that more people died in car accidents every year according to statisticians who kept such statistics. Just taking off in a plane nearly killed him.

He tried Cameron's cell phone, but after several minutes, gave up. Either Cameron was on his way to the cabin resort and couldn't hear the phone above the noise of the snowmobile, or he was already beyond where he could get a signal.

Gavin ran his hands through his hair. At least he could convey the information to Cameron about the gray pickup when he caught up to him. Although he was more interested in the woman Cameron had his sights on rescuing this time.

Gavin shook his head. Cameron would never learn. He punched a few numbers on his phone and said, "When is your next flight to Bangor, Maine?"

The snowstorm intensified as Cameron and Faith drove their snowmobiles slowly along the unplowed road, the visibility less than a quarter mile, the wind blowing faster than they were driving. Pine and spruce trees lining the wide road were draped in white, like snow giants protecting the dwellers of the forest.

Cameron and Faith had considered staying at the lodge in Millinocket for another night, but both of them were impatient to get on with their business. Cameron still wondered exactly what Faith's business here was. He didn't believe for a minute she was here to relive her father's snow-filled adventure. Not in the beginning, and then when Officer Adams mentioned the sociology business, Cameron wondered what that was all about, since the police had taken an interest. Not only that, but Faith had been reluctant to mention it. Curiouser and curiouser.

He was still wondering about his friends, too. Were they in some kind of trouble? From what Gavin had told him about the conversation with Owen, it didn't sound like it. And with the difficulty Owen was having with talking to Gavin because of the remoteness of the area, that might have been the whole problem. They'd gotten stuck some place where they couldn't make phone contact and were perfectly fine. If Owen and David were now quitting the hunt, maybe they'd get home before

Cameron could even locate them. Which put a whole different slant on the situation. What if he now could make a vacation out of this instead of work? He hadn't taken one in over three years. Maybe he could share Faith's adventure, help her to relive the time her father had spent here?

He snorted. He didn't believe that was what she was here for in the least. And he was determined to learn the truth sooner or later. But another thought occurred to him. Why was she worried about the gray pickup? Even though he'd called the license plates in to Gavin to have him investigate, Cameron knew he wouldn't hear back from him for a while, what with communications being so spotty where they were going. But Faith seemed to think something wasn't right about the vehicle, and he wasn't leaving anything to chance.

And the police officers? That was another concern. Of course every department had its own procedures, and every individual officer had his own way of dealing with a crime scene, but he thought both acted strangely unconcerned. Almost as if they were trying to appear that way to cover up their true feelings. He'd observed Officer Adams's expression for the briefest of instances when he'd first seen the dead man, as if he had more of a tie to him than he wanted to admit. But then his look had swiftly changed to all business.

More than that, they seemed to recognize Faith before she even told them her name. From what Cameron understood of the situation, she'd never been to this part of the country. So it seemed odd. Even if they'd heard of her father, it was as if they had a whole dossier on the family, current photos included. The comment about her being a wanted woman threw him, too. Even though he shouldn't have made anything of the guy talk, he couldn't help wondering if Adams was referring to Cameron wanting her, or someone else.

Shifting his thoughts to where they needed to be, Cameron concentrated on the road, trying to stay in the center while he followed Faith, unwilling to go first and risk losing her behind him, when he saw a flash of something to his right. Jerking his head that way, he tried to see into the forest, but the snow was blowing so hard, he couldn't make anything out. Probably nothing of importance. But he still couldn't help wondering what it was or if he'd just imagined it.

Watching Faith again, he hoped she was warm enough from the heat distributed from the manifold through foot-rest grilles and heaters placed on the steering handles on the snowmobile. She was wearing those stretchy, clingy ski pants that, on her figure, were flattering and way too sexy. Even her ski jacket was short-waisted, showing off her curves a little too much.

Not that he didn't enjoy looking, but he could have beaned the guy restocking shelves at the grocery store for eyeing her a little too hard. And the "kid" at the snow-mobile rental place made a big deal out of the fact she wasn't wearing a wedding ring and when she returned to Millinocket, he could sure take her out to some fun places. That was until Cameron did his I'm-with-the-lady routine to keep the vultures away. Whether she wanted him to or not.

Actually, she'd seemed a bit amused. If any guy thought he'd make any moves on her at the camp, he'd let them know just how wrong they were.

She slowed her snowmobile down a little, and he matched her actions. He suspected they were getting close to the resort when he thought something moved again to his right. But when he looked hard in that direction, all he saw was blowing snow, snow-laden trees, snow piled against them, nothing but white.

He glanced back at the road and a one-story log lodge appeared up ahead with a majestic prowlike front and covered wraparound veranda. Cedar rocking chairs sat all along the wooden deck, the arrangement welcoming guests to sit and visit while taking in the panoramic mountain and forest view. But the large picture windows were dark, no light filtering through, and the massive stone fireplace was cold, not a trickle of smoke.

Faith drove up to the porch and paused for a minute, not turning off her engine. He parked beside her and saw what it was that had stopped her: a note pasted on one of the windows from the inside.

Closed due to family emergency. Keys in cabins. Be back later. Charles and Elizabeth Roux.

Faith pulled her ski mask down under her chin so she could speak more clearly. "Guess we're on our own."

"Good thing we brought supplies with us and didn't count on eating at the main lodge first thing. So, which cabin do we hole up in for now? White Wolf or Black Bear Den?"

"How good are you at starting fires?"

He smiled. "Eagle Scout. Although, I have to admit I always carried a lighter with me on campouts as a boy."

She laughed and even though her sweet voice was half drowned out by the roaring wind, her laughter warmed him deep inside.

"Come on, boy scout, before we freeze our buns off out here. We'll go to whichever is closest."

"Black Bear Den. Yours."

He hoped she'd be amenable to letting him remain the night. It wasn't that he was so needy, but he didn't like the idea that a woman would be staying alone in a cabin in the wilderness with no one about. Especially in the midst of a blizzard. Well, truth be told, he was feeling a bit needy, too.

They wound their way along a narrow forested trail on their snowmobiles, the trees helping to shield them from the blowing wind, until they reached the first of the small log cabins facing the frozen lake. Through the clearing, bitter cold wind whipped off the ice.

A carving of three whimsical black bears holding a sign that said, *Welcome, Black Bear Den*, attached to the door of the cabin, indicated they were at the right place.

As he recalled from the map Charles had sent him when Cameron booked the reservation, his own cabin was quite a distance from Faith's. Each of the cabins had a screened view of the lake with plenty of trees in between to provide them enough privacy from their neighbors. Which was another reason he didn't like it that Faith would be alone.

Snowdrifts were piled against the side of the cabin all the way to the windows, at least a foot of accumulation covered the deck, and the roof was bearing a heavy load. Although it was midday, the blizzard made everything look gray, cold, and foreboding.

Which made it imperative he started a fire right away to heat up the place. As soon as she was inside, he hauled in his stuff behind her. No sense in leaving it out to freeze in this weather even if he wasn't staying the night. When he put his bags down on the knotty pinewood floor, she raised her brows and gave a funny little smile.

"Not snowproof," he said, as if answering her unspoken question, then headed back outside before she could retort. When she followed him to get the rest of her stuff, he waved her inside. "Go set up housekeeping, Faith. I'll take care of the rest of your bags. Dressed the way you are, you're way too much of a distraction."

He loved the way the skin underneath her eyes crinkled when she grinned, shook her head, and returned to the cabin. His attention then focused on the skin-tight ski pants hugging her derrière. The thought came to mind how much fun it would be to ski with her in the great Northwest, share a hot toddy at the ski lodge, and snuggle together with her in a spa, the snow piled up around it. And then work out all the kinks from a day on the slopes in a soft bed made for two. He shook his head at himself, grabbed the rest of her bags, and returned to the cabin, shutting the door against the howling wind.

Faith had pulled off her ski hat, mask, goggles, and gloves but was still wearing her jacket as she looked inside the cabinets. The log cabin was ice-cold, with unadorned large picture windows facing out on the frozen lake. The walls were made of logs, but insulated. Cameron didn't feel a bit of wind coming through the walls, which he was grateful for. At least once he had a fire going, the place should warm up pretty quickly.

"Have a fire started in a jiffy. As soon as I can find my lighter."

Faith had already started a tea kettle on the gas stove. "Fire here," she said, pointing to the flame under the kettle. "Did you bring coffee? I've got green tea."

"Coffee." He knew he'd forgotten something. Although he figured he could have gotten some to drink at the main lodge, the thought crossing his mind that cuddling with Faith early in the morning would negate any need to get up to have any for sometime anyway.

"You didn't bring any?"

"No. Forgot all about it."

"How about hot cocoa then?"

"Either is fine." He finally got the fire started in the wood-burning stove, turned on the fan to blow heat into the room, and looked around. One double-sized bed and two twin beds in two bedrooms off the living room. Although a queen-sized suited his height better, a double was better for snuggling with a sweet feminine body on cold winter days. No bedding or linens on the bare mattresses, which is why they had to bring their own sleeping bags, and he considered how well his would fit on her mattress.

She caught him eyeing the bed. His ears burned with chagrin, and he smiled. Hell, he was caught in the act, and he was pretty sure she could read his transparent thoughts. Women often could.

"So, I offered to fix lunch. Or have lunch with you. But since it appears this is where we'll be eating, what appeals?" She took off her jacket and laid it on a chair, then started pulling out cans of spinach, green beans, corn, asparagus, salmon, and the package of tuna.

"How about you pick out the vegetable and we can fix my salmon steaks?"

He looked around the kitchen. Sink, no running water. "Ice box, but no refrigeration. They'll have to supply us with ice, but looks like no one's around to do that today."

"We could gather up some snow and put it in the ice box. But the salmon sounds good to me."

"No breakfast for me, so it sounds fine."

She cast him an annoyed expression.

He smiled. "Yeah, I know that look. You didn't wait too long for me at the restaurant this morning, did you?"

"No, just ate and left." She turned her back on him and emptied the contents of the can of spinach into a saucepan.

"Ah, good." He didn't believe a word of what she said. She'd waited for him. In fact, he suspected, she had gone straight from the restaurant to Back Country Tours. So she must have waited a good half hour for him at least, which made him feel like a cad to an extent. But his partners' welfare, he believed, had been at stake. "I thought I had a lead concerning my friends so I ran out at five thirty this morning. Turned out to be a dead end. I figured by the time I found that out, you'd have left the restaurant, so I headed to Back Country Tours. And lo and behold, here's my favorite lady."

She hmpfed. "Panicking over a dead body."

He moved in closer and with her back still to him, he rubbed her arms, the soft peach sweater sliding a little, her subtle sweet fragrance tantalizing. "You looked a little pale, and you were doing the smart thing by leaving in a hurry when you heard an intruder in the place, but you did it with true grit. Any other woman I've known would have run out of there screaming."

"Not the screaming type. *Normally*. Although when I found a snake curled up in my wet laundry in the washing machine once…" She pulled out a broiler pan for the salmon. "I'm sure you could have heard me all the way to Seattle."

"Fear of snakes?"

She smiled up at him. "Only when I reach for a handful of wet clothes to put in the dryer and feel something solid, wet, round, and slimy that shouldn't have been there." She sprinkled lemon and pepper seasoning on the salmon. "About the dead guy though, he had a needle mark in his chest. I think you were right in figuring he was injected with something. But there was the oddest thing next to the puncture wound."

Hell, he wished he'd taken a look now, too.

"A drop of what looked like a silver solution," she continued. "I would have loved to have taken a sample of it and analyzed it. But I didn't want to tamper with the evidence, and besides, I don't have any equipment here to do the analysis anyway."

He admired her for having investigated the situation when he left the office. He never suspected she had. "Silver? Mercury, maybe?"

"Hmm, no on the mercury poisoning. A year ago, we had a case of an attempted suicide who unsuccessfully used an intravenous mercury cocktail. It didn't lead to acute systemic toxicity. Or in laymen's terms, it didn't overload his system causing death."

That was a new one on him.

"But silver poisoning?" she said, raising her brows. "Yes. You can find silver remedies that claim all kinds of health cures. So they're not hard to come by either online or in health food stores even. Argyria is the name of the condition when people ingest silver and silver poisoning can turn skin gray. It's permanent. So slow poisoning is visible to the naked eye; not a good way to murder someone on the sly. In high amounts though, it can kill someone also. I investigated a case where the husband injected his wife with 50 mg of silver salts because of the life insurance policy he had on her, and she promptly died. But in another instance, a quack doctor injected a pregnant mother with silver nitrate for an abortion and killed the mother, too."

Cameron was speechless at first. He and his partners could really use someone like her on their team. "You could be handy in an investigation."

"That's what my coworkers always tell me. So did you see anything in the offices that you checked?"

"Papers strewn all over the place. Looked like someone was searching for records of some sort."

"Anything on your friends?"

"No. At least not that I could find on such short notice. The records were in a shambles, so they probably were there in the mess."

She stirred the spinach. "I hope your friends are okay."

"They're former police officers, too. I'm sure they can handle themselves just fine. But I have to be certain. Where had you planned on going exactly? Do you know where your father actually went while he was out here?"

"No. Trevor Hodges knows though. If I can find him. The man who owns this place? Charles Roux? He runs the dogsledding part of the business here also and said he could take me to see Trevor at his campsite beyond Baxter Park."

"Ah, so then why were you at Back Country Tours?"

"You know," she said, running her finger along Cameron's sweater-covered chest, then gave a little tug on his belt hidden beneath the sweater, "you sound just like a cop."

Loving the way she touched him with a hint of flirtation, suggesting she wanted more, he was ready to delay the meal. "I've always sounded like a cop. Ever since I was a kid. Heck, one of the Boy Scouts in my troop stole money from several of us. I had to prove who the culprit was." He combed his fingers through her hair, loving the soft texture, enjoying the small smile playing on her lips.

"Didn't you feel like a tattle tale?"

"No. And I doubt you would have felt that way either." If he had her figured right. He wrapped his arms around Faith, and to his delight, she melted against his chest. He breathed in her heavenly scent, loved the feel of her pliant body pressed against him.

"You're right. If a girl in my Girl Scout troop had been stealing from any of us, I would have set a trap, taken pictures, or videotaped it, and caught her red-handed."

Just envisioning Faith in her super-sleuthing activities as a kid, he laughed, surprised that she was a Girl Scout. "Right is right and wrong is wrong. I've never had a problem with seeing the difference. So what made you get into the business?"

"The truth?" She pulled away from him and motioned to the salmon. "I'd better turn them before they're blackened."

He didn't care as long as he could cuddle with her longer. He hadn't felt like that toward a woman in eons, but the way she spoke, he sensed some darker reason had catapulted her into her chosen career field. He was sure he wouldn't like it.

"The ten-year-old girl across the street disappeared when I was sixteen. I helped put out fliers, helped look for her in the neighboring communities, brought food to the distraught family." Faith stared at the spinach for sometime before she spoke again. "They found her four days later, dead. The search for Christine was over, but looking for her murderer?" Faith let out her breath. "I couldn't do anything more for the family, so I decided right then and there I'd help find Christine's killer. Took me nearly ten years."

Now that, he hadn't expected. Gavin's father had been on the police force and had died in a robbery shoot-out. That's what made Cameron and Gavin join the force. David had always had a sense of adventure, so it was either that or join the military. When the rest of them decided to join the force, he was not one to be left out. And Owen? His father had been in enough barroom brawls that he was always on the opposite side of the law. Owen didn't want to follow in his father's footsteps and much preferred being the arresting officer. But Cameron didn't even like thinking of the danger Faith might have been in, searching for her neighbor's killer.

She offered Cameron a sad smile. "We got him. The bastard was an older cousin, who didn't like it that she had loving parents, lots of everything, when his dad was an alcoholic and his mother was never around much. I thought it might have been him, the times I'd seen him treat Christine meanly when he came to visit. But we had to have proof. And after I was trained in forensic science, I was able to obtain the proof in the cold case files after sorting through boxes of evidence that had sat idly for years." She sighed. "What about you? What made you go into the business?"

"Nothing as dramatic as your situation. But Gavin's father had always been like a surrogate dad to me since my own died in a car accident when I was a teen. So when Gavin's dad died in the shootout, I wanted to become a cop, too."

"I'm sorry about Gavin's father. And yours also."

He didn't want to tell her that even when his dad was around, he wasn't much to brag about. Gavin's father was a different story. War hero, all-around nice guy. His father? Womanizer, carouser, gambler, all-around deadbeat. But it didn't seem the time to talk ill of the dead.

He glanced around at the cabin. Fabric with black bears on plaid covered the pillow cushions on all the seats. Pictures of real black bears in the woods, fishing in a stream, hung on the walls. And a mixture of real-to-life black bear carvings and whimsical ones sat on a shelf. Cuddly, oversized teddy bears added to the black bear theme of the cabin.

He could imagine what his cabin looked like. The intense amber eyes of white wolves watching every move he made, strategically placed everywhere in the cabin.

Faith motioned to a plastic jug. "At least they left us some water before the staff took off. The five-gallon container should last us a while. If we run out, you can go get yours."

Glancing out at the storm, not letting up in the least, he shook his head, having no intention of leaving Faith and the toasty cabin, unless they were in dire need. "We'll have to make this last for now." But if he didn't read anything wrong in what she was saying, did she plan to let him stay?

He intended to change her mind if she didn't want him to and made himself useful, setting out the silverware, the plates, only glancing back at her in the kitchen when she stopped rattling pans around. She was watching him, a small smile percolating on her lips. She held his gaze as if measuring him for a job, licked her full sensuous lips like she was readying them for a well-placed kiss. And he was damn well ready to kiss her again.

He hadn't entertained a thought about a woman in such a way for months—not with the self-imposed sixty-hour work weeks he'd been putting in. Not to mention his former girlfriend jilting him several months ago. Just about the time he began working lots of overtime. Yet he was more than intrigued with Faith. Which he thought had something to do with the way she handled herself at a crime scene and how knowledgeable she was in figuring out clues. And not flighty when she came face-to-face with a naked stranger. Her endearing story of her neighbor and the way she helped out impressed him also. Plus, he'd never have figured her for the kind who would manage roughing it in a place like this.

His ex-girlfriend would have thrown a fit not to have an attached bathroom and running water and linens for the bed. And no maid service or room service or television either. Nope, Marjory would have given him notice before they even arrived at the place once she learned she couldn't use the Internet or phone her friends. One of whom happened to be the guy she took off with.

Distracting him from his thoughts, Faith turned and flipped the salmon again and switched off the oven.

If his intuition was right, he was certain Faith was considering letting him stay the night, although he was ready to convince her if she had any doubts that it was the best thing for all concerned—for safety's sake, of course.

"Meal's ready." She began to dish out the spinach, when they heard someone yell out somewhere in the woods.

He looked out the window but didn't see anything or anyone. Immediately he worried someone had been ice fishing and fallen through the ice. "Stay here," he said, jerking on his coat and gloves.

"Maybe I should go with you."

He shook his head. "Lock the door after me. Probably nothing, but I've got to check it out." He yanked on his ski mask and hat, then headed outdoors, hoping he wouldn't find anybody in any real danger. He didn't like leaving Faith alone, but he had to make sure no one was in any real trouble.

Faith scooped the spinach back into the saucepan and kept it on low heat. Then she returned to the window to watch for any sign of anyone, but mostly for Cameron. She liked it that he was a take-action kind of guy, but prayed no one was really in any trouble. His story about Gavin's father endeared him to her. But it made her wonder what the deal had been with his own father because the concern he shared with her reflected much more sorrow for Gavin's father than his own. She sighed. Maybe his father had been like her mother. Not there to really count on for anything.

After locking the door, she began making the bed. His double-wide sleeping bag and her single sleeping bags unzipped fit the double-sized bed nicely. Even though it was a bit presumptuous of her to think he would stay the night, she figured he was hoping. They might as well share the place and meals, keep each other company while they dealt with the staff of Back Country Tours.

Tomorrow, they could straighten out the cost and, well, since Cameron was going to go broke if he didn't choose the cheapest brand of tuna—she smiled—this would save him a little money.

She returned to the stove and poked at the salmon again. At this rate, it would be overdone and cold by the time Cameron got back. Then one of their snowmobile's engines began to rumble, and for a minute, she thought Cameron had come back for it. But when hers started up, she assumed the worst. Someone was stealing their snowmobiles. She grabbed a large cast-iron frying pan, hurried to the door, and opened it, just in time to see two men sitting on the sleds, both backing up from the cabin in the wind-driven snow.

"No!" she screamed, and, wielding the pan, she raced out to stop them.

Chapter 4

THE FIRE GLOWED IN THE MASSIVE STONE FIREPLACE AS Kintail Silverman paced across his lodge's great room miles from where his new troubles lay, wondering how the hell he was going to remedy this mess while other members of his pack kept an eye on Owen and David in the den.

Kintail glanced at Lila Grayson. She looked a little contrite for once and he frowned. "You were supposed to be watching Owen. David will do anything we say, but Owen... he's trouble. How many phone calls did he make before Trevor caught him? And twice, he's tried to escape. The only good thing about any of this is we're too remote for him to get word out, he doesn't know his way around out here, and he doesn't have a clue how to deal with the shapeshifting aspect." Kintail stared out one of the picture windows at the blowing snow, the cold so invigorating, even now he wanted to shift and run like the wolf he was.

He couldn't kill Owen, not yet. He knew the man needed some time to adjust. If only his partner, Cameron MacPherson, wasn't on the way to rescue Owen and David now. That's what was causing him all the heartburn.

Lila cocked her head in her arrogant way, yet he knew insecurities about something in her past fed her actions. Given time, he figured she would eventually come around.

"You shouldn't have changed them. Or at least David."

She smiled. "I don't think Owen's forgiven me for biting him."

Kintail liked it when she smiled, as if a part of her gentler nature was trying to reveal itself. But now wasn't the time to concern himself about his issues with Lila. Neither David or Owen had any family left in Seattle. Kintail hadn't thought one of their partners would look into the situation.

Kintail shook his head. "If we didn't have so many hunting parties scheduled for the next several weeks, we'd leave early for Yellowknife. Take them with us and isolate ourselves. But we can't split up the pack, and we can't leave right now. Not without hurting our business and ruining our reputation here."

He loved living here half of the year, flaunting what they were while the locals and tourists didn't have a clue. Except for the Cree in the area—they knew, but they revered the wolf, which worked to Kintail and his people's advantage. "I'm sure nowhere else in the States can a werewolf pack show off their pack members in broad daylight, anywhere and everywhere, and get away with it."

Lila stretched her arms above her head, then crossed them. "I agree, and that's what's so much fun about living here in the winter, being around people who are clueless as to what we are, thinking that our wolves are like old good-natured dogs. But what about this Cameron MacPherson? Can't we just change him, too?"

Kintail didn't care for the interest in Lila's tone of voice or the expression on her face. He knew her well enough to recognize she was intrigued with the man. Did she think maybe she could convince Cameron to take over the pack and then mate with her just because Kintail wasn't freely mating with her? Cameron? A newly turned *lupus garou*? She had to be nuts if she thought Kintail would lose against the newcomer. Besides, her secretive past was what was keeping her from letting Kintail get close to her. He doubted she could get close to Cameron anymore than she could with him.

"If he's coming to rescue his partners, he's sure to be an alpha. There's only one way to deal with him."

"Hmm, well, can't we just make an offer first? Then if he says no, whatever happens to him is his own damned fault?" she asked.

Kintail gave her a hard look.

She lifted a shoulder and pushed her hair back into a ponytail, and he inwardly groaned at how enticing the woman looked. "You're the boss of course. But it seems to me if we can get him to join us, that would be the best scenario." Then she curled her lips down, and he knew what was coming next. "What about the woman? She's been snooping around, asking about Trevor. Looking for information on her father's trip here."

"Trevor swore Kenneth O'Malley didn't see anything, but Hilson says he has evidence that her father saw one of us shapeshifting."

Lila sat down on one of the velvet couches. "So… my question, again, is what do we do with her? What we should have done with her father when he was here before, is my way of thinking."

Kintail gave Lila a sly smile. "She could make a nice addition to the pack." Lila had only joined his pack two years ago from a group in Finland. He still wasn't sure what her deal was, except she had been born a *lupus garou* like him. But she hadn't allowed any of his pack members to get close to her. Especially not him. Unless she thought she could get him to bend to her wishes. She really didn't know him that well. Yet.

"We have enough females in the pack," Lila snapped.

"We can never have enough females what with the shortages there are. Besides, Hilson wants to deal with her."

"Hmph, if he'd dealt with her when he first staked her old man out, we wouldn't have this new situation. What's your brother's problem? She's not too alpha for him, is she?"

Kintail rubbed his chin and looked back out the window. He wondered why his brother hadn't already taken the woman for his own. Maybe she was too alpha for *him*.

—◆◆◆—

Cameron didn't see anything near the lake where he'd heard the man yell, although the way voices traveled, he might have been much farther away. But when the sound of snowmobiles started up at the cabins, his intuition immediately kicked in, warning him something wasn't right.

He trudged through the knee-deep snow as fast as he could manage in the blowing wind, retracing his steps as much as possible to make it easier to run. The snowmobiles sounded like they were leaving the area around Faith's cabin. Which he assumed meant only one thing. At least two people were stealing them.

But as soon as he saw Faith racing around the side of her cabin half dressed, wearing no parka, gloves, or ski hat, shouting, "Bastards!" his heart nearly froze.

"Faith!"

She whipped around, her brows knit in a deep frown, her mouth curved down, her bare fists held tight at her sides. "They stole our snowmobiles!" She stiffly waved down the road.

"Go inside," he warned, as the snow covered her hair and stuck to her sweater, the wind still not subsiding, and he figured she'd catch pneumonia the way she was dressed.

She waded through the deep snow, stopped, looked down, then fished a cast-iron frying pan out of a snow drift, whisked around, and returned to the porch. In disbelief, he watched her. Hell, the woman was lethal. Despite the circumstances, he smiled, then hurried around the cabin and looked down the road. The snow-mobiles were long gone.

When he stepped inside and closed the door, Faith was busily jotting down information. "Blue parka, black ski mask, scrawny build but tall, jeans, cowboy boots, black gloves, yellow goggles. Other guy—black parka, black ski mask, heftier, same approximate height, jeans, snow boots, brown gloves, 9mm," she muttered under her breath.

"One of the bastards had a gun?" Cameron pulled off his gloves, parka, and hat, setting each of them on the chair near the wood-burning stove, then lifted a blue floral towel she'd hung over the log footboard of the bed.

"Yeah, pointed it at me when I started chasing them."

"Before or after you pitched the frying pan at them?" He joined her and ran the towel over her wet hair. She melted a little under his ministrations, and he leaned over and kissed her cheek, her skin still cold. "Hell, Faith, didn't they ever teach you not to chase armed men when you don't have a weapon of equal or superior might?" he scolded, dropped the towel on a chair and pulled her tightly into his arms.

She turned her head and frowned up at him. "I didn't know he had a gun at first. Not until he pointed it at me. Bastards."

"The snowmobiles *are* insured."

"Well, yours has a slight dent on the tail end now. But it doesn't make me any less angry knowing they're insured."

"You hit my snowmobile?" He released her and began massaging her tense shoulders, her sweater soft, slippery, and springtime fragrant. She leaned into his touch, and he was ready to carry her off to bed, to sooth his frayed nerves... in his own way.

"I aimed for the guy, but that frying pan weighs a ton so it didn't have the lift I'd hoped for." She growled, then purred as he continued to massage. "Good thing you brought your stuff in or they would have stolen your gear, too."

"All I care about is they didn't steal *you* away." Even now his heart was still racing from worrying she might have come to harm. "Did they do anything other than take the machines?"

"Not that I saw. What about you? Did you find anyone in trouble out there?"

"It might have been a diversion to draw me away from the cabin. They might have suspected that if only one of us was here, they could steal the snowmobiles."

"One of us. You mean the weaker sex." She pulled away and dished up the spinach.

Chuckling, he squeezed her arm to reassure her he didn't feel that way in the least about her, then served up the salmon on hefty-sized dark brown plates. "Believe me, I don't want to ever make you that angry. Weaker sex? How much damage did you do to my snowmobile with that frying pan?"

She gave an evil smile. "At least if I see it again, I can recognize it better."

When they sat down to eat, Cameron wondered if his insurance or hers would cover the damage to his snowmobile given the circumstances for the bash. He was about to cut into his fish when he spied his couple-sized, down sleeping bag spread out over the mattress like a welcome mat through the open bedroom door. He tried to conceal his smile before she caught it, but what could he say? His motives were usually crystal clear when it came to women.

"Trying to take all your stuff to your cabin in this storm without the use of a snowmobile isn't a good idea," she said, matter-of-factly.

He nodded, very serious-like, as he took a bite of his salmon. But the thing of it was, she had to have laid out the sleeping bag earlier, before the machines were stolen. Had to have, because she wouldn't have had time to do it afterward without his catching her when he came inside.

"I wholeheartedly agree."

"*Besides,* you owe me breakfast and there's no way I'm traipsing in the cold all the way to your place at six in the morning to have it."

"Six in the morning?" Hell, he thought that was just this morning's schedule, a way to get ahead of the incoming snowstorm.

"Yes, that's when I'm always raring to go."

"I thought this was a vacation for you." Now maybe he'd get the truth out of her.

The sound of her laughter was lighthearted and fun-loving. "My internal alarm clock wakes me at five every morning. It's amazing what I can accomplish by getting up early."

"Maybe you just haven't had the right incentive to stay in bed yet." He was afraid his smile was a little too wolfish when her cheeks blossomed with color, but the coy smile she offered in return made her eyes sparkle with humor.

She saluted him with her cup of green tea. He saluted her back with the awful stuff.

Yeah, he'd make it worth her while to stay in bed until it was a decent wake-up time in the morning. Especially if he couldn't have a cup of coffee first thing.

Now, he was glad he'd brought his made-especially-for-couples sleeping bag. And to think the reason he'd taken that one and not his single sleeper was it would serve more like real bedding while he stayed in the cabin, and truthfully, it was lighter weight and easier to compress than his old one. For the first time, he didn't mind that an earlier girlfriend had ditched him before they had the chance to try it out. Or that his latest girlfriend wouldn't have taken a step in any direction that had to do with sleeping bags.

If he could just get a good fix on his friends and maybe even help Faith with whatever reason she was really here, this could turn out to be a nice little getaway. Notwithstanding that they had to get word to the police in Millinocket whenever they could that their snowmobiles had been stolen.

After eating lunch, Cameron helped clear away the dishes. Without snowmobiles, or the lodge owners in residence at the moment, there wasn't much else to do with the snowstorm still pelting them, but hunker down in the cabin... or...

Cameron glanced back in the direction of the main lodge. The cedar hot tub was supposed to be fired up nightly. Two heated shower facilities with flush toilets were connected to it. Since no one was here to object, maybe he'd heat up the hot tub a little early.

"Did you bring a swimsuit?" he asked.

Faith stopped putting some of her sweaters in a drawer of a small three drawer chest and looked at him as if he'd lost his mind. "Lake's frozen solid. And I'm not a member of the polar bear swim club either."

"I was thinking more in the line of a hot tub."

Her expression brightened considerably. "Oh, I forgot about that." Then she seemed subdued again. "But the owners aren't here." She returned to the kitchen and pulled the cans of groceries from a plastic sack, then tucked them under the cabinet.

"And the owners should be in residence. Besides, we wouldn't do anything they wouldn't do if they were here. So I figure, why not?"

She shook her head. "I thought you were an Eagle Scout."

"I am, but..." He shrugged. "So, do you have a swimsuit?"

Looking thoughtful, she pulled a golden curl behind her ear, which made him want to nibble her lobe, right then and there.

"I wonder how many other guests are here?"

She was going for it! And he bet she didn't have a swimsuit.

"Not many. Looked like at least half of the eight cabins were under renovation, closed tight. I saw lights on in one of the remaining ones. None on in the other. And of course there's mine, which is vacant. Otherwise, that's it."

"One renter. Could be an active family with tons of kids. What if they showed up about the time we did our illegal firing up of the hot tub in the late afternoon? Here we'd be, snuggled down in the hot soupy water, and kids with floaties would pour onto the deck, chattering, and laughing, and—"

"I'll heat up the hot tub and be right back." He didn't wait for another objection—if she was even going to offer one—shoved his jacket on, and hurried outside.

He thought about what she might wear for their excursion. Something pink and lacy? White, maybe? Daring red? Black and seductive?

The stiff wind hit him with a blast of snow. He wished he hadn't been in such a hurry and had taken his goggles and ski hat. Next trip, when he escorted his date to the spa, he'd be better prepared.

When he reached the deck attached to the shower house, he plowed through the snow and retracted the cover on the spa. Steam rose from the heated water. He pulled off a glove and stuck his hand in. Warm, not really hot. After turning the heat up and the jets on, he pulled his glove back on and rubbed his hands. Billions of bubbles popped up, creating a white foam, soon hiding the Caribbean blue marble effect on the walls of the circular tub.

He would have opted for one that was couple-sized, but the spa looked like it could hold six to seven adults, not half as cozy as he would have liked. And the awful thought it could be filled with lots of kids came to mind. He turned on the lights around the edge of the tub, then found a snow shovel in a utility shed, and cleared as much of a path on the deck as he could up to the cedar-surrounded spa from the changing rooms. He envisioned Faith in the tub with him and how hot things could get if he and Faith could have more privacy. Too bad they didn't have one inside their own cabin.

Then he went inside the changing room to warm it up so they could shed the majority of their clothes. A gust of bitter cold wind blew in through the doorway and he turned, thinking Faith couldn't wait to join him. But no, it was some other woman, and he felt a pang of disappointment. If she was a guest, that was the end of his plans to share some private time with Faith. But then he wondered if this woman was one of the owners ready to give him a dressing down for heating up the hot tub without permission.

"Lila Grayson," she said, slamming the door shut behind her with a lot more force than needed.

Lila Grayson, the one from Back Country Tours—it hit him as odd that she'd arrive here of all places. Wearing ski boots, an ivory wool sweater, and ski pants, she looked ready for cold weather expeditions, minus the ski jacket. Tangled by the wind, her platinum blond hair drifted past her shoulders. Her golden eyes wary, she was a looker, with skin the same color as her clothes and ruby lips glossed for show. High angled cheekbones gave her the look of a movie star, but her tiny nose contradicted that image. She pulled off her glove and extended a hand.

"Cameron MacPherson," he said, shaking her hand. "You run Back Country Tours?" Now maybe he'd get some answers concerning his friends.

She lifted her nose and sniffed. "You were in my office earlier today? Along with a woman friend? Found one of my employees dead, according to the police?"

So, she hadn't just happened to run across him here. She was investigating him.

"Yeah, I was looking for you or your partner, Kintail Silverman. Two of my friends went on a hunt and haven't returned."

"Owen and David are quitting. Haven't they told you?" She raised a brow and smiled just a hint, but it was icy like her whole demeanor.

"Quitting the hunt."

"No, quitting *your* business. They're going up north with us, joining our hunting guide team. They're tired of the P.I. work. Didn't they tell you?"

Cameron stared at the woman as if she'd managed to turn him into a frog. "I'll hear it from them first."

"Owen said he called your partner, Gavin. Said he told him they were quitting the business. Since you were…"—she smiled—"checking out our office, I figured you might not have gotten the official word yet."

"I'll get the official word directly from them."

"Hmm," she purred and took a step toward him, and he envisioned a lioness on a hunt, her eyes fixed on him, just waiting for the right moment to pounce and rip out his jugular. She reached her hand out and trailed her fingernails down his sweater. "Maybe you could quit your job, too. Come join us."

That's when the door suddenly opened and Faith stalked inside, a frozen smile on her lips, her eyes narrowed in a confrontational way. She looked as though she was ready to punch out her competition, and he loved it. "Forgot your towel, honey." Faith waved the blue towel at him and slid her arm around his waist, snuggling up next to him. She gave Lila a get-lost look.

He was ready to play the lover's role for real.

Lila sniffed the air. "She's the one with you at my office this morning. Are you looking for his partners, too? Or something else?" she asked Faith.

Faith stiffened. "Office? You're from Back Country Tours?"

"Lila Grayson."

"I'm looking for Trevor Hodges. He works for you, right?"

Her smile faked, Lila said, "Not of late. What did you want him for?"

"He guided my father on a… tour. I wanted to see the route they took."

Lila narrowed her eyes. "And you are?"

"Faith O'Malley."

The woman's eyes widened a little in recognition. Then she smiled slyly. "Well, old Trevor Hodges could be anywhere out there." She waved her hand around in the direction of Baxter Park and the surrounding woods. Then she glanced outside at the steamy spa. "Don't want to let your water get cold." She smiled again at Cameron. "Offer still stands, if you decide to come work with us."

"Have David and Owen meet me at the lodge, and I'll hear for myself if they plan to quit our partnership."

"I'll be sure to give them the message." Lila whipped around and headed out of the building, shoving the door against the wall as she left the place.

Faith hurried to close the door against the blowing wind.

"Why did she recognize your name?" Cameron asked, pulling off his sweater.

"Dad seems to have made an impression on a lot of people. And she might have met him when he hired Trevor to take him on the tour." Faith dumped her ski coat on one of the cedar benches.

"I thought maybe there'd been some trouble when your father came on his trip here. At least the way Lila responded it sounded that way."

Faith tossed her sweater onto her coat. "What was the business offer she proposed to you?"

The fact Faith changed the topic so quickly made him wonder even more what this was all about. "She wanted me to become one of her guides."

"And you don't believe your friends would quit the partnership like that?"

"Nope. We've been friends since grade school. Always talked of having a partnership. And even if they did want to jump ship, they'd never do it like this without discussing it with us, and then giving us time to downsize or get a couple of new partners."

"Hmm, so it sounds like Lila Grayson and probably her partner, Kintail Silverman, have something going on."

"Yeah." *But what was the deal with Faith, her father, and Trevor Hodges?* "Do you believe that Trevor Hodges no longer works for Back Country Tours?"

"Nope. No more than I believe your friends are leaving you and your other partner high and dry without saying so face-to-face." She unbuttoned her blouse.

He felt like a kid in a candy store, waiting to see all the treats. He turned around and pulled off his shirt to give her some privacy. When he tugged off his jeans, the door squeaked open and shut, and he looked around to see she'd left him. Smiling, he hurried to join her outside. The cold wind whipped across his bare skin, as she quickly slipped into the hot water with a splash. He got an eyeful of blue bikini panties, a matching blue bra cut nice and low, and pristine peach flesh covered in goose bumps. She lowered herself into the bubbling water, the swell of her breasts lifted above the foam. Her gaze moved lower, her expression bemused; his body was certainly responding. He hoped he wouldn't embarrass himself.

"Warm enough?" Although as hot as she looked, he figured she could heat the water right up.

"Hmm, perfect." She closed her eyes and rubbed the hot water over her neck and shoulders and sank lower into the tub.

Yeah, perfect was right. No matter what the woman wore, or didn't wear, she was a sight for deprived eyes.

Cameron climbed into the water and settled next to Faith, wanting to make the night with her something special. The warm water and powerful massaging jets that targeted his lower back and calves were only half the fun. The sound of gentle moving water through amplifiers built into the tub casing covered the noise of the jets. "This makes the cold and the trip well worth it."

Before he could settle in nice and close to her and take advantage of her soft expressive mouth, a gray-haired old lady waddled from the back side of the building in a coat and short snow boots, but her white, hairy legs were bare. She smiled. "Be right out, folks." She entered the changing room and shut the door.

Cameron scooted even closer to Faith, his body touching hers, the image of her half naked sitting this close to him in the heated water, stirring up a raging need. Before the woman returned, he shifted restlessly, his gaze moving from the shower house to the object of his most fervent desire. *Faith*. Her lips wore a tentative smile, but her eyes—they challenged him to take the first step. He couldn't help being irritated with the stranger, to say it mildly. But he wasn't about to let the woman stop what he had in mind to do.

He leaned over and pressed his lips against Faith's mouth, savoring the velvety softness, the way she woke to his touch, lifting her chin to accommodate him, closing her eyes, her hands clutching at his forearms. He touched her supple breasts and she moaned softly, but the moment was all too short.

Shattering the mood, the older woman exited the room, wearing a tent-size bathing suit in hot shimmering pink and the furry boots. "Charles must have fired up the hot tub earlier than usual, although I haven't heard a peep out of his sled dogs. He must've figured we couldn't get out in this weather to ice fish. Always so considerate of his guests. I'm Mary."

"Faith, Cameron," he said, pulling away from Faith, although his leg and hip still rested against hers. His hand shifted to her thigh, caressing, enjoying her silky skin, and the way she leaned against him. But even though her eyes were smoky with desire, the newcomer's presence caught Faith's focus. All he could hope for at this point was that Mary would tire of the tub quick enough and leave so he could get back to business.

"On your honeymoon?" Mary asked, smiling as if she were a woman in the know.

Faith said yes as he said no. The old woman laughed. "I've been there, done that myself."

As soon as she had her boots off, the sound of crunching snow from the direction of the backside of the shower house warned them others were coming. Faith gave Cameron an I-told-you-so look, and he figured it was time to leave before the woman's grandkids showed up with the floaties. Except that the way the newcomers moved, the footfalls sounded more like adults' and not overzealous kids'.

Three men around Cameron's age came into view and gave Faith interested looks, then went inside the changing room.

"Do you want to leave?" Cameron asked, figuring she'd want to, as he certainly did.

She patted him on the leg and leaned over to speak in his ear, her whisper soft voice rousing him even more, which made him wish the others would just vanish in a puff of mist. "I hate to be run off, Cameron. The jets feel so good on my back." She snuggled closer and kept her hand on his thigh.

Hell, now he was really ready to take her back to the cabin and try out his new sleeping bag for two with her. "Are you sure?" He ran his hand over her arm and kissed her cheek, hoping to coax her away so they could have more privacy.

She gave him an interested smile. Yeah, she was game, but she still wasn't leaving the warmth of the hot tub. Couldn't blame her there. The heat and pulsing jets were only part of the draw though—the sexy, nearly naked body snuggled up beside him, soft and malleable and hot and wet—that's what inspired him to stay a while longer.

The raggedy-looking guy with frizzy red hair and a shaggy beard exited the building and gave Faith a wink, his green eyes challenging her to join him— later. Barefooted, the other men hurried out of the shower house and across the snowy deck to reach the tub pronto.

Cameron wrapped his arm around Faith's shoulders and gave her a squeeze, not caring if he was showing his possessiveness. Besides, he was keeping Faith warm, in case she needed him to. She responded by leaning her head on his shoulder and caressing his thigh, way too erotic for all the company they had, although with all of the millions of bubbles rolling to the surface of the water, no one could see a thing. Speculation was another story, and he imagined everyone was speculating away. "He wasn't no Bigfoot," the redhead said to his companions as he climbed into the sauna and sat next to Mary.

The old lady laughed. "Bigfoot, Chris? When I was a girl, three of my friends and me saw him. Or might've been a her. Twelve foot tall he was. Hairy, slouched over like a bent-shaped man, only naked and bigger. He glimpsed us in the woods, sniffed the air, then hurried into the shelter of the trees, and disappeared. I wanted to follow him. See where he went. But the other kids were too chicken."

"You saw him around here?" Faith asked, at once her body stiffening with interest, surprising the hell out of Cameron.

He really didn't think she'd be interested in hearing about fairy tales, since she was a forensic scientist, dealing in scientific fact.

"North of here. Toward Baxter Park," Mary said, nodding vigorously, as if she'd gotten a live one to listen to her tall tale.

The black-haired man of the three shook his head and looked over at Faith. There was something about the way he observed her, not as if he was interested in her sexually, but something else. Almost as if he were a cop, watching for her reaction. "Not Bigfoot this time," the guy said. "It's one of those others, and we need to take care of business."

"One of what others?" Faith asked, sounding a little too interested.

Don't encourage them, Cameron wanted to say. Hell, next they'd be talking about little green men and being poked and probed on a spaceship from a galaxy far, far away.

Chris smiled at her, then looked at his friends, but the expressions on their faces said that this was still a secret and they weren't about to share their findings with a couple of strangers.

Cameron was just as glad. But Faith persisted. "What was it you saw?"

Chris cleared his throat and gave her a half smile. "Maybe we can talk about it in private sometime."

"Ah, Chris, can't you see the two are together?" Mary teased.

"Her loss," he said, grinning at Faith.

Cameron wanted to wipe the grin off Chris's face, and although he wanted to take Faith out of here pronto, he couldn't now. It had to be her call, or he'd look like a possessive, overbearing lout.

Chris turned to the black-haired guy who was patting the bubbles on the surface of the water, his nearly ebony gaze still on Faith. "Should we tell her, Matt?"

Matt shook his head. "Privately, if she wants, just like you said." His voice was cold and calculating, and Cameron didn't like it one bit.

Faith stared Matt down, and then turned her head and looked up at Cameron with the most adoring expression. He thought it was faked just for their audience's benefit, but he was willing to believe. "Ready to call it a night, honey?" she asked, her tone seductively enticing.

Well past ready, but his heated gaze wasn't in the least bit false.

"It's about that time. Wait, and I'll get your towel." What he wanted to do was kick the men's asses out of here while Faith got out, and he would have, too, if she'd agreed.

He climbed out of the hot tub, grabbed her floral towel, and held it down close to the water so she could leave without showing off her wet bra and panties. No one said a word, and he suspected the guys were watching her in rabid fascination, but he was too busy trying to shield her from them to see. With the towel wrapped around her, she headed into the women's shower room, and he entered the men's room.

Once he was dressed, he left the changing room, out of view of the hot tub to wait for her near the path they would take to her cabin, when he saw three feral-looking white wolves in the trees near the main lodge, the blowing snow almost disguising them. Lila stepped out of the forest to join them, her red lips turned up in a half smile. "Kintail told me to bring you to our hunting camp. You can see Owen and David there."

He wanted to speak to them. But not like this. Not off in the wilderness somewhere that he couldn't communicate with authorities if need be. Not without some kind of backup.

"I'll take your suggestion under consideration. In the meantime, I've told the police about my missing friends."

Her lips curved up even more. "Good for you. I imagine they were readying the search parties right away."

The woman had him there.

She snorted. "Didn't think so. See you around, Cameron."

She turned and took a few steps in the direction of the snow-cloaked spruces, and he swore, dressed all in white still, she evaporated into the snow-filled wonderland. Her wolves eyed him longer, then one by one, they whipped around and vanished, too.

"Cameron!" Faith hollered from around the backside of the shower and hot tub building, sounding distressed and in need of his help.

In full rescue mode, the adrenaline pumping pell-mell through his blood, Cameron dashed around the building to save her.

Chapter 5

FAITH WAS POINTING AT THE SNOWMOBILES PARKED BEHIND the shower and hot tub building, the one snowmobile's back end dented. But that's not what got Cameron's full attention. The wolf lunging in their direction, materializing out of the snow without any warning, made his heart nearly stop. He wasn't sure which one of them the wolf was aiming for, but he didn't have time to do anything but block Faith's body with his own, and throw his arm up to protect his throat. She screamed. The wolf bit through his jacket and into his arm.

"Your gun!" she shouted.

"In the cabin." He never thought he'd need it at the hot tub.

He tried to shake loose of the wolf as if it were a friendly old dog with a big bone, playing tug-of-war, growling, eyes narrowed, hair on the back of its neck standing on end, but just in good-natured fun. Only Cameron's arm was the bone and it hurt like hell as the pain radiated up and down through every nerve ending. Plus he felt the blood seeping from the wound, the tear in his parka letting in the chilled air.

Suddenly, Faith swung a snow shovel, striking the beast in the hip. He yelped, released his hold on Cameron, and jumped back from Faith. For a second, his eyes stared at hers as if he was reading her inner soul and every thought she had.

She stomped at him and swung the shovel in an effort to hit him again, and this time Cameron swore the wolf smiled. Then the beast bent down, whipped around, and melted into the snowy woods before she struck him again.

Faith dropped the shovel and grabbed Cameron's good arm. "We've got to get you some help."

The pain in Cameron's arm throbbed even harder now. "You mean, ask for it from those clowns in the hot tub? When Charles Roux returns, we can get him to send for help. Just take me back to your place for now."

She didn't listen to him and instead helped him to the hot tub. Everyone had left. She opened the door to the changing room, letting some of the heat out. The place was empty. "No one here," she said.

"Guess when you left, the party was over."

"Oh, Cameron, your face is so pale. I'll get you to my place, but I don't have any first aid kit, and I didn't see any in the cabin. What about you?"

"Bandages for blisters, but nothing for wolf-sized bites."

"Then we'll have to check out the main lodge."

He was going to object, but Faith had a mind of her own and helped him to the main lodge porch, then up to the door. She tried the handle. *Locked*.

He could have told her it would be. Otherwise, people like him might just wander in and make themselves at home.

"Sit here, for a second, Cameron. I'll see if any of the windows are unlocked." She helped him to one of the knotty pine rockers, put her ski cap on his head—which reminded him he should have brought his own—then she started tugging on windows.

Watching for any sign of the wolf that attacked him, he let out his frosty breath, cradled his injured arm against his body for warmth, and tried to ignore the streaks of sharp pains like needles jabbing into the muscle.

Faith tried to open the rest of the windows on this side of the lodge.

When she began to venture around the backside, Cameron said, "No, Faith. I don't want you out of my sight."

She frowned at him. "It'll only take me a minute. If I can find an unlocked window, they might have antibiotics and better bandages inside. I have to try."

"No, it's not worth it. If the wolf's still lurking out there… it's just not worth it to me. Come on. Take me back to your cabin so we can get warmed up." His blood had soaked his shirtsleeve and sweater and it had chilled him even further. Now, due to the shredded parka sleeve, everything that had been wet was coated in ice. Shivering uncontrollably, he didn't think he could get any colder.

Still frowning, Faith helped him down the steps and back to the cabin. "I can use my towel maybe, to stop the bleeding. How bad does it feel?"

"Not too bad," he lied, afraid she might still try to go after the windows on the other side of the lodge once he was settled in her cabin. "With as many layers of clothes as I'm wearing, he didn't hurt me too much."

"A German shepherd can crush a bone. I imagine a wolf could do even more damage. Are you sure you're not too bad?"

"I *was* feeling better."

She chuckled, a little hysterically.

"Sorry. I guess I shouldn't have told you that."

As soon as they reached the cabin through the path to the woods, she assisted him inside and helped him to one of the dining room chairs, then locked the door. After removing his coat, she pulled off his sweater and stared at the blood and rip in his shirt.

"Not too bad," he said. "It's not even bleeding any longer."

A flitter of concern slipped across Faith's face, but she quickly removed his shirt and wrapped the towel around the wound without saying a word.

"Tetanus shot up-to-date," he said. But he knew that probably wasn't what was worrying her. Rabies. What if the animal had rabies, and that's why he'd attacked?

"We have to go back to town tomorrow if Charles doesn't return to the lodge by then."

He agreed with a nod. Now that their snowmobiles were back and if the weather had cleared up by then, he figured that was the best move.

"Wonder why the men stole the machines, then brought them back," Faith said, as if she was trying to get his mind off his injury. "Really bizarre."

"I don't know. What made you go around that way when the way I went was closer to your cabin?"

"I was drying the edges of my wet hair when I looked out the window and saw the snowmobiles. I didn't really think they were ours. How weird would that be? But I had to check it out. Do you think it might have been somebody joy riding who doesn't have a snowmobile here at the camp?"

"Who first threatened you with a gun?"

"Well, then, maybe somebody stole them from these guys and brought them back." Faith helped Cameron into bed, pulled off his boots and socks, and covered him with his sleeping bag.

"Highly unlikely," he said.

"Well, you're a former cop. What do you think?"

He gritted his teeth against the pain in his arm, but when Faith caught his action and glanced out the window, he started talking to distract her from leaving him to seek help. "It's hard to say why anyone would do what they do. I rode around with some petty criminals once while I was undercover. Their reasoning for not stealing a young woman's purse? She had a kid. Not that morality had anything to do with it. They figured the kid would scream and attract too much attention. Another scenario? A woman was carrying a big purse. Which to them meant she had lots of money."

"You're kidding? A woman with a big purse might not have a bit of money, just lots of useless junk."

"Right. So you see, it's hard to predict what goes on in the criminal mind." He patted his sleeping bag on the mattress. "Are you going to join me?"

She rubbed her arms, her brows furrowed. "I'll add some more wood to the fire."

"Don't go outside."

"Enough wood is stacked in a basket by the stove. Just sleep, Cameron. I'll get you help as soon as I can."

"Don't leave the cabin, Faith," Cameron reiterated in his police officer's voice, obey or else. No way did he want her to risk going outside alone to get help for him. But they needed to get word to the other guests also. Later though. He figured no one would run around much in this weather, and he wasn't in any shape to go anywhere, nor did he want Faith out in it by herself.

Faith's cold hand touched his forehead. She gave him a worried smile. "No fever."

"No, I'll be fine. I just need some rest." Tired beyond belief, he closed his eyes, a dull pain throbbing from the wound and radiating down to his fingertips, the thought of cuddling with her still lingering in his thoughts despite the pain.

She moved away from the bed, added firewood to the stove, paced across the wooden floor a bit, her footfalls muffled when she walked on the braided rugs. He wished she'd join him in bed, still worried she might leave, but then he drifted off into the world of snow and wolves. The wind howled and then the sound shifted, changed, morphed into the howl of a wolf. One, the alpha male, deep and low and long. Then another joined in, and more until a whole chorus of wolves sang their lonely song. One part of him longed to join them, but part of his conscious mind warned him the consequences could be deadly.

"Hmm," Lila said, lounging before a roaring fire in the great room of Kintail's lodge, her bare foot rocking up and down off the sofa, her manner an attempt at seductive, and Kintail wished she really was up to seducing him.

The woman was a master manipulator when she wanted her way, or just plain sarcastic and antagonistic when things weren't going her way. He noted the subtle change in her demeanor since he'd had the run-in with Cameron earlier today.

He knew sarcasm was her ploy this evening before she even spoke further. "So you bit Cameron but you didn't kill him. And his feisty girlfriend struck you with a snow shovel."

Situated at the massive oak dining room table that overlooked the sitting area in the great room, Kintail lifted another spoonful of hot and spicy chili to his lips. Feisty, that's the way to describe the woman named Faith O'Malley. But seeing her in her low cut bra and bikini panties before she entered the hot tub, gave way to more erotic fantasies. He hadn't liked the way Cameron was kissing her in the tub and Kintail had the notion of biting her instead of Cameron, get it over with, change her, and see what transpired, but she had to call out to Cameron about the snowmobiles. Kintail hadn't predicted the guy would race around the building as if the world was on fire and get in Kintail's way.

Served him right to get bitten first. Still, Kintail couldn't quit thinking about the woman. She might be trouble, but she was damned intriguing. And here she'd only just met Cameron, but instead of screaming for help after Kintail had bitten him, she'd slugged Kintail in the hip with a shovel to save the guy.

Kintail hadn't expected that. The bruise would heal up soon, so no big deal. But he liked her character, protective, loyal in the face of danger, striking in the flesh. An alpha female.

He finished the bowl of chili and motioned to Trevor to get him some more.

"Well?" Lila snarled.

He knew she wanted him to kill the woman. Competition. Good competition, too. Faith was the first woman he thought might have enough gumption to fight Lila and win. Not that he wanted Lila hurt, but he needed a mate, damn it. And she wasn't cooperating one iota.

Trevor set a fresh bowl of chili before him, his gaze shifting to Lila.

"She's intriguing," Kintail said, knowing his words would antagonize Lila. They had sort of a love/hate relationship, and he supposed some day he'd have to take her for his mate. Unless he could find someone else he truly cared for, if he couldn't break the impenetrable barrier Lila had erected around her heart. Miss O'Malley was growing more interesting all the time even though he'd never considered changing a human to suit his purpose. Those born as *lupus garous* already knew the role they had to play in their society. Much easier to deal with. Normally.

"Intriguing, my ass. She's real trouble. And why did you just bite Cameron and then let him go? I saw the way you looked at that woman and didn't attack her when you easily could have. No damned shovel would have stopped you. Particularly when some weak human woman was wielding it. One lunge and she would have dropped the shovel and fallen flat on her backside. Then we could have been done with her."

Even though Lila sounded tough, he noted a hint of insecurity in her voice, which couldn't help but trigger his interest in her again. He liked her better when she let her vulnerability slip, and suspected she could be right for him if she ever let go of her past hurt.

He thought again about the way Faith clobbered him with that shovel and it wasn't in the least bit done meekly. She let the whole force of her slight body go with the flow. Of course if he'd seen it coming, he would have nimbly dodged the blow, and at most the shovel would have only glanced off him. Next time, he'd be more prepared for the woman's tactics so the outcome would be much more agreeable.

"When have I killed a man for the sake of killing him?" Kintail asked, fingering a slice of buttered French bread. "Even with the intent of keeping our people's secret safe?" He took a bite of the crunchy bread, then scooped up another spoonful of chili.

"I'm sure you used to."

"A long time ago. Before there were that many people. When we had to. Not now. What do you think would happen if someone found his body and thought one of our wolves killed him? With DNA testing of hairs and saliva left at the crime scene, they could pin it on an Arctic wolf. And who else has Arctic wolves in the region but us? Is that what you want?"

Lila rolled her eyes. "I just wondered if you'd decided to let Cameron join our little merry gang of wolves."

An alpha male? Not on Kintail's life. But he'd draw Cameron into the wilderness where human traffic rarely went, somewhere no one would ever discover his body, and fight him wolf to wolf. Much more sport that way.

The wolves' howls faded into the misty snow and the moan of the wind returned. Cameron jerked awake, feeling strangely unsettled. Faith was curled up against his chest, her breathing light in sleep, her body soft and huggable. He held her with his good arm, reached over with his bad, and stroked her golden hair. But she was sound asleep, and he didn't want to wake her. His

wounded arm didn't even give him a pinch of pain now.
Maybe it hadn't been as bad as he thought.

But what he couldn't comprehend was the restlessness stirring deep inside him. He'd never felt that way
before. On cases he was close to solving, he might not
be able to sleep, his mind working overtime in solving
the puzzle. But this was something more primal, more
physical. He was torn between staying with Faith and
enjoying her comforting heat, the sound of her steady
heartbeat, and her subtle fragrance—and squelching the
craving to ditch his clothes no matter how cold it was
and run through the snow.

Trying not to disturb Faith, Cameron slipped out from
under her, making sure his sleeping bag still covered her,
and then he left the bed. He was surprised to experience
no dizziness or fever from the wolf's bite. He stretched
out his arm, but no matter how he moved it, the ache was
completely gone.

After pulling the towel off his arm, he examined
where the wolf had bitten him. Except for faded bite
marks, dried blood, and light bruising, he was nearly
as good as new, although it had seemed so much worse
when he was first bitten.

He went to the door and opened it, stared out at the
moonlight reflecting off the snow, the clouds having
moved away, the storm spent and gone, leaving moun-
tains of snow in its wake. It looked as though the day
was already upon them instead of the dead of night.
Mystical, magical, even romantic, if Faith had been
awake and here to share it with him.

But the moon compelled him to do what no sane man
would ever have done. He couldn't repress the urge

he had to—well, he wasn't sure what he wanted to do. Leave. Maybe. But it wasn't exactly that either. Despite not being able to see the actual moon, he could feel its presence. Like the moon's gravitational pull on the tides, he felt an odd connection. A seduction, a caress of wills, his against the moon's. *Come to me, and I'll make your dreams come true. Fight me and you'll suffer.*

He was going mad.

Without another second's hesitation, he stripped out of his jeans and boxers, and stood watching the tree limbs stirring in the breeze. The bitter cold surrounding him shook him to the marrow of his bones, but then dissipated when a strange warmth quickly worked its way through every fiber of his being, his muscles twisting, bones reshaping, all painless, effortless, exhilarating.

He stood on four pads, a thick, double white coat covering his skin, making him impervious to the cold. He stared at his large front paws, black wicked-looking claws touching the wooden floor. He sniffed at his fur, which smelled of spicy aftershave.

The moon again called to him, the branches of the trees waving at him, beckoning him to join them. Without another thought, he lowered his forequarters, keeping his hindquarters straight and did a slight bow, then raced out the door, bounding over the piles of snow left by the storm and took off through the woods.

Cameron raced through the forest, brushing against the snow-covered branches of towering spruces, shaking loose torrents of snowfall. The snow falling down on him didn't touch his skin though. A thick coat of fur kept the snow from melting, and he felt toasty warm. He expected the snow and cold to chill his "bare" feet, but it didn't bother his paws, maybe, he thought, because of the fur between the pads.

He ran on the tip of his toes, which seemed weird, but it lengthened his stride, and he covered more ground that way. Whenever he began to slip on an icy patch, he instinctively spread out his pads, increasing the surface area that he stepped on, the additional friction preventing him from taking a spill.

A fresh coat of snow, looked to have been a foot or more, covered everything, but he found that he didn't sink into the fluffy white stuff as he would if he was running as a human. The freedom this gave was exhilarating as he raced through the trees, only stopping momentarily to smell a whiff of a rabbit or bird and fresh clean air.

When he came across a fallen tree angled toward the sky, propped against another tree, he would have had to climb slowly over it in his clunky human form, but instead, he leapt, his feet sprawled, gripping the trunk with ease, propelling him over the top. And then he was down again, running on his tippy toes.

He'd run for miles, although it hadn't seemed like any time at all, when he heard the sound of voices. Curious by nature, but even more so now, Cameron headed toward them.

"Hell, she was interested," a male voice said, and instantly Cameron recognized it as the guy who'd joined them in the hot tub. Chris, the redhead with the unruly hair.

"Interested in Bigfoot. Sure. But she might not be interested in what we've found. And besides, the fewer who know what we're doing, the better," said Matt, the guy with the cold, calculating voice.

Then a woman spoke up. Mary, it sounded like. "Chris doesn't *just* want her to be on the team. He's looking for something a little hotter than that, Matt, I suspect."

"Her father was writing a research paper about Bigfoot. When we got separated, I swear he saw something like we have since then. Hell, I'm sure she already knows all about them. That's why she questioned us more about what we knew. She wanted in." Chris sounded annoyed with his companions, ready to take them on.

"Says you," Matt countered. "We can't just trust anyone, especially when it's your dick talking for you."

Cameron drew closer to the mammoth-sized tent in the small clearing. A stovepipe vented smoke out the top of the tent, while lanterns inside shown through the orange tent fabric, silhouetting four figures sitting inside. Were they talking about Faith? About her father? According to the police, her father was conducting a sociology study. About Bigfoot? Cameron would never have guessed. Was that why Faith hadn't wanted to talk about it? But if he could discuss it with these men, maybe he could find out what they knew. Then, perhaps Faith would have some of the answers she was seeking. But then again, maybe they were talking about someone else, not Faith at all.

He moved in even closer, wanting to clear his throat to warn them he was here, before he intruded or startled them too much. But all that came out was an alien huffing sound.

"What the hell was that?" Chris said, as all of them began to stand.

"I've got my gun," Matt said, and that's all it took.

Chapter 6

HAVING BEEN SHOT ONCE IN THE LINE OF DUTY WHEN HE WAS on the police force, Cameron didn't need to be reminded how much that hurt, nor did he want to be injured way out here in the middle of nowhere, if Matt or his buddies decided to shoot him.

Cameron whipped around and headed away from the tent the way he had come, following his trail back through the woods, surprised to find his footpads had left a scent for him to track.

Chris exclaimed, "Shit, it was one of them! One of the wolves. Look at all the damned tracks! Break up camp before they come back for us. Hurry!"

The panicked group hurried to strike camp, but Cameron kept running, following his tracks, keeping his paws in his original footsteps so that he could make better time. The tracks looked huge in the snow, like his paws were much larger than they were. Which probably contributed to tales of wolves that existed as gigantic beasts.

He raced on and on, realizing now he'd traveled a distance much greater than he'd first suspected, yet he felt free and wild, not tired and cold as he might have imagined.

After a good long while, he smelled smoke from a wood-burning stove and knew he was getting closer to the cabin resort, when he nearly plowed into a wolf. He stopped on the proverbial dime and stared at the wolf, russet in color, his brown eyes shining in the dark, his expression surprised more than anything. As much as Cameron himself was surprised.

He expected a confrontation, but the red wolf just studied him with interest, sniffed the air, and remained standing in place, not moving an inch in any direction, his ears alert, twitching back and forth. His posture seemed relaxed though, unlike Cameron's. His was stiff, apprehensive, unsure of what would happen next.

He sensed the wolf was an alpha, holding his tail straight out behind him, not tucked, his head held high, not bowed. Cameron was standing in the same manner, waiting to see what the other wolf would do first. He couldn't get over the fact a red wolf would be in the area. Gray maybe, living somewhere in the wilderness. The white wolves, Kintail's, absolutely. But not a red wolf, that he thought was extinct in most areas.

Then the sound of snowmobiles zooming off through the woods from miles away, caught their attention. Chris and his buddies, Cameron suspected. He twisted his head around to look in that direction. When the snowmobiles headed farther away and weren't driving in his direction, he turned back to observe the red wolf, but he was gone, vanished, like a flake of snow against a snowbank.

Cameron looked around, didn't see any sign of the wolf, sampled the air but couldn't get a whiff of him the way the breeze was blowing. He thought about Faith, about the bed, about snuggling, and felt the adrenaline rush begin to drain off, then loped toward the cabin resort.

When he reached her cabin, he stared at the wide open door. For an instant, he worried that someone had

broken in. Then he wondered if he was the one who
had left the door open. He headed inside and nudged it
closed with his nose and paws. Then he jumped on the
bed and joined Faith, although he didn't attempt to crawl
into the sleeping bag with her. Too much trouble and he
was plenty warm enough.

Closing his eyes, the last vague thought he had was
he'd experienced one hell of a dream.

Faith snuggled closer to him and sighed. The dreams
and Faith's touch finally faded away, but before long
Cameron bolted upright in bed and stared at the cabin,
the hour still early, his whole psyche turned upside down.
Thankfully, Faith's face was cloaked in blissful sleep,
and he hadn't awakened her. He swept his hand down
her hair, every ounce of his physical being craving her,
and yet, now, for some unfathomable reason, another
part of him warned she was dangerous and to avoid
entanglements with her at all costs.

So why the hell was he wanting to prove she wasn't
in the least bit dangerous?

He climbed out of bed and found he didn't have a
stitch of clothes on, when he thought he was wearing at
least his boxers and jeans when he fell asleep last night.
He vaguely remembered Faith carefully removing his
parka, shirt, boots, and socks like an angel to his rescue.
The braided rugs were wet, too, and he wondered when
that had happened. Maybe Faith had spilled water before
she retired to bed.

He tugged on a pair of jeans, but didn't bother to
secure his leather belt or the top button and zipped them
only far enough to keep them on his hips as if he might
want to shed the pants any moment, so why fasten them

all the way? He walked over to the window and stared out at the bleak white landscape, wondering why he was feeling so unsettled. He wasn't feverish, yet he didn't feel right. But he couldn't pinpoint what was wrong. Cabin fever maybe? Too bad the most vivid, unreal dream he'd ever experienced hadn't resolved the bizarre feelings snowing him over. Yet he kept wondering, what if the dream was true? That he'd really heard the guys in the hot tub outside the cabin last night and incorporated their ramblings into his dreams?

He let out his breath. Nah. Just a case of recalling situations he'd been in earlier in the day or past several days and mixing them up in a dream. Although he couldn't account for why he'd envision a red wolf. Then he recalled watching a program about the ones reintroduced into the wilds of North Carolina a week ago, and saw *Wolf* with Jack Nicholson the night before last, and then the *Howl of the Wolf* after that. And then? Cameron dreams he's a wolf?

He shook his head. No way had he turned into a white wolf during the night. After being attacked by the one, and seeing them with Lila, that was the reason for the surreal dream.

Man, he'd had his fill of wolves for a lifetime.

"Are you feeling all right?" Faith asked from bed, her voice silky with sleep.

He didn't look at her. Didn't want to. He hated feeling out of control, out of sorts.

"Much better." Which was the truth, to an extent. His arm did feel better, but his mind was in turmoil.

"What's wrong?" Her voice warned him she understood him as well as he knew himself.

"Nothing. We're snowed in." He pulled the door open, let in the cold air, some part of him wanting to freeze the unwarranted emotions he was feeling now out of existence.

The snow halfway blocked the entryway except where something had run through it. He stared at the sight, trying to figure out what would have made the impression, and noticed then how wet the braided rug was next to the door. Hell, Faith must have left the cabin sometime during the night despite him telling her not to.

He attempted to see beyond the piled-up snow, but it was stacked too high to observe what had happened clearly.

The box springs squeaked, and then Faith's footsteps padded across the floor. Cameron turned to look at her and couldn't help raising his brows. She was wearing a footed one-piece sleeper contraption covered in white bunnies and pink flowers on a lilac background. Her blond hair appeared tangled from a night of restless sleep, or a lover's tryst. She looked soft and huggable in the chilly room.

Frowning, she hurried toward him. "Are you sure you're all right?"

His gaze shifted to her bunny outfit and the long, lilac zipper that reached from the neckline all the way to the pubic bone. His thoughts instantly switched from running in the wild, to pulling that zipper down as far as it would go. "Plenty of food and firewood. We'll stay warm enough."

The craving to be with her overriding the urge to leave, he shut the door and locked it.

She reached out and touched his hand. "What about your wound? We need to get it checked out."

"Feels good as new." His voice had already taken on a husky tone, and he sifted his fingers through her silky hair, wanting to feel every inch of her, to breathe in her scent, to taste her. Already, he seemed to sense more—her own interest in him—but it wasn't the expression on her face. She looked worried, not sexually ready. But it was her scent that indicated she was interested. A subtle change in the way she smelled was all it took to make him want her even more. As if the scent was a trigger of acceptance and willingness.

Not to be thwarted in her concern for him, she said, "It's still really dark in here. How can you see anything?" She turned on a gas lamp, then examined his exposed skin, her lips parting slightly, looking damned kissable.

As much as he hated to admit weakness, he explained what had been bothering him.. "I felt I needed to get out of here."

"Maybe it's cabin fever." Her eyes took in his naked torso, shifting downward to his pants, only partially zipped. Her gaze shot back up to his, but he didn't think she was shocked as much as intrigued. She touched his shoulder in a reassuring way, her fingertips leaving a streak of heat behind, then ran her hand down his arm until she reached his fingers and took hold. "I've been snowed in for a few days, but it doesn't bother me. Maybe we can play games or something."

"Or something." Despite his brain warning him to keep his distance, he wanted to kiss her and much more. He settled his hands on her shoulders, his thumbs caressing them in little circles, his gaze focused on that sensuous mouth of hers, curved up slightly.

Every nerve ending was attuned to the way she felt, the soft fuzzy fabric of her pajamas, the curve of her shoulders, the swell of her breasts rising and falling with every breath, even her nipples protruding, begging to be fondled, and the way she relaxed under his touch as if she savored his strokes as much as he did stroking her. She tucked her hair behind her ear, the motion surprisingly sensual. Nibbling her creamy earlobe came to mind. His libido ratcheted up another notch.

"I promised I'd keep you in bed longer this morning," he said, his voice deep and raspy as he swept his hands down her arms to her fingers. He lifted one of her hands to his lips and kissed the top of her hand, and then with the same kind of appreciation, the other, her skin delicate like peach velvet.

She smiled coyly, her green eyes narrowed a bit. "Are you sure you're all right?" Her voice was husky with need, too, and he smiled with the knowledge.

"Only one thing will make me feel better." He leaned down and wrapped his arms around her back, pulling her closer, his body barely touching hers, yet every inch that did, sizzled with heat. He kissed her lips, gently at first.

But gentle wasn't what she seemed to have in mind as she slipped her arms around his waist, hugged him even closer, molding her sensuous curves against him, and licked her lips, making them glisten in the low lantern light. Her eyes looked deeply into his, challenging him to play with her. He would have dived right in, but he was too intrigued and let her have her way.

In the beginning.

She kissed his lower lip with just enough pressure to stir him up. And then he intended to do his part, but she kissed his upper lip, her eyes now focused on his mouth. He savored the heat and fullness of her sweet mouth, the way she teased him with her light kisses. She opened her mouth and tongued his lips, exciting his senses even more, the scent of her arousal filling him with rampant desire. But when she withdrew her tongue, her lips still parted, offering him a deeper connection, he took the initiative, licked her velvety mouth and took advantage of her offer. His tongue slipped into her mouth, tasted of her, memorized the hot wetness, the softness of her tongue and lips and mouth.

She slipped her fingers underneath his waistband, her nails skimming his naked skin, dipping toward his erection. His skin on fire, his senses staggered, completely scattering what he had in mind to do next. Nothing else intruded on his thoughts—the cold room, the wet braided rug beneath his bare feet, the aroma of the salmon cooked the afternoon before still lingering in the air. All vanished as he braced for what she would do next, her touch so pleasurable he was momentarily paralyzed into inaction.

Her long nails slid deeper and she smiled when she discovered he didn't have anything on underneath the jeans. She pulled her hands free from his pants, but before he could again take the initiative, she traced his erection hard beneath the soft denim, making it jump with her touch, the tip now exposed from the zipper riding so low and from her working him up. Despite trying to show restraint, he shuddered with her touch. He'd never had a woman work to pleasure him and the experience was astonishing.

With one hand, she dragged the zipper the rest of the way down, her fingers stroking his heavy arousal at the same time, while her other hand slid down the back of his jeans and cupped his ass. But then she pulled his waistband down and exposed him even further, the tip of his penis wet, ready to penetrate her.

Wanting to get her in bed and underneath him now, he slipped his hands down her back, intending to lift the vixen up and wrap her legs around him to carry her to the mattress, when his fingers discovered an intriguing secret. A flap at the back of her bunny britches. Quickly feeling around to determine a way in, he slipped his fingers inside, touching the curve of her naked derriere, and felt her tremble. He pulled his hands free, found the snaps, and with several pops, exposed her sweet, little ass. She smiled and slid her hands down his spine, until she reached his waistband, and slipped her fingers underneath his jeans, cupping his bare buttocks and squeezed.

Slow and easy, work her up the way she needed, he figured, but she was making it awful hard on him. And she knew it, too, the way she rubbed against his arousal, the soft flannel of her nightwear teasing him. He was hard with need, and he wasn't going to last with the slow approach at seduction. He slid his hands over her ass, lower still until he found her drenched curls between her legs. She shifted her feet so he could get better access and he obliged, stroked her deep, bringing forth a moan of uninhibited desire from her. Then he kissed her open mouth with his, speared her with his tongue, and pressed her harder against his erection, wanting to be inside her now.

She groaned and he capitulated. Lifting her off the floor, he carried her to the bed, his hands still cupping her exposed ass, her feet wrapped around his waist. But he soon had the bunny gear off, and her skin bared to him, peachy silky delight, her breasts perky and full, the nipples pebbled, her legs spread apart, offering him entrance.

He reached into his jeans pocket and pulled out a rubber. "Let me," she murmured, her eyes hot and sassy.

He jerked off his jeans, and he crouched over her, his engorged penis reaching out to her as he leaned forward. She slid the rubber up his shaft, her hands moving it with a firm stroke. He sucked in a breath, barely able to do anything but concentrate on every touch to the nerves so close to the surface. When she was done, he threaded his fingers through her hair, then shifted his hands to her breasts, his thumbs stroking her nipples, pulling and pinching. She moaned in response, arching her pelvis toward him. Her eyes remained fastened on his cock as if she was ready to devour him. Just her expression of intrigue and the way her hands worked miracles on his arousal nearly sent him over the edge.

Unable to wait a second longer, he nudged the thick head into her opening. Slowly he penetrated her tight sheath, allowing her to expand to his size, and pressed deeper as she wrapped her legs around him.

"Are you okay?" she whispered, as if she suddenly remembered the injury to his arm, pausing as she touched the skin below the bruising.

He groaned in response, eliciting a naughty smile from her lips. For the moment, he felt as if he'd never been bitten, nothing was hemming him in, the world was right again.

He tilted off her a bit so he could reach her most erotic spot, loved the way she tightened her hold on his

waist as he stroked her into ecstasy, her pink feminine
lips wet with need. She arched into his hand, begging
for more, faster, slower, harder. And then she let out a
shudder, a satisfied sigh, her face and nipples flushed,
her body trembling, gripping his erection with the most
erotic sensation as he renewed his thrusts.

Deeper, faster, he found she was the maker of heady
dreams, the one he'd been needing to sate his sexual
desires since he'd had any interest in the opposite sex.
But she'd aroused something more primal, something
darker, something that he couldn't identify. He wanted
her, craved having her for something longer-term. Crazy.
The blood from his brain had slipped into his cock and
that was what was making him feel so light-headed, so
powerless under her spell.

Her fingers dug into his butt, and he swore she came
again. And that did it, with her hands squeezing his flesh,
her inner muscles wringing his erection, he came with a
final thrust. Spent, satiated, the most content he'd been
in forever, he collapsed on her possessively, spreading
his legs over hers, pinning her to the mattress, his erection still inside her. *His*.

"Hmm." She skimmed her nails down his back in
tantalizing caresses designed to stir him up again, like a
sexy siren bent on seducing him.

But she didn't need to make the effort. She'd caught his
attention the minute she'd walked in on him when he was
naked, towel-drying his wet hair in his hotel room. And
he'd wanted her then, the offer of dinner only the beginning.

He chuckled and kissed her lips, tonguing her tongue,
already wanting more. "If you'd stayed last night, I
wouldn't have seen your erotic bed wear."

She laughed and pulled at his earlobe with a gentle tug. "I'll have you know I only wear that on snowy excursions when I'm going to be alone. Or at least think I'm going to be alone. It was a gift from a girlfriend for when…" She paused and a flicker of darkness fluttered across her face. But she didn't say anything further.

Not wanting to ruin the mood, although he desired to know what she was going to say, he kissed her cheek and rolled over, pulling her with him to cuddle against his chest, her legs spread provocatively over his, his hand stroking down her back to the cleft in her sweet little derriere. "Absolutely works for me." In fact, anything she wore, or didn't wear suited him fine. "I should start a nice hot fire."

The place was much too cold, and although he was still enjoying the heat of her body, he felt her tremble from the chill in the air and chill bumps were rising on her arm. He was ready to warm up the place and take another long winter's nap with Faith since he'd had such a fitful sleep last night and having sex with her had finally settled his unfathomable desire to run off into the woods.

But she was already pulling away. He should have expected it, because she'd said she was a morning person, but he wasn't, and he wanted to enjoy her in bed a good deal longer.

She glanced at her watch. "I was thinking about running back to the trailhead and reporting Lila's wolf attack and that someone had stolen our snowmobiles. Take you in to see a doctor also."

"Since whoever it was already returned the snowmobiles, I doubt the police would care. And my arm is fine now." He held her tight, still wanting to keep her in bed, to possess her, to prevent her from leaving. "Why don't you stay here until I get the place warmed up at least?"

That's when the sound of dogs barking in the distance caught his attention.

Instantly, a new primitive need ran amok through his system. The need to dominate the pack.

Chapter 7

CAMERON ACTED AS THOUGH HE WANTED TO KEEP FAITH IN bed forever, which was a heady kind of feeling she had to squash before she got used to the idea of having him around. Already the thought of returning alone to her home in Portland seemed cold and unappealing, when normally, being alone suited her fine, once Hilson took off. But God, she'd never had a man who could send her to the moon and back like Cameron had done. And despite her usual need to get up and get to work early in the morning, before the dogs had gotten Cameron's attention she probably would have snuggled with him longer. And more, if he'd wanted more. Which she didn't doubt for a second he would have wanted.

She sighed. Even though nothing would come of a fling with Cameron, maybe there was hope she could start over again with someone new, eventually.

But as soon as Cameron heard the dogs barking, his whole demeanor changed. At once, he acted much more interested in where the barking was coming from— probably his P.I. instincts. Was it Charles Roux and his sled dog team? She imagined it had to be.

The sound of snowmobiles drawing closer filled the air next. Before Faith could get free of Cameron and the bed, the snowmobiles parked outside her cabin, and a few seconds later someone pounded on her door, giving her a start.

"Maybe it's Charles bringing our ice for the ice box and another five-gallon container of water," she teased, not believing it, as early in the morning as it was, but if the dogs they'd heard barking belonged to Charles Roux and he'd returned home, he might be dropping by to complain if he'd discovered Cameron had fired up the hot tub without his permission.

"It's about time we got some service around here," Cameron said with a wink, although he didn't sound like he believed it either as he climbed out of bed and jerked on his jeans.

Faith hurried to get dressed. She quickly ran a brush through her hair as Cameron finished buttoning his shirt and looked over at her. "Ready?"

She nodded.

As soon as Cameron opened the door, she saw two policemen standing beyond their snowed-in entryway—Adams and Whitson. The same ones who had spoken to them in Millinocket when they'd been at Kintail's office and found the dead body. She closed her gaping mouth. With them coming all the way out here this early in the morning, it couldn't be a social call.

Officer Adams flipped through a notebook. "Faith O'Malley? Cameron MacPherson?"

"Did you learn anything more about the dead man?" Faith asked, hoping this was good news and nothing more that was bad.

"May we come in?" Adams asked, his tone more of a directed suggestion rather than a question.

This smacked of an investigation—as if Cameron and she were under the gun.

Cameron motioned for them to enter, although getting through the piled up snow for them was a trial.

Then a man appeared in a parka, his fur-trimmed hood framing his darker skin, his dark eyes focused on Cameron as he trudged into the snow piled up on their porch. "Charles Roux, owner here. I'll bring a shovel and clear the snow away. Return later to talk with you folks," he directed to Faith and Cameron.

Talk to them later about what? The hot tub?

She suspected they were in more trouble than that, if the police had anything to do with it. The officers came inside and shut the door.

"Green tea?" Faith asked the men. She was shivering between the cold in the cabin from the fire going out and letting in the frigid air from outside. At least the wind seemed to have stopped and the snow was no longer falling.

Cameron quickly shook his head. "I'll have some coffee at the main lodge later." Then he rubbed her arm and kissed her cheek. "You're shivering. I'll start a fire."

"Thanks, Cameron." She glanced at the police officers. Adams and Whitson took deep breaths, then looked from Faith to Cameron. "Tea?" They both declined. Faith started the kettle while the men waited. "So what did you find?"

"Where were the two of you between yesterday afternoon and early this morning?"

Faith put the box of tea bags down and paid more attention to the officers. She and Cameron were suspects in something else now?

Shoving a couple of logs into the wood-burning stove, Cameron took the lead, not sounding in the least bit troubled. "We were snowed in here. I left Faith for a few minutes when I thought I heard someone yell out near the lake. But I didn't see anything or anyone. And then I headed back to the cabin when I heard a couple of snowmobiles, concerned that someone was taking ours."

"Yes, two men stole our snowmobiles. Here's the description I have of them." She headed to the dining table and offered the note to the closest officer. "We were at the hot tub for a while also. We had witnesses. A lady named Mary, and three guys. One was named Matt and another, Chris. We didn't get the last guy's name."

"Were they guests of yours?"

Faith looked at the officer as if he'd gone mad. "Of course not. Cameron and I arrived first. Then Mary. Then the three guys. We hadn't met any of them before."

"Uh-huh." The officer raised his brows at Cameron, who was lighting a fire in the stove.

Cameron shook his head. "Didn't know any of them."

"Can you describe them?"

Faith poured hot water over her tea bag. "The lady was maybe sixties, gray hair, gray eyes, large build. The guys—Chris had bushy red hair, green eyes, scrawny. Matt, had nearly black hair and eyes, more muscular, and the last, light brown hair, blue eyes, medium build, late twenties. He didn't offer a name. They were lightly dressed and wore boxers into the hot tub. Mary had on a bright pink swimsuit."

"Uh-huh."

"Well, all you have to do is check their stories at the other cabins."

"According to Charles Roux, the only others staying at the cabins are a Leidolf Wildhaven of

Portland, Oregon, and a Hilson Snowdon of the same location."

Faith clamped her gaping mouth shut, set her tea mug down, and sat before she collapsed.

"Mean anything to you?" Officer Adams asked, knowing damn well it did from her reaction.

Cameron was watching her just as closely. God. What the hell was Hilson doing here? He was supposed to have been at the other cabin resort a couple of miles away that was booked solid or she would have stayed there instead. And Leidolf? Was he with him? What were the odds that two men would be here from the same city in Oregon that she was from?

"Then where did the other people go? The ones that came into the hot tub?" she asked, hoping the officer would believe that was the reason for her shocked reaction.

"What's this all about?" Cameron asked, rejoining Faith, his hand resting reassuringly on her shoulder.

Not answering Cameron, Officer Whitson pointed at Cameron's parka hanging over one of the dining room chairs, the sleeve torn and stained with blood. "Your coat didn't look like that earlier yesterday when we first met. Care to explain?"

Faith really didn't feel good about this. Something else had to have happened if they were being considered as suspects in some kind of criminal activity.

"A wolf bit me. A white wolf. And since I'd seen Lila Grayson with some earlier in the day near the same area, I figured it had to be one of hers," Cameron explained. "I suspect you don't have any in the area otherwise. I'm glad that you paid us a visit though. Before her wolves bite anyone else, I want to press charges." The officers traded conspiratorial looks, but the impression Faith got from the exchange was that Lila and her wolves were either above suspicion, or Lila and Kintail brought too much business into the area to warrant an investigation. Small town politics. At least that's the way she felt.

"Care to show us your injury?" Officer Adams asked.

Cameron obliged, pulling up his sleeve to expose his skin, but nothing on his arm indicated he'd been bitten. No bruising, no bite marks, nothing.

Faith stared at his arm in disbelief, his expression just as surprised. "It was bad last night," she said, "but he healed up quickly, and this morning all that was left was bruising and shallow bite marks. You can see a little dried blood still. And my bloodied towel." She pointed to where Cameron had left it on the kitchen countertop. "I'd wrapped it around the wound."

Officer Adams frowned at Cameron. "Mind if we take it with us and have it checked out?"

Whitson continued to be the strong, silent type. Although now he warily watched Cameron, no longer keeping his attention on Faith.

"Why? What's happened?" Faith asked.

"Charles Roux found a dead body not far from here. He went on in with his dog sled and reported it at Skidoo Rentals at the trailhead. They passed the word along to us since there's no reception out here for phones."

Not believing another dead body had mysteriously turned up, Faith cleared her throat. "Who died?"

"Not sure until we positively ID him. No papers on him."

"Did he die in the same way?" Faith asked.

"Can't say. Ongoing investigation." Officer Adams tilted his head to the side. "You wouldn't know how the other man died, would you?"

She folded her arms. "Not sure unless I did lab tests." She was used to being asked her opinion about how victims died, but not as a key suspect!

"You say you saw Lila Grayson with some of her wolves," Officer Adams directed to Cameron as if he had never mentioned the fact that one of the wolves had bitten him. "Did she tell you where your partners are?"

"Hunting, she said. She told me they were quitting the partnership, but I don't believe it. I want to hear it for myself, so she said she'd let them know. Problem is I'm not sure she's telling the truth about any of it."

The officer jotted down something, then looked up at Cameron. "Maybe you should have a look at the dead man. Just in case it's one of your partners."

Cameron's jaw tightened, but he didn't say a word.

Faith took hold of his hand and squeezed. "Can I go, too? As a courtesy? I can have a look at him and see if I notice anything about the body that might help you in your investigation."

"We have our own investigators on it, but thanks for the offer, ma'am," Officer Adams said. He didn't sound sincere.

"I don't want to leave Faith here by herself," Cameron said, squeezing her hand back. Was he really worried about her safety? Or did he think she might see something he'd miss?

"She can't go. Not without permission from our head honchos, and we can't get it out here. Maybe she can visit with Charles Roux while we take you out there. You say your snowmobiles were stolen?"

"Yeah, and then they were returned behind the shower building," Faith said. "Really bizarre. When I saw them, I hollered for Cameron, and when he came around the building, the wolf attacked. So we never did have a chance to bring the machines back here to my cabin."

"We'll take a look at them. Are you ready to go with us, Mr. MacPherson?" Adams asked.

"Faith?" Cameron said.

She nodded and pulled on her ski jacket. As soon as Cameron was out of sight, she was going to have words with Hilson and get her father's flash drive back. *Pronto*. And although she wanted to see Trevor Hodges to learn more what went on, if she could get the flash drive, she would be happy enough to leave and forget about the cold, about Trevor, about everything. Except for Cameron. But what if the spark she felt for him was a case of instant rebound from Hilson's betrayal? What if having a fling with Cameron was nothing more than a way of validating that any man would want her?

That's what she was afraid of as she headed to the lodge with Cameron to see Charles Roux, when all she wanted to do was find Hilson's cabin and give him a big piece of her mind.

Cameron escorted Faith to the main lodge, despite her telling him he didn't need to take her all the way there. But he seemed on edge and wanted to speak to her privately. She assumed it had to do with the reaction she had when she heard Hilson was staying in one of the other cabins, but Cameron hadn't wanted to bring it up in front of the police.

"Do you know either of the men who are staying at the other cabins?" he asked her, his voice hushed as he walked her up onto the lodge's porch.

Yeah, she guessed right. What would he think? He might be pissed that she didn't tell him she and her boyfriend had just split up.

"Hilson Snowdon is my ex-boyfriend. I didn't know he was here."

Cameron stared at her for a second, his face wearing a mask of disbelief. "This was recent? That the relationship was dissolved?"

He seemed more than troubled by the news, as if he had more of a long-term interest in her. No, that wasn't it. Something else seemed to be eating at him.

Cameron added, "If he's followed you here, I assume he wasn't the one to do the ditching."

That came out harshly. And the notion suddenly dawned on her that he might have had a relationship that ended badly for him recently, too. Great. She hadn't intended to hurt anyone, but she couldn't deal with this right now.

Cameron seemed cold and distant, while the police officers watched them both with too much interest, and although she didn't think they were close enough to hear the conversation, they seemed to be trying anyway. Hell, her affairs were her own and had nothing to do with Cameron's problems in the least.

"Our relationship was... complicated. And for your information, he left without a word a couple of days ago."

"A couple of days ago?"

"Yeah, Cameron. Why don't we just leave it at that for now?" She hadn't meant to sound hurt and angry. But she couldn't help it. Cameron's whole expression was one of accusation. That she'd pushed Hilson away somehow maybe. Either that or Cameron didn't care for the fact it had been recent and Hilson was here, as if he had followed her and was still in love with her. But she didn't want to explain that he'd stolen her father's research in front of the police officers, who wouldn't do anything about it anyway. All she needed was for Hilson to turn up dead, and then they'd figure she really was the guilty party, as mad as she was at him for stealing her father's flash drive.

But then she wondered if Cameron's reaction wasn't tied to worrying if the dead man was one of his partners and in some bizarre way, he was unloading on her. Pretending that his tone didn't bother her, she said, "I'm sure your friends are safe."

"I believe you're right." But he didn't sound convinced, which made her think he probably had a better take on the situation than she did. "Stay with Charles here at the inn, and I'll be back in a while, Faith."

To talk more about her relationship with Hilson? No thanks.

He turned and headed off to where the police officers waited with their snowmobiles. He didn't look back at her, or even make eye contact with her one last time, as if she'd already vanished. His attitude? He'd made a mistake in getting to know her even for the brief interval they'd been together; time to cut his losses and run.

Faith rubbed her arms in the winter chill, ground her teeth in frustration, then waited until Cameron was out of sight. She had half a mind to dump his bags onto the porch, move him out of her life pronto, take care of business, and return home just as she intended. She didn't need any more drama in her life that involved men with an attitude.

Hell, she had enough problems.

Then, for a minute, she was torn. Talk to Charles Roux and find out Hilson's cabin name, or find it herself? She figured she might as well talk to Charles. But after she walked inside, she found the lodge empty. Figuring he must be out with the dogs or doing something else for one of the guests, she left the lodge.

With no time to lose, she headed for the tree-lined path beside the lake, leading to the other cabins, determined to discover which one Hilson was in, and have her say with him, confiscate the flash drive, and now, maybe even return to Millinocket before it got too late today.

She trudged through the knee-deep snow, some in drifts as high as her shoulders, not that she'd traverse those. Past her place, she finally reached the White Wolf Den, marked by a carved painted wolf sign that looked like the wolf that had attacked Cameron. Which brought to mind Cameron's wolf bite—she still couldn't believe he could heal that fast.

She peered into the windows of his cabin. The place was dark, and when she tried the door, she found it was locked. She continued on past it, winding her way through the spruce trees until she reached the next cabin, also facing the lake. She was glad her place was closer to the main lodge and shower facility. What would other guests do if they had to go to the bathroom in the middle of the night?

The next cabin, complete with a tower, was called the Eagle's Nest. She went up to the door and knocked. No answer. She peered into the window, hoping she wouldn't see the occupant, Leidolf Wildhaven, staying here, instead of Hilson Snowdon. The living room, kitchen, and dining room looked unoccupied. But then Hilson was a neatnik, so it still might be his place.

All she needed to find was his bag, clothes, anything to identify this was his cabin.

She reached for the doorknob, but something flashed by her in the woods. Something. Everything was so white, surely she would have seen if it was a person dressed in something other than white. But nothing. She didn't see anything but the snow-covered firs. Barely a whisper of a breeze caressed the snow-laden limbs. And everything was silent. At least in summer, the lake water probably rippled on the shore, but now it was solidly frozen. Eerily silent.

Although she was bundled to the hilt, she suddenly felt cold, chilled, like when she thought the gray pickup had been following her. And then she realized she hadn't spoken to Lila about who might own the pickup. One of her employees? Or maybe Kintail, since Faith didn't figure anyone else would run around with a wolf attached at their hip except for the owners.

She stood frozen on the porch, watching for any movement in the woods. *Nothing*. She took a deep frosty breath and turned back to twist the doorknob when she saw movement inside the dark cabin. She pulled her hand away from the door and froze.

Whoever it was had headed out of the bedroom and paused in the darkness as if he suddenly realized a woman was peering in at him. Even in the low light, she could see a mouthful of white teeth. She didn't think it was Hilson. The guy was as tall as Cameron, but not as tall as Hilson. And he appeared to be the same build as Cameron, not as husky, as far as she could see in the dim light. She whipped around and meant to leave and look for the next cabin when the occupant of the Eagle's Nest opened the door in such a rush, she gasped.

"Well," the man said, his voice deep and charming, "to what do I owe this unexpected pleasure?"

Faith turned and faced the man occupying the Eagle's Nest cabin, his chestnut hair tinged red, green eyes full of mystery and intrigue.

His mouth curved up a trace, but at the same time his eyes darkened a bit, and the next question from his lips pinned her with accusation. "Are you lost?"

Chapter 8

THE BODY WAS LYING FACEDOWN UNDER A SPRUCE, HALF buried in snow. He was the right build and was wearing a gray-green parka that could mean the man was either of Cameron's friends. His heart beating faster than he wanted to admit, Cameron came around to the right of the man to see his face.

He was a stranger, a beard covering his cheeks and chin, now matted with snow, his pale brown eyes lifeless. Cameron took a deep breath, relieved it wasn't Owen or David. "Not either of my partners."

"So are you certain you've never met Miss O'Malley before?" Officer Adams asked, slanting a glance at Whitson, while a couple of investigators were searching for clues in the snow farther away.

Cameron ignored the question as he leaned over to get a whiff of the dead guy, although he thought Adams's inquiry odd. Like he really wasn't as interested in him identifying the body as he was prying into Cameron's relationship with Faith.

He considered the dead man further. He was too frozen to decay, but he smelled like a wolf. Which didn't make any sense. For one, why could Cameron smell such a thing, unless it was because of being bitten himself and the close encounter had given him a new awareness? And why would he know that it was a wolf smell and not some other? But he didn't smell exactly like the one he'd had the run-in with either. Something different about him, but he couldn't pinpoint what it was.

"See anything?" Adams asked, drawing closer.

"No, I just… nothing. He's not either of my partners, so if you're done with me, I'll head back to the lodge."

"Which wolf bit you?" Adams asked, the question so out of the blue, Cameron stared at him blankly.

Then he gathered his wits and responded. "He was one of Lila's wolves. An Arctic white wolf."

Adams shook his head. "Size? Male? Female? Shorter hair, longer? Full coat? Raggedy? You're a former police officer. What made him different from the others?"

Cameron was used to analyzing people's looks and behaviors, but wolves? "How would I know? He was big. Maybe bigger than the others but they weren't around at the time so I could compare them. He had a thick coat that made him appear as though he was older, more mature, if that's what you mean. Not a juvenile. Otherwise, they all looked the same to me. No different markings. All pure white. But if you must know, I was concentrating on his bared teeth, not checking if he had balls, when he lunged."

Officer Whitson bit back a chuckle, while Adams gave his partner an annoyed look. "Did the wolf… was he attempting to kill you? Or did he just bite you and then run off?"

"I didn't ask, but the way he lunged at me, I'd say he went for the throat—for a kill—but I blocked his teeth with my arm. If Faith hadn't clobbered him in the hip with a snow shovel, he might have eventually given up on my arm and gone for the jugular again. So yeah, I think he intended to kill me, not just play with me."

His eyes wide, Whitson cleared his throat. "What did the wolf do when Faith hit him?"

Cameron glowered at the officer, not liking that he still seemed interested in Faith. "After *Miss O'Malley* struck him, he looked surprised. I expected him to growl at her, but instead I'd swear he smiled."

Whitson shared a look with Adams, who closed up his notebook.

Although Cameron figured he wouldn't get a response that would satisfy him, he asked anyway. "So now are you going to put an All Points Bulletin out on the wolf and its owner?"

"It's just your word that the wolf intended to harm you. You might have made a move that to him meant you intended to hurt *Faith*," Whitson said, "and he was protecting her. Or he might have thought something you did meant you wanted to play with him. Kintail's wolves are good-natured and wouldn't hurt a soul, unless provoked. Did you provoke him, Mr. MacPherson?"

Cameron clenched his teeth, unwilling to get into a pissing match with Whitson. He knew the officer didn't like that he had any kind of relationship with Faith and so was bound to be antagonistic toward him. On the other hand, Adams was looking at the dead body as if he was uninterested in the conversation. But it was only a ploy. Cameron knew that whatever he said Adams was considering as important to any investigation.

"If a dog bites someone, no matter its motive, it's considered vicious, unable to live safely amongst humans. Even if one was provoked, the charges against the animal would be taken seriously. We're talking feral wolf here. Not some centuries-tamed family pet. It wouldn't matter if they'd been raised as a second- or third-generation house pet either. They're wild animals. Period."

Adams finally spoke up. "We'll talk to Kintail about it. But if you don't even know which wolf it was, we couldn't very well put down his whole pack, now could we?"

"Whole pack? How many damn wolves has he got?"

"At least two make a pack," Adams clarified. But he didn't enlighten Cameron any further about numbers.

"How many *does* he have?" Cameron insisted, figuring from Adams's response, the police officers knew.

Adams's gaze pinned Cameron with warning. "You'd have to ask him. But he's touchy about his wolves. So I'd ask real nice if I were you. You're not from around here. He brings a lot of business into the area, so we take care of our own, if you get my meaning."

"If you mean you can get away with murder if you have enough money and connections, I completely understand. Works that way where I'm from also. Universal policy." Without evidence that he'd been bitten, just Faith's word, Cameron figured he didn't have much of a leg to stand on anyway though. "But next time, I won't just play with the wolf."

For the first time, Adams offered a slight smile, on the sinister side. "Your business. Just be sure to stick around in case we need to question you further."

"I'll be here, and if I find my friends and get ready to return home, I'll let you know." Cameron gave Whitson the same icy hard stare, then returned to his snowmobile and headed back to the lodge.

He patted the gun under his coat. He didn't like shooting animals, any kind. He'd never been a hunter, just of the predatory human variety. So killing a wolf didn't appeal. But he'd shoot it, if the wolf attacked again, just to make sure it didn't harm anyone else, whether Kintail liked it or not.

As he reached the resort, he saw Charles Roux putting a snow shovel up at a shed and veered his snowmobile in his direction.

The man turned to look at him. A few gray strands running through his dark hair braided behind his back. His round face, darker skin, and dark eyes looked Native American, and since Cameron had heard many of the tribes felt some kinship to the animals of the wild, he wondered about Charles's take on Kintail's wolves.

"The word is you're looking for Kintail." Charles's gaze quickly shifted to Cameron's bloodied and torn parka sleeve. "You were attacked?"

"By one of Kintail's wolves. Although they were with Lila. Two of my partners went on a hunt with Back Country Tours. They haven't returned and I haven't gotten word from them. So yeah, I'm looking to speak with Kintail. I haven't had any luck with Lila."

Approaching snowmobiles garnered their attention. Adams and Whitson headed their way.

Charles responded to Cameron's concern. "Communications in these parts are pretty sketchy."

"I understand, but I have to make sure that they're all right." Which brought to mind another concern. *Faith.* "Can you tell me anything about one of your guests? Hilson Snowdon? When he got here?"

Charles looked back at the police officers who were nearly there. "Officer Adams, Whitson," he said in greeting.

"Tell your sister we'll be back when she's made some more of that chocolate cream pie of hers," Adams said, tilting forward on the snowmobile.

Charles gave them a stiff nod. "Will do."

The officers gave Cameron another hard look. Adams said to Cameron, "We'll keep in touch." Then he and Whitson drove down the road in the direction of the trailhead.

"So what do you know about Hilson Snowdon?" Cameron asked Charles again.

"You can talk to him when he's around. He might be at his cabin now, or off on another excursion. Folks come here to get away. I don't ask their business. Does Miss O'Malley still want to see Trevor Hodges?"

Cameron frowned and looked back at the lodge. "Didn't she talk to you about it already?"

"I've been busy shoveling snow so I haven't been up at the main lodge. She's probably talking to my sister, while she prepares the next meal, unless she's off seeing to something else. Work's never done around here in the winter." Charles motioned to Cameron's bloodied and torn parka sleeve. "About the wolf that bit you, which one was it?"

"I figure it was a male, as big and aggressive as it was." Cameron couldn't understand why everyone seemed to think that he should know which wolf it was as if they all had names and separate identities.

When he'd raised a litter of Labrador retriever pups, they all looked similar, too, although, as they grew, personalities began to appear and some physical differences were noticeable—one was chubbier than the rest, one taller. But the only way to tell the difference for most of the rest was to observe them for some time. The brief encounters he'd had with Lila and her wolves were just that—way too brief.

"Do you know how many wolves Kintail has?"

Charles's eyes widened a bit. Then he frowned and rubbed his chin. "No. A few."

"Lila Grayson was with a few of them earlier. They ought to be put down if they attack people, and Lila ought to be brought up on charges."

The old man didn't respond one way or another, so Cameron couldn't get a feel for what Charles was thinking. But he was surprised when Charles asked, "How do you feel?"

"Better. The bite's all healed up."

"Come with me while I feed my dogs. We need to talk."

He led Cameron to a barn where he kept his dogs and sleds. A slew of huskies greeted Charles as soon as he and Cameron entered the building, licking and poking their noses at Charles's hands and legs.

Immediately, Cameron had the overwhelming need to show them who was in charge. Which wasn't like him. Befriend the animal? Sure. But make sure they knew he was boss? Not him. Whoever the dogs' owner was, as far as he was concerned, served as the boss man.

But this time, the oddest feeling snowed him under, forcing him to acknowledge each and every one of them eye to eye with a glance—not a confrontational stare at first—but then he considered them closer, looking for the leader of the pack. And when he found the bigger male, Cameron stood taller, stiffer-legged, and pinned him with his gaze, acting as though he was in charge. As if he instinctively knew this would work with the alpha dog of the pack.

The dogs sniffed Cameron from a distance, looking wary, which surprised him. Dogs and kids always gravitated to him. But the alpha leader lifted his head, lowered his tail, and arched his back slightly in submission, and Cameron knew he had won the confrontation. He didn't feel superior to the dog for the rapid change in pack dynamics, just that it was the natural order of things.

Charles turned on a lantern, although it was light enough in the building that Cameron was surprised he would bother. Then Charles opened a hefty-sized canister and poured food into dog trays. "Best sled-pulling huskies in the territory. One of these dogs weighing in at only forty pounds can pull over eight hundred pounds." He pointed to their bootie-covered paws. "The huskies are strong, but their feet aren't meant for this kind of weather. So they wear polar fleece booties to keep them warm."

Cameron counted sixteen huskies. "So is Faith navigating a sled, or are you taking her for a ride when you look for Trevor?"

"She just wanted me to take her to see Trevor."

"I'll be going with you."

Charles looked up at him. "Has she agreed to allow you to go along? I had the impression the matter is personal to her. She wouldn't even enlighten me as to why she wished to speak with him."

"She's agreed." At least Cameron figured she would once he gave his reasoning. "So how will we work this?"

"The five-foot-long wooden sled's not big enough for three. We have several sleds and can divide up the dogs, but I doubt either of you are trained in mushing.

Although, that's what I do. Give rides and teach folks how to handle a team. Faith can snuggle up in the sled bag on my sled, but of course if the going gets tough, we'll all be walking. How are you with dogs?"

Charles gave Cameron a look as if he were judging him for the job.

"Good. Never found one that didn't like me." He reached down to pet one of the darker-faced huskies. The animal bowed its head to him as if she was afraid.

"That's Nikki. She's a real beta and pretty shy, but for her to greet you first indicates she really likes you." Charles packed the rest of the dog food into a sturdy can. "Bear-proof. A bear can smell dog food through anything. One broke into my barn and tore it up good, but at least he can't get into one of these. Nothing worse than reaching my place and having no food for the team."

"I can imagine. Ever try a husky/wolf breed?"

Charles snorted. "These dogs love to pull a load and they love to please humans. Plus they get along with each other great. A wolf mix?" He shook his head. "Wolf blood made the wolfdogs skittish and aggressive with one another. But mostly, they like their freedom. Pulling a load for a human? Forget it." Charles took a deep breath. "What I wanted to talk to you about was the wolf that bit you. Normally, when a wolf like that bites someone, the pack takes the person in."

"A wolf pack?" Cameron wasn't following him.

"Has anyone talked to you about, well, ahem…" Charles looked back at his dogs and began stroking one of them on the head. "Has Kintail talked to you since you've been bitten?"

"I haven't met the man."

Charles looked up at Cameron. "Seeing the extent of damage to your parka and the fact no one's talked to you about what's happened, I'm assuming something else is going on."

"You mean that Kintail has trained wolves to attack certain people? Like attack dogs?"

Charles shook his head. "No, that's... not exactly what I'm trying to say. I'm Cree, if you were wondering. In ancient times, my people believed that when the aurora borealis danced across the night sky, magical or divine wolves came to earth. In many Native American cultures, wolves have been revered. Wolves take care of their packs, much as we take care of our families, our tribes. My people much admired wolves' superior hunting skills in cooperating with one another. And like the wolves, in ancient times, we would keep outsiders from invading our territory." Charles smiled as if he was remembering the stories passed on by his elders.

Then he sighed. "The Inuit tell the story of an old lady, abandoned, who became a wolf. The Navajo believed a man or woman who wore a wolf's skin would transform into the wolf. The Sioux believe the wolf has a powerful spirit. The Pawnee were often known as the Wolf People, who, like some other tribes, stored their magical tools in wolf skins. Unless I'm mistaken, one of these wolves has infected you."

In disbelief, Cameron raised his brows. "A magical wolf?" The wolf was big, but there wasn't anything magical about it. Just one mean-spirited beast, although the way Cameron healed so quickly was pretty bizarre.

"Have you… experienced any changes? Heightened senses? Or feel anything out of the ordinary, like cabin fever?"

Hell, that was what was making Cameron so antsy. His senses were on higher alert. Everything from seeing well in the low light of the barn before Charles turned on the lantern, to smelling the differences between the dogs. Normally, they would have all smelled like wet dog, period. But now, he noted subtle differences—one had rolled in something. And how he should know that beat him. Another's breath smelled bad, although the dog was not anywhere close to him. It was more than that though.

It seemed as though every gland associated with each hair follicle produced an individual odor signal that he could easily recognize. And pheromones that cast off a different smell—more of a form of communication—like when one of the bigger dogs, the alpha male, maneuvered closer to the food that was left. As soon as he did, the dog next to him lifted its nose, sniffed the air, and moved out of the bigger male's way.

Sounds were more pronounced also, now that he thought about it.

Charles eyed Cameron closely. "Do you feel any different?"

Yeah, although Cameron wasn't a runner, he had the worst urge to stretch out his legs and run for miles. Hiking, swimming, and skiing were more his style. "Nothing that can't be explained."

"Don't you have any… empathy for the wolf now? More so than you might have had before?"

"What I feel is irritation that anyone would stick up for a wild animal that bites people unprovoked."

Charles just shook his head.

Cameron took another tack, figuring that wolf lovers couldn't understand unless maybe one bit them. "So what is a magical wolf's bite supposed to do to me?"

Charles cleared his throat again. "Have you had any cravings to rip off your clothes and run like the wolf?"

———

Faith considered Leidolf Wildhaven as he stood in the entryway of the Eagle's Nest cabin, his amber eyes studying her just as much in return. "Uhm, no, I'm not lost. I'm looking for someone," she said.

"Ah. Did you knock? I didn't hear you."

"Yes." She had, although probably not hard enough, wearing her gloves, which had muffled the sound.

He wore a hint of a smile, as if he was saying he knew very well she was planning on searching his place without his permission. But then again, maybe she only thought so because she was feeling guilty.

"I'm sorry. I'm at the wrong place."

She started to step off the porch when Leidolf said, "Watch out for the Arctic wolves, young woman. They can be troublesome in these parts."

She turned around. "You've seen them? My friend got bitten by one. But the evidence of the bite marks are already gone. Do you know Lila Grayson? She owns the wolves. And Kintail Silverman, I guess. They run Back Country Tours."

"I'm Leidolf Wildhaven. And you are?"

"Sorry, Faith O'Malley." She walked back over and extended her hand.

He studied her way too closely, took a deep breath, and smiled a bit ominously, belatedly shaking her hand with a firm touch. "Your friend? The one who was bitten? Is he a very *close* friend?"

Closer than she would admit to a perfect stranger. "We just met."

"Ah. So you have separate cabins."

The statement was more of a question, but she treated it as a statement, and none of his business. "You didn't say if you knew Lila Grayson."

"No, I don't know of the woman or this Kintail. But I've seen their wolves. Your friend, where is he staying?"

She hesitated. Hell, she was lousy at lying. "He's at White Wolf Den."

"Appropriate. His name?" When she hesitated to say, Leidolf added, "I've been bitten by a wolf before, and maybe we can swap stories. Sometimes it helps to air our concerns with someone who has experienced the same... trauma."

Faith hadn't even considered that Cameron might have been traumatized by the attack and thought it was a great idea, warming up to Leidolf instantly. "Cameron MacPherson. I'm sure he'd love to talk to you."

"You said he was your friend, that he stayed at White Wolf Den, which means you were looking for someone else?"

"Yes. I thought maybe this was his cabin. But obviously not."

"He wouldn't happen to be Hilson Snowdon, would he?"

"Uh, yeah, do you know him?" From Portland? Friends? She hadn't known Hilson to have any friends in Portland. But it seemed like too much of a coincidence that they both were from there and now here, at the same time.

"I ran into him while he was pacing down by the lake. He seemed to be bothered by something. Didn't like it that I intruded on his privacy. Although from what I understand, he's the only other one here right now. So I assumed he was either Hilson or Cameron. And since White Wolf Den isn't occupied yet, or I should say until more recently, the one I met must have been Hilson."

"Dishwater blond hair? Amber eyes?"

"Yep. That would describe him. And irritated. I'm not sure he's in the mood for company. Would you like me to walk you back to your cabin? Or to the main lodge?"

"No, thank you. Is his place in this direction?"

"Next cabin over. Porcupine Cove. The other four places are under renovation. Or at least will be when the spring thaw comes."

"Have you seen three men in their late twenties, and a gray-haired older lady around? Or had any trouble with theft?"

Leidolf looked darkly amused that anyone might try to steal from him. "No. Why?"

"They were at the hot tub last night, but apparently they aren't staying here. And two guys stole our snowmobiles, then parked them behind the shower facilities."

"Sounds like pranksters to me. Using the facilities, but not belonging here."

"But in the storm last night? Where would they have been from?"

He seemed vaguely interested. "I don't know. But I'll keep an eye out for them. Are you sure you don't want me to escort you back to—"

"Thanks, but I've got to run." She hurried off the porch, not having any doubts about what she had to do next and not wanting to delay the inevitable.

"Be careful, young lady," Leidolf said, his voice a warning.

Something about the man seemed mysterious. She couldn't put a finger on what made her feel that way. Something inherently protective. Even though he seemed intrigued with her, he seemed just as willing to help out her "friend," Cameron. Which she so appreciated. She wasn't sure after the way Cameron had reacted to the fact that she'd had a recently ended relationship that she could call him a friend any longer, though.

And that bothered her a lot more than it should have for just having met the guy. But she felt some kind of connection with Cameron and... Well, hell, she was not willing to dwell on that issue, because once she got the flash drive from Hilson, she could just pack her bags and go, and get her life back together where she belonged.

She thought about something more that Leidolf had said. Hilson was pacing and agitated. Why? Had he learned she had followed him here? Or had he tried to sell her father's research and hadn't been paid?

She couldn't imagine he would want to use the research for himself, no matter what it was about. He was a stock broker, although because of the stock market, he'd lost a lot of money recently. Enough to make him want to steal her father's work for a tidy sum? She hadn't thought about that.

Plowing through the fresh snow and getting way too much of it into her boots, she noted that no one had walked anywhere in this area since the blizzard had subsided. Everything was perfectly pristine. Which meant Hilson should be home and hadn't ventured out. Or he left during the blizzard or before it began. She should have asked when Leidolf had seen him last.

What of the men and woman who had dropped by the hot tub? What if they were staying at one of the cabins that was closed due to renovations? It would make sense that they would be from some place close by and slip into the hot tub. Something else she should check out. But a nagging worry warned her she should have Cameron with her for that excursion.

When she finally reached Porcupine Cove, she stared at the bristly, fat little critter carved on the sign. The place was dark, just like Leidolf's cabin had been. Maybe Hilson was taking an afternoon nap. He often did because he was such a night owl. Before she reached the porch, she saw dog tracks. No, not dog tracks. She'd bet her IRA that they were wolf tracks. All around the area, into the woods, up to Hilson's porch. Lots of wolf tracks. She thought it had to be several, or one very antsy, hungry wolf.

She glanced around, suddenly feeling a flush of adrenaline, worried a wolf might be watching her. Not any wolf, but the one that had bitten Cameron. Not seeing anything, she hurried up onto the porch and raised her hand to the door. And hesitated.

Steeling her back, she wondered if Hilson would hand over the flash drive without a fuss. He'd always seemed to genuinely care for her. But how could she be sure of anything where he was concerned now? She growled, then banged on the door as hard as she could.

No answer. *Hell*. She twisted the doorknob. *Locked*. She hurried around the place, trying every window, peering inside. Everything was sealed tight. And just like Leidolf's place, this one was neat, bed made, no dishes on the kitchen counter, no sign of any bags, as if no one had ever stayed here. But Leidolf had said he'd met Hilson, so he had to be around. She looked back in the front window. If she broke a window, and managed to get inside, what would that accomplish? There was no sign of any of Hilson's belongings. But what if his bag was under his bed, and his clothes in the drawers?

She wouldn't know for sure unless she made the effort. If she could find the flash drive, she would have done what she came here to do, make her father proud, and learn what he was up to for so long. He would have enough time to prepare his presentation, and that's all that truly mattered. Plus, she'd make a million copies of his research in the meantime, in case Hilson had a mind to snatch it again before her father gave his presentation.

She searched for something to break a window, then spied a log stacked on a rack, half buried in snow. She struggled to get one of the logs off the top, where it was frozen to the others. After several minutes of trying, she broke it loose, stumbled back, and lost her footing. Landing in a pile of snow, she was glad it softened her fall.

She scrambled to her feet, grabbed the small log, and headed for the porch. As soon as she readied it for a good hard window-breaking swing, she heard someone rapidly approaching from behind.

Chapter 9

HOLDING THE LOG IN HER CLUTCHES LIKE A WEAPON, FAITH whipped around, her face white with fright. Then she let out a frosty breath as if she'd found an angel instead of the devil.

"What are you doing?" Cameron asked, closing in on the porch. He'd followed her trail here, although a stop at Leidolf's place had given him the information that she had gone to see Hilson at the next cabin on the path around the lake.

He assumed she might have decided to return to the ex-boyfriend to renew her relationship with him, which didn't sit well with Cameron, even though he shouldn't have cared one way or another. On the other hand, he thought she might be planning to have words with Hilson. And although it wasn't any of his business, he wanted to make sure she was going to be all right. That this Hilson Snowdon wasn't a violent type. But he never expected to see her like this.

She lowered the log and frowned at him. "What are *you* doing here?"

He chuckled darkly and joined her on the porch, then took the log from her. "Apparently, I'm here to stop a breaking-and-entering criminal trespass in progress. What's going on, Faith? What's the deal with you and Hilson and Trevor Hodges, your father, everything?"

"I thought you were pissed off at me and didn't want to talk."

He tossed the log into the snowbank off the side of the porch and reached out to run his gloved fingers over her cheek, red again now from the cold. "I want to know what's going on. Maybe I can help."

"The... the man who was dead that you went to see, he wasn't one of your partners?"

"No. I have to think they're both fine." But he appreciated that whatever issues she was dealing with, she was still concerned about his situation, even if it meant she tried to sidetrack him about her own troubles. For some reason, he wanted to talk to Faith about the strange way he was feeling, and about the odd conversation he'd had with Charles. Something about Faith made him want to share with her things that he didn't even want to disclose to his partners. Not even with his former girlfriends. "Faith, we've got to talk. Hilson doesn't appear to be here, so why don't we head back to your place and get warm and discuss this?"

"You were angry with me over Hilson." Her eyes flashed annoyance along with the accusation.

He wrapped his arm around her shoulders and held her tight as he guided her off Hilson's front porch. Angry, yes. He couldn't help thinking she had unfinished business with Hilson that meant she might end up going right back to the bastard. The first girl Cameron had dated had done the same to him. He sure as hell didn't want to fall into the same trap again

But somehow this whole scenario was different. He wasn't willing to let her go back to Hilson, if she had half a notion to get sidetracked in that direction. And why he was even thinking along those lines, he wasn't sure. Maybe that he figured the guy didn't deserve a second chance.

He noted the wolf tracks all over the place and eyed the woods, looking for any sign of the wolf or wolves now. Nothing. Yet, a trickle of concern wormed its way into his blood, the feeling that any second now the wolf that had bitten him might materialize out of the snow-filled scene and attack. But he didn't worry about himself, as much as he worried about protecting Faith.

As they crunched through the snow back toward her cabin, Cameron kept an eye out for trouble, trying not to alarm her. But he wanted to know what her deal was with Hilson, so he figured he might as well share his own story first. Maybe that would encourage her to talk. At least he hoped so.

"One evening, my girlfriend, Marjory, was talking to me about a vacation we'd planned to Canada, and then the next morning she called it quits."

"I'm so sorry, Cameron."

He shrugged, although he hadn't gotten over the hurt. Not exactly. "My fault."

She looked up at him, her eyes filled with tears.

"Ah, Faith, I didn't want to upset you." He figured she must have been through the wringer with Hilson recently and the parallel was making her feel badly, but he wanted to get this out in the open. "Later that night when I was on a stakeout of a house where a guy lived who'd been skipping child support payments, he grazed me with a single shot fired. Marjory decided she couldn't deal with the life-and-death dangers I might be involved in. I could understand that to a degree. But, there was someone else."

Faith shook her head. "Like my mother."

Cameron looked down at Faith, not expecting that. She didn't say anything more, just watched her boots as she navigated the trail of tracks they'd left in their wake the first time.

When she didn't speak, Cameron figured he'd have to coax it out of her later and continued. "Gavin, one of my partners, discovered the truth. He'd just happened to see Marjory at Starbucks with another man. He didn't think anything of it at first, but the guy was acting a little too intimate, hand on her thigh, head leaning in toward hers to whisper something in her ear. So although I didn't know it, Gavin began following her, assuming I'd be pissed if I learned of it. But he's like that, can't let a notion go. And he wanted to prove to himself she wasn't being unfaithful. He didn't want to see me going down the same road again."

"This happened to you before?"

"Yeah, guess I'm just a magnet for cheating women." Cameron squeezed her tight as they trudged through the snow, loving how her body warmed his, wishing that he hadn't upset her though. He wondered if this was what rebound was all about. He supposed that Marjory had been the reason for such a whirlwind romance after Katie had dumped his butt. Now was Faith the same to him? There to fill the void in his life, but when he had his act together and she did, too, they wouldn't suit?

Getting way ahead of himself, Cameron cleared his throat. "Gavin followed Marjory and her boyfriend to the guy's apartment. And after that, every time she said she was supposed to be one place or another, Gavin would jot down exactly where she'd been. With this guy."

"Who was he? Anyone you knew?"

"Gavin wouldn't tell me at first. But I warned him I'd find out myself. So he explained who it was, but only on the condition I wouldn't kill the bastard."

"Someone you knew?"

"Former police officer friend."

"That sucks."

Cameron kissed her forehead. "Yeah, so she was trading me in because she was afraid I'd get shot in the P.I. business when this man is still on the police force."

"He can't be half the man you are, Cameron." She smiled up at him, her expression much brighter.

"No. He's a loser. But then I guess that's what she needed. Someone she could boss around, and I'm not very bossable." This time he smiled down at Faith, feeling much more lighthearted than he had since Marjory left him several months ago.

He hoped Faith would feel like sharing her story with him. But when she opened her mouth to speak, she was back to being concerned for him. "Did you see Leidolf? He's staying at the Eagle's Nest cabin. He said he was bitten by a wolf, too, and wanted to talk to you about it. He seemed real nice."

Cameron gave her a heart-warming squeeze. "He didn't say a word about it when I came looking for you. He seemed a little amused, but not surprised that I was chasing you down. He also was worried that you were alone and so didn't say anything except where you were headed, and that he'd tried to talk you into letting him go with you to keep you safe."

"I told you he was a nice man."

As long as he wasn't *too* nice. As they neared the Eagle's Nest cabin, Cameron suddenly thought back to what Faith had been saying. "Did Leidolf tell you one of Lila's wolves had bitten him?"

"No. Just that a wolf had bitten him." Faith's eyes grew big. "You think he might collaborate our story, that the same wolf bit him that attacked you? Or one of Lila and Kintail's other wolves?"

"Yep, that's exactly what I'm thinking. Let's pay Leidolf a visit." He led her up the steps to Leidolf's deck, but when he knocked, there wasn't any answer.

"Maybe he's gone to the lodge." Faith glanced at her watch. "They should be serving early lunch there now."

"Okay, let's go. You can talk to Charles about finding Trevor, too."

Faith didn't say anything and he got the impression she had other things in mind. "You still want to go, right?"

"I… thought if I could talk to Hilson, I might not bother with Trevor."

Cameron stopped walking and pulled her to a stop. "So what's really up, Faith?"

She let out her breath. "Hilson stole my father's flash drive containing his research. Hilson's been gone for a couple of days now, but I located him in the area by discovering his password and finding his itinerary."

Research, like the police officers had mentioned her father was doing. Cameron shook his head. "Breaking into someone's computer and…"

"Hey," she said, poking his chest with her gloved finger, feigning annoyance, "did you hear what I said? Hilson stole my father's research paper. And Hilson's computer was at my place and he abandoned it, *and me*. So fair play."

Cameron took her hand and wrapped her arm around his waist, then hugged her tight, looking down into those sparkling green eyes. "What am I going to do with you?"

She gave half a shrug. "Treat me to lunch."

"We've got some other business to take care of first." He didn't often use his lock picking kit, but every once in a while, a situation justified the use. He turned her around and headed back toward Hilson's cabin.

"What are we doing now?"

"We're going to see if Hilson has your father's flash drive."

Faith frowned at him. "But the place is locked tight. I didn't think you believed in breaking and entering."

"Not the way you were going about it. That would add charges of destroying property."

She tightened her hold on Cameron and gave a relieved smile.

"So, Faith, what's the research about that's so important Hilson wanted it?"

"I have no idea why it would be so important. But something Dad had witnessed while he was on his sociology research project with Trevor Hodges was what spurred him on to write the paper. He's supposed to be speaking on it in just a week. So I have to have it to him before then."

"He didn't have any other copies?"

"On his hard drive, but Hilson stole that also, and Dad wouldn't tell me what it was about. Super hush-hush. All I know is that initially he went on a hunt for Bigfoot out in this area with a group who really believed in the elusive creature. My dad didn't. He was just doing a study of the group's behavior, how they goaded each other on, how that affected what they might find. Of course they didn't know he was a nonbeliever and that he was studying *them*. But something happened while he was out here. He was shaken when he first came home, wouldn't talk about what he'd seen, thought he was being followed even, and then dove into writing the paper with such enthusiasm, I was thrilled to see him interested in his research again. But no matter how many times I asked, he just wouldn't tell me what it was all about."

"But Hilson must have known."

Faith didn't say anything in response and that's when it dawned on Cameron. The guy had used her to get to her father's research. Then again, maybe not. Maybe he'd just learned of it while he was seeing Faith and thought he could make a quick buck off it if he could find a buyer.

"How long ago did you say Hilson stole it?"

"A couple of days."

Cameron frowned.

"I know. Hilson's probably already sold it. But I still have hopes I can find it. And if not, Trevor's my next best bet. Maybe he can help me reconstruct what had happened. I thought if I learned what happened from Trevor's perspective, I could help my father put the pieces back together in time for his lecture if I couldn't get the flash drive from Hilson."

"I'll help in any way I can."

She looked up at him, her smile dazzling. "Thank you, Cameron."

He shook his head. "That's another of my problems. Helping women in distress."

She chuckled, the sensual tone triggering another bout of deep-rooted need. "Seems I have the same problem, except I help men in distress—rescuing my father from failure, and you from a wolf."

"For which I'm grateful." He didn't think his friends would ever let him live the fact down if the word got out that a petite lady like Faith had saved his butt from a big, bad wolf attack.

When they reached Hilson's cabin, Faith acted as lookout, and Cameron used his lock pick to unlock the door. But, inside, the place was empty. No bags, nothing out of place. Either Hilson had already vacated the place, or he hadn't actually moved in. Faith's shoulders slumped forward slightly.

Cameron rubbed her back. "Come on. Let's get some lunch and talk to Charles about leaving to see Trevor."

He locked the place up and escorted her in the direction of the lodge. But they hadn't gone very far when they saw Charles stalking toward them on the path. "I've gotten word that Trevor is at a campsite about three hours from here and wishes to see you, Faith, concerning your father's trip."

Faith took in a deep breath, exhaled, and smiled. "When can we go?"

"Now, if you want to grab a bag." Charles looked at Cameron. "Still going?"

"Yep."

"Are you certain, Cameron?" Faith asked, looking worried, but he noted a hint of hopefulness in her expression that he truly wanted to go with her. "What about your partners?"

"Trevor works for Kintail as a guide, and maybe he knows something about David and Owen. Plus, I can help you gather information about your father's research while we're at it." He just hoped Trevor would enlighten him and not give him the runaround like Kintail and Lila.

"Are you a friend of Kintail's?" Faith asked Charles as they trudged back through the snow, and Cameron wondered why he hadn't thought to ask. Faith was really good at this investigative work and he couldn't help but admire her for it.

"I… respect him. He's taken a rag-tag group of people and given them purpose, jobs, an income. I do business with him from time to time. He takes hunting groups out, but sometimes he has inquiries from people looking to go dogsledding. Since he has a bigger operation and much more business, he directs interested clients my way. Nothing more than that." He looked at Cameron's torn parka sleeve. "But sometimes one of his wolves gets a little cantankerous."

"Cantankerous? He could have killed Cameron. He *would* have, if I hadn't clobbered him." Faith folded her arms. "Kintail's wolves might be okay where some people are concerned, but not with us."

"You hit the wolf?" Charles stroked his chin. "I'm not one of Kintail's men. I respect what he does, who he is, but I don't work for him. But he's super-protective of his wolves. I wouldn't want to be on his bad side and…" Charles just shook his head, as if he thought better of saying anything further. As if he wanted to warn Cameron of trouble, but he was afraid, or maybe just loyal to someone who sent business his way, who he respected, and lived nearby.

But the connotation was there. Cameron was on Kintail's bad side. He smiled a little. No one wanted to get on Cameron's bad side either.

"Do you know Trevor Hodges very well?" Faith asked Charles.

"He's an old-timer who's worked with Kintail on hunting excursions forever. Get your bags and join me at the barn." Charles eyed Cameron for a minute. "You sure you feel all right?"

Cameron thought it odd he'd ask again. "Yeah, I'm fine." For the moment, he was ready to get this show on the road. Maybe just the notion he could get somewhere where his friends were concerned and help Faith with her difficulties was all he needed to make him feel right again.

When Faith and Cameron entered her cabin, she packed up a bag with a few items of clothing. "Do you really think you'll locate your friends through Trevor?" Faith asked, heading for her sleeping bag.

Cameron hadn't unpacked his bag, so he just set it by the door. "I think he'll have seen them and reassure me they're just fine." But he wasn't about to speculate any further than that. Before Faith could roll up her sleeping bag, he halted her. "We don't need to take your bag also, if you don't mind sleeping in mine again with me."

"Sure, stay warmer in the cold that way. Okay, I'm ready."

He handed her his sleeping bag since it was lighter and more compact, then he grabbed the bags with their clothes and other items and headed outside. She locked up the place, but way before they even reached the barn, the sound of dogs excitedly barking made them both smile.

"Sounds like the dogs are ready to go," Cameron said, but just their enthusiasm was making him feel the unfathomable urge to run again.

"We used to have a standard poodle, and when we said the word go, whether we were talking about taking her for a car ride or walk or anything, that dog would act crazy, hopping around, poking her nose at us, ready to go."

"Sounds like a Lab I had. He would sit by the truck if I mentioned taking a ride."

She smiled. "Someday, I wouldn't mind having another dog, but I'm living in an apartment right now and no pets nor children are allowed."

Cameron raised his brows a hair, wondering if he'd read Faith wrong. "A swinging singles place?"

She chuckled. "Not sure about the swinging part and there are a lot of couples… working couples."

"Ah. Just sounded kind of interesting." He winked and she grinned back at him. But again that strange feeling of possessiveness washed over him, of not wanting to hear that a ton of single guys were hitting on her where she lived.

Trying to quash the unreasonable feelings bubbling up inside him concerning Faith, he led her into the barn where Charles was harnessing one of the teams. "If you can, Cameron, just copy what I'm doing. I'll check to make sure you've done it right after I'm finished here."

Cameron strode across the floor and began harnessing the first of the dogs, but they were so excited about running, they wiggled and thrashed about so wildly, it was hard to do the job right. In the oddest way, Cameron knew the feeling of wanting to run so badly, he could taste it. As if he was a runner in a competition, and yet he'd never been interested in competitive sports before.

Nikki poked her nose at his bare hand and gave him a warm wet kiss on the cheek while he was working on aligning two of the males. "You get to be on my team, Nikki."

Faith rubbed one of the dogs between his ears. "Looks like you have a new girlfriend already." She raised a brow, her lips curving up slightly.

Cameron gave her a small smile in return. No way was a pooch stealing his interest away from the tantalizing woman.

"At least they're well fed and had a little rest." Charles hitched the first team to the sled.

When his dogs were ready, Charles came over to check the harnesses Cameron used on the team, then helped him to hitch them to the sled. "A couple of tips. When we start out the team, you say, 'Hike.'"

"In the movies they hollered 'mush.'" Cameron wondered if that was another Hollywood-ism.

"The sound is too soft, not a distinct enough command for the dogs. Make a loud kissing sound to get the dogs to speed up. 'Gee' means turn right. 'Haw' is for left turn. 'Whoa' means stop. 'On by,' to pass another sled team or some other kind of distraction. And just remember, to the sled dog, you're the leader of the pack."

Cameron didn't need to be told that. Dogs naturally seemed to want to please him, and these even more so. Plus, now that he had come to an agreement with the leader of the pack, Cameron was it.

"Also, we don't talk while we're sledding, unless giving orders."

The dogs were so hyper, the air felt electric with their zeal—ready to run, ready to gratify their masters. The thrill of the impending trip electrified Cameron's blood and in the worst way the craving to run with them grew.

"Faith will ride with me up ahead, so I can show the way, and if you take a spill, she'll be safe," Charles said.

Cameron's jaw tightened. He couldn't pinpoint why he was feeling so acutely possessive of her when he knew Charles wasn't interested in anything but her safety. Although no matter how much he tried to crush the feeling, the stirrings of wanting to protect her nearly strangled him.

"He's at a campsite located twenty miles northeast of here that will take us about three hours to reach. That's where Trevor is planning to be for the day and overnight. I've packed lunches, dinner, and food for the dogs for the trip."

"Good," Faith said, but the unsettled sensation that raced through Cameron's blood hadn't gone away, he had to admit, and he barely heard what Charles was saying.

Despite realizing how crazy the notion was, Cameron had the most awful urge to rip off his clothes and run through the snow, not as a naked human, but as a... *wolf*. As if something alien possessed him, or someone had slipped him a drug that was making him feel so strange. And yet the vivid dream he'd had during the night reminded him he'd felt the very same way before and then it was as if he had stepped into his dream and made it real.

He thought back to Charles's comments about this very matter. How had Charles known how he'd feel? Cameron's attention shifted to the way the dogs were bouncing around, which stirred his own compulsion to get on with business.

Faith climbed into the heavy canvas bag filled with wool blankets on Charles's sled and she looked warm and cozy, but most importantly, safe. He should have been satisfied. She looked over her shoulder at Cameron and smiled—sexy and sirenlike. He wanted her on *his* sled, and he couldn't conceal the annoyance he felt as he glowered at Charles.

Charles looked from Cameron to Faith and gave a slight shake of his head.

Cameron felt he could drive a sled well enough and that Faith's safety wasn't an issue, but he gave in to the older man's decision. Cameron climbed onto the two ski-like blades attached to the bottom of his sled and grabbed hold of the horizontal bar in front of him, his body tensed for the new experience. The dogs continued to bark, their muscles taut like tightly coiled springs, readied for when he gave them the magic word.

Charles glanced back at him. "Ready?"

Cameron bowed his head slightly and lifted it. Charles's eyes widened. Then Charles turned and yelled to his team, "Hike!" and his dogs took off.

Cameron shouted, "Hike!" and his team yanked the sled in the direction Charles was moving. A rush of adrenaline instantly flooded his veins. Losing his balance, Cameron quickly compensated for the sudden movement by crouching a little and gripping the bar tighter.

The sleds sped across the snow with a soft, creaking sound, away from the resort, down an unplowed road, the snow-laden spruces and pines stretching out to them on either side of the road. The dogs barked, bellowed, and yelped starting out the trip. But as they journeyed onward, they grew quiet, all business, the crisp sound of the sled runners whooshing, no noisy sputtering engine roar like when they rode the snowmobiles. The dogs' booty-covered paws thudded gently on the snow while their frosty breaths wafted in the air.

Every bump shot through the blades and up Cameron's legs to his hands, every dip, making his heart drop and rise again. *Exhilarating*. Then Charles picked up the pace and they practically flew over the snow. Cameron was glad his mask and ski glasses protected his face from the bitter cold wind.

One of the dogs turned and nipped another, and Cameron immediately yelled, "No, Trigger!"—glad Charles had introduced him to each of the dogs by name earlier. The dog instantly minded. "Good dog!"

As soon as he said the words, the whole team perked up. He smiled. The team was a dream to work with.

Then Charles made a sharp turn ahead of him onto a narrow path through the forest. Cameron tried to copy the maneuver, but he nearly tumbled off his sled. So much for thinking he could keep Faith safe. Quickly shifting his posture to lower his center of gravity, he regained his balance and again wished he was running alongside the team on his own power.

The soothing whispered sounds of the skis crunched on the snow, but everything otherwise was softly silent, filling him with awe as he thought about his friends and the next step he would take if Trevor didn't have any clues for him. He was sure Lila was right, that the police wouldn't do anything unless something clued them in that his friends were in real trouble.

But an hour and a half into their journey, Charles suddenly called out "Whoa!" and stopped.

Up ahead, a tree had fallen and blocked the path. Charles checked it out, while Faith climbed out of her snug sled bed and joined him. Cameron crunched on the snow to reach them as Charles had gone into the woods a ways. He looked up at Cameron and pointed to where the tree had been cut, the tree over forty inches in diameter and branches spread out several feet in every direction. "Recently," he said, touching the trunk. "Still warm from the chainsaw blade." He looked up at Cameron. "Can you smell who did it?"

Chapter 10

CAMERON TOOK A DEEP BREATH, SAMPLING THE BREEZE, BUT he didn't smell any sign of who might have cut down the tree in their path. "Did you get a whiff of cologne or aftershave or something?" he asked Charles as Faith took a deep breath, her chin tilted up.

Charles shook his head at Cameron as if he was hopeless.

Not sure why Charles should think he would smell something when the old man couldn't, Cameron glanced around at the woods, looking for tracks in the snow. Boot prints could be seen all over the place. "We have axes, right? We could cut the tree up to clear the road."

"Would take too long. Too much work. We'll go another route. Through there." Charles motioned to a narrower path.

Cameron didn't like it. They had switched from a major unplowed road, to a smaller one, and now just a trail, from the looks of it. "Are we being railroaded?" Cameron asked, wondering if they were being forced to take this route for some sinister reason.

Rubbing his chin, Charles stared at the downed tree. "No reason I can think of that someone would do such a thing. We don't have to go, if you don't like it. We can always return to the resort."

"No, I want to see Trevor," Faith said, frowning. "As long as this trail will get us there, I'm all for it. Don't you think it'll be all right, Cameron?"

He studied the trail. "If Charles thinks it's all right, it's fine by me."

Charles headed for the sled and everyone took their places and then they were off again. Only this time the woods reached out so close to the trail, they sometimes touched Cameron, calling to him, every shadow as the day drew on, every whisper of movement, a bird startled by their presence, fluttering off, the breeze making the branches tremble, a rabbit bolting from underneath a spruce close to the trail. Instead of riding down the man-made path on the sled, he wanted to explore the woods on foot, smell the scents of animals and plants, identify everything with his senses that seemed to be so much more highly attuned.

Conquering that urge, he continued to follow Charles and avoided thinking of anything but what he had to do when they reached Trevor. After half an hour on the trail, they came to another downed tree, cut in the same manner, only it had been sawed down earlier. Charles peered into the forest and didn't say anything for several minutes.

Another trail came off this one, but where would it lead? A dead end? The wrong direction?

From Charles's reaction, it appeared it wasn't a good thing.

"Can we cut this one up?" Cameron asked.

"Too big. Take too long. We go back and try another way."

"Who would do something like this?" Cameron asked, walking with Faith and Charles back to the sleds.

"Someone who doesn't like snowmobilers, possibly. Cross-country skiers maybe." Charles pointed to ski tracks. "They can easily traverse the tree. Hard to say."

Faith looked disappointed, although she tried to hide the expression. They'd already been delayed over an hour. Now this would add another hour to the trip.

But the most worrisome concern was whether or not they were being delayed on purpose and if so, why. Or if the situation was more of a case of being forced to go in some other direction, which again led to the question of why. Although the downed trees might not have had anything to do with them at all.

When they reached the small road again, Charles motioned to the tree lying prone in the road. "We'll cut it up."

About time. Cameron grabbed the ax off his sled and stalked over to the tree. For a quarter of an hour, Charles and Cameron chopped off branches, and Faith hauled them into the woods. Another hour and Charles and Cameron had chopped enough of the trunk away to maneuver the dogs and sleds through the partially cleared path.

When they were on their way again, Cameron mulled over everything that had happened since he'd met Faith. He couldn't stop thinking about the way she'd beaten the wolf off him, or how she'd taken care of him afterward with such a tender, caring touch. And then this morning, the way she'd wanted him like he'd wanted her, settling his strange desire to leave the cabin and run through the woods with a few well-placed kisses and… well, hell, he had to admit she wasn't anything like the other women in his life. He even admired her for hauling off the branches while he and Charles chopped away at the tree. Marjory would have looked at her long fingernails and said, "No way." Katie would have pouted.

From roughing it, to trying out the spa in the bitter cold, to investigating a crime scene, to nearly creating her own as she readied a log to bash in her ex-boyfriend's cabin window, to standing up to Lila when she thought she was making the moves on him, Faith was the kind of woman he could really go for. Even though they barely knew each other, he felt a connection existed between them that made him feel as though he'd known her for so much longer. And yeah, he wanted to be there for her, to help her father out in his time of crisis while he searched for clues concerning his friends' whereabouts.

He shook his head at himself. He just hoped he wasn't being a sucker for lost causes again.

It didn't even seem like another two and a half hours had passed when Charles called out to his team, "Easy!" His dogs instantly slowed to a walk.

Cameron surveyed the two-story lodge in the distance and gave the same command to his team. Surrounded by spruce, the place looked like a rustic dwelling, probably having been inhabited for a couple of hundred years. Even Charles's main lodge had been built in 1860, according to the brochure.

"Trevor's campsite is about another hour west of here since the secondary road we took moved us out of the more direct route. This is Kintail's lodge and I thought you might check in with him to verify that Trevor was still at the campsite, although he might not know. But it looks like nobody's home." A hint of warning was in Charles's voice and Cameron wondered why.

Probably had to do with Cameron threatening to press charges about the wolf attack.

Like Charles's lodge had been when they had first arrived at his resort, the windows were dark, no lights on inside, and there wasn't any smoke coming out of the chimney. So it didn't look like anyone was home, which rankled. He'd really hoped to talk with this Kintail and get some answers about his friends.

When they finally reached an outer building, Charles pulled his sled to a halt, a good three hundred yards from the main lodge situated on the banks of a frozen lake.

Charles said, "Wait with the teams. Since Kintail and his people know me, I'll check the place out first. He wouldn't like it if strangers were snooping around the place without permission if they're not home." He handed Cameron a canvas bag. "Give the dogs treats while I'm at it, and they'll love you for life."

Without a backward glance, Charles hurried to the lodge while Cameron helped Faith out of her canvas bag.

She watched Charles trudge through the snow to the lodge. "He seemed kind of on edge, didn't you think?"

"He thinks I have issues with Kintail. And why wouldn't I? The guy's wolf bit me and he likely knows my friends' whereabouts, but isn't forthcoming with the location. At least his partner, Lila, isn't."

Faith shivered and Cameron reached over and rubbed her arms, but she turned her attention to the metal building. "Wonder if it's locked."

"Why?"

She looked up at him. "After we feed the dogs, we could stand in there out of the wind."

But the expression on her face was much more devious, and he assumed she had it in mind to do a little investigative snooping. Just his kind of woman.

He glanced back at Charles as he neared the lodge and hoped Kintail was home despite the way it looked.

"Sounds like a plan to me." Cameron gave her a handful of doggy treats, then headed to his team while Faith offered her portion to Charles's team.

Faith assumed Cameron had figured out her real reason to visit the outer building. Just the slight glint of recognition, the tilted up chin, his eyes lighting just a bit, and then the devilish smile. Yeah, he was all for it.

After giving Charles's dogs their treats, Faith stalked across the snow to join Cameron as he gave the last dog on his team a hug and back rub. She shook her head. "You're just one of the pack."

"The alpha leader."

She grabbed his arm and hurried with him to the barnlike building. "Did I tell you I like alpha males, and I love the way you handle the dogs, firmly but kindly?"

"If I didn't know better, I'd say you were ready for another kiss."

And more, if the circumstances were more suitable. She smiled as they entered the outbuilding, but as soon as he closed the door, she headed for a stack of crates underneath a window that was about eight feet off the ground. "Looks like just some camping supplies," she said, lifting the lid of one wooden boxes. "Probably for their hunting excursions."

Cameron was checking out a box across the room, situated next to a couple of snowmobiles with the name, *Back Country Tours* painted on the side with a white wolf logo.

"Tents here." Cameron poked around some more as Faith pulled out a sleeping bag.

A little crinkling noise from inside the bag caught her attention, and she unzipped it to find out what it was. A candy wrapper. But deeper down in the bag, a receipt.

"Finding anything?" Cameron asked, surrounded by a growing mound of tenting gear.

"You sure know how to make a mess." She smiled when he did. She opened the receipt. The handwritten note listed food and other items from the grocery at the trailhead. "Nothing that would help. This receipt is dated yesterday for food supplies. But it only has the last numbers of a credit card, so no telling whose it could be." Something shiny caught her eye, and she reached in to pull out a can of pepper spray. "This could come in handy."

"Good as a deterrent for some wild animals if the wind's blowing in the right direction. Why don't you hang onto it? Nothing in this mess." Cameron began gathering up the tents and shoving them back into the box. But something hard in one of them stopped him. He pulled out the tent again and fished out a credit card from an inside pocket. "Trevor Hodges. Bet he doesn't even know it's missing."

"What are the last four digits on the card?"

"Four, nine, nine, two."

"Not the same as this receipt." She was about to drop the receipt in the bag and zip it back up, when something leathery caught her eye. She reached in and pulled it out. A gun holster. "David Davis," she read engraved on the inside.

Cameron dropped the tent he was about to shove in the box and stalked over to join Faith.

"David's," Cameron said, and the way his voice hitched a little, Faith knew this wasn't real good news.

"He'd never leave his gun or holster behind. I don't like this."

The door lock made a clicking sound. Cameron raced to the door and twisted the knob. It didn't budge. "Shit."

Outside the building, Charles suddenly hollered, "Hike!"

"Son of a bitch!" Cameron rushed across the building to join Faith as she scrambled to climb on top of the crate to look out the window, but it was too short to reach.

"Was it Charles who locked us in?" she asked. She got back down and assisted Cameron in sliding another crate over, then helped him lift it on top of the other.

"Looks that way." Cameron sounded pissed.

He gave her a little boost up on top of the stacked crates. Using her gloved hand, she wiped away the dust on the window and peered through the still dirty glass. All she could see was the lake from this angle, not the dog sleds or the lodge. "Nothing." She hated to ask, but wanted to know what they were up against. "Did you bring your gun?"

Cameron patted his side, glad he'd been prepared. "Always." Except for when he went to the spa with Faith. But on an excursion like this, absolutely. No telling what they might have run into. Although he was thinking more of wildlife problems, like an attack wolf, not real human troubles.

Trapped in a snare is the way Cameron felt and his blood heated with anger. Just like the time he and Gavin were locked in a storage building when they discovered illegal smuggling. Only that time, the building had no windows, just metal walls that were weak and rusted.

After a few well-placed kicks, he and Gavin had managed to knock out part of a wall. But thankfully, the district was empty, not a soul around. Although before long, Cameron figured they'd have trouble waiting for them outside this building.

Faith suddenly looked below. "Holy crap," she whispered. "Two wolves are pacing beneath the window."

Hell. Cameron searched the building for another weapon. Finding a shovel, he returned to the crates and handed it up to Faith, then climbed up to the top to join her. Slowly, he slid the window up, but the wolves looked in their direction, their ears perked, alert and ready.

"We can climb down to the ledge below and from there it's an easy drop," Cameron said.

"But the wolves—"

"Use the pepper spray. You make a run for the sled. If I don't make it, you leave me, Faith. Do you understand? If my friends have come to harm because of Kintail and his people, we're sitting ducks here. You leave if you can and return to the cabins. Take the snowmobile and get to the trailhead. Once there, grab your rental vehicle and report this…" He reconsidered. "If you report it to Officers Adams and Whitson, they'll no doubt discount our claims, unless we find a body. Leave Millinocket and go to Bangor. Get outside help."

She shook her head. "Got it all planned out, I see."

"Yeah, well, you're a forensic scientist. I'm a former police officer. You're not trained for this kind of work." Although he had the most awful urge to take the wolves on wolf to wolf.

She climbed down, muttering something that sounded suspiciously like she wasn't leaving him. But that *wasn't* an option if things didn't turn out well. She waited on the ledge, clinging to the side of the building, and shivered. He joined her.

The wolves watched them. Anticipating their move. Ready.

"I'll go first, swinging the shovel. You jump down right after me. Spray their faces and run for the sled."

As soon as he jumped, one of the wolves lunged. Cameron swung the shovel and connected with the wolf's nose. It yelped and darted away.

Faith jumped down next to Cameron, sprayed the other wolf in the face, grabbed Cameron's arm, and ran with him. The wolf sneezed and pawed at his nose and eyes. "Come on, hero of mine. I'm not leaving you behind. What if I need you again?"

The sled dogs barked like crazy, wanting to run, too. Charles had taken off with the sled Cameron had used earlier. What the hell was he up to?

As soon as Cameron got Faith to the sled and she was safely in the sled bag, he jumped on the runners. Throwing the shovel aside, he yelled, "Hike," and made a kissing sound to get the dogs to hurry.

The one wolf was still pawing at his face, sneezing and coughing, and the other was limping toward them, but not making any real effort to chase after them.

"Maybe Charles didn't do this to us. He couldn't have locked us in," Faith shouted over the dogs' excited barking.

Cameron chastised himself for going along with her on this trip. He felt *he* was the reason for her being in danger. "Maybe." But he wasn't convinced. Maybe Charles figured he'd better cut his losses and run since he was in business to a degree with Kintail. Although, Cameron couldn't believe Charles would leave his other sled team behind.

They shot across the snow in a madcap race to catch up to Charles. But Cameron couldn't help worrying that Kintail's men would learn of their escape soon. Hell, he should have done something to mess up the snowmobiles in the shed so they couldn't use those at least.

Riding snowmobiles, how long would it take for Kintail's people to catch up to them?

—∿—

After an hour, Faith and Cameron still hadn't caught up with Charles, yet she saw his sled tracks clearly. The sun was fading and the dogs needed to rest. She was glad Cameron had so quickly mastered handling a dog sledding team, but she still couldn't believe Charles would have left them behind and not waited for them somewhere along the way.

When Cameron finally pulled the team to a stop, Faith frowned at him. "We're not going any further? What if it snows in the middle of the night? Or the winds pick up even more and we lose his trail?"

"I'll find it. Even though the dogs are naturally nocturnal, they need a rest."

Cameron seemed so sure of himself, but she wasn't so positive. "I'm not certain we even have a tent."

"Underneath that bag you're sitting in. I noticed it earlier when he pulled out his ax."

"Why would he desert us like that? Leave the rest of his dogs, his sled? They're his livelihood." She crawled out of the bag and felt chilled to the bone. "Not to mention I'm sure he's really attached to them."

"He likes wolves, too. They're… magical, powerful," Cameron said sarcastically. "But if you want to know the truth, I think he was attempting to draw the wolves away from us. Or, he figured we'd have a better chance if we left separately, the one not blocking the other's escape that way." Although he wasn't sure either scenario could be the truth.

And who had locked them in the building then? Unless Lila had done so and hightailed it back to the lodge until Kintail and his men arrived, leaving the wolves to guard the place in the interim so Faith and Cameron couldn't escape.

He began unloading the sled and found food for the dogs, while Faith pulled out the double-walled tent, red and orange, like a brightly colored pergola he'd seen at a Renaissance fair.

"Hope there's something for us to eat also on this sled. I'm starving since we missed lunch and breakfast." She searched on the sled while Cameron erected the two layers of tents, then went about setting up a stove and pipe to vent the smoke.

"Food! Salami, ham, cheese, cookies, bread, bottled water." She sighed. "Charles gave me a book to read on how to take care of a team on a race while we were traveling. Good thing I read it, too, because we're sure going to need the help." She glanced up at Cameron as he paused to watch her. "It's almost like he figured we'd need to know how to do this alone."

"I'm sure he was just being prudent, making sure that if we got in a bind like this, at least one of us would know the ropes."

"Yeah, but I was with him, not you."

Cameron didn't say anything, and Faith could tell by his darkened expression he'd had the same thought already. "So what do we do with the dogs while we lie down?" He carried his sleeping bag into the tent, while she dug around on the sled.

When she found what she was looking for, she grabbed a handful of straw just as Cameron reemerged from the tent.

"The book said to lay this down for the dogs, take off their tug lines, and booties and massage their feet and leg muscles."

"I'll take care of the dogs. Why don't you carry the food into the tent, and I'll join you when I'm done? Maybe I'll even massage something of yours?" He raised a brow.

She chuckled. "Too cold to remove anything." Although if it hadn't been, she'd sure take him up on it. "I'll help you with the dogs so we can get done with the chores faster." She handed him a tube of ointment. "For their feet."

Then she grabbed up the cooker to heat up some snow, and once it melted, she mixed it with bits of chicken. She glanced at Cameron as he pulled off their booties while they licked his face.

He massaged their feet as the ones waiting for his attention continued to bump him with enthusiasm. She smiled. He fit right in.

He grinned at her. "See how much they appreciate me?"

She laughed. "Yeah. Snuggling I can do. Licking your whiskery face, uhm, not tonight."

"Guess that's why a dog is man's best friend." He rubbed one of the leader's legs, and glanced up at Faith with a wicked look on his face.

"And diamonds are a girl's best friend."

Cameron shook his head as he fed the dogs the kibble and melted snow. "Haven't even had a real date, and she's already talking wedding rings."

"Who's talking weddings? I just like diamonds." She brought over the cooked food for the dogs. "Here, make some more brownie points with them, and I'll cook us something hot to eat. Might not be five-star restaurant worthy, or as good as the dogs' food, but it won't be cold."

She cleaned out the cooking pot and melted the cheese over the ham and sausage, then served it up between two slices of bread. "Ready?"

Cameron gave her a look like he was interested in more than just eating, but took a bite of his sandwich and nodded, his eyes smiling. "Good stuff. Where'd you learn to cook on campouts?"

"Truthfully? I didn't. Just used what we had available. Except for day hikes, I've never camped out."

"Could have fooled me."

Yeah, she wasn't used to this. At least there were no bugs. But camping in snow and ice was for the polar bears, and even *they* had sense enough to hibernate. She'd prefer a nice warm hotel room, comfy bed, and room service. Her thoughts shifted to Charles. Although she didn't want to undermine Cameron's plans, she wondered if they should be following Charles, or just heading back to the cabins and doing what Cameron outlined if she had been on her own.

She cleared her throat. "You think this is the way to go? Not return to the cabins instead?"

"I have to believe that Charles didn't steer us wrong. That he wanted us to follow him this way, and I figure eventually we'll locate Trevor or end up back at the resort."

But his expression said he wasn't completely sure that was the case.

They finished their meals, checked on the dogs one last time, then retired to the tent, which was nice and toasty inside from the heat in the stove.

"What are we going to do if Kintail comes for us? We don't have much in the line of defenses," she said, pulling off her jacket, gloves, and boots.

"The two wolves weren't in much condition to run off and alert Kintail. I doubt he was around or we would have seen him when we escaped." He slipped off a boot, then the other, watching her snuggle in the bag, and she hoped to hell they wouldn't have any trouble while they napped. He climbed into the bag with her and pulled her into his arms, then stroked her hair. "Get some rest. We'll leave in a couple of hours and run by moonlight."

"Are you sure you can find the way at night?"

"Yeah, we'll make it now."

She sure hoped so because she didn't relish sleeping out in the open another night. At least a building would offer them further protection.

Then she nestled tighter against Cameron's warm body. If Kintail or his men tried to follow them, they didn't have sleds or dogs, and Faith and Cameron would hear snowmobiles from a mile away forewarning of their approach. That was if they used snowmobiles, and not skis.

She tried to close her eyes, to rest, to shut off her mind, but she couldn't. His eyes closed, Cameron was still touching her hair with one hand, his other stroking her back, his fingers drawing lower to the tip of her spine, stirring a compulsion to feel him deep inside her again. She lifted her head and he looked down at her, his expression half quizzical, half hopeful she wanted him again. She reached up and kissed his lips, his mouth soft and warm. His skin smelled soap fresh, and his body heat wrapped around her in an enjoyable way. A shiver of pleasure stole through her. But his blue eyes were what caught her attention the most—dark and beautiful, and quickly turning from intrigued to lustful. She nibbled his lower lip. His mouth curved up slightly.

He closed his eyes, slipped his other hand around her back, and pulled her tight against his chest. His full-blown erection speared her belly, and she rubbed her body gently against his arousal. A low moan escaped his lips and he took charge, licking the seam of her mouth, tugging at the waistband of her pants, trying to lower them past her hips. And she responded, touching her tongue to his, licking his lips back, pressing her mouth to his. Her hands jerked up his sweater and then his shirt so she could feel his skin.

The aching need he'd awakened in her pushed her to roll off him and reach for his jeans. Verging on panic, she yanked at his belt buckle, but he quickly unbuckled the belt and continued the sensual onslaught, pressuring her mouth with his, getting her worked up, her panties growing damp in response. His breathing and hers were labored, her body burning with need. Every touch sent her head spiraling, making her want more. Before she knew it, their tongues were mating in a teasing, heated dance again, as she struggled to pull off her pants.

They bumped heads as he tried to help her remove her panties next, his actions just as frantic as hers. The air from the stove kept the tent warm and a slight breeze brushed against the silky walls and rustled through the branches of nearby trees, but mostly all she noticed was Cameron, his hands yanking at her sweater to remove it, his fingers fumbling with her bra—now she wished she hadn't worn one.

She struggled to help him remove his sweater and shirt, but he wasn't cooperating. Instead, his hands were on her breasts, weighing them, massaging them, playing with her nipples, his smoldering gaze slipping from her nakedness to her eyes. Something about the look on his face warned her their relationship had taken a drastic turn, that he didn't plan to let her go anytime soon. Which was crazy. They didn't even live in the same state.

But for the moment, she didn't care. And when he drew her down onto her back and pressed her legs apart with his knees, nothing mattered, but feeling him deep inside her. The tautness in his actions fed into hers, her hands reaching to touch his skin, to feel the muscles in his arms beneath her fingertips, tensing as he centered himself between her legs.

And then he thrust deeply with raw desire, no measured moves, no gradual accommodations. Too late for anything but primal fulfillment. She surrendered to his frenzied pace, drove herself to meet it, her pelvis angled to feel the urgency, to glory in the experience. For the first time in her life, she felt wanted, needed, loved, as crazy as it might sound.

She felt the exquisite peak of the sexual experience just beyond reach, and then as if he instinctively knew, he slowed his pace, slipped his fingers between her legs and touched her. Just that simple touch nearly pushed her over the edge. But she wanted more and pushed against his fingers, begging for fulfillment. And he obliged, rubbing and stroking and didn't let up until she moaned out with pleasure.

He watched the expression on her face, as if her orgasm was the most precious thing he could have ever done for her. Her lips curved up a bit, her skin flushed, her fingers instantly grappling for him to finish what he'd begun.

He didn't hesitate, diving into her again and again, his mouth on her lips, the nape of her neck, her breast. Then he groaned out loud, "Sweet love of…"

But he didn't say another word as he tackled her mouth one last time, thrusting again until he was done. Spent, and looked totally satiated, a small smile lifted his lips, his eyes saying she was the best thing in his life right now. Rolling over on his back, he pulled her tight against his heated body. "I don't… think… we needed the heat from the stove," he said, brushing her damp hair behind her ear. "God, you feel good."

"And you," she whispered, loving his sentiments, not wanting to break the spell. She hugged him tight, wondering where their relationship was headed, but despite feeling he wanted something more, she wasn't sure if it was still just a case of rebound—for both of them.

That's when she realized that in their enthusiasm, they had forgotten to use a condom this time.

———∿∿∿———

Faith slept half on top of Cameron snuggled in his double wide sleeping bag. He was torn between staying with her and enjoying her comforting heat, the sound of her steady heartbeat, and her subtle fragrance, the tantalizing smell of her arousal still lingering—and squelching the craving to ditch his clothes no matter how cold it was and run like one of the sled dogs.

The dogs were quiet and he planned to leave in another hour or so after they'd had some rest, concerned Kintail or his people might still catch up to them. Plus, he did worry about losing Charles's tracks if the winds grew. But he couldn't suppress the restlessness growing in his blood again.

Trying not to disturb Faith, Cameron slipped out from under her and ducked out of the tent.

He wanted to run in the worst way, to stretch his legs, and something new—claim the area while they stayed here as if he was a conqueror and wanted to leave his mark.

Giving in to the urge, he started pulling off his clothes as if it was the most natural thing in the world to do. And at once, he had the eerie feeling he'd done this before. The cold chilled him instantly, the dogs all watching him with interest, expectant, their eyes alert, ears perked. Then heat sifted through every muscle, through every blood vessel, and Cameron stretched his arms out as if he were reaching for the moon, visible in the distant sky.

In the next instant, he was standing on all fours, his fur white, his body perfectly warm, his elongated snout sampling the crisp, cold air. His footpads felt fine against the snow, which made him look back at the dogs, all sitting up now.

Why would they need booties when he didn't?

When he started to leave the campsite, the dogs ran after him, but he growled at them to stay behind, to protect Faith. They stopped and stayed.

He swung around and raced off again. He didn't have to look to see their reaction. They were silent, standing there still, waiting, like he'd commanded them.

It didn't take long for him to cover about a mile. His toes digging into the snow, he lifted his nose and smelled the scents—a rabbit, fishy odor of the frozen lake they'd left behind, even the dog's food, and—Nikki's scent. What the—

He whisked around and she bowed her head slightly to him. She hadn't been with his team. Initially, yes. But now she was supposed to be with Charles.

Hell, Charles and his team had to be close by. Cameron opened his mouth to ask where Charles was, but as soon as he tried to speak, his words ended up sounding like a huffing noise, not quite a bark, more like a woof, a breathy cough. Nikki circled around in front of him as if she was trying to tell him something, but he wasn't sure what she was attempting to say. She gave a little bark and pranced around some more. He huffed back, wondering why his bark didn't come out the same. Then Nikki headed away from him and when he didn't follow, she returned, wagged her tail, and turned and headed in the same direction.

Follow her, that's what she was trying to tell him. But as soon as he ran up behind her, the dogs in his team began barking, warning of an intruder.

Faith. His heart in his throat, he raced back toward camp in hunting-to-kill mode.

It was only another dream, he reminded himself. A really vivid dream, but he couldn't help feeling Faith was in danger. And what about Nikki? How had she found Cameron? Was Charles in trouble?

More dogs barking. Hell, it was the other team from somewhere in the distance. *Charles's team*.

His heart wildly pounding, Cameron had another eighth of a mile to go when he spied Faith emerging from the tent. Four wolves were skulking toward her.

His blood on fire, Cameron would kill every one of them before they touched her. The dogs circled the wolves, barking and growling in a mad frenzy, protecting Faith, protecting their territory. Cameron bolted for the wolves.

Faith dove back into the tent, but the lightweight fabric designed for cold weather conditions wouldn't deter the wolves. She reemerged with the pepper spray and his gun, and he couldn't believe her tenacity. She was no match for a pack of feral wolves. Neither were the dogs. She had a chance against one of the wolves, maybe. But she couldn't fight this many.

Racing toward them as if his life depended on it, he vowed to reach her before any could hurt her.

One of the bigger wolves tried to cut Faith out of the pack. Cameron's heart pounded even harder. *Hold on, Faith. Hold on*.

She hesitated to shoot the predator with either weapon.

The wind is blowing the wrong way. Don't use the pepper spray!

And the gun. She couldn't aim with any accuracy without using both hands.

Faith.

The wolf separated her from the huskies, snarling and snapping his jaws, his nose puckered, his hackles raised, pelt bristling, creeping closer, ready to lunge.

Cameron did what he never thought possible, leapt nearly sixteen feet into the air at his prey, his own fur raised, his canines bared—ready to kill.

Chapter 11

WITH HER HEART IN HER THROAT AND NO SIGN OF CAMERON, Faith backed away from the Arctic wolf targeting her. Her chances of survival were slim at best. The way his narrowed amber eyes pinned her with promise—glowing menacingly in the moonlight—she'd be dead within seconds.

But she had to save herself, the dogs, and find Cameron.

The wolf crept toward her, separating her from the dogs that were charging and growling at the other wolves. Like a predator singling out the weakest link, the wolf bared his daggerlike teeth, snarling, crowding her. Her heartbeat spastic, her hands trembled as she tightened her grip on the can of pepper spray in one hand and the gun in the other.

The damned wind was blowing in the wrong direction. She couldn't chance choking herself or the dogs with the spray. If she could work her way around to have the wind at her back… but dogs and wolves blocked her path, and the tent was hindering her in the other direction. Plus, she was unable to fire the gun accurately without using both hands. She shoved the pepper spray in her pocket and wrapped her hands around the gun. Having had weapons training in her line of business, she knew how to shoot, but practicing at targets was one thing. Killing a live animal or a person…

The aggressor wolf paused, his expression changing. No longer growling, he smiled—if a wolf could smile. Her finger on the trigger, she hesitated to fire the weapon. Since he'd quit pursuing her, she hoped she could scare him away—although she figured it was a futile exercise—but giving it a try, she stomped her foot, yelling, "Ha!"

He crouched in response. An icy shiver stole down her spine. Readying to leap, he behaved just like her standard poodle would when he was a puppy, crouching before the pounce.

But more than that, she envisioned the wolf that had lunged at Cameron, then bit him in the arm.

She aimed the weapon again, took another step backward, and stumbled on a pile of snow. Her heart nearly seized. Falling on her butt, she dropped the gun.

Everything seemed to freeze in time. The dogs and wolves quit growling and barking, their mouths snapped closed, their attention diverted to something behind her. The one ready to leap on her, straightened, his ears perked, his gaze focused to her left.

She didn't have time to turn to see what was coming, when a huge wolf sailed past her shoulder, nearly hitting her. She jerked away from the great white beast and rolled over the mound of snow.

The new wolf, bigger than any of them, pounced half on the wolf's shoulder, his hind feet landing firmly on the ground. He knocked the other down. The pinned wolf tried frantically to get to his pads, before the newcomer seized his throat.

Not wanting to see any of the animals fighting or injuring each other, she feared the outcome should either win.

The other wolves and the huskies all observed the
pair as if the newcomer was attempting to become the
pack leader of a mixed bunch of wolves and huskies,
and they wanted to see who came out on top.

Faith scrambled to her feet and shoved her gloved
hands into the piles of snow until she located the gun.
She shook the snow off her gloves and aimed the
weapon at the fighting wolves. Their incisors bared,
snarling, lunging, and biting, the ferocious sound
chilled her blood.

Patches of blood covered both wolves' fur and stained
the snow in places.

Desperately, she wanted them to give up fighting and
run off. But the two continued to circle each other. Then
the biggest wolf attacked the other, tore his ear. When the
wolf yelped and jumped back, the biggest one went for his
throat like an animal possessed by the devil. The newcomer
seized the other's throat and the wolf went down.

The victor's head swiveled around to look at her.
Immediately, she raised the gun and pointed it at
him. But she couldn't pull the trigger. If they were all
Kintail's wolves—which she believed to be so—why
did the biggest one kill one of the others?

For an instant, the animals were silent. Then the other
three wolves began to growl low. So, they didn't accept
the newcomer as the pack leader. But at the same time,
the dogs began to bark at the wolves, growling and
lunging. The big wolf's chest heaved for a few minutes
while he stood still, turning his attention toward the rest
of the animals.

Although he had helped her and the dogs, she worried
he still might turn on them.

The dogs pounced on one of the wolves, while the other two wolves shied back, then ran off. They'd tell Kintail. That's what she figured. They'd alert him to where they were, leading them back here like bloodhounds on a prey's trail. Then she and Cameron would be in bigger trouble.

Bleeding at the shoulder, the big wolf crouched low, targeting the last of the aggressors. The beast continued to show his aggression, his ears straight up, his tail stiff behind him, snarling at the dogs. The huskies ran at him, snapping their jaws. He lunged in retaliation. They darted out of his path.

The victor wolf growled threateningly low. The sound made the hair on the nape of Faith's neck stand at attention, even under her parka hood.

The final aggressor had been fierce and full of bravado when facing the dogs, but she swore he looked like he was about to die now. His tail suddenly lowered, his ears flattening as he turned to face the real threat—their wolf savior.

The big wolf crouched. His tail was slightly raised, the tip twitching to one side, his ears and fur erect. As soon as he made his move, he would kill the other. The smaller one had to be a male also, aggressive and single-minded in his urge to fight. Because of his size, the larger wolf had to win.

Without further warning, the victor lunged. The two slammed into each other. Their front legs lifted off the ground, their teeth clanking as they bit each other's mouths. They landed on their pads, but the victor didn't hesitate to attack again. He grabbed the aggressor's throat and killed him. The animal dropped to the ground with a thud.

Everything was whisper soft with the breeze blowing against the tent, and the animals now standing silent. The victor quietly watched Faith. He stood still, panting, his white muzzle tinged with blood, his eyes amber, the wildness in them softening. Her heart was beating hard and she felt panicked, unsure what to do, but she didn't want to kill him. Not after he'd saved them from two of the wolves. And not while he didn't act threatening toward the huskies or her.

For a minute, no one made a move. Then the dogs barked in excitement. Jumping at each other, they licked him in the face in greeting. He continued to watch Faith's reaction, his tail now pointed down. She barely breathed and wanted to get the huskies away from him before their overexuberant attentions irritated him, and he attacked them. The dogs treated him as if he was a war hero and they were cheering the wounded veteran. He didn't seem bothered by them, but eerily kept his attention on her.

But then a husky nuzzled its face against the wolf's ear. Recognizing the husky, Faith's mouth dropped open. "Nikki?"

Nikki. What had happened to Charles and the rest of the team? And Cameron? Faith's gaze searched for any signs of him and saw Cameron's parka and the rest of his clothes piled up on top of the sled.

"What the…?"

The wolf lifted his nose and sniffed the air, then turned his head south. With the dogs still yipping, he tore off. Nikki followed him, along with two of the other dogs.

Dashing to the others to grab their collars and make them stay with her, Faith hollered at the rest to come back. But the wolf's influence overrode hers and the dogs ran with him until they disappeared from sight. She prayed they'd come back and that Charles and his team were all right. That the wolf wasn't leading the dogs into an ambush like the one did in one of Jack London's wolf tales.

But what of Cameron? She had to locate his tracks in the snow. Something surely had gone wrong with Charles and his team, too. She glanced at the dead wolves, their blood coloring the snow red. What if the blood attracted predators? She shoved her outer gloves back on and hurried to the sled to search for a shovel.

In the distance, an eerie howl sounded.

After he killed the first of the wolves, Cameron reluctantly concluded he wasn't living a dream or a nightmare. The taste of blood and fur was too real. The smell of dogs and wolves. The way he recognized their fear, anger, and jubilation in every action—the raised tails and the drooped ones, the ears forward, or back, or flattened, the narrowed eyes, or widened. Every action signaled a defensive, or aggressive, or excited posture. The way he understood their barks, growls, and yips. The feel of the cold breeze whipping across his face and the burning in his shoulder from the new wolf bite. The iron smell of blood—of his and the ones he'd killed. All were very real and too unreal to ponder more closely.

Still in shock over the whole changing-into-a-beast scenario—had to have been twice now—he couldn't figure out what the hell had happened to him. Except it probably had something to do with Charles's comments about magical wolves coming down from the aurora borealis. But he didn't want to think about his bizarre situation beyond that for now. All he knew was he had to locate Charles pronto, make sure he was safe, and find out more concerning the magical wolves.

He was a white Arctic wolf, just like the one that had bitten him, and the ones he'd killed.

But right now, more than anything, Cameron hoped the older man was all right and the dogs were, too.

Nikki ran with Cameron, then turned west. He followed her along with the other dogs and heard Charles's team barking in the distance again. The sound was in greeting, not warning of danger. Which gave him a small sense of relief.

Then it occurred to him that the other two wolves had taken off before he could kill them—the one howling their whereabouts. What if they circled back around to the camp and Faith? Hell, if only he could be in two places at once. He had to hurry, not wanting to leave Faith on her own for long.

When he neared the camp, his original husky team raced to greet him, but there was no sign of Charles, just his sled, tent, and the bed of straw he'd made for his dogs. Cameron loped toward the erected tent, the door flap blowing in the wind. He poked his head inside and saw Charles lying in his sleeping bag, deathly quiet. After walking inside, Cameron nuzzled Charles's face with his nose and pawed at his chest, but Charles didn't wake. Cameron concentrated on the man's breathing, his heartbeat. And he smelled blood. But Charles was alive, thank god. Although he needed help and Cameron couldn't give it to him—not like this.

Then a blood-curdling scream shrieked across the snowy woods from the direction of Cameron's campsite. The dogs began barking. His heart thundering, Cameron raced out of the tent. *Faith*. Kintail's other wolves. Or maybe Kintail and his men had arrived.

Hell, what next? He had to take care of Faith, and then Charles, but how could he take care of anyone while he was in the form of a magical wolf?

Cursing his situation, he tore off across the snow again, heading straight back to Faith. A couple of the dogs had followed him from the other team, and so did his own, making him truly feel like the alpha leader of the pack.

When he finally reached the campsite, Faith was gone. Or maybe she was hiding inside the tent. There was no sign of anyone else, and he realized then—there had been no sounds of snowmobiles approaching the area. Then the wolves had to have returned.

The dogs that had remained behind greeted him and their teammates. It wasn't until he got around them to head for the tent when he saw what probably had shaken Faith.

Kintail's men lay naked in the snow where Cameron had killed the two wolves. He stared in disbelief. That could have been him, if they'd gotten the best of him instead. Shaking loose of his surprise that they had the same affliction he had, Cameron rushed over to the sled, wishing he could turn back into his human form and dress and see to Faith. They had to get the team together and take care of Charles.

Cameron closed his eyes and concentrated. *I want to be human again*.

He opened his eyes. Nothing had changed. Hating not being in control, he growled low. He nudged at his clothes with his long wolf's snout, pawed at them, wanting to put his things back on, to be himself. But still, he didn't change.

Without another plan, he loped toward the tent, hoping Faith was all right inside. But when he pushed the flap aside, he found the tent empty. *Hell*. Trying not to panic, he attempted to smell where she'd run off to. Or *had* someone managed to take her?

He found no signs of any tracks other than wolf prints, and the impression in the snow made by her small boots. He raced after her, hating not being able to holler her name.

When he found her, if he found her, what then? She'd think he was the same kind of wolf that he'd killed, most likely. Some type of alien aberration.

The sound of footfalls followed him, and he whipped his head around to see all the dogs chasing after him. His breath frosty in the breeze, he paused and sniffed again. Straight ahead. He bolted in that direction, his tail straight out. The tracks indicated she'd stumbled and fallen several times, running at first, then slowing her pace as if the need for flight had dissipated.

When he finally saw her not very far from camp, she was sitting in a pile of snow, her white parka and clothes nearly blending in. She looked back, her eyes widening when she saw him with the teams. The dogs raced to greet her, and Cameron moved in close with them, hoping she wouldn't shoot him, or wouldn't attempt to with the other dogs surrounding him.

Tears sparkled in her eyes and streaks of tears trailed down her cheeks. But the dogs were so enthusiastically licking her and poking her to go with them, their actions stirred her from where she sat. He wanted so badly to take her into his arms and hold her tight. Damn what he'd become.

Warily, she watched Cameron, then patted some of the dogs and rose to her feet. She didn't pull the gun on him, *yet,* but she kept her eyes on him as she headed toward him in the direction of the camp. *Good.* Maybe he could nudge her into hitching up the team and joining Charles until Cameron could figure a way of changing back. *If* he could. Hopefully, he wouldn't have to die first. Damn, what if Kintail somehow changed people through these attack wolves and then once they changed, there was no turning back?

No, Cameron had done it before. Damn, then that meant that he really had seen Chris and his friends in the tent that one night. Oh hell, if they hadn't seen Bigfoot, had they seen someone like he was now?

When Faith neared him, she made a wider circle around him as the dogs escorted her back, some racing ahead, some running by her side. Cameron inched in closer and nudged her gloved hand with his nose in greeting. She looked like she was about to run.

Don't run, Faith. He'd take chase. He could already feel the urge rising in his blood. He didn't want to scare her, but the instinct was too great.

She was already walking as fast as she could, trying to get away from him. He stayed close. *Don't run, Faith.*

But as soon as she got near enough to camp, she dashed for the tent.

Had she left the gun in the tent?

Hell, maybe. His shoulder already hurt like the devil, and he didn't need her shooting him, too. Beyond that, he had to convince her to take care of Charles, who could be dying for all Cameron knew.

He bolted for her, the thrill of the chase coursing through his blood. The dogs barked with glee and Cameron lunged for her.

As soon as he pounced on her back, she screamed and fell face first in the snow. And then, lay very still, but he didn't move either. If he released her, she'd go for the weapon. She continued to remain motionless. From the sound of her too-rapid heartbeat, her heavy breathing, and her slight trembling, he knew she hadn't passed out, but rather was playing possum. He wanted to smile at her clever deception.

The playful urge to take her down gave way to something deeper, more primal and possessive. How could he want her now when he was a wolf? But the more he tried to deny his feelings, the greater his need to have and protect her surged through him.

The strange feeling that had consumed him, rushed through him again, the heat, his muscles and bones stretching, until he was butt naked and his backside was freezing as he pinned her down.

How the hell did he change back? And worse, how was he going to explain to her what had happened to him?

He cleared his throat. "Faith, I'm going to let you up, and we have to get the team hitched. Charles is not far from here, but he's been hurt and isn't responsive. We need to hurry and give him first aid."

"Cameron?" Her voice was muffled in her ski mask, kind of a squeak.

"It's me. Cameron." He spoke close to her ear, huddled against her for warmth. From the surprise in

her voice, he guessed she was thoroughly confused. Why wouldn't she be? He still couldn't get over the change himself.

Then a new thought occurred to him. What if she thought he had bolted out of nowhere and shoved her down, protecting her from the big bad wolf that was chasing her?

He groaned. Then what? Tell her, or keep it a secret a while longer if she hadn't put two and two together?

"I have to dress. Why don't you take down the tent while I do that, and then I'll get the dogs together?" Cameron let her up and raced over to the sled, trying not to think about how cold he was, hoping she didn't go after the gun and shoot him in the back. But if he didn't get dressed quickly, he was going to lose some body parts to the frigid air. Beyond that, his new wolf bite shot streaks of throbbing pain from his shoulder straight to his brain, and he was having trouble concentrating on much else.

When he'd donned everything but his parka, he looked back to see her staring at him, her eyes dark and wide. He hoped she'd realized what had happened so he wasn't left with trying to explain, or keeping his strange condition secret. Deep inside, he knew he shouldn't tell her what had become of him, that it would be safer for him, and for her. "Hurry, Faith. We've got to help Charles."

Her expression changed slightly, from still in shock to all business. She whipped around and went into the tent. He hesitated to do anything, his first thought she was going for the gun. But then she came out holding his rolled sleeping bag up and headed for the sled. "Hurry, Cameron. You have some explaining to do."

Well, that decided that. He closed the distance between them and pulled her into his arms to give her a comforting hug.

At first, she was stiff, but then she melted, wrapped her arms around him, embracing him as if she had found her long-lost love and never wanted to let him go. Still concerned that she might be in shock, he leaned down and kissed her forehead, then ran his gloved hand across her cheek. "Let's get you settled in the sled bag. I'll take care of everything else."

"I'll pack the tent." Her gaze fixed on his, making her seem determined to get through this on her own.

He leaned down and kissed her cold lips and hugged her with a bear of an embrace. He still worried she might be in shock, but when he tried to steer her toward the sled, she shook loose. "I'm... I'm all right." But he could tell by the hesitancy in her words, she was putting on a front.

He let her go, but while he rushed to get the dogs' booties on, and harnessed the team, then hitched them to the sled, he watched Faith dismantling the stove pipe from the stove, then working on the tent, to ensure she truly was all right. She seemed to be, and afterward, he packed the stove and tent on the sled. But then he caught Faith's gaze focused on the dead men lying in the snow.

"I'm sorry, Faith."

"You're injured," she said, changing the subject, her voice more sure now, and he was glad to hear it. "We have a first aid kit and I'll take care of you after we see to Charles."

"It's a deal." The burning in his shoulder from the fresh wolf bite hurt like hell now and every move added a twinge of excruciating pain through the muscles.

He wondered if Faith was in denial though—if she truly didn't believe he was the wolf, or if she did and just couldn't acknowledge it. He sure had refused to believe it. Well, still did to an extent. Now that he was back to his normal self, he couldn't imagine being able to shapeshift again. At least the urge to run as a wolf was gone for the time being.

Glancing at the dead men, Cameron took a deep breath. "I'll clean up the camp a bit. Be right back."

He grabbed the shovel she'd dropped in the snow and buried the two men. It was as proper a burial as he could give them, but he figured Kintail and his men would come for them eventually. For a moment, he stared at the mounds, wishing it hadn't come to this. Figuring he'd killed a couple of wolves, wolf to wolf, he never imagined...

The wolf part of him felt no remorse. He had to protect Faith and the huskies. That was a given. The human side of him...

Then he remembered Faith's terrified expression. The wolf would have killed her. The man-wolf. It didn't matter what form they had taken. Cameron wouldn't have let any of them harm her.

Letting out his breath, he hurried back to the sled. He slipped the shovel on the sled and climbed onto the runners. Even if she couldn't see that he was one of them, she knew the others were. No words could express what had happened to make it any less unreal.

In pain and worried about Charles's condition, Cameron shouted, "Hike!"

The dogs took off and they raced past the grave mounds.

"Haw!" he shouted, steering them left, toward Charles's camp.

He hoped Faith could deal with all that had happened, and that she wasn't too traumatized. She needed to manage the other team, if they were going to get both sleds home. He prayed Charles would be all right when they got him to Millinocket. *And* Cameron hoped that he didn't have a sudden urge to turn into a wolf again *ever*.

He made kissing sounds at the team, encouraging them to run faster.

When they reached Charles's camp, Cameron hollered, "Whoa," and the dogs came to a halt.

"What's wrong with Charles?" Faith climbed out of the sled bag and seemed much steadier now.

"Not sure. I couldn't rouse him." Cameron grabbed the first aid kit and hurried into the tent.

Charles was sitting up, his eyes glazed.

"Hell, you're alive." Thank God for small miracles. Cameron knelt beside him and took his wrist to feel for the strength of his pulse, although he concentrated more on listening to Charles's heartbeat, but he couldn't let Faith know that. Strong steady pulse, not raspy like he'd feared.

Charles's gaze shifted to Cameron. "What… what happened?"

Cameron glanced at the sleeping bag and saw blood where Charles's head had been.

"You tell me. You took off and left us to fend for ourselves." Cameron examined the back of Charles's head as Faith knelt beside Charles and held his hand.

"Ambush," Charles said and started to lie down.

Cameron stopped him. "Wait, let me see where you're injured." Then he found the bloody swelling centered on the very back of his head. "Who struck you?"

Charles moaned and closed his eyes.

"Kintail? One of his men?"

Charles didn't respond, but with the way he was struck from behind, he might not have even seen who hit him. Cameron pulled bandaging out of the first aid kit and wrapped it around Charles's head, trying not to hurt him any more than he was already. But Charles winced and groaned.

"What's wrong with him?"

"Someone struck him from behind." Cameron eased Charles down on the sleeping bag and covered him with the blankets.

Faith rubbed her arms. "He wasn't bitten, was he?"

"No, he wasn't bitten. Here, you can feel the knot on the back of his head. Probably got a concussion. He's pretty out of it."

"Kintail's men?" she whispered.

"Good bet."

"So what do we do now? Find our way by ourselves? Wait until he's better?"

"We'll be right back, Charles." Cameron took Faith's arm and led her from the tent to the sled. "We can't go the way we came or we'd have to run by Kintail's lodge. We'll have to find our way to the main road that had been blocked. Since he's in bad shape, we'll stay here, let the dogs rest, then head for the cabins. I'll set up our tent and—"

"I'll stay with Charles. To make sure he's okay during the night."

Again he wondered if she had a clue about the wolf and him being one and the same, about his being naked in the snow. And why she hadn't asked him anything more about it. "All right. Go to him then. Let me know if he gets any worse." He headed for the dogs.

"I'll help you with the huskies."

He thought she'd ask him what had happened at their camp. Instead, she talked lovingly to the dogs and helped get them settled. Then, much to his surprise, she assisted him in setting up the tent. When they were done, they shared an awkward moment of silence. He wanted to kiss her and give her a hug, to reassure her that they'd all be fine. But before he could take her in his arms, she said good night, whipped around, and quickly escaped to Charles's tent.

He couldn't reproach her, although he couldn't stifle his desire for her, no matter how much he tried. Normally, if a woman wasn't interested in him, he wouldn't have followed up. Although no woman had ever acted afraid of him. Except for the case where he'd questioned a woman who had everything to hide—including a dead husband and stolen money from work—but he didn't think he would have anything to do with a woman who feared him. So what the hell was making him want Faith even more?

The need to prove he was the same person as before? The same man that she'd found as desirable as he found her? But he wasn't the same, either. He was some kind of aberration. And he still wanted her. Craved her as if she was his lifeline to reality.

Inside the tent, she asked Charles, "Are you going to be all right?"

Cameron hesitated to hear an answer. Charles didn't respond, much to Cameron's disappointment, then he ducked into his own tent.

His shoulder was throbbing with a deep ache and after settling into his sleeping bag, he tossed and turned, reliving the night's events. He thought about Kintail and his wolves and how they were not at all what they seemed. Which meant?

Hell, Kintail was probably one, too. And David and Owen?

Cameron raked his hands through his hair.

If they'd seen Kintail's people shapeshift, had he had them killed? Or were they now what he was?

Chapter 12

UNABLE TO SLEEP AFTER ALL SHE'D WITNESSED, FAITH rolled over and felt Charles's pulse again. Normal. His breathing was steady. She sighed and hoped in another couple of hours, he'd be feeling well enough to make the journey. And that she could drive a team without any problem.

She bumped against something plastic, wondered what it was, then realized it was the first aid kit. *Damn*. She'd meant to tend to Cameron's wound.

She couldn't get the look of hurt in Cameron's expression out of her mind—although he'd quickly hid it when she'd chosen to stay with Charles instead of him—but she had to watch over Charles. Beyond that, yeah, she couldn't have stayed with Cameron. She just couldn't have—not in light of what had happened. She didn't want to think about why he was naked either, or how he could have survived in the cold that way for long. Only one conclusion she could come up with, and that was too bizarre to contemplate. But the wolf had been chasing her and then all of a sudden she was pinned beneath Cameron's naked body? He hadn't shouted to her he was coming to save her, nothing. Just one pounce and she was facedown in the snow, and then he was on top of her, heating her backside.

Not only that, but their savior wolf had miraculously vanished. If he hadn't, she still would have wondered what Cameron was doing freezing his naked ass off in the Maine wilderness. And how had he been injured? Wolf bite for sure. But when and where? He sure hadn't freely offered any explanations either and that didn't bode well.

But even so, she'd meant to treat his injury.

Grabbing the first aid kit, she crawled out of the sleeping bag and tent. Several of the dogs lifted their heads and watched her. She shushed them before they ran to greet her.

She peeked inside Cameron's dark tent, but she couldn't see anything. She hesitated. Maybe this was a stupid idea if he was sleeping soundly, and she should just skip it. But his bite wound had looked nasty, she'd promised, and besides, it might soothe his pride that she hadn't stayed with him.

She crawled into the tent, opened up the first aid kit, and pulled out the ointment and bandages. Then she reached for Cameron's arm, to shake him slightly and wake him so she could ask him to turn on his lantern, and she'd doctor him.

Bad plan. Her fingers felt fur and lean, mean wolf instead. As soon as she touched him, she about had a heart attack. He growled, whipped his head around, and bit her.

She screamed and fluorescent amber eyes peered at her in the dark, then the shine in them faded. Her heartbeat pounding, she jumped back, favoring her throbbing hand, and ran into one of the tent poles. The pole toppled and the tent collapsed.

Feeling suffocated, Faith scrambled away from the center of the tent, trying to extricate herself from the tomb of polypropylene fabric. Her hand touched fur again and she jerked back, afraid he'd bite her once more. She thrust her hands out madly in another direction. The canvas elevated near her. He'd slipped in front of her, like a dangerous predator, unwilling to let her escape.

A tongue licked her injured hand, and she gasped. *The taste before another bite?*

Again, she crawled toward what she hoped was the tent opening, but all she found was more tent, and then Cameron's soft bedding. Her heartbeat thundered in her ears as she scrambled over his blankets and sleeping bag and tried to locate a way out.

And then she touched bare skin—Cameron's thigh?

Before she could jerk away, a large hand grabbed her wrist and held on tight. "Stay."

God, Cameron. Barely breathing, she didn't move.

"I'm sorry, Faith. I didn't mean to bite you." He sounded remorseful, but worried, too.

Her hand was stinging so badly, she was sure he'd broken the skin. Her heart pounded like a sledgehammer while she tried to come to grips with the truth. *He* was the wolf. It made the only sense and yet no sense at all.

But he was the wolf—he admitted biting her, had been chasing her earlier, had saved the dogs and her from the other wolves—which was the only reasonable explanation that fit. The dead men—the ones who had been wolves before Cameron had killed them—they were like him. He was one of them.

She groaned and collapsed onto the bedding. Could Cameron's bite have transferred whatever he was to her, and she'd be like him now?

"What were you doing in here?" He pressed her hand against his face and breathed deeply.

She swallowed hard, trying to calm her racing heart, to drum up the courage to speak. What *was* she doing in here? Oh, yeah, his wound.

"I was going to put some salve on your injury."

"Do you still want to?"

What a disaster. She closed her eyes to still the pounding in her head. "We need to erect the tent first. But I can't see anything."

As if he was afraid she'd escape, he didn't release her, but moved away slightly and turned on a lantern. But she wasn't exactly afraid of him. Not after what he'd done for her and for the dogs. He'd risked his life to protect them.

That's when she saw every muscled naked bit of him as he elevated the tent with his free hand, then released her and pushed the lightweight fabric upward with the other, like Atlas only the world wasn't on his back.

She'd gotten an eyeful when he went to dress in the snow, but that was only his remarkable backside, toned from his back to his butt and legs. But now, she got to see all the goods again from his corded chest all the way down to his well-toned thighs. Despite the cold, he was totally aroused. Her gaze shifted to his face and he raised his brows, waiting for a response.

She cleared her throat, glanced back at his glorious erection and said, "I'll get the tent pole."

He smiled a little, and pointed with his head toward the bedding between his legs. And sure enough, there was the pole sitting between his feet.

"Oh."

His wolfish grin made the heat rush through every nerve ending.

She hurried to set the other tent pole, knowing his injured shoulder had to hurt something awful, and he had to be freezing.

He released the tent with a groan, sat down on the bedding, and pulled his wool blanket over his lap.

She examined the bite as he watched her. "It doesn't look half as bad as the other bite did."

He didn't say anything, but reached up to touch her cheek. His gentle caress felt like a prelude to something much deeper.

This was *so* not good. She knew he wanted her and she knew it wasn't right, not when he was whatever he was. "I'll just cover the wound with this salve."

When she smeared the smelly stuff on, he hissed, and she looked up at him. He gave her a half smile. "Stings."

"I'm sorry. Hopefully, it'll kill any germs." She instinctively clasped her hand on his forehead, but his skin was normal and not feverish, thank god, and she hoped it stayed that way. She pulled the bandaging from the first aid kit and began wrapping it around the injury, trying to be gentle, although his muscle was rigid as she worked, and she feared she was hurting him.

"Hasn't anyone ever told you not to touch an injured animal?" He relaxed a little and leaned his head closer to hers, his face touching her hair with an amative hint of a nudge.

"You're not a wolf now." She couldn't help that her voice was tinged with annoyance. What did he think? She was stupid? Of course she knew to be careful around an injured wild animal. Even a pet that had been hurt could react viciously to helping hands. "*Furthermore*, how could I have known you were a wolf when I came in to take care of you? Besides, it's too late for the warning."

"Do you often go into dark places without regard to your safety? What if I'd thought you were one of Kintail's men?" he scolded.

"I smell too nice. Besides, I've got the gun and pepper spray."

His brows rose in a roguish way. He tenderly touched her cheek with the back of his hand. "You'd actually use those on me? But I know martial arts and could have you just where I wanted you in a matter of seconds."

The vision of him flipping her onto her back with an expert martial arts move, the can of pepper spray tossed one way, the gun the other, and the aroused hunk landing squarely between her legs, pinning her to his soft bedding flitted across her brain. Just the images that brought to mind started an ache between her legs. She grabbed his wrist, stopping him before things got out of hand. Before she changed her mind and let him get out of hand, rather.

When they'd made love before, it was one thing. She didn't know what he had become. Now, she did. But then she frowned at him. Had he already known?

His eyes were clouded with desire, his voice coated in lust. He definitely had sex on the brain. Not that she wasn't having a tough time keeping her own mind on business. Trying to take care of his injuries, she had every intention of returning to Charles's tent before she got herself into more trouble.

"Stay with me. For a little while?" He took her face in his hands, his brain definitely now residing in the lower part of his anatomy.

She closed her eyes and breathed in the cold air, the slight cologne Cameron wore, and opened her eyes. "Do I have a choice?"

"About what's to be? I doubt it. About staying with me? It'll always be your choice."

Before, she was afraid to become too attached to the hunk, and then they'd go their separate ways. But now… now how could she knowingly make love to someone who was part wolf, part man? On the other hand, what if she was half and half now, too? She didn't feel any differently except her hand throbbed with a vengeance. She didn't feel like she was having any symptoms of cabin fever like he'd had which she was now thinking had all to do with what he was. But then again, he had experienced those symptoms several hours after the first wolf had bitten him.

"Do… do you have any control over it?"

"When I'm around you, I want to be human and it seems to work."

"Seems to? You don't know for sure?"

"I've only changed three times, and every time when we were close to each other, I changed back."

Close. She didn't think it had to do with him being close to her as much as he was lusting after her—at least the times as far as she could tell, first when he pinned her to the snow. The second time after he bit her, she thought it was more because he felt badly and the emotions swamping him precipitated the change. Unless it had to do with her being on his bedding, and he wanted her again. "Three times? When was the other?"

"Middle of the night. I thought I was dreaming. Oh hell, Faith, I overheard Chris and his friends talking in a tent. They might have been discussing you."

"What about? Why didn't you say before?"

"I thought it was a dream." He sighed. "They were talking about a man doing research and how Chris believed his daughter would join them."

"Join them? In what?"

"Finding the magical wolves? They were looking for Bigfoot when your father went with them. But he must have gotten separated from them when he saw what he did. Then he was shaken up, and no wonder, and returned home to write his paper."

"So what if Kintail learned of it and sent someone to spy on him? Hilson." She let out her breath in exasperation. "Do you think he could be one of Kintail's people?"

"Maybe."

Well that decided that. So he did want the research and not her.

She looked up at Cameron. "I need to return to Charles. To watch over him."

"Lie down with me, Faith, for just a little while."

He half pleaded and half commanded. The commanding made her think of Hilson. Always in charge. Always bossing her around. But the pleading, *that*... was another matter entirely.

She came to her senses and shook her head. "You'd better get something on before you freeze." Hating to reject him further, she decided she had to leave because she was certain she'd hate herself more if she stayed.

Besides, Charles needed her, as badly injured as he was. She'd never forgive herself if he got worse, and she wasn't there to monitor him closely. And they required some answers from him also, soon.

But before she exited the tent, Cameron groaned, and she glanced back at him. He'd slipped into the sleeping bag, his face white with pain. And then she was really torn. Stay with Cameron for a little while, just until he fell asleep?

Or return to Charles pronto and save herself?

Chapter 13

FAITH'S WISHFUL EXPRESSION MADE CAMERON THINK SHE was trying to decide whether to stay with him longer or not. But her soft green eyes shifted to the opening of the tent, and he knew he was losing her.

He reached out and touched her uninjured hand, wanting desperately to pull her into his embrace, to hold her tight, to make everything that had happened in the last several hours fade away, but he couldn't force her. Her jaw clenched.

"Faith." He meant to say her name softly, but it came out as lust-drenched pleading to his ears.

"Just for a little while. But I've got to go to Charles before long." Her gaze flickered to Cameron's and she looked down at the bedding.

Then she crawled into the sleeping bag with him, and laid her head on his chest, her arm over his waist, and even one leg propped over his. For an hour, she rested with Cameron, his hand stroking her hair as he held her tight. But she seemed tense. He could tell from her breathing she wasn't sleeping, her body stiff, but she laid against him just the same, her body heating his. This had to be enough for now, and he was grateful for any concession on her part, but then she pulled away so tentatively, he was certain he could still keep her close, if he just pushed a little harder, even though he didn't want her that way.

She had to accept him for what he was even if it killed him to see her go. He was certain her reluctance didn't mean she hadn't wanted to be with him. Maybe that she was truly worried about Charles. Or maybe that she was unsure of being with Cameron. That bothered him as much as her not staying with him for a little while longer.

She rubbed her injured hand again, then slipped out of the tent, leaving him to face the bitter cold. With her there, the tent had seemed so much warmer, full of her light. He ground his teeth and sank against the bedding.

The damn pain from his injury wouldn't subside, and he wanted her. And every inch of him was freezing. He growled and jerked his sleeping bag aside, then yanked his clothes on, feeling like he was sitting in his freezer. He couldn't understand why he desired Faith so badly. Not that he hadn't been interested in her from the beginning, and he admired her tenacity and resolve despite all that they'd been through. But everything about her triggered a deeper interest, a need to possess, to make her his, when he didn't think he'd ever feel that way about a woman.

He doubted her resolve to tend to his injured shoulder had everything to do with it. His hang-dog expression had upset her, and she'd been feeling badly about abandoning him. Come to think of it, no one had ever nurtured him so far as he could recall, which endeared her to him even more.

Then he had to change into the blasted wolf again, and worse, bite her. He'd tasted her blood, knew he'd broken the skin. He prayed he hadn't infected her with the magical wolf's virus, or whatever the hell it was.

Damn the change and his lack of control over it. He jerked the sleeping bag to his chin, and slammed his eyes shut, but sleep wouldn't come. Not with the way his mind kept working over all that had occurred since he'd first met her. All he wanted was the siren curled beside him, her head resting on his chest, his arms wrapped around her bundled body, listening to her steady heartbeat, breathing in the fragrance that was all Faith—a hint of something floral, and definitely something sexual. More than anything, he desired her acceptance. And now what? Had he changed her also? Annoyed with himself for his lack of restraint, he curled his fingers into fists.

Unable to sleep, Cameron wanted in the worst way to look for David and Owen and search the area to ensure none of Kintail's wolves lurked nearby. Or Kintail and his men either. Which now he wondered if they were all one and the same.

But he needed to rest, too.

He rolled onto his side, then his stomach, the pain in his shoulder giving him fits. He tossed onto his back and stared at the tent ceiling. "Hell," he growled.

He stripped off his clothes and willed himself to shift.

It didn't happen right away. He thought of claws and teeth, of fur and a long menacing snout, of ears sitting atop his head that twitched back and forth, listening to sounds. And then he felt the heat circulating through every blood vessel.

This time when his fur coat covered his bare skin, and he was standing on the bedding as a wolf, a new sensation filled him with an uncontrollable need. The urge to howl.

—///—

Faith woke with a start, unsure what made her stir. She hadn't thought she'd ever fall asleep, as upset as she was about Cameron biting her. Well more than that, that he was whatever he was and Kintail's wolf had turned him that way.

She thought back to when she was in the camp alone—most of the dogs had run off with the wolf that had killed the others. Fearing the dead wolves' blood would attract a predator, she'd meant to bury the wolves. But when she'd found the two naked dead men in the wolves' places, she'd nearly had a stroke. It didn't dawn on her that Cameron was the wolf that had killed them either, just that he'd vanished. Even when he'd pounced on her, then began talking to her in his human form again, trying to reassure her, her brain had a hard time assimilating the information. He was human, a bit of a rogue, dangerous even, if someone threatened his safety, but a man who could turn into a wolf?

She ran her hands through her tangled hair. Even now, it seemed more like a dream, well, nightmare, especially once he'd bitten her. Although the bite wasn't hurting any longer. Hopefully, it was only that—a small bite that wouldn't amount to anything.

Charles mumbled something. That's what had woken her. She sat up and touched his cheek. "Charles? Can you hear me?"

He didn't respond.

His temperature appeared normal, his breathing also.

Glad he wasn't in distress, she sighed. But they still needed to get him to a doctor.

Not wanting to leave her warm sleeping bag, Faith finally crawled out, the call of nature too great. The worst part of winter camping in the middle of nowhere, besides the constant cold, was that there were no outhouses. She slipped out of the tent, glanced at Cameron's tent and the dogs, but Cameron must still be sleeping. The dogs lifted their heads. She shushed them, then walked away from camp. She headed deeper into the woods, but not too far, perfect for privacy in case Cameron exited his tent. Although she was surprised he wasn't up already, tending to the dogs. But then again, she was the morning person, and he seemed to be more of a night owl.

Then she worried about his new wound. Hell, what if the bite had made him terribly ill? No way could she manage taking two injured men back to Millinocket, maneuvering two sleds and all the dogs. Planning to check on Cameron as soon as she took care of business, Faith found the perfect spot, a huge spruce shielding her from the campsite. She was about to get on with business when something moved in the woods off to her left. She jerked her head that way. A big white wolf with light brown eyes stood watching her. Don't run, she warned herself, the image of Cameron flattening her against the snow in his wolf form flitting across her brain. Yet the instinctive urge was there—to flee the danger.

On the other hand, maybe it was just Cameron in a magnificent ice white coat, same tall stature, longer legs and healthy body, unlike the scrawnier wolves he'd fought. She folded her arms and faced him down. He paused some distance from her, panting, his ears twisting back and forth, probably listening to sounds only he could hear, his tail slightly wagging, and his mouth almost smiling.

But then the sound of one of the dogs running up behind her caught her attention. She turned slightly to see another white wolf. Her heart nearly seized. The two wolves were matched in size and looked very similar.

If the one coming from camp was Cameron—must be because the dogs didn't react—then—

She glanced at the other.

He'd vanished. Her heart racing, she stared at the trees, the snow piled up against them. Anyone of them could be hiding the white wolf.

The wolf behind her nudged her hand, and she swallowed a scream. "Cameron?"

He bowed his head.

"Jeez, I thought the other was you." She rubbed her arms, her whole body trembling. "I need some privacy."

Instead of returning to camp, he took off to check out the woods in front of her, and then she wished she hadn't wanted him to leave, fearing he'd find the other wolf and tangle with it.

After taking care of business in a hurry, she waited for Cameron to return. But when he didn't, she hurried back into camp. Once she'd retrieved the gun and pepper spray—which she scolded herself for not carrying with her all along—she rushed back to the woods.

Silence greeted her. Not even a whisper of a breeze. Her heartbeat now pounded in her eardrums, the can of pepper spray in her gloved hand as she took a few steps in the direction Cameron had taken.

What if she found a wolf? What if it was the wrong one? She pushed forward, her boots sinking knee deep in the soft snowdrifts. If she had to run, she'd be in a world of hurt. But she wouldn't abandon Cameron either.

Growling pierced the frigid air and she stood stock still. And then another sound, snowmobiles? The engines' roar in the distance... headed their way?

Rescue? Her heart lifted. Or Kintail's men? Her hopes took a dive. She stared at the spruces, figured she'd better get back to protect Charles and the dogs, and prayed Cameron would be all right.

With no sign of the snowmobiles yet, although they were headed this way, she raced to feed the dogs, who pranced and danced around her, eager for breakfast.

Hurry back, Cameron. Now, she silently pleaded.

After putting food out for the dogs, she returned to Cameron's tent to get the first aid kit and change Charles's bandage before the snowmobiles arrived, three of them, she thought. They continued to roar toward them and as they drew closer, the dogs let out a chorus of wild barking.

Listening to the noisy snowmobiles, she loved how much quieter and in tune with nature dog sledding was. Then as she saw the three machines in the distance, she felt the heavy metal gun in her pocket and held onto the can of pepper spray.

The three men drove into camp, wearing ski masks and snow goggles, their fur-trimmed hoods hiding their faces so she couldn't see their expressions. Then Cameron, or at least she hoped it was, loped back into camp as a wolf. He eyed the newcomers, sniffed the air, moved in closer to her in a protective mode, bumping her leg, nuzzling her. She was glad to have him on her side.

"Where's Charles?" one of the men asked, climbing off the snowmobile. He glanced at the wolf, but he didn't seem surprised.

He knew Charles? Had to be a friend the way he sounded worried. Which would have eased her concern but the fact he didn't act shocked to see a wild wolf in camp meant he knew Kintail and his wolves. But then again, it seemed everyone knew of Kintail and his wolves.

"He's been injured. How do you know him?"

"I'm his cousin. He didn't tell us he had paying customers for an overnight sled ride, and he's late arriving home. His sister is worried sick about him. How was he injured?"

A cousin. Relieved, Faith motioned to the tent. "It's a long story. We became separated from him and when we found him, he'd been hurt. He was struck in the head and appears to have a concussion."

"Separated?" The man frowned at her, then stormed inside the tent and spoke in French, but she couldn't understand what he said.

At once, she felt as though they thought Cameron and she were party to a crime.

The other two men dismounted and began taking care of the dogs, putting on their booties, packing up the sleds. The dogs' barking was nearly deafening.

His brow deeply furrowed, Charles's cousin exited the tent. "I'm Michael Roux. Charles is conscious and said you need to return to the cabins, pack your bags, and leave for Millinocket at once. You and my brother, George, can take the snowmobiles in. The rest of us will follow with the sleds when we've finished packing."

Cameron loped past them into his tent and after a few minutes, reemerged in his human form, dressed for the weather. Faith closed her gaping mouth. *Guess he had the wolf change business under control.*

Michael and the others took notice, but didn't say a word. They knew. She wondered how many other local area residents knew about Kintail and his wolves. Or were Charles and his cousins also some of the same kind of creatures?

Cameron hauled out his sleeping bag, and Faith's and his bags, avoiding looking at anyone, appearing uncomfortable as hell. Faith hurried to help him.

"You must be with Kintail," Michael said to Cameron as he worked on the dogs' harnesses.

Faith felt her blood pressure rise.

Cameron sliced him a glare. "Not in this lifetime."

Michael and the other two men stopped harnessing the dogs, and he glanced back at Charles's tent and swore under his breath, "Damn, Charles." He considered Cameron's torn parka sleeve. "When did it happen?"

"A couple of days ago."

Michael considered Faith. "Were you bitten also?"

"Not by one of Kintail's wolves." Faith avoided eye contact with Cameron.

Cameron threw their bags on one of the snowmobiles. "Yeah, she was... *by mistake*."

Michael shook his head. "Best if the two of you leave the region pronto, if you know what's good for you."

Cameron gave him a caustic look. "I'm still looking for two of my friends."

"We admire you and your kind." Michael bowed his head slightly in reverence. "Kintail and his people have been here for centuries—magical creatures, powerful and at one with nature. They have always lived in peace with our people, the tales passed on from generation to generation, while we have honored their ways. Which means we don't interfere in their… your business. What goes on with Kintail's pack, territorial disputes, internal encroachments or external ones, will be decided by you and your kind."

Faith closed her gaping mouth. Kintail *was* one of them. For centuries this had been going on? It had to have been what her father's research was all about!

What about what the men in the hot tub had said? They hadn't found Bigfoot, but something else? The man killed in Kintail's office… with silver. Hell, he was a… werewolf?

The fairy tales were true? But then again, silver in high amounts could kill anyone.

"We appreciate your helping us out, and we'll take it from here." Cameron took the gun from Faith and shoved it in his pocket.

The notion they were out on a twig of a limb without a safety net crossed Faith's mind. This was so not good. Wanting to thank Charles and say good-bye, she stalked into his tent, but his eyes were shut and when she crouched next to him and spoke, he didn't respond.

"Thank you, Charles, for everything." She kissed his cheek and pulled the blanket higher. "We appreciate everything you did for us, and if I can ever pay you back… just contact me." She hoped he was really awake, or enough so that he could hear her. But she intended to check on him after they returned to Millinocket later.

When she reemerged from the tent, she asked Michael, "Will Charles be all right?"

"That hard head of his has taken a lot of knocks. Yeah, he'll be fine, but he shouldn't have gotten into Kintail's business. He knows better."

"I can't understand how you can treat Kintail as if he should get away with this," she said, waving toward Charles's tent, "as if you don't care." Faith's voice was much higher pitched than she meant it to be, but she couldn't believe Charles's family would allow such brutality to one of their own. Maybe they didn't care about Cameron's friends, but Charles was their cousin! "You act as though Kintail's a god!"

"I'm certain you'll come to understand Kintail's ways before long. All I can say is that we were not put here to judge him or his kind." Michael turned to George. "Get them to the resort and make sure they leave for the trailhead after that. We'll be headed that way shortly. And don't talk to anyone. We don't want any more trouble."

George barely let Faith and Cameron mount their snowmobiles before he took off. He drove so fast she wondered if it was because he didn't want Kintail or his people to catch him aiding them, he hoped to lose them, or he just wanted to get back as quickly as possible to help Charles.

She glanced at Cameron driving behind her. Was he getting the wolf change more under control? She hoped so or he'd have to live like a mountain man. Find a job where he could work out of his home. No dealing with people on a regular basis. Only private eye investigations under the cover of dark.

Then she worried about her own situation. What if *she* began to change? There went her job, too.

She didn't feel any urge in that regard, though. Thankfully. Through her balaclava, she smelled the air, crisp, clean, and cold. Nothing unusual about it. Maybe the only time someone like Cameron had the wolf sense was when he was a wolf. That would be understandable. At least as much as turning into a wolf could be believable.

But the whole time back, she worried about what they would report to the police. That a wolf attacked Cameron, changed him into something mythical? And maybe she was in the same boat, too? That he'd killed two wolves defending her who happened to be men also? That Kintail or one of his men had nearly killed Charles?

Officers Whitson and Adams would believe every bit of it. *Right.*

In half the time it took to travel with the dogs, they arrived on the snowmobiles back at the cabins. As soon as they dismounted at the lodge, Faith hoped to understand more of what they were up against. She asked George before he could run off, "What do you know about Kintail's wolves?"

He cast a disgruntled look her way. "You're not one of the Cree and you're not an accepted member of Kintail's pack. If I were you, I'd do what my brother suggested. Get out of here before Kintail or his people make you vanish for good."

"But Cameron *is* one of them," Faith insisted.

George shook his head and took the keys to the snowmobiles from them. "Kintail hasn't made him part of his pack and none of his people will welcome him here while the leader wants him dead. My own people won't willingly take sides with an outsider who's one of Kintail's kind but on his terminal list. So Cameron will have to leave and…" He lifted a shoulder. "… maybe start his own pack. Since Cameron bit you…," George said, his lips lifting slightly, "for all practical purposes he's already claimed a mate."

Faith's mouth gaped, and she quickly looked at Cameron.

He cleared his throat and took her hand. "We don't know that you've been infected."

George looked like he didn't believe she'd escaped Cameron's fate. "Kintail's pack rules this territory. The best thing for the two of you to do is return to your own region. Although blending in someplace else might be hard to do when the shift occurs. No Arctic wolves in the States, except for Alaska. Unless you manage to win the populace over like Kintail and his people have here, pretending that the wolves are pets."

George's expression darkened. "The problem if you go to Alaska is it's the only place in the United States that animals can be shot from an aircraft through some loophole in the law. So, hunters will either kill from the air, or run the wolves or other hunted animals down until they're too exhausted to escape, land the aircraft, and shoot their prey. A magical wolf would then be just as much at risk of being hunted down while in its wolf form. Many hunters oppose aerial hunting because it violates the ethics of fair chase, but the ones who don't…" His jaw taut, George shook his head.

"You can leave the keys to the cabins on the kitchen counters." Then George went inside the lodge and shut the door.

"You might be all right, Faith," Cameron reiterated. "You might not have contracted my… condition."

But she wasn't just concerned about herself. "What will you do? And what about your friends?"

Cameron took Faith's uninjured hand, walked her past the shower facility, and headed for the path through the woods to her cabin. "I can't leave until I find them. It appears you don't need to stay here any longer though. Seems your father might have seen something of what I've become while he was doing his research. And I doubt that even if the flash drive still exists, Kintail will want your father sharing the information with the world. In fact, it's too dangerous for you here. Until I can get you on a plane out of here, you'll stay with me, but then you need to return home."

She frowned at him. "I agree that my dad probably found out about Kintail and his people and that's what he wrote about. Maybe someone was following him like he thought because of what he'd known." Faith pulled Cameron to a stop. "What if Hilson is dead? If he tried to blackmail Kintail with the information, he or his people most likely would have killed him. Maybe that's why he's no longer at the cabin. Or maybe he's one of them." She took a deep breath. "But even so, I can't go, not now."

"Listen, I've got to find my friends and free them from Kintail's clutches if they're still alive. *Somehow*. It's not going to be a walk in the park. But I can't be watching your back also. It's too dangerous."

She "humpfed" and headed off to the cabin. "For your information, Cameron MacPherson, I may already have your, uhm, problem, condition, whatever. So I'm not about to get on an airplane and fly home before I know for sure. What if I changed in the middle of the flight? No pets allowed, and certainly no feral wolves.

"I could see myself having an *episode* and having to hightail it to the bathroom. Then the seat belt lights go on, and I'm stuck in the privy as a wolf. The stewardess is pounding on the door, trying to get a stubborn passenger to retake her seat. And I can't say a word. The stewardess uses a key on the door, afraid there's something terribly wrong. And there is. I've got big sharp teeth, an extraordinary sense of smell, and better vision—all the better to see, smell, and eat her with. So I'm staying here until I know the whole story."

He didn't say anything for quite a while, his hand still tight around her arm as he held her close, helping to keep her warm from the bitter breeze. Then he cleared his throat. "Okay, but you continue to stay with me for the time being. And," he turned to look at her and added, "if you don't show any signs of what I have, you go home, pronto."

She glowered at him. "It would be my pleasure." Although she didn't mean it in the least. Had to be a case of immediate rebound. Hell, she was ready to settle down with a wolf-man?

"What if this *condition* affects people differently? What if I take longer to change?"

Cameron let out his breath in a frosty huff and hurried her faster toward her cabin, but didn't reply. Then he mumbled, "I shouldn't have gone with you and Charles. I put you at risk."

Surprised, she glanced up at him. He was feeling this was all his fault? "Right, you protected me from the big bad wolf behind the shower room."

When he raised his brows at her in disbelief, she frowned. "He was coming for me. You got in his way. So you just delayed the inevitable. He still got me, only through you." She gave a half smile. "Besides, I've been in worse predicaments."

He opened his mouth and she figured he planned to contradict her.

She shook her head. "Okay, maybe not anything worse than this. Although I did have a mad killer after me once."

He snorted.

"I did. In my line of work, sometimes the crazies go after the forensic scientists. He didn't want me to learn how he'd murdered three of his victims."

A look of admiration crossed Cameron's face for a second, then he was back to being annoyed. "Okay, so that was one mad killer. This is a pack of them. And I'm serious about sending you home." Cameron took Faith's hand and continued walking her down the path to Black Bear Den cabin. But as soon as he stepped on the deck, he paused to smell the air, and frowned.

She smelled something, too. A hint of spice, and something else.

Cameron pulled the door open.

Leidolf Wildhaven, his brows lifted, stood in the middle of the cabin amongst Faith's colorful bras and panties, which were strewn about the floor.

Chapter 14

"WHO THE HELL TOLD MY MEN TO GO AFTER CAMERON and the woman at their campsite?" Kintail asked Lila, suspecting she had everything to do with it as he glowered at her, and then he switched his deadly look to the rest of his pack.

Twelve males and six females stood around his great room, their expressions wary, looking rebuked. The only two who didn't seem that way were David and Owen. But then they wouldn't have had anything to do with it. And if anything, they seemed pleased to hear that things went so well for their partner and friend.

Kintail growled. Two people murdered at the hands of fanatical killers and two more dead because of this damned Cameron MacPherson. Although Kintail didn't blame him. The newly turned wolf was protecting what he felt was his property. But she wouldn't be for long.

"Who?" Kintail asked again, his voice just as hard. No one spoke. He motioned to one of the older women. "Katina was the only one who did what she was told. Well, she and Vance and Luke." He bowed his head slightly to them, glad they'd been so quick thinking when Charles appeared out of the blue with his sled teams and Cameron and Faith. Katina locking Cameron and Faith in the barn while they were snooping around couldn't have been better planned, and Vance and Luke guarding the building in their wolf forms was the perfect touch. Even if it didn't work to keep his hostages where he wanted them, at least some of his people were making the right *effort*.

"Despite that he's newly one of us, Cameron is an alpha, folks, if any of you are too shortsighted to see that. He's not one to mess with. But from what I could see of the track marks at their campsite, Baker targeted Faith. To kill her? Or to have her? Since he's dead, the case is moot. But if anyone else tries to touch the woman, you won't only have her newly turned protector to deal with, but me. Understood?" He gave Lila a hard look.

Her expression sulky, she lifted one brow, not to be cowed.

David and Owen exchanged glances.

"As to the ones murdering our people without provocation, I want them brought to me alive. Understand?"

Officer Whitson and Adams shifted a little in their stances. Hell, why have a couple of his people on the police force if they weren't going to learn who the murderers were pronto? Except for getting his wolves out of hot water when need be, this was the first real test of trouble, and they hadn't been able to do anything about it.

Although Kintail suspected Faith might have a clue. "Get the woman to share her theory about the killings, Adams."

"But you said not to involve them."

"They're involved up to their hairlines, damn it. Find out what Faith suspects. Maybe as a forensic scientist, she can uncover the truth."

"She'll cause problems," Lila said, sounding as if she hoped the woman would.

Kintail suspected she was going to be trouble, but in a different way than Lila was. He had every plan to keep Faith under his control better than he had Lila.

"And Cameron? He's a private investigator and former police officer. We checked his credentials and he's been at this a lot longer than we have," Adams said.

Kintail should have gotten Adams and Whitson on the force and trained a long time ago instead of just six months ago. "How long has he been in the business?"

"Eight years."

Hell, no way did he want to solicit the outsider's help. On the other hand…

Kintail nodded. "Yeah, see if he can shed any light on the situation." Once they located the murderers of his people, Cameron wouldn't be needed any longer.

"What about that nosey red?" Adams asked.

"Leidolf? You were supposed to question him. What did he say he was here for?"

"He explained he was on vacation. But he wouldn't say anything further."

"Vacation, my ass. And where's Hilson?"

"He's around. But making himself difficult to locate." Adams looked back at David and Owen. They both perked up. Adams turned his attention to Kintail. "We have another situation."

Before Adams said what it was, Kintail knew.

"Their partner, Gavin Summerfield, booked a flight and is on his way to Bangor."

Owen shook his head. David raised his brows at his friend.

Kintail pondered the situation before he spoke. "Where are Cameron and Faith now?"

"Michael Roux told us he sent his brother George with them to return to their cabin rentals. Charles wants them gone. He figures he's upset you."

"None of my people better have injured Charles." Kintail looked over at Trevor. "Faith wants to speak to you about her father's work. They won't fall into the same trap twice. Go to her. Make up a Bigfoot story. Appease her. Unless she's learned what we are. Then tell her whatever satisfies her. I want Cameron and Faith to stay right where they are. It's easier to monitor their movements than if they're back in Millinocket. Until we have some answers about the murders committed recently, I want their help. Gavin's, too, if he can provide it."

"What about them?" Adams asked, motioning to David and Owen.

"They stay here, out of sight, and away from harm. The four men together would be too much of a risk. Not when they're still learning pack rules." Kintail cast a small smile at Owen.

The guy was trouble, but at least he had David in line.

"I can't believe Gavin's coming here," Owen said to David as they were locked in the basement again, the windows barred, the room smelling of mold. Owen sneezed again. "I'm afraid I really blew it this time." He slumped on a mattress resting on an iron bed frame that looked like old Army issue—olive drab blanket, scratchy bedsheets. Hell, he was used to the kind with the silky high-numbered thread count—courtesy of a former girlfriend who'd hated his own rough sheets. Now he couldn't get used to anything else.

"Don't be so hard on yourself. You were only trying to save Cameron's ass. You can't help it that communications are so spotty out here. And you know Gavin would have come out anyway if he never could get hold of Cameron. Besides, together, they'll be able to do more." He sighed. "You know the more you create problems, the more they watch you though."

"Yeah, and while you're doing nothing, they figure you're a real beta, complacent, willing to do whatever they say." Owen couldn't help sounding disgruntled. He was always a man of action, take control of a situation, push for a solution no matter how difficult the trials. In that respect, he was more like Cameron. David? He was the ultimate laid-back kind of guy. But Owen couldn't be like that, no matter how much he tried. And who has the heart attack? The no-stress guy. But on the other hand, maybe David's no-worries attitude was all a façade, and all this time he'd held the stress in.

"What do you think they'll do when Gavin reaches Cameron?" Owen asked, clenching his hands into fists, wishing the hell he had his gun, but recalling belatedly it wouldn't help anyway. Not against these wolf types.

David reclined in the bed, arms beneath his head, and stared up at the concrete block ceiling. "Not sure. Sounds like Cameron's got his hands full, protecting some new little lady in distress. I'm kind of surprised after the way Marjory stiffed him. I just hope Faith doesn't put him through the wringer, too."

"Hell, what about these werewolf hunters? At least if Kintail would let us, we could put our heads together and deal with them." He growled, hating to be locked in the basement for most of the time. At least he'd gotten the shapeshifting business pretty well under control. He wondered how Cameron was taking it. "Cameron's been turned," Owen said, tapping his fists on the bed frame. "He's got to be pissed."

David closed his eyes and yawned. "No more than you are. As for the werewolf hunters, we can't do anything about it. But as many people as Kintail has guarding us, we shouldn't have to worry. Relax. If we seem like we're not going any place, Kintail and his people will get sloppy. Then we'll make our move."

"What about Elizabeth?" Owen raised a brow at David. When David ignored Owen, he persisted. "She's got the hots for you. You might use it to our advantage." Although he knew David was the kind of man who wouldn't use a woman no matter what the circumstances. Owen took a different approach and shrugged. "Once we get out of here, you could always send for her if you're that interested." He knew David was. He'd seen the shared glances. The shy intrigue on Elizabeth's part. The way David tried to hide his interest in her. But Owen recognized she meant something to him.

David slipped his hands behind his head. "Lots of guys in Kintail's pack are interested in her."

"Yet she only has eyes for you. You heard that police officer, Adams. He was peeved as hell. Said she hadn't made those fudge brownies or that special stew of hers for anyone in the pack until the two of us arrived."

David smiled. "Damn good, too. But who says she made them for me, and not because of some whim of hers? For you, even?"

"She watched you to see what you thought of her cooking. Of course you made a big impression when you went back for thirds."

"They were good."

"Yep. And she has the hots for you. So you ought to use it to our advantage."

———

Don't jump to conclusions, Faith warned herself as she stared in disbelief at her clothes strewn all over the cabin while Leidolf Wildhaven stood on the braided rug among a pink bra and four pairs of panties ranging from matching pink to black. He didn't look like a guilty man caught in the act, which may have been the reason for her thinking he had nothing to do with messing with her stuff. But he did have a hint of a smile on his lips and in his gaze, which irritated the hell out of her.

She noted, too, that not one thing of Cameron's had been touched.

"What are you doing in my cabin?" She stormed into the place and started to grab up a sweater, when she smelled the odor of urine.

"You've made an enemy," Leidolf said, matter-of-factly. "Female. She left her calling card."

Now, Faith was *really* ticked off. "Who?" But as soon as the word was out of her mouth, she figured who. *Lila Grayson.* And despite being the type who was always civilized even under the most uncivilized conditions, Faith wanted to pay her back.

"Don't know the woman to match her with the scent." Leidolf sniffed the air and raised his brows. "We need to talk."

"You don't smell like one of us," Cameron said, yanking a plastic bag out from under the kitchen sink. "What's your story?"

Faith stared at Leidolf. He was from Portland. He couldn't be an Arctic wolf also.

"You saw me the other day. In my wolf form."

"A red wolf?" Cameron's eyes widened.

"A red wolf?" Faith parroted, helping Cameron to pick up her things. Clothes that hadn't been peed on, she deposited on the bed. The rest of the stuff went into the plastic trash bag, while she cursed silently to herself. "You said you were bitten by a wolf, too. Not one of Kintail's?"

"No. He and his people are Arctic wolves. I'm a red. Then there are grays. Arctic wolves are a subspecies of the gray. Beyond that, I wasn't bitten and changed like the two of you. Not that I haven't been bitten before. That comes along with the territory as a pack leader."

Faith snapped her gaping mouth shut.

Cameron flicked his gaze Faith's way.

"The two of us? You know for sure I'm one also now?" She collapsed on one of the dining room chairs. She didn't feel any differently, well, except for a sudden bit of light-headedness, but that wasn't from *being* a wolf, but *being told* she was one. "How... are you certain?"

"It's subtle. You have a special scent. You're one of us now. Guaranteed."

Faith looked a little ill. Cameron had prayed he hadn't infected her. He guessed it was as she said, everyone's system reacted differently to the change, although he'd been trying to sense anything that might have altered about her. He'd hoped since her wound had been nearly superficial that she might not have been infected. But he couldn't break free of the gnawing at his gut that he was responsible for her condition.

Part of him felt like he had to keep and protect her, since she was like him and he'd made her that way. Part of him worried she'd hate him for what he had done to her. And since they had both recently weathered dissolved relationships, he figured that might create even more problems. Yet he couldn't deny how much he wanted her.

He joined her and rubbed her back. She relaxed a little, but just stared at the floor, and he assumed she was thinking about how much this was going to affect her. At least for himself, he couldn't quit thinking about how he could live amongst humans and continue to work with his partners the way he was now.

"How could you have been born this way?" he asked Leidolf.

"My mother and father and all their ancestors, or most of them, were *lupus garous*. So that makes me one, too. Or rather a royal, one who has barely any human genes." He gave a small smile, arrogant, as if everyone could figure that out.

Faith looked up at Leidolf. "Why are you here? Charles's cousin, George, said that Kintail's pack controls this area. Since you're a red from Portland…" She didn't say anything further.

Portland, where Faith was from. As much of an alpha as Leidolf appeared to be in his wolf form, Cameron assumed he ran his own pack in Portland.

"You've seen the killings. The one at Kintail's offices, and the one out here. What did you make of it?" Leidolf questioned in response.

"You're investigating them? With Kintail's permission?" Cameron asked, not figuring that Kintail would have given it, unless Leidolf had special qualifications to deal with something like this.

Leidolf offered another subdued smile. "Not exactly. But it's my business because it also involves my pack, so…" He shrugged.

Cameron frowned. "Your pack out of Portland?"

"That's where I'm from, now. Do you want her?" Leidolf asked Cameron, but before he could answer, Leidolf responded for him. "It's obvious you do."

The pheromones Cameron was giving off must have clued Leidolf. Cameron could smell Faith's, too. Although he wasn't sure if that was purely a biological issue, or if something deeper down triggered it.

"What I'm getting at is do you want her for your mate? *Permanently?* We take a mate for life, no adulterous affairs, no divorces. Once we've mated with one of our own kind, that's it. Although in a couple of rare cases, researchers discovered pack leaders among the wolves with two mates at the same time; it's not the case with us. Partly it's an inborn thing with us—one mate at a time, no desire for another. Maybe our genetic predisposition evolved that way because we haven't had enough females to go around as it is. But I've always suspected it goes a lot deeper. My sister would say it has to do with finding your soul mate. Although I'm not certain I'd go as far as believing that."

Leidolf seemed deep in thought for a minute. "Then again, maybe she's right. With our werewolf kind, if we can find one, we're able to select a mate. It's not just left up to the alpha leaders like in most real wolf packs. And if we're able, we can have our own offspring. But like with real wolves, in a rare instance, one of our kind might deviate from the norm and take a second mate while already having one. Just like with any species where one of its kind does something that isn't normally done."

From Leidolf's glum expression, Cameron assumed he knew someone who *had deviated from the norm*. Which made Cameron curious as to the outcome.

"I take it you know someone who had a couple of mates at the same time. What happened?"

Leidolf's face darkened. "Let's just say it didn't have a happy ending." Taking a deep breath, he added, "Before you're mated with one of our kind, you can have sex with any number of humans. We're immune to their sexually transmitted diseases and normally can't get a human pregnant. As long as we don't get ourselves killed off accidentally, we live long lives, aging a year for every thirty once we reach eighteen. So be sure of what you want. I only mention all this because I assume the one who bit you and intended to kill you didn't give you any insight into the way we live."

Not saying a word, Faith left her chair and began heating the water in the tea kettle.

Cameron wondered what kind of a mess he'd gotten himself into. He figured there'd be a big learning curve, but not that he would have to adapt that much. Mainly, control the timing of the shifts, but the werewolf politics was another matter.

As far as taking a mate for life… he glanced at Faith, saw the vulnerability in her sparkling green eyes. Whether it was right or wrong, he craved having her for his own. From the moment he had walked out of his bathroom and saw her standing in his hotel room, her boots on the floor as if she was getting ready to stay, he'd wanted her.

"I don't know how it is with Arctic *lupus garous,* but with red and grays, we have a severe shortage of females. So…" Leidolf shrugged. "… finding another mate could be difficult, if you and Faith aren't itching to become mates. Once Kintail's bachelor males discover a new, unclaimed female *lupus garou* is in his territory, better watch out. Of course, that's saying there's a shortage of females in his pack."

Crap, what else? He had intended to send her home for her own protection from Kintail and his people as soon as Cameron knew for sure she hadn't been turned. But he'd never expected the unmated population of Arctic magical wolves in the area might try to claim her for their own.

"If a pack leader had it in mind to kill me and I was newly turned, I'd be leaving this area pronto." Leidolf removed his parka. After folding it over the couch back, he took a seat on one of the kitchen chairs. "So what can you tell me about Kintail and his people?"

The concept was probably preposterous, but Cameron had to ask. "There's no cure for this condition?"

Chapter 15

FAITH JERKED HER HEAD AROUND TO SEE LEIDOLF'S RESPONSE, but the smile on his lips told her all she needed to know. No cure existed for the werewolf condition.

"No sense in fighting what we are. You are what you are. Of course being a red would be preferable to an Arctic wolf. Limits where you can live in some regards."

"Red wolves aren't all that common either," Cameron said, sarcasm in his voice and Faith smiled at him, thankful he'd had a swift comeback when she couldn't think of one for the life of her.

Leidolf shrugged. "You're right of course. I'd still rather be a red than anything else. You'll both have a new lifestyle to an extent, but for the most part, I'm sure you'll adjust well enough. However, you'll need to live with an established pack while you learn our ways. You might have to go to Alaska to find one. Since Kintail's from the Canadian Arctic, from what I understand, you won't be able to join his pack up there. Unless there are others in the area."

"So what exactly are you here for?" Faith asked, offering Cameron a cup of hot cocoa, then another to Leidolf. She was not in the least bit interested in joining a werewolf pack in Alaska or anywhere else.

"Have you heard of the Dark Angels?"

Faith already didn't like the sound of them as she

sat down at the dining table and sipped her cocoa, then shook her head.

"I discovered them on the Internet, describing some group that searches for abominations—Bigfoot mainly. No problem. But then there was some interest in werewolves. Usually someone in a pack monitors stuff like that. This group listed some information about real werewolf trials, which and of itself could mean nothing. But they are extremely focused on the possibility we exist."

"Real werewolf trials?" Of course Faith knew about real witch trials, but trials for werewolves?

"Sure. For centuries, trials have been conducted all over the world. Really bad in France during the witch hunts in medieval times. One of the documented cases was about a John Grenier, only thirteen, who confessed to being a werewolf. No torture involved. At the time a reddish feral dog had been attacking villagers. But because of his age, and that he came freely to the court to confess, they didn't sentence him to death." Leidolf shook his head. "The boy wore a wolf skin and confessed to killing a dog, a baby, and a young girl. He tried to kill another, but she beat him off with her staff while she was shepherding. He tried to murder a young boy, but his uncle rescued him."

"But… werewolves aren't supposed to kill just for the sake of killing, are they? If he was a real werewolf…"

Leidolf drank his cocoa and set the cup aside. "Most of our kind believe he wanted to be one of us, probably saw a *lupus garou* changing and thought killing innocents was what it took to become a werewolf. He was nothing more than a murderer, a cannibal."

"But, they released him? How could they?"

"The president of the court said that lycanthropy—the ability to change into a wolf, and kuanthropy, someone who changes into a dog, were hallucinations, that the boy was of too tender an age, and that he was too dull-witted to know what he had done was wrong. So instead, he was incarcerated for life at the monastery of Bordeaux, where he could learn morals and Christian teachings. They say he ran around the cloister and garden on all fours, devouring a bloody pile of offal—you know, the entrails and internal organs of a butchered animal."

Cameron shook his head.

"He died when he was twenty, his mind completely gone. So that's why we figured he wasn't truly one of us, just a mad youngster who wished to be."

Faith let out her breath. She'd never considered people would turn to cannibalism in the guise of being werewolves. "Still, he wasn't really a werewolf."

"Right, but the problem is that people like that give us a bad name. Some think that we truly exist. Some think those tried for being werewolves, truly were werewolves, but the authorities wouldn't believe it because of church doctrine. Then hunters of werewolves suddenly appear from time to time, reciting these old trials. Another case was Gilles Garnier," Leidolf said, getting up from the table and making himself another cup of cocoa. "He was a poor farmer who had been a hermit, then married and moved his wife to an isolated home. But he wasn't used to feeding more than himself, and he couldn't afford to feed a wife, so he started foraging for food. That's when he killed a girl, a boy, wounded another girl who was rescued but died later, and again was caught after murdering another boy. What shocked the court the most was that he planned to eat the boy on a Friday, against Catholic doctrine."

When Faith's mouth gaped, Leidolf explained, "Fish only on Fridays. There never was any sign of wolf attacks. Just a human claiming, under torture, that he was a were-wolf. His story changed so many times that who knew what to believe. He was found guilty of lycanthropy and witchcraft and burned at the stake. So it's interesting to note that in one place in France, the president of the court didn't believe in lycanthropy and in another, he did."

"But he really wasn't one," Faith said.

"No, he wasn't. In another case, a man in Russia was accused of being a werewolf, and he told the court that he and his werewolf pack killed demons. He was sentenced to ten strikes with a whip for idolatry and superstition, then released."

"Was *he* a werewolf?"

"No. If he had been one, he wouldn't have admitted it. None of us would ever willingly give our kind away. Remember that. But now it seems we have a group who believe we exist, maybe who have even seen our kind shapeshift, and are killing them. They are trying to start a cell in Portland. That's why I'm here. To get at the root of the evil. Eliminate it here and stop them from causing trouble in my region."

"And Kintail knows this?" Cameron asked. "I wouldn't think he'd like your interference."

"He doesn't have to like it. I'm here to get the job done, then return to my pack, not before that."

"Then what if you help us and we help you?" Cameron asked.

Leidolf studied Cameron, then glanced over at

Faith, who was watching his expression closely. Could he be trusted?

"You want me to help free your friends from Kintail's pack?" Leidolf asked.

"That's the gist of it," Cameron said.

Please, please say yes, Faith said silently to herself.

"I can't." Leidolf leaned away from the table. He exuded confidence in his mannerisms, the way he smiled, the intensity of his look, all alpha, and just as arrogant. He might seem relaxed, but Faith was quite certain if he was threatened, the man would be the devil to deal with. And that's why she figured having him on their side would help significantly in confronting Kintail and his people.

"It has to do with pack politics. I'm here about my own situation concerning danger to my pack. It has nothing to do with Kintail or his people. I can't interfere with his pack or how he runs it."

"But he's taken Cameron's friends hostage! They weren't part of his pack and he can't claim them." Faith scowled at him. "We'd help you!"

Unruffled by her outburst, Leidolf bowed his head slightly. "If you located the men who are doing the killing, you would help yourselves. Any of us are at risk. And if you want to get right down to it, both of you belong to Kintail's pack."

"Because his wolf bit me," Cameron said.

"Right."

"But Cameron bit me," Faith said, still frowning at Leidolf.

Leidolf smiled a little. "Then it seems you're Cameron's, if you're agreeable. Or if not, Kintail will surely want you. As for Cameron? I suspect Kintail doesn't want him or he would have taken him into the pack right away once one of his people bit him."

Faith looked over at Cameron, not liking any of this one bit. Cameron was masking any reaction, making her feel he wasn't part of this, or was afraid to show what he was truly feeling in front of her.

Leidolf cleared his throat. "Mate with her, and she's yours. If you don't, she's considered available. If you do mate with her and Kintail or one of his people desire her, they'll have to kill you before they can have her."

"That's barbaric." The more Faith heard about the pack rules, the more she thought they needed major revamping.

"We mate for life. The wolf's instinct is ingrained in us. It's our way." Leidolf rose from the table. "I'm going to do some exploring in the woods, then return to Millinocket for a time. I think that's where these men are from. Either of you want to come with me?"

"As a wolf?" Faith asked, hoping not, but expecting the worst.

"As a wolf."

Faith gripped her mug tightly. "I haven't changed before. And I don't plan to if I can help it."

Leidolf appeared mildly amused, then he looked at Cameron. "You?"

"We're returning to Millinocket. Charles wants us out of here." Cameron got up from his chair and joined Faith. "Good luck on your hunt." He offered his hand to Leidolf and they shook on it.

"Thank you. Good luck on yours." Leidolf headed out of the cabin and shut the door.

Faith wished Leidolf would have helped, figuring he

knew the wolf ways a lot better than they did. But since it wasn't an option, no point in worrying about it.

"We can't leave here," Faith said, tugging at Cameron's hand. "What about your friends?"

"Like I said, we return to Millinocket. We can use the Internet there and I'll get in touch with Gavin. I'll find David and Owen and get them back. I don't need some red's help."

She wasn't so sure they couldn't use Leidolf's help. And she noted she was left out of the equation, but she figured as soon as she shapeshifted, and Cameron was assured she was an Arctic werewolf like him, he'd change his mind. Maybe it was fate that threw them together, or maybe it was a total mistake. But the idea she'd return without Cameron and live like this on her own, well, hell, he needed her as much as she needed him and she had no plans to return home alone!

She started to pack her bags, then considered throwing out the items that Lila had sprayed with urine. Yeah, no sense in taking them with her. Nothing that she couldn't replace. She dumped the trash bag on the floor next to the door. "I'm ready, Cameron. Let's go."

She hoped they wouldn't encounter Kintail or his people on the ten-mile trip to the trailhead and have even more difficulties again. But the way things were going for them, she halfway counted on trouble.

Leidolf's words rattled around in Cameron's brain, over and over again, like a computer program attempting to make a connection. Cameron had bitten Faith. She was his. That much he got, whether Leidolf had said so or not. But no matter how many times Cameron told himself Faith was as much his to keep and protect, he didn't like her being with him. Although there was nothing he could do about it for now. He had to get her safely to Millinocket. And from there, he hoped to get her to Bangor and on a plane for home. Werewolf killers and mate-hungry bachelor werewolves all made it too dangerous for Faith to stay here. Later, he'd hook up with her, and they'd work something out. But for now, the priority was leaving and getting a safe place in Millinocket.

Faith was too quiet as she packed up her snowmobile, and he figured it had something to do with the fact she was just like him now. The concept still hadn't completely sunk into his own brain that he was now a werewolf. He could imagine how she was feeling. Or maybe not. Being a woman, she might feel a little differently. Especially the part about how a bunch of werewolf males might be after her, and Kintail was leading the pack at that.

Before Cameron could say anything to her, she got on her snowmobile, pulled her ski mask up and her ski glasses down, then headed down the road toward the trailhead.

All he could think of on the way here when they first ventured to the resort was how he wanted to ensure his friends were all right. Now he was pretty sure they weren't. He was a werewolf, the woman he'd traveled with was one, too, and werewolf hunters had killed two of his kind. He shook his head at the whole nightmarish and unreal concept and hurried to keep pace with Faith. At least this time, they weren't traveling in a blizzard.

But only a few miles from the resort, Faith suddenly sped off into the woods. That's when he saw that a tree had been felled across the road. *Hell*. Cameron veered into the woods to follow Faith. She'd slowed down some to maneuver between the trees. And that's when he heard the snowmobile in pursuit of them.

What next? Kintail's men? The Dark Angels? Only one thing he could think of to do, set a trap to stop their pursuers. He slowed his snowmobile, turned it around, wished he could flip off the headlights—but he dared not turn off his engine and waste even more precious time—and waited, hoping Faith wouldn't get too far ahead of him. The sound of the engine grew closer, the halo of light widening in scope.

After removing his outer gloves, he readied his gun— time to terminate the pursuit. Thankfully, he had plenty of bullets. At least enough to put an end to this madness. Not that he wanted to kill anyone. A minor injury would be enough to make his pursuer cease and desist. At least he assumed.

But then the sound of two more snowmobiles pelted the vicinity, much farther off, headed this way. Cameron ground his teeth. *Damn*. Well, he could get rid of the first driver and then take down the next two. Good thing they weren't any closer to the first one. All three at once could take some fancy maneuvering. The sound of the snowmobile's roaring engine drew closer. And closer. He aimed his gun straight ahead.

The engine sound grew louder. The vibration in the ground sent shimmers of the stalker's pursuing vehicle through Cameron's snowmobile and up through every one of his nerve endings. He responded by tightening his grip on his weapon, his finger poised on the trigger.

"Let's get this over. Come to Daddy."

He hated the delay—every precious moment he idled his vehicle, the sound of Faith's machine faded away. "Come on, damn it."

The stalker didn't deviate from his course. Cameron gave a bitter smile. As soon as he appeared in his sights, Cameron would have his man.

Fearing whoever had felled the tree wished them harm, Faith tried to find a way back to the main road around the downed spruce, but the forest of trees didn't cooperate. The farther into the woods she drove, the farther it seemed she was headed away from the unplowed road. She glanced back for a second to see if Cameron was keeping up with her, but all she saw was her tracks in the snow, trees laden with the white stuff, and no sign of Cameron. Although she could hear him in the distance. She slowed to a stop and waited.

That's when Faith heard the snowmobile headed for her in the opposite direction. "Shit."

She glanced back Cameron's way. Still no sign of him. If she drove off in a different direction she was afraid she'd lose him, not to mention she might lose her own way. Navigating by street maps, no problem. Navigating her way through woods was not her forte.

The snowmobile in front of her grew closer. She reached into her pocket and gripped the pepper spray. And waited, praying Cameron would hurry up and join her.

That's when she heard a snowmobile behind her, but still too far away. And she thought a couple more were behind that one. Damn it, they were being hemmed in from all sides.

The snowmobile appeared in front of her, moving slowly, the driver male, tall, bulky, and if she wasn't mistaken... But no, the ski mask and hat hid his hair color and face. It couldn't be.

The man pulled in front of her with several feet separating them. She tightened her grip on the pepper spray still in her pocket.

"Faith, honey. What are you doing way out here? Looking for me?" His voice was deep, dark, and full of warning.

Hilson. Come a little closer. But she was afraid while he was wearing a mask and goggles that protected his face, the pepper spray wouldn't have any effect on him.

"Hilson?" she asked, trying to sound clueless, as if she truly didn't know who he was in his wintry gear. Although she didn't recognize the clothes. But then again, he'd never worn winter clothes like that before. Suits, yes, as a stock broker. In fact, he'd never worn anything much casual. Jeans were out. Sneakers? No way. She wondered now if he wasn't even a stock broker though, or something else.

Hilson fell for her ploy and drew the mask under his chin and pulled up his goggles to rest on his ski hat. "It's me, honey. In the flesh. Missed me, eh?"

At least her glower was hidden behind her mask and ski glasses. But she was sure her voice would give away her ire once she spoke. He had to know damned well that she was madder than hell at him.

"You weren't supposed to follow me here. I would have come back for you eventually. Didn't you get my note that said I would return in a couple of weeks? That I had some important brokerage deals I had to handle?" He folded his arms and leaned slightly back on his machine.

Thankfully, he didn't approach. Maybe because he thought she looked ready to bolt.

"I must have missed the note." She'd found it all right, but she hadn't seen it until she'd discovered he'd stolen her father's flash drive and hard drive. So she hadn't believed for a minute that he would return.

As much as she wanted to take another glance in the direction of the trail off to her right, she didn't want to give away that she was considering detouring in that direction. She figured if she kept heading that way, she'd end up at the frozen lake eventually. Probably not the direction she wanted to go.

"How did you manage to find me so quickly? Break into my computer? I left it there so you would know I was returning to you. But I hadn't expected you would learn my password. Kintail says you're an investigative genius."

She didn't care what Kintail said about her, and she didn't say anything in response, stalling for time, hoping Cameron would hurry and arrive with the backup weapon. Even though the bullets he had weren't silver. Not that she wanted Hilson dead, just stopped in whatever he had in mind to do.

"You've really caused some problems coming here, you know?" Hilson leaned forward, his amber eyes narrowed, the same look he'd give when he caught some guy hitting on her, and he meant business. "Lila wants you dead. Kintail wants you, period."

"What do you want, Hilson? I thought I meant something special to you." It sounded like Hilson had given up all claims to her. She desperately wanted to look behind her. Wanted to see if Cameron was nearly there. Had to stall Hilson before he did anything she'd regret.

"I know. Whirlwind romance. Three months of great times. You're lucky I didn't just eliminate your father. That's what we do when someone learns what we are. We terminate them or turn them. There wasn't any good reason to make him one of us."

Her father. She felt sick to her stomach. They hadn't killed him, had they? "My father," she said half angry, half choked with emotion.

"He's not the one to worry about right now. You know about us, don't you? Kintail says that prick Cameron told you." He sighed. "Damned newbie *lupus garou*. Don't know when to keep their mouths shut. It's supposed to be instinctual, preservation of the species type of thing." He shook his head. "I knew it would come to this eventually." He pulled off his ski mask and goggles.

"What are you doing?" She tried to sound scornful, but her armor was slipping. She guessed what he was doing, just as soon as he began unfastening his coat.

He was getting ready to shift. And then he would bare his teeth before the bite.

The snowmobile roared around the bend in the trees and slid some distance to a stop. Goggles and a black ski mask hid the driver's expression, but Cameron could pretty much guess the gun was a deterrent in the man's pursuing them. Cameron hadn't heard Faith's snowmobile in sometime now and hoped to hell he could locate her quickly once he dealt with their pursuers.

Then the driver of the snowmobile jerked up his goggles and pulled down his mask and grinned like a lunatic. *Gavin*. His red brows raised, he motioned behind himself, and Cameron instantly lowered his gun.

"Cavalry's coming. Where's the little lady?" Gavin asked.

"Up ahead."

"Let's set up a roadblock. They're not far behind." Gavin hurried off his idling snowmobile, and Cameron did the same. Gavin glanced at Cameron's shredded parka sleeve. "You all right?"

"Yeah." Switching the subject, Cameron warned, "No ax."

"Looks like we have enough fallen trees that together we can create a makeshift stopgap."

That's what Cameron always liked about Gavin. He was an optimist extraordinaire, and he could MacGyver anything together if he had the time and resources. Sometimes even when he had neither. Their current predicament reminded Cameron of some of the missions they'd been on.

"So what's she like, Cameron?" Gavin asked, as the two of them hauled a heavy tree onto the trail behind Gavin's snowmobile, but he glanced again at Cameron's torn coat, and Cameron figured he'd have to start making up stories to appease his friend, as much as he hated doing so.

Looking at the mess they were creating, Cameron hoped to hell they wouldn't have to backtrack this way anytime soon.

Gavin dumped another armload of branches on the trail. "Faith O'Malley, the woman you've hitched up with this trip. Believe me, I was surprised as hell. She must really be something."

"Faith O'Malley?" How the hell had Gavin already learned so much about her?

"When I arrived at the lodge where you stayed for the night, the clerk gave me an earful about giving the key to your room to a cute blonde, that she suspected you were now friends with since her room was across from yours. The clerk sounded a little wishful that she'd had the key to your room instead. Then I learned Miss O'Malley had some business with Lila Grayson and Kintail Silverman concerning Back Country Tours also. That made me wonder if it had anything to do with you calling and having me check out the license plates for a gray Ford pickup."

Cameron paused as they pulled another tree in place. "What did you learn?"

"It belongs to Back Country Tours in the name of Kintail Silverman. And since you were investigating the same outfit, I figured you might have hooked up together in the romance department. Although the way you were feeling about Marjory, I wasn't sure you'd take the plunge again so soon—even if it's been several months. So what's the story?"

The information about the registration for the pickup didn't help much, although it looked like Kintail had been following Faith's progress all along. Cameron was damned glad Gavin was here, but the realization hit him again that he couldn't explain all that had happened. He wanted to, as close as he'd been to his partners. But internal warning bells went off concerning what he was now. And instinctually he knew for the preservation of his kind, he couldn't reveal the truth to Gavin.

He didn't answer Gavin, but considered the tangle of trees and branches they'd gathered now blocking the trail and figured it would take their pursuers a while to clear a path. "She's up ahead. Let's go."

Gavin would assume that Cameron was in a hurry to protect the woman. But soon, he suspected more would be at stake. He just hoped the reason there was no sound of a snowmobile's engine grumbling in Faith's direction was because she was stopped, waiting for him to catch up.

As soon as he climbed onto his snowmobile, he tore off toward Faith, Gavin following a distance behind. No matter the bizarre set of circumstances now, Cameron was glad to have his partner at his back. He just hoped Gavin wouldn't learn the truth about the werewolf business, or they'd have a hell of a new mess to deal with.

Trevor stalked into Kintail's lodge and the hangdog expression meant things hadn't gone as planned. Kintail at first thought the problem was that Faith wouldn't speak with Trevor. But Trevor quickly explained, "Before Officer Adams and Whitson could reach the cabins, Cameron and Faith had left. The officers are in pursuit, but they wanted me to report back to you to tell you what had happened. Once they convince Cameron and Faith to return to the cabins, I'll visit with her there." He stroked his gray beard, his gray eyes watching Kintail's reaction.

Kintail ground his teeth. Couldn't anyone in his pack do anything right? He wanted the woman to discover who the killers in their midst were, and then he wanted her. Period.

"Another thing."

Kintail refocused on Trevor, the man's posture defeated, and Kintail knew he wouldn't like this other thing.

"Or, a couple of things, I should say. The red, Leidolf, was seen exploring the woods near the lake. We think he's investigating this matter of the *lupus garou* killers also. But why, we don't know."

"Fine. He's welcome to help in the investigation if that's all he's here for."

Trevor cleared his throat and Kintail knew the next bit of news would not set well with him either. "Hilson's after the woman."

Kintail drew himself taller. "My brother didn't claim her. Didn't mate with her. He didn't eliminate her father, who could be a real threat. He has no right to the woman."

"He's been with her for three months," Trevor reminded him.

"Only to get closer to her father, to learn what he was up to, despite *you* saying Kenneth O'Malley hadn't seen any of us shapeshift."

Trevor didn't flinch. Kintail liked that in him. No matter how many times he'd questioned Trevor, he hadn't been able to bully him into telling a different story. Either Trevor really didn't think Mr. O'Malley had see them change, or he was protecting him. If it was the latter, it meant something about O'Malley's actions must have triggered a sentimental side of Trevor to appear suddenly. Where kids and pets were concerned, he had a soft spot. But adult human males?

Kintail just couldn't figure the situation out. But his gut instinct told him Trevor saved O'Malley's ass from being eliminated. Hilson had thought the same and of his own accord moved temporarily to Portland to watch O'Malley. But observing him from a distance was getting him nowhere. That's when he targeted the daughter.

Trevor took a deep breath. "Lila cares for you."

Kintail stared at him as if he'd lost his mind.

"I overheard her talking tearfully to Katina about losing her mate and son."

Kintail clenched his teeth, not sure he wanted to hear how much she had loved someone else, telling himself that's why she couldn't love him. But he held his tongue and waited.

"She's scared she's going to lose you, and she's scared she can't show you how much she cares before it's too late. As an alpha female, she puts on this act to hide her true feelings, afraid to show her vulnerability."

Kintail looked out the window. Maybe so, but would she ever come to grips with her past? She wouldn't even speak to him about it.

"As to Faith, she wants Cameron and he wants her. You won't ever change that. If you kill Cameron, Faith will want to kill you."

Glancing at Trevor, Kintail wouldn't be thwarted in his mission. If Lila could come around before it was too late, so be it. Otherwise, Faith was his. "Where the hell is Hilson now? No one's been able to get hold of him."

"He's after the woman. George Roux told us that when we were looking for Faith and Cameron, Hilson had arrived twenty minutes before us, looking for the woman, then he headed into the woods to find a way to stop her."

"She's mine to turn, damn it." Kintail began jerking off his clothes. "Where the hell are they now exactly?"

Standing against the wall, waiting for the door to swing open and hide him in their basement prison, Owen warned David, "It's now or never."

The aroma of beef, potatoes, gravy, and spinach wafting down the stairs made his stomach rumble in anticipation. But he wasn't planning to eat the lunch this time, no matter how much it appealed. This morning only an older woman, Katina, had brought their food, no guard. If it happened again, they'd be in luck.

David reclined on the bed, looking perfectly relaxed like he wasn't about to go anywhere. But the effect was an illusion. Owen could see the tightness in David's face, even if others couldn't. He noted the tension in David's body, and knew that if the chance availed itself this time, he'd spring from the bed and aid their escape.

So when the door opened wide and David's placid face turned to a frown, Owen knew the circumstances weren't exactly right for an escape attempt. But damn it, Owen was ready. And he'd already played his hand, so they'd be wary of another trick in the future.

But as soon as Elizabeth entered the room, Owen wondered what the difficulty was. Although she stopped short to see Owen wasn't in the bed or anywhere else in the basement. David quickly smiled

at her and reached for the tray, trying to distract her.
Owen figured they could tie her up and take off.
Or take her with them. But right after that, a man
followed her into the room and turned to see where
Owen was once he saw he wasn't anywhere else in
the small basement room.

With no time to lose, Owen clobbered him with
his fists, bringing him down, only he was carrying the
second tray of food and the dishes clattered to the floor.
But worse, a third man was right behind the first. David
was up and out of bed in an instant, knocking the second
man out. Elizabeth looked like she was going to die, but
quickly set the tray on the bed, and moved out of Owen
and David's path.

"Do you want to come with us?" David asked, taking
hold of her hands.

"Hell," Owen said, hating that they'd made such a
racket and hoping whoever else was in the lodge hadn't
heard. "This isn't the time, David. Let's get a move on."

"Do you?" David asked.

"They'll kill us," she said, but nodded. "I can guide you."

"All right, let's go." Owen raced up the stairs as
Elizabeth followed him.

David locked the door to the basement and hurried
to join them at the top step. "Place is quiet," he whispered, suspicious.

"Maybe they're out looking for the killers." At least
Owen hoped they were.

"Several are, but not everyone. Lila's here, too, taking
a nap," Elizabeth warned.

Even though she was petite and seemed shy, she'd
targeted David from the beginning. As if she'd wanted

him and when the time was right, she'd have him. Well, the time might not be right, but he was all hers, for now. Owen just hoped she would be a help and not a hindrance.

Heavy footfalls headed their way. Owen bolted through the kitchen and jerked open the door that led outside to a small garden with David and Elizabeth following on his heels. The garden was covered in snow, but from what he'd overheard, Kintail and his people left here before the weather got too warm, and returned to their native stomping grounds in the Canadian Arctic, so Owen imagined the garden never was ever planted. Unless a small contingency of his people remained behind.

"Somehow we've got to join forces with Cameron," Owen said, racing through the snow, in the direction of the outer building, wishing he had gloves and a hat at least. Kintail's people had confiscated their parkas, gloves, ski masks, goggles, anything they could use to keep them warm in the cold out-of-doors in the event they managed to escape. He glanced at Elizabeth. Wearing jeans and a soft sweater and boots, she wasn't in any better shape clothing-wise than they were. Already he was having misgivings about this.

"We may have to shapeshift," David warned, "as much as I don't want to."

Elizabeth stayed close to David, not saying a word.

"I thought you liked being a wolf," Owen shot over his shoulder as they made their way through the deep snow to the barn. "Maybe a couple of the snowmobiles are still in residence, and some of our gear is in there."

"Being a wolf is fine. I love the freedom, the hunt, the attuned senses we have now. But trying to communicate to Cameron is another thing. And then what do we do about getting some clothes in case we decide to shift back? Even though we're getting better at this, we still don't have the shifting completely under control. I can imagine us in the middle of nowhere, stark naked."

"Yeah, well, that's true enough." Although Owen hated that it was, that they still hadn't gotten the shifting under complete control.

"If you can control it, I agree we'll need to shift," Elizabeth said, "but there may be some spare clothes in the barn in the event either of you can't."

Trevor had warned them it might take months to get the hang of shapeshifting, sometimes years, depending on the personality of a newly turned *lupus garou*.

Owen jerked open the outer building door and hurried inside, briefly noting the empty place where a couple of snowmobiles had sat. "Damn." He started rummaging through a box, but it appeared to contain just tents. And a credit card. He lifted it up and smiled. "Trevor Hodges's. Might come in handy, if we can use it where no one knows him."

"He's probably lived here for eons, and everyone would know him. But sure, take it just in case. It might come in handy."

"Everyone knows him," Elizabeth said, digging through another box.

David dove into another one. "Sleeping bags in here. Yours and mine, too, Owen. But no sign of any winter clothes."

"Well, hell. Let's get out of here before someone sounds the alarm."

That's when they heard angry shouting from the main lodge.

"Too late for that," David grumbled.

David grabbed Elizabeth's hand and they bolted out of the barn with Owen and ran straight for the cover of the nearest woods.

Chapter 16

THE WOLFISH GRIN ON HILSON'S FACE TOLD FAITH HE MEANT business as he jerked off his jacket. Only she was afraid he intended to turn her when she'd already been turned! She didn't relish getting bitten again. But then she heard two snowmobiles headed in her direction. Cameron! But someone else, too, and she didn't think it could be anyone who would help them. Kintail's men, or…

Something crashed some distance behind her and curses carried through the woods like a long-distance echo. Thank God, not Cameron's voice. Hilson glanced in that direction, his expression turning from wolfish intent to red-faced anger. "Adams," he growled under his breath.

The police officer?

Then another crashing sound and more curses. Some from the same man, some from another.

"Hell, and Whitson."

She didn't know what to think if the men following them were the police officers. All she knew was if she waited for Cameron, and Hilson changed before she could leave, he'd bite her. Even if she tried to outrun him, he'd be able to keep up as slowly as she had to maneuver between trees on the snowmobile. And in his wolf form, she figured he'd have the advantage.

Then she swore she saw a red wolf's amber eyes peering between spruces, watching her, watching Hilson.

Leidolf? If it was him, would he come to her rescue if she needed him to?

Hilson was stripped down to his shirt and pants and boots. She made the decision right or wrong, turned her machine, and headed in the direction of the lake—unfortunately, farther from her destination.

Hilson swore at her and she was sure he was ripping off the buttons on his shirt as he tried to finish undressing quickly, although she couldn't hear it over the roar of her machine and didn't dare look back. When she'd gone some distance, the vehicles behind her stopped suddenly, but then shifted in her direction. Cameron to the rescue. She and he could stop whoever was following them next. But in the meantime, she pulled her snowmobile into the woods off the trail and waited for Cameron, hoping Hilson would run off in another direction, afraid of what could happen if he messed with Cameron.

Except for the approaching snowmobiles, the woods were quiet and still and deeply shaded. They smelled of evergreen and a chilled wetness. She glanced back at the white woods, the sudden urge of wanting to blend in with them overwhelming her, as if a wolf guardian angel was nudging her in the right direction. Before she could control what she was doing, she began yanking off her own clothes. The cold tightened her skin as she tossed her sweater and shirt. Chill bumps raised up on her arms. She jerked off her boots and then her pants. Cold, freezing cold. Standing beside her snowmobile, completely naked, she knew then the wolf bite had made her go insane.

When she thought she'd die from exposure, her body began to warm. A heat, like what she imagined a hot flash to feel like, invaded every inch of her body. That's when Cameron came into view on his snowmobile. Just before her body twisted painlessly, effortlessly, like giving a good stretch to knotted up muscles. Then she dropped down on four paws and stared at her black claws against the white snow in disbelief. Her legs were skinny and long and covered with white fur. This was just too damned unreal.

"Faith," Cameron yelled, right before Hilson lunged as a wolf, or at least that's who she assumed it was, and knocked Cameron off his snowmobile.

Her heart nearly quit beating. But before she could come to his rescue, a man driving a snowmobile behind him shouted, "Cameron! Damn it!" He jerked his machine to a stop, drew a gun from beneath his parka, and fired at the wolf, hitting him four times, before the wolf bolted into the woods.

Faith stood stock still as the man turned his attention to her, afraid the man would shoot her next, although she wanted to make sure Cameron was all right. The man held his gun aimed at her, but didn't fire. Faith didn't move, just whimpered at Cameron, wanting reassurance he was all right.

He stirred from his prone position, face first in the snow. He raised his head, groaned, and saw her. "Faith," he whispered, and she noted the deep regret in his voice.

Yeah, well he'd done this to her, but it was her own damn fault, too.

Cameron turned to the other man. "Don't shoot the wolf, Gavin. She's all right."

Gavin? The partner Cameron had left back in Seattle? She hoped Hilson would survive his partner's bullets, but she was glad Gavin was here to help Cameron locate their other partners.

"Why are Arctic wolves out here?" Gavin asked, his voice full of disbelief as he holstered his gun, then climbed off his snowmobile. "You all right?"

"Yeah." Cameron shook his head, dislodging some of the snow from his hat and ski mask and glanced back at Faith.

She wanted to approach him, lick his cheek, and nudge him to see that he truly was all right. He appeared a little dazed. Certainly, if he'd been perfectly all right, he would be on his feet already.

"How do you know this one's okay, when the other attacked you?" Gavin asked, helping Cameron to stand.

Cameron leaned into Gavin, and she knew then Cameron had been hurt.

"Faith," Cameron said, reaching his gloved hand out to her, his attention focused on her eyes, his concern for her evident.

Appreciating his gesture, she still didn't move. Gavin could have killed Hilson, and she didn't relish getting shot also. Just one wrong move and the cowboy would pull his gun. Guaranteed.

"Faith," Cameron said again, and he tried to move toward her, but he seemed to be in pain. His face was hidden by the mask and goggles, but he was leaning so hard against Gavin, she assumed he must have hurt his leg or hip or something.

She inched toward him, ready to bolt if Gavin reached for his gun. She probably couldn't outrun the first bullet, but maybe subsequent ones she could. Hilson seemed to have been too focused on taking Cameron down to notice Gavin had hit him right away. She wouldn't have that problem.

She smelled a hint of wolf nearby, carried to her on the breeze. A hint of… red wolf. *Leidolf*. Was he just curious what would happen? Or was he watching out for her in case she needed him? She liked to think he was there for her, if need be. Although he seemed kind of mysterious, willing to help, but then again, not wanting to get mixed up in Cameron and her affairs.

"Are you sure…" Gavin said, his hand reaching under his parka.

"Don't shoot her," Cameron ordered, his voice angry. "She's mine."

Gavin chuckled a little under his breath. "You haven't had a dog since old Dusty died. But at least she was a Lab. An Arctic wolf?" He shook his head. "I'm sure there's a story behind all this. Can you make it, Cameron? Can you ride?" He glanced back at the clothes lying behind the snowmobile and frowned. "Was Faith driving this snowmobile? Hell, what happened to her?"

Cameron just shook his head. "She's okay. She'll be fine. We need to get to Millinocket," he said, his gaze focused on Faith's. "That's where Faith will go."

But how could she go there dressed in her wolf coat? And what if she decided to change back all of a sudden out here in the middle of nowhere without a stitch of clothes. She'd freeze to death. Not to mention embarrassing herself to death. And if anyone saw her shift, she'd put the whole werewolf world in jeopardy—which she still had a hard time believing existed beyond Kintail's pack, and now maybe Leidolf's.

"You have to follow us, Faith," Cameron said, pleading with her.

"You named the wolf after the woman you're running around with?" Gavin asked, his voice incredulous. "Does she know?"

"Grab the clothes and bags off the snowmobile. We'll have to return for the machine later." While Gavin did as Cameron asked, Cameron crouched, groaning with the effort and reached out his hand to Faith.

She couldn't reconcile the emotions swamping her. She was a wolf now, and no matter how she looked at it, this was just plain bad news. Usually, she felt pretty well in control of her life. Not now. Now she was a danger to others of her kind and a danger to herself. And there was nothing she could do about it. She didn't move toward Cameron, as much as his eyes pleaded with her to draw closer. She didn't want to be petted like a damned dog. She didn't want him to hug her and try to reassure her everything would be all right, because it wouldn't be. Leidolf might have been right in saying they were what they were now. But having been born a *lupus garou*, he can't have known how it would feel to someone like Cameron or her.

She took a step away from Cameron, hating the look of hurt in his eyes. But she couldn't accept his comfort. Not like this. Not as a damned vicious Arctic wolf with teeth that could crush bones.

She lifted her nose and sampled the air, smelled Leidolf drawing closer, but still out of sight. She understood why. He probably had seen what Gavin had done to Hilson.

Gavin was watching the two of them now, her clothes and bags in his arms. "She's still a feral wolf," he said, his voice gentled. "Let her go."

"You're mine," Cameron said softly. "You have to go with us, Faith. You can't stay out here alone. Kintail's men…" He rose unsteadily, his jaw clenched, eyes narrowed. "You can't stay here. Follow us."

She waited for him to limp to his snowmobile, waited for him to climb on, waited for him to look back at her once more, pleading more than demanding that she obey him. And then she decided what she would do. She'd follow him, for a brief time, then find Leidolf. She couldn't run to the trailhead and risk turning into a human somewhere along the way. If she could make it to their rental vehicles, maybe. But not out in the open like this.

She followed Cameron for a little while as he drove his snowmobile and tried to find a way back to the main road. He kept glancing back at her, making sure she was still there, loping slightly behind his snowmobile, while she kept looking for the best place to bolt where the trees wouldn't allow a snowmobile passage.

Gavin was an even further distance behind, and she noted he was watching her, too. Wary, she suspected. If one wild wolf could knock Cameron from his machine, why not another? Only she was female and not half as big as Hilson. Although she assumed if she bared her teeth, she could scare the most stalwart of men.

She glanced back at the woods, knowing Gavin figured what she was up to. Cameron, too, but she hoped he wouldn't see her take off until it was too late. And then she spied a flash of red fur. *Leidolf*. He must have realized she might need help. At least she hoped that's why he was stalking them.

With one last look at Cameron, she silently wished him well, then bolted for the woods. She half expected

Gavin to warn him that she had taken off, but he didn't. Probably figured she needed to run wild and Cameron shouldn't have interfered with her natural instincts. In any event, it worked well for her.

Cameron would no doubt give him holy hell for it, too. But Faith didn't think she could make it to the trailhead as a wolf. She couldn't risk it.

Faith ran deeper into the woods, the sudden realization that no matter what else was wrong with her life, she enjoyed the sense of adventure she now was experiencing, the freedom to move as a wolf, the way her fur coat protected her against the elements without her having to wear tons of clothing to keep warm. Freedom, that's what she felt.

But it would be short-lived if anyone from Kintail's pack caught up with her. Or she ran into the werewolf killers.

--- ∿ ---

Cameron was certain Faith would run off, but he hadn't expected his good friend, Gavin, not to tell him the moment she did. He glowered at him again, as the two trudged through the trees on foot, pursuing her tracks, unable to follow on the snow machines. He had to admire her ability to solve problems no matter what the circumstances. He only hoped they wouldn't find her naked, freezing to death along the way. And he hoped that if they did catch up to her, she wouldn't be in any other trouble and would be willing to follow his lead this time. Frustrated with his own inability to take care of her while she was a wolf in the wilderness, he was damned thankful Gavin hadn't seen her shapeshift and that he could avoid the problems that would have entailed.

A blurring of two exquisite shapes, like the northern lights mixing in surreal colors, that's the way she had appeared to him, blending from the beauty of a naked woman into that of a furred white wolf. The woman one instant, the wolf the next. Even though she shifted quickly and even if he hadn't chanced to see the blurred effect, she wasn't the same after the process was done. The woman vanished, the wolf took her place. So there was no mistaking it if Gavin had caught a glimpse of the switch. Although he probably would have assumed he'd been hallucinating.

"I don't understand why you feel we have to chase after the wolf, Cameron. She probably took off after a rabbit, and she'll be back."

Cameron sliced his friend another glare.

Gavin looked back at the tracks. "You already bit my head off about not warning you sooner. But hell, she's a wild wolf, and this is what they do." He paused and leaned over a little. "Damn, there are two tracks now."

Cameron stared at the impressions in the snow. "Broader paw, larger wolf. Male." He swore under his breath.

Gavin chuckled. "She could be in heat and interested in him and having little wolf pups in the spring."

Cameron hauled off and socked his friend in the jaw. He didn't know what came over him to knock Gavin off his feet. Except the raw emotions he felt toward Faith were sitting at the surface, and he couldn't contain them any longer.

Gavin winced and stared up at him. "Hell, what is wrong with you? I know you've got to be tied up in knots over the guys' disappearance, but this wolf? What's gotten into you?"

Cameron couldn't even make the effort to apologize like he should have. He wanted to shift. In the worst way, Cameron wanted to go after her, tear into the male wolf who was with her, and show the world of wolves she was his.

After the male wolf met up with Faith, her paw prints disappeared, and he knew she was following the male, using his tracks to make her journey easier. Incensed, he wanted to shake her, make her realize he was the only one for her.

He vaguely noticed Gavin rejoining him, still caressing his jaw. "You still have a damned hard punch. Want to tell me what's going on?"

He wanted to. They'd never kept secrets from each other before, except for Gavin's clandestine operation concerning watching Marjory's extracurricular activities. But he knew this part of his life he couldn't disclose to Gavin. And now, he was afraid he might have to dissolve the partnership, or get his friend into the trouble he and Faith were in already.

But *after* they located Owen and David. After they made sure they were safe.

Which brought another troubling thought to mind. If Owen and David had been changed, and he suspected at this point they had been, the three of them could continue to be partners in their business. How would they be able to eliminate Gavin from the partnership as close as they had all been over the years?

He shook his head. No matter the scenario, he couldn't think of an uncomplicated way out of the mess.

Gavin followed behind Cameron. "Guess you don't want to discuss it. I could understand your not wanting to tell me about your new girlfriend. But hell, your relationship with a wolf?" Then he hurried to catch up. "Did the wolf rescue you?" He shook his head. "Knowing you, you rescued the wolf and now you feel this connection, like you always do when it comes to rescuing damsels in distress. But I never thought in a million years the situation would have extended to a wolf."

"They've headed back to the cabins," Cameron finally said, noting the path the wolves' tracks were taking. "Let's return for our snowmobiles and find a way back to the main road. It'll be faster that way."

"What about Faith, the woman?" Gavin asked, taking a handful of snow and holding it against his jaw.

That's what Cameron worried about more than anything. Faith, the woman, and the mess she could be in now.

"It'll be faster if we shed our clothes and run like wolves," Owen said, racing through the woods ahead of David and Elizabeth, half freezing to death, rubbing his numb fingers, then shoving them back in his jeans pockets, his trouser legs stiff with clinging snow. "You still think we should go straight to the cabin resort where Cameron is staying?"

"Yeah. I know that Officer Adams and Whitson and that Trevor Hodges are on their way there, but it's the only way we can get to Cameron. They'll stop them from leaving for Millinocket, and we've got to let Cameron know we're all right. Although Kintail will most likely assume we're headed that way also and try to have us intercepted before that." David looked at Elizabeth. "What do you think?"

"I agree with everything you've said." Elizabeth had kept up with their longer strides, while David's hand remained wrapped around hers the entire time, pulling her along, making sure she didn't fall, and she hadn't once complained. She looked worried, of course. She knew Kintail better than they did.

But Owen was surprised when David had asked her if she wanted to come along. He figured David would have been more concerned for her safety. Maybe he was using her a little as she'd kept them headed for Charles's cabin resort when Owen had tried to steer them wrong. Deep down he didn't think so though. Maybe David had the hots for her as much as she did for him, only like usual, he was hiding his feelings.

Suddenly David asked, "Think we can start our own pack in Seattle?"

Owen shot him a get-real-look over his shoulder. "We'll be lucky to find a place in Alaska where as Arctic wolves, we will fit in more. But I doubt we'll be safe there either. And what if the areas are tied up with packs already, just like Kintail's, and they don't relish the idea of two more full grown males joining them?"

"Kintail's got the people believing his pet wolves are perfectly tame here, so everyone's used to seeing them around, off of leashes, completely compatible with the human populace. Why couldn't we do that back home?"

"In Seattle?" Owen shook his head. "Can you imagine dropping into Starbucks for your favorite cup of coffee, with me in tow as a guide wolf?" Owen let out his breath in a puff of frigid smoky vapor. "So do we do it, or not? Can you force the shift?"

"I can do it. I'm just not sure I want to."

"When we arrive at Cameron's place, he'll have a change of clothes for us. He's already one of us. He'll recognize us. His girlfriend, Faith, should have clothes for Elizabeth. We'll be warmer. My hands are already numb. Most of the heat in my body, I'm losing through my head without having a parka, a hood, or hat to keep me warm. I can barely see because of the sun reflecting off the snow except where the trees shade the area. Plus, trudging through the snow is slowing us down. We'll be able to run a hell of a lot farther and faster with our lighter weight as wolves situated on top of the snow rather than in our human forms plowing through it. And we'll be a lot less visible in our white fur against the snow-filled backdrop than we are now."

"He's right," Elizabeth said.

David said, "All right, all right. Cameron just better have a change of clothes for both of us." He gave Owen a disgruntled look as he began pulling off his wool sweater.

Owen and David turned their backs to Elizabeth while they stripped. Even though it was a natural occurrence for the members of the pack to shed their clothes in front of each other if the occasion called for it and no one paid any attention to it, David and Owen weren't there yet. And even now, Owen was feeling a little self-conscious with exposing his backside to Elizabeth.

"At least his clothes will fit you. With my height, it'll look like I had a growing spurt and hadn't had time to buy new clothes," David added.

Owen smiled and finished ditching his clothes. Once he was stark naked, he hurried to bury his things underneath the snow before he felt the shift taking place. He hadn't even willed himself to do it. He figured it might have been a need for self-preservation, that once his skin grew too cold, the wolf coat kicked in.

David was soon at his side nudging him with his long wolf snout, and the two greeted each other like a couple of old wolf pals, noses touching, tongues licking, a show of camaraderie, of solidarity. They did the same with Elizabeth, only David was a little more amorous and if Owen could laugh, he would. Then he took off at a run.

Kintail had told him they could run flat out at tops forty miles per hour for several miles, and easily cover sixty miles in a night at a trot. He loved the way he felt as a wolf, capable of anything. His paws gripped a fallen tree and he bolted over it, knowing David and Elizabeth were right behind him. The three headed down a trail where dogs and sleds and Cameron had once traversed, their scents still lingering behind. They'd find him soon. And then?

They'd return to Seattle, changed men. Poor Gavin—odd man out now. If they made it home safely, what could they do about him?

Chapter 17

AFTER AN HOUR, CAMERON REACHED THE BLACK BEAR DEN with Gavin, but the place looked lifeless, deserted, just as he and Faith had left it. His heart in his throat, he hurried to enter the cabin, smelled Faith's sweet fragrance still lingering in the air, but there was no indication she had returned here.

"Maybe she's watching us from the shelter of the woods," Gavin said, glancing at Faith's soiled clothes in the garbage sack.

Maybe. But Cameron figured she'd show herself now that he was here. Maybe Gavin was the one who scared her. Hell, sure he did. He'd shot the wolf that had attacked Cameron, and then pointed the freshly fired gun at Faith.

"Listen, Gavin, why don't you go up to the main lodge and see about Charles's condition. Say that Cameron's asking, but don't tell anyone I've returned."

"Are you sure? I know that look in your eye. You're going off investigating Faith's disappearance on your own. Why don't you let me come with you? If nothing else, I can watch your back."

Cameron shook his head. "She may be afraid of you after you shot the other wolf. Just check on Charles. I'll return to this cabin after a while. You can meet me back here."

Gavin looked a little worried, but Cameron motioned to the lodge. "I'll be fine. See you in a few minutes."

"All right, but if you're not back here in half an hour, I'm coming for you." Gavin trudged off, muttering under his breath about friends and not keeping secrets.

Cameron got back on his snowmobile and hurried off toward his own cabin, calling out Faith's name. But she wasn't at his place either, although unless she'd shapeshifted, she wouldn't have been able to get inside. Then he thought of Hilson and his place. Damn, why hadn't he thought of him before? Cameron raced toward the Porcupine Cove cabin, but was in sight of Leidolf's place when the man opened his door and waved to him to come inside without saying a word.

Faith. Cameron parked and jumped off his vehicle, then rushed up the steps to the deck.

Before he could step inside the cabin, Leidolf warned, "She's here and she's sleeping. But we've got problems."

Hell, tell him something he didn't know. Cameron shoved past Leidolf into the cabin and headed straight for the bedroom. "On your way out, run by the lodge, will you? My partner Gavin Summerfield's there, but I want him to know where I am and that I'm with Faith, the woman, so don't want to be disturbed."

Leidolf gave him a knowing smile and didn't seem to be offended that Cameron was ordering him about, then closed the door to the place and locked it from the outside. He strolled on past the window in the direction of the main lodge.

Thank you, Cameron said silently, and opened the door to the bedroom as quietly as he could. Faith looked like an angel, sleeping soundly on the bed, her shoulders bare. Hell, she was still naked? Leidolf didn't give her anything to wear?

The place was comfortably warm though, and she looked like she was sleeping well. Still, he wanted her to know he was here now, and although he was pissed that Leidolf had had to rescue her, he was glad he had done so and seemed to have her best interests in mind.

Cameron sat next to Faith and leaned over and kissed her cheek, his hand caressing her shoulder, wanting to make the contact, wanting to assure himself she hadn't come to any harm. "I'm here," he said, his voice soothing, low and dark, not wanting to wake her, but just to reassure her he was with her again.

She stirred, her eyelashes fluttering. He ran his hand over her hair and kissed her lips this time. Her eyes popped open, her expression startled, and then she smiled, the most delightful smile he'd ever witnessed. Then she frowned and reached out to take his hand, her fingers grasping his protectively. "Are you all right? You were injured."

He sighed and stroked the nape of her neck. "Seems the werewolf genetics heals minor sprains and twists quickly enough. Why didn't you keep following me?"

"I didn't think I could keep from shifting again. I couldn't chance it. I barely made it to Leidolf's cabin. Where's your friend Gavin? He didn't see me shift, did he?"

"No. If he had, I'd never have heard the end of it."

Frowning, Faith touched Cameron's cheek. "We're in trouble. Officer Adams and Whitson? They were following us and were injured when Adams' snowmobile plowed into a hastily constructed barricade across the trail, and Whitson slammed into him right afterward. They'll live, according to Leidolf, who got the news from Charles's cousin, George, but they both were injured pretty badly. Broken arms, legs, Adams has got a concussion. And the worst of it all?"

"They want to arrest Gavin and me?" Cameron couldn't believe this could get any worse.

She shook her head. "They were trying to catch up to us to tell us Kintail needs us on the investigation. Whatever it takes, he would like us to find out who the killers are, and then he'll deal with them. And he wanted us to stay here at the cabins while we're doing the investigation."

Cameron cursed under his breath. "Kintail fancies having you. And if he wants both of us on the investigation, why did a wolf try to kill me in the woods just a half hour ago?"

Faith's cheeks turned a little pink. "That most likely had to do with me and nothing with Kintail's orders."

"You?" Before she could say what she meant, he cursed again. "Hilson. Hell, the ex-boyfriend scorned?"

"Yeah, well, he's an Arctic wolf, too, although I had kind of guessed he might be, after I learned they existed and that their kind, well, our kind wouldn't want to be exposed and that was the reason he stole my father's research. But what will we do about my father? We have to make sure he doesn't try to put another paper together about werewolves or our kind will most likely kill him."

"It seems there's only two choices we have—change the person who witnesses the shift, or kill him or her."

"So will you bite him?" Faith asked, running her hand over Cameron's.

He took her hand in his and squeezed. "After biting you, I wouldn't want to be responsible for turning another soul."

Faith looked away from Cameron. "Hilson will live, too, according to Leidolf. He said he'll go off and lick his wounds and it might take a few days, but he'll be as good as new, as long as the bullets Gavin fired at him weren't silver."

"Unless there's something about Gavin I don't know, the bullets weren't silver."

"Hey, Cameron!" Gavin shouted outside the cabin, banging on the door.

"Damn it, Gavin," Cameron said to himself more than to anyone else and then added for Faith's benefit, "I'll be right back." He stalked out of the bedroom and closed the door, then headed for the front door.

Unlocking it, he scowled at Gavin. "I told you to wait for me. Leidolf was supposed to tell you—"

"A Trevor Hodges is at the main lodge. He said Faith wanted to talk about her father's research concerning Bigfoot." Gavin raised a brow, then gingerly touched his swollen jaw again. "Anything you want to talk to me about?"

Bigfoot, my ass. But then again, the hunter guide might know about David and Owen's location. And that was the leverage they needed. If Kintail turned over their friends, they'd locate the killers. Working as a team, they could do it. Except now they had a new partner, much prettier than the rest of his partners. And if Leidolf wanted to come along for the ride, he was welcome to tag along. "Tell Trevor to meet us at Faith's cabin. We'll be right there."

Lila fumed as she paced across the great room at Kintail's lodge. She'd just managed to overhear some of what Kintail and Trevor were speaking about and knew for sure now Kintail planned on taking that damned O'Malley woman for his mate. What did he think? That Lila would just go along with it? A newly turned *lupus garou* would become the alpha leader's mate?

She didn't think so. And she couldn't believe Trevor had overheard her crying when she'd talked to Katina. Wasn't anything she did private? At least she knew Katina hadn't said anything to anyone about her distress.

But how was Lila to thwart Kintail from taking Faith for his mate? Then again, Cameron was looking more appealing all the time. She smiled at the thought he'd put Adams and Whitson in their place. Once Kintail had gotten them on the police force, the two had thought they were better than anybody else, not accountable to anyone—except for Kintail. They knew where they stood when it came to the pack leader.

But damn it, before that, they'd listened to her, too. Probably because they'd initially thought she'd be Kintail's mate. Now they weren't sure.

She stalked to the picture window and stared out at the woods where a few of Kintail's men were still searching for David and Owen. Kintail might think he was in charge of those two, but she could have told him David wasn't so much willing to go along with the scheme of things as he put on. She knew that he wasn't being just thoroughly grateful that he was still alive after suffering a massive heart attack. They were a lot alike in many ways—she was openly honest about some aspects of her life, and secretly dishonest about a lot more. But she couldn't help it. Some of her past life, she just didn't want to expose and didn't want to deal with.

David seemed that way to her, too.

But Elizabeth? She never suspected the woman would turn traitor and run off with the men. Yet she should have seen the signs. She'd seen a glimpse of Elizabeth observing David when she thought no one was watching her. But Lila hadn't put two and two together. Too wrapped up in her concern over Kintail. Yet in Lila's heart, something stirred. A desire to be like Elizabeth. To do what the woman had done, defy an alpha pack leader to choose a man she wanted to be with. Not that Lila truly wanted anyone but the pack leader. But she just wished she could show that side of herself again—that she wanted him, no other, and would stake her claim. What if she lost him though? That's what she thought she couldn't handle the most. Another mate's death.

She glanced down at the statue of an Arctic wolf sitting on a chest—a gift she'd given to Kintail. She tried to show she cared about Kintail. He was the typical arrogant alpha male leader who ran the pack, made the decisions, was in total control of everything that went on. And that appealed to her. But her past thwarted her when it came to having any kind of a relationship with a man.

And she suspected he sensed that, maybe concerned she'd never grow to love him. Which was probably why he hadn't mated her yet since she joined the pack two years ago, despite the fact that although there were several available women, none of them was alpha enough to lead the pack like her. She'd hoped when Trevor had told Kintail on her, the leader would have understood her better when she was having a devil of a time explaining herself to him. Even though she hadn't wanted Trevor to tell him her secrets like that. But what did Kintail do? Said he was going to take Faith for his own anyway. She jammed her hands in her pockets and growled.

Cameron she liked. Instantly. There was just something she admired about him. And she wanted him. But what if it all had to do with that she didn't know him that well, and he didn't know her? What if it was that she could only want attachments that weren't real? That once she got to know him, she'd have the same difficulty showing any affections toward him as she did with Kintail, too?

She ground her teeth, irritated that she couldn't get on with her life. She just had to get rid of the woman who was a constant reminder that both Kintail and Cameron coveted the cute little forensic scientist. And neither desired Lila. Yet.

Eliminate one threat, maybe Kintail would come around and give Lila another chance.

Baker had missed his calling. She didn't know how he botched his assignment so badly, failing to kill Faith at their campsite, but he did. She ran her fingers down the condensation on the window and stared out at the snowy setting, the forest perfectly still. Not a soul in sight. The lodge itself was eerily empty. The few men who had been left here who weren't trying to locate the killers of their pack members were running around in the woods, searching for their escapees now.

Time for her to change into the wolf and see if she could somehow isolate Miss O'Malley away from the others and do what Baker had failed to do. She reached for her sweater when snowmobiles zoomed up to the kitchen on the other side of the lodge, and she hesitated. Should she stay and see what news the others had? Maybe they'd located David or Owen or both. She'd have a good reason to go to Charles's resort then in the event she ran into Kintail. With news of the men's recapture. Or news of their escape and continued success at evasion of being recaptured, if no one had gone in search of Kintail to apprise him of the situation yet.

She'd warned everyone who had seen Elizabeth take off with the men that the woman had been forced to go with them. Even though a couple of the men seemed reluctant to spread that tale, she'd finally convinced them that David had hold of Elizabeth's hand and was tugging her along. That she hadn't gone of her own free will. Kintail would forgive Elizabeth, if Lila asked him to.

David and Owen? They were another story. She didn't think he'd listen to her about them. Even though she'd speak up for them, again. Kintail didn't like it when she'd let Owen get away with phoning Gavin. But she thought maybe he'd get the message across that they were quitting the job and Gavin would let them go. Didn't work, but she'd tried to help.

A door creaked open to the kitchen. But she didn't hear anyone speaking, which she thought odd. Whoever they were noisily tromped on the tiled kitchen floor, and then loud male whispers reached her ears—but not of anyone she recognized. And no one she knew would have spoken in hushed voices at the lodge.

The hair on her neck stood on end.

—⁓—

Kintail had one thought in mind when he arrived at Charles's cabin resort—turn Faith O'Malley before his brother did. When he focused on a single area of interest, he got results. Plain and simple. Until he reached Charles's lodge and saw Charles's cousin George, his eyes widening at the wolf sight of Kintail. George knew him, knew Kintail wasn't any threat to George and his people. But the expression on George's face meant Kintail could expect trouble.

Except not as much as he ever bargained for.

Silently, George waved for him to come into the lodge. Kintail loped inside, his temper already rising.

"In here." George motioned to Charles's office. "I'll get you a change of clothes."

Kintail paced. What the hell had happened now?

It seemed to take forever for George to return with a handful of clothes. He set them on the leather love seat by the window and then bowed his head slightly and left the room, closing the door behind him.

Kintail shifted faster than he thought possible, and quickly shoved on the trousers, not bothering with the shirt or sweater. "Come in," Kintail hollered, not liking any of this one bit.

George pulled the door open and hesitated to enter until Kintail motioned him to the love seat. "What's happened?"

George was Charles's younger cousin, definitely not an alpha, and if Charles wasn't still at the hospital under observation for the blow to his skull, he was certain, George would have much preferred Charles to talk to him. Kintail wondered where George's older brother, Michael was, who was always in charge if Charles was absent. Maybe he was with Charles.

"Tell me."

George took a seat and wrung his hands, his eyes avoiding Kintail's glower. "Officer Adams and Whitson were injured badly in a snowmobile accident. Michael took them both to the hospital. We couldn't wait to get word to you to send your people here to take care of them. But they'll both be all right, several broken bones, Adams had a concussion."

Kintail stared at him in disbelief. "How did it happen?"

George shook his head, still not looking Kintail eye to eye.

"Guess."

George's gaze flicked his way, and then returned to study the floor. "They were following Cameron and Faith. We think they might have run into a barricade."

"A barricade."

"Yes, hastily made on a trail through the woods. A felled tree had blocked the main road, probably dropped down by whoever is doing the same on other roads and trails in the area. It appeared Cameron and Faith took a trail into the woods to go around the obstacle. Adams said that Cameron was joined by another man. I later found out it was his partner, Gavin Summerfield."

"Where's Faith now?"

"She's at Leidolf's cabin, but she and Cameron are returning to the Black Bear Den to talk with Trevor."

The way George fidgeted, Kintail suspected there was other news. "What else?"

George rose unsteadily from the chair. "Your brother's been shot. He was in his wolf form and knocked Cameron from his snowmobile. Cameron's partner, Gavin, shot Hilson four times, afraid the wolf planned to kill Cameron. Hilson's resting in Charles's bedroom, feeling well enough to demand three meals already, but not in any shape to go anywhere. Because of the bullet wounds, we couldn't risk transporting him to the hospital and the questions that would follow."

Kintail clenched and unclenched his fists. Half the time he was perturbed with his brother, and he couldn't help being annoyed that Hilson had gone against his wishes, but when it came right down to it, he was Kintail's brother. Damn it.

Cameron and Gavin were dead men.

Kintail hated to ask, although he couldn't imagine anything else could have gone wrong. "Anything else?"

George paused at the office door, his gaze finally focusing on Kintail's. "Cameron's partners escaped your lodge. Elizabeth's with them."

Chapter 18

As soon as Owen and David heard snowmobiles, they darted deeper into the woods with Elizabeth, knowing Kintail's people wouldn't give up on trying to return them to Kintail's lodge. They'd dodged them several times already, and Owen was slightly worried the men were trying to corral them. But he was pretty sure he, David, and Elizabeth were getting closer to Charles's resort also.

That's when he thought something was different about the men in pursuit of them. The snowmobiles were plain noisy, no masking the sound. But they had never heard a peep out of the men stalking them in silence, just like wolves on the hunt. And Owen felt a kinship to them, understood their ways.

Now he heard shouts of glee, "Woohoo!" "There they are!" like kids at a circus. And that's when he felt in his bones, the predators had changed. They might sound like silly ass kids, but his gut instinct told him they were a hell of a lot more dangerous than Kintail's people.

David tensed, his hackles raised, his ears twitching back and forth. He recognized the change in their circumstances, too. And Elizabeth appeared almost frantic, running between David and Owen, panicked. He didn't believe she'd feel that way about her own people.

They had to reach the cabins. There, they could join forces with Cameron and Gavin, if he'd already arrived. There, they stood a chance.

—∿∿—

"Trevor can't be here to speak to us about Bigfoot," Faith said, getting dressed while Cameron watched her in Leidolf's bedroom. Cameron looked like he could devour her in one wolfish bite. She raised a brow at him as she pulled on her pants.

He smiled back, the look just as devious.

"Pay attention, Cameron. We can't allow Gavin to be in the same room with us when we talk to Trevor."

Cameron ran his hands down Faith's sweater-covered arms, then held her hands tightly. "I don't want to lose you ever, Faith."

She gave him a coy smile back. "I have news for you. You're not getting rid of me that easily."

He pulled her into his embrace and squeezed the breath out of her, his hands sweeping down her back, his body pressed against her, already hard and wanting. If they hadn't had important matters to take care of, she would have been willing to relieve both his needs and her own right this very minute.

"I thought I might have lost you. I even clobbered poor Gavin when he mentioned you running off with Leidolf and having wolf pups."

Faith's lips parted slightly. "Wolf pups? What next?" She didn't even want to think about that scenario. Although if Leidolf's assumption was right, the mistake she and Cameron had made with not using a condom the last time wouldn't have mattered, not if a werewolf couldn't get a human pregnant.

Cameron held onto her tight as if he was afraid he truly had lost her, and she loved the way he was—protective, desiring her and only her, and a little bit jealous that anyone else might want her.

But with Gavin in the next room, and unable to focus on much more than getting this business with Kintail over with, she pulled free from Cameron's embrace. "Let's see what Trevor has to say."

Cameron slipped his hand over hers and held it tight, his gaze saying other issues were at stake and just as important to him. But for her, business always came before pleasure, although she snuggled up against him to reassure him she was just as willing. That seemed to relieve some of his tension, and he hugged her close as he opened the bedroom door.

As soon as they left Leidolf's bedroom, the appraising look Gavin gave her and the small smile that sparkled in his eyes told her he approved. She noted the bruise on the side of his jaw, though, and hoped he and Cameron weren't too mad at each other. He probably couldn't figure out what had set Cameron off like that. If only he had known.

She squeezed Cameron's hand and the three headed out of doors.

"So," Gavin said as he mounted his snowmobile, and Faith climbed onto Cameron's with him, "I understand Cameron named a female wolf after you."

Faith smiled, closing her arms around Cameron's waist, hugging him tight. "Yes, sweet of him, wasn't it?"

Gavin looked to see Cameron's reaction, but he seemed deep in thought because he never said anything in response, but she wondered if he'd made the slip inadvertently or deep down, he wanted his friend to know she and the wolf were the same.

When they arrived at the cabin, Leidolf and Trevor were standing on the deck, watching their approach. At least that's who she assumed the gray-haired man was. His gray eyes seemed wary when he observed Gavin, but he seemed pleased to see Faith, although his eyes widened a bit and then he seemed surprised as she, Cameron, and Gavin joined him on the deck.

"I wish a word with only the young lady, if you don't mind," Trevor said, speaking to Cameron.

Cameron put his arm around her shoulder. "We stay together."

Trevor flicked a glance Gavin's way, then said to Cameron, "It's private."

"I'll talk to him." Faith wanted to hear the news Trevor had from Kintail, but if the hunter insisted, she'd speak with him alone. They couldn't include Gavin; that much was clear.

"Leidolf and Gavin can wait out here for us, but I stay with the lady," Cameron said, his voice a barely controlled growl.

She was beginning to think his losing her for a while when she turned into the wolf had really affected him worse than she'd first thought. "The two of us, then."

Trevor bowed his head slightly, although he looked displeased.

Cameron opened the door for them, and after closing it behind them, they took seats at the dining room table.

"Who bit you?" Trevor asked first.

Cameron tensed at once. She folded her arms. "You were supposed to tell me about my father's trip out here."

Trevor took a deep breath and leaned back in the chair. "All right. I suppose it really doesn't matter who bit you, but Kintail will be displeased." His eyes remained focused on Faith's as he continued. "I really liked your father. He had a great sense of humor, spoke privately to me about his real purpose here, to observe the Bigfoot hunters while he did a research paper. On the hunt, we spotted nothing but a bird occasionally and a rabbit. Until the guys on the expedition found wolf tracks and thought they might have been a small Bigfoot, although from what I've ever heard, the footprint is supposed to be more like a human's print, not a wolf's. But since we weren't finding anything else, and the prints were old, I allowed the men to follow them. At the same time, your father took copious notes on the group's behavior, casting me small smiles unobserved by the others on the team. Although they were grown men, they behaved like excited teens playing a video game."

"But my father saw something he shouldn't have."

"I was supposed to perpetuate the Bigfoot myth with you, but Kintail doesn't know you're one of us now. So yes, your father and I became separated from the team. They'd run off wildly into the woods after the old wolf trail. Your father got a stitch in his side and I waited with him, figuring I could catch up to the team members if they got lost, when I spied Lila in the forest. She was stripping out of her clothes, then shifted into the wolf. I don't know what she was up to, didn't want to tell Kintail in case it was something he didn't want to hear, and I didn't speak of it to your father. I hoped he had been too busy writing notes to have noticed. Well, he was busy writing, but I hoped it was about the team and their behavior rather than anything he had seen with respect to Lila."

"You didn't ask him?"

"I'm not dumb. Self-preservation for our kind is tantamount. I did like your father, but exposing our kind to the world is not something any of us want. So when everyone was asleep in the tents that night, I read through your father's notes. He said nothing about what he'd seen. But he was strangely quiet the rest of the time. As if he had seen Lila shift. As if he had seen me observe her. But most telling, I said nothing. Which for him—for a sociologist—was just as telling. I couldn't know that for sure, though. Just speculation on my part."

"But if you didn't tell anyone, how did Hilson learn of it?"

Trevor snorted. "Here I was afraid to get Lila in trouble, and she managed to turn the trick. Probably figuring she better do so before I did. Anyway, she wasn't supposed to change in the open like that, and certainly not with so many humans close by. But I denied that your father saw anything. Hilson took it upon himself to watch your father, following him all the way back to Portland."

"And when he couldn't get enough information from him from a distance?"

"I imagine he approached you."

"So now what do we do? My father is at risk, isn't he?"

Trevor didn't say anything.

Faith took in a deep breath. "I don't want him killed."

"It's not up to you."

But it was, damn it. Fine, no way did she want to bite her father and turn him into what she was, but she didn't want him dead either. "What about Cameron's friends?"

Trevor had been sitting so regally, so confident, until she mentioned that part of the equation. Then he fidgeted a bit, his hands on the table, then back off the table, on his lap, hidden. He glanced Cameron's way and looked back at Faith. "Both of you are in danger if you remain here. Kintail…"

"Where are they?" a man roared to Leidolf and Gavin, stalking across the deck outside.

Immediately Trevor rose from the table and said under his breath, "Kintail."

The door flew open and a giant of a man barged in, as tall as Hilson, but instead of being an overstuffed teddy bear, this guy looked like an enraged polar bear standing in the entryway, filling the entryway, blocking out the sun. Blond hair nearly white, square jaw clenched, his narrowed pale yellow eyes shifted from Trevor to Cameron… to Faith. Clenched fists swung at the polar bear's side as he strode into the cabin where Cameron had already pulled Faith to his side, close, protecting her. The hulking man got in their space. Maybe it was fine for a wolf's space, or the way an alpha showed dominance, but it was much too close for Faith's liking and as tense as Cameron was, he didn't like it either.

Faith felt the heat of Kintail's body, the smell of the fresh wind on him, saw specks of black in his eyes that seemed to expand and consume the pale yellow color as he turned his angry gaze from Trevor to Cameron.

Cameron didn't move until the man flicked a look Faith's way, the same kind of threatening expression— yet there was a hint of something else, interest maybe?

Intrigue? Garnering her attention again, Cameron tightened his hand on Faith's back, squeezing her closer.

The man growled something under his breath, jerked his lethal eyes back to Cameron, then turned to look at the open doorway. Both Gavin and Leidolf had moved inside, waiting, anticipating trouble, ready to be of service.

"This is private," he snapped at Gavin, ignoring Leidolf.

Faith felt badly for Gavin who wanted to stick by his partner's side, but was being dismissed by everyone he came in contact with, even his own partner.

"Do you want me to talk to Gavin about the situation?" Trevor offered, his voice rather meek, and Faith hated that he seemed cowed before the great Kintail.

"Yes, take him up to the lodge." Kintail glanced at Gavin. "We have a pack of serial killers on the loose. We could use your services since you and Cameron put two of the police officers working the case, who were coming to ask your aid in solving this crime, in the hospital."

Gavin looked a little gray. Cameron motioned for him to leave with Trevor. Kintail glowered at Leidolf. "He can go with you also."

Leidolf gave Kintail a sinister smile, then bowed his head slightly and left with Trevor and Gavin, shutting the door behind them.

"Where the hell are my partners, Kintail?" Cameron asked, his hand rubbing Faith's shoulder, but his whole body vibrated with anger.

"They're gone, slipped away. My people haven't located them yet."

"You want our help finding your killers, then we do this my way," Cameron said.

"Our way," Faith corrected him. If she was going to be an alpha pack leader's mate, it would be an equal partnership. She smiled at Cameron when he frowned down at her.

For the first time, a hint of amusement crossed Kintail's face. But then he was back to being dour again. "You can't have your men—"

"I want them here with me. With the four of..." Cameron paused. "... five of us, well six if Leidolf wants to still help, we'll catch these killers. But we won't bother otherwise. Our sole focus is locating my partners and getting them out of here."

"Are you quite finished?" Kintail asked, folding his arms.

"I don't want my father killed," Faith said, choking a little on the words when she had planned to sound as firm and forthright as Cameron.

"It's not up to me," Kintail said, his words softening.

"What do you mean it's not up to you? You sent Hilson after him, right?"

"No, he went on his own, but Kenneth O'Malley is in Leidolf's territory. He'll have to deal with him now."

Faith just stared at Kintail, the words sifting through her brain but not making any sense. Why didn't Leidolf say anything before this? Because he thought she would be upset if she heard what he intended to do? She was torn between racing to the lodge and forcing Leidolf's response and staying with Cameron to provide a unified front until they got his concession concerning his partners.

"We'll talk to Leidolf, Faith," Cameron said, then kissed her cheek. The threat in his voice indicated they'd get their way on this so not to worry. But she did worry. What if they weren't in time? What if they were already too late?

Cameron focused again on Kintail. "Do we have a deal? My partners released to me in exchange for our help in finding your serial killers?"

"I told you, they escaped. They're on their own now, most likely headed in this direction."

"But you have men trying to recapture them, don't you?" Cameron asked.

Kintail abruptly sat down at the table and drummed his long fingers on the oak top, his gaze fixed on Faith, his unspoken word speaking volumes. He wanted Faith, and he was bound to have her. As for Cameron's partners? He didn't seem willing to give them up easily either. Which meant?

Cameron was a dead man.

She refused to back down from Kintail's impertinent gaze, furrowed her brow and gave him the devil back. His lips lifted slightly.

Very low, very dark, and very meaningfully, Cameron said, "She's mine."

She squeezed his waist, glad he'd stand up to Kintail.

Conceited, all knowing, Kintail's gaze slowly switched to Cameron as if he were an insignificant gnat. "You're a newbie, don't have a clue what you're doing, or the ramifications of what you are now. She needs someone with experience. Someone like me." But he didn't emphasize the *someone* as much as he did the *me*.

"We're mated," Faith said.

Kintail raised his brows at her.

"Leidolf said that if wolves are mated, they can't seek anyone else. So Cameron and I are mated. You'll have to stick with Lila or someone else who can put up with you."

This time Kintail's smile was slightly more than a hint, as if she'd really amused him, and as if he wasn't used to showing a lighter side of his personality and didn't know how to do it. But the smile wasn't a good indication because it meant—at least to her way of thinking—he either didn't believe she and Cameron were mated, which according to their werewolf traditions, they weren't, or he didn't care. In which case that reverted back to the case of—Cameron was a dead man.

~~~

The snowmobilers were running David and Owen ragged as they tried to protect Elizabeth, but to no avail. If the two men hadn't had such healthy hearts after they'd been turned, Owen figured they'd have been run to death by now. When he smelled wood smoke and the lake, he guessed they were close to Charles's resort. But they couldn't move any closer. Every time they tried to dive through the spruces, another snowmobiler hemmed them in.

Then one of the men pulled in front of Owen and yanked out a gun. If they were the guys who were killing the werewolves, the bullets would be silver and the three of them were good as dead. Kintail's men never resorted to guns, except on a hunt. But never to track Owen down, even the last two times he'd escaped.

He lunged, ready to kill the man when something hit him in the flank with a sharp stab of pain. He yelped. And fell in midair, landing on his belly. What the hell, he thought, his mind drifting like the sparse clouds in the darkening blue sky.

David nudged his face with his nose as if telling him to get up. He could smell David's fear, but then a shot was fired again, and David collapsed against his legs. Elizabeth growled and lunged for one of the shooters and a third shot was fired. She yelped and collapsed. David growled low from his prone position in the snow. Owen wished David had been given the chance to have had a life with Elizabeth. Owen always figured he and a partner might die together on a mission. He only wished they'd accomplished it, ensured Elizabeth's safety, and seen Cameron and Gavin one last time.

———

Incarcerated at some unknown location, Lila stalked back and forth across the basement that smelled like wet cement, musty and moldy. If she'd had allergies, she figured she'd be sneezing her head off. She glowered at David, Owen, and Elizabeth sleeping still as wolves in the big cage against the wall, angered they wouldn't wake up, as many times as she'd poked at them through the bars with a cane she had found behind a bunch of old crates.

She began pacing again. Fourteen steps led to the door to the basement. Forty steps across the main floor both ways. The windowless room was dark, but she could see just fine. She stopped and listened. Traffic noises. They were in a town or city. Millinocket maybe?

She paced again. Thankfully, they didn't think a female werewolf was as dangerous as a male, and so they'd taken her without drugging her. She hadn't fought them either, because a female in human form was no match for three human males. So they'd treated her like a lady. She knew they had to be the ones who killed Sutter at their office, from the scent the redhead had—deodorant not working, aftershave smelled like pine floor cleaner—but they couldn't get a scent of the killer at the other crime scene. Not with the blizzard wreaking havoc with it.

But once Kintail and his men got through with these killers, she was ready to return to the frigid Canadian Arctic for a vacation. At that instant, she realized Kintail was the one she looked for to rescue her. Not Cameron, the newly turned wolf. But Kintail, centuries-old Kintail, who would locate her and free her, and if she played her cards right, she would show him just how much she appreciated the rescue. Some part of her finally recognized she'd been holding onto the past, unwilling to let go, feeling as though her mate and child's death were her own damn fault. Yet deep down, she knew it wasn't. Knew her mate wanted the role of alpha pack leader, knew he couldn't win it. She'd only wanted him, but he hadn't been happy as the second in command. And he'd died for it.

She paced across the floor some more. So why did she feel at fault? She was an alpha female, and he felt inferior not being the alpha leader. But she knew he'd never make it against the leader. And little Tristen just got in the way when the two men fought. No one could protect him when her mate and the leader tore into each other.

Lila closed her eyes and rested her hand against the wall for support. It wasn't her fault. She hadn't pushed her mate to fight the leader. She'd been assisting another female in labor, so her mate was supposed to have been watching Tristen. It wasn't her fault.

Wiping away tears, she climbed the creaky stairs again, pressed her ear against the wooden door, and listened.

Kintail still had a thing for that Faith O'Malley. If Lila eliminated her, Kintail would know it. He'd condemn her to death or send her far, far away.

Which made her take stock of what she had… a winter lodge here, a summer lodge up north, a bunch of pack members that treated her like the alpha pack leader's mate, even if she wasn't Kintail's chosen mate, yet. And what of Kintail?

Two years ago, he'd tried to encourage her interest in him when she'd fled the pack, where the politics were brutal, her mate murdered, and her child killed. She hadn't known how to live. Or love again.

Kintail had been so patient with her, waiting, watching, and finally giving up on her when Faith O'Malley suddenly appeared. But she wondered if some of his attraction to Faith had to do with his brother wanting her first. Lila didn't really think Hilson loved her or he would have turned her and mated with her three months ago. Or maybe Kintail's interest in her only had to do with Lila's refusal to show him any real affection.

She growled at her inability to change back to the person she was, the person before her beloved mate and son were murdered.

She reconsidered Faith and what she had to offer Kintail. The woman was a neophyte. It would take eons for her to understand their ways. Kintail couldn't want that. Maybe he was trying to get Lila to give up her loss, her secrets, to move on, forcing her by showing an interest in another woman.

Then she heard movement somewhere in the house, footfalls walking from one room to another. No voices though. She wanted to hear voices, to get details. A house number and street name would be nice. A warning to the others that Kintail was on his way to free her would also be welcome news.

She waited, just as if she was on a hunt, patient, all ears, waiting.

She thought back to how she'd gotten here, tried to recollect anything that might help her pinpoint the location. They'd pulled a black hood over her head, but she'd memorized the amount of time she'd spent on a snowmobile, and then in a vehicle, the roar of the engine sounding like a pickup, and the amount of time on the road. That's why she thought she was in Millinocket. Not too far away, but far enough. The killers' home base.

She knew how many steps it took from the front door of the house, or a back door, into a long hallway, and then to the basement door. Waxed wooden floors that were a little slick, the smell of gingerbread cookies baking in the oven, the sound of New Age music drifting from another room had greeted her when she arrived. The place had been almost uncomfortably warm, but not the basement.

As soon as she was taken to the basement, the temperature had dropped a good thirty degrees. When she had asked if they could give her a coat, the redhead

Chapter 19

CAMERON DIDN'T TRUST KINTAIL ONE BIT, BUT MAYBE, JUST maybe if Cameron could help the pack leader with his troubles, Kintail would change his mind. If Kintail didn't, Cameron assumed there was only one way to deal with it—wolf to wolf. And ancient or not, Kintail would not win this battle. Not when Cameron had so much to lose.

"All right," Kintail said, and rose from the table. "I'll call off my people and let Owen and David make their way here under their own power. From the time they left the place, and if they're running as wolves, they should be here within the next hour or so. Find the bastards who killed my men, but let me deal with them in my own way."

Cameron shook on it, although he didn't know what he'd do when the time actually came. The idea of just killing the men in cold blood didn't appeal. Yet if he and his kind were exposed now, he was sure that they would have an even worse nightmare.

Kintail whipped around and headed out the door, slamming it behind him.

Faith let out her breath and wrapped her arms around Cameron's neck, her gaze worried. "What do we do first?"

"We're going to have a problem with Gavin." Cameron stroked his hands down her sides, attempting to reassure her. "We can't tell him what we're exactly just smiled. "Grow a fur coat," he said, his companions all laughing, then they left her alone in the basement in darkness.

Which suited her just fine.

About two hours after that? They brought in this huge cage bearing the Three Stooges. Sleeping a long winter's nap like a bunch of damned polar bears. David, Owen, and Elizabeth. Kintail's people didn't recapture them… nope, the killers had to.

She let out her breath as she stared down into the basement at the three wolves, glad the killers hadn't eliminated them or her, yet. She wondered why they took them into custody this time. Why didn't they just kill them outright?

Hopefully they didn't plan to dissect them or torture them into telling the truth about their existence. What if that's what this was all about now? The Dark Angels didn't plan to rid the world of the scourge of werewolves now, but wanted to make a real name for themselves. The famous Dark Angels who discovered the real existence of werewolves.

She ground her teeth and listened again at the door, figuring if she could ever wake up the sleeping beauty trio and conjure up a way to get them out of the cage, they'd show the Dark Angels how dangerous it was to deal with darkly angered *lupus garous*.

up against. He'll think these bastards are crazy, and he can help us locate them, but beyond that, it'll be too easy for one of us to slip up and show our true nature now."

Someone walked up onto the deck and knocked at the door. "Yes," Cameron hollered.

"It's me, Gavin."

"Come in."

Gavin opened the door, smiled when he saw Faith and Cameron in a hug, then closed the door. "I don't understand what's going on. Trevor said David and Owen are still hunting and that communications are just not available where they are. Which is understandable. I researched the place and read where the owners of several lodges told guests to leave laptops and cell phones behind because they don't work out here. No land phones, nothing. Now, this Kintail has asked us to search for serial killers, but from what I gather, he's a winter resident here, not even a permanent year-round resident. He's not a police chief or anything. So what's the deal?"

"Which as private investigators is why it's right up our alley," Cameron said smoothly, offering Gavin a chair. "The two men who were killed were employees of his. That's why he's so concerned. He's afraid someone is targeting his people, and if we don't catch these bastards soon, there'll be more deaths."

"Want some green tea or cocoa?" Faith asked, moving to the kitchen to turn on the stove.

"Cocoa," both men responded.

"So it's not an official investigation?" Gavin asked.

"The police are definitely looking into it. They've had two murders, one out here by the lake and one at

Kintail's office in Millinocket. But they don't have the resources to analyze all the clues or find the killers."

"Then it must be connected to his hunting business." Gavin looked in Faith's direction. "What about the little lady? Isn't this kind of out of her area of expertise? I mean, this could get dangerous, and I wouldn't think you'd want her involved."

Faith didn't look in his direction, but smiled a little.

"She's a forensic scientist, works for the police in Portland."

Gavin stared at her. "Well, hot damn. Beauty and brains all in one package. Send you on a rescue mission and instead… hey, wait, so what was the deal with the guy in the gray pickup stalking her?"

"Just Kintail's people wanting to get in touch with her about her father's research here."

"Which was about Bigfoot?" Gavin smiled. "Did Cameron tell you we went on one of the Bigfoot hunts in Washington State once?"

"You did?" She raised her brows at Cameron.

He shook his head and joined her at the stove, resting his hands on her hips and kissed her cheek. "Yeah, but they're not real, you know."

"All four of us went," Gavin continued. "We were actually tracking down a deadbeat ex-husband who owed child support. We heard he was on one of those Bigfoot hunts so we hoped to catch him."

"Bigfoot or the deadbeat husband?" she asked.

Cameron wrapped his arms around her waist and pulled her snug. "The deadbeat husband. We always catch our man… or woman."

She smiled back at him. "And Bigfoot?"

Gavin cleared his throat. "Missed him completely. But you know, hunters can go on hunts looking for known prey in an area and still not run across them. Even if the prey really exists. So what's the plan now? Trevor said you'd already been to both crime scenes, so what's the verdict?"

"I've only been to the one at Kintail's office." Faith stirred the cocoa into the mugs, then handed them to Cameron. "At least that one appeared to have been killed by silver poisoning."

When Gavin stared at her in disbelief, Faith shrugged. "Lots of silver remedies claim all kinds of health cures. So you can get them either online or in health food stores. When people ingest silver, the condition is called Argyria. But it's not a good way to kill someone. Slow silver poisoning can permanently turn skin gray."

"Sounds like you've got a keeper, Cameron," Gavin said with a wink.

But he knew from the slight sarcasm in the tone of his voice, Gavin didn't think Cameron had what it took to make this relationship work either. But he and Faith had more in common than they ever thought possible. And he planned to hang onto her. The problem was, retaining Gavin in the partnership. He wondered, too, if David and Owen had changed any personality-wise after being turned. Would they be able to stay together as a team after all this was over with? If his friends were even all right?

"So what's next?" Gavin asked.

"I think the three men who were in the hot tub with us the one night, are the ones who killed the men," Faith said.

Again, Gavin looked surprised.

Cameron smiled a little. "Like you said, she's a keeper."

"What makes you think the three men had anything to do with it?" Gavin asked her.

"They said so, in so many words. If Trevor didn't tell you already, the killers are werewolf hunters. They believe that werewolves exist just as much as Bigfoot does. So they injected at least the first of the two men with silver, believing that he was a werewolf and it would destroy him. The only thing is, it can kill anyone, so his death isn't really proof that the guys are werewolves. They've seen Kintail's Arctic wolves and believe they're werewolves and anyone who has anything to do with them are, too."

Gavin switched his attention to Cameron. "Did you ever find your wolf?"

"She's back with Kintail's pack."

Gavin leaned his head back and opened his mouth to speak, then looking as though he thought better of it, he closed his mouth and said, "Hmm."

Yeah, that would take some explaining. First, Cameron's frantic about "his" wolf, and now he didn't care anything about her because she was back with Kintail's pack. He could see how complicated things were going to get without telling the whole truth of the matter.

"So then what do we do first?" Gavin asked.

Faith pointed the spoon she'd been stirring the cocoa with at Cameron. "What if the guys in the hot tub were the ones who stole our snowmobiles? You said that the man yelling was a distraction that drew you from the cabin so that while you were gone, they could steal the machines."

"Because you were the weaker sex." Cameron smiled when Faith did. He turned to Gavin. "You should see what she did to my snowmobile."

"You mean that huge dent in the backside?" Gavin asked. His expression showed even more admiration for Faith.

"She wields a heavy cast-iron frying pan like an Olympic disc thrower."

"Ha! If I could do that well, I would have hit the driver, not the vehicle."

"Probably would have killed him. I take it you had another theory about them stealing the machines?" Cameron asked.

"Yeah, what if they were afraid you were going to find the body, and so they took off with our machines to divert our attention. That way if the man was still alive, he would have frozen to death overnight. The police came in the morning and asked us where we'd been during the night. After the men stole our machines, they get in the hot tub with us, and voila! The machines are around the backside of the shower building. They probably had... wait! I was thinking, what if they were staying at one of the cabins while it was closed for renovations. But I didn't want to check it out without you being there. Then we got distracted when Charles said he'd take us to see Trevor."

Cameron rose from his chair. "Where did Leidolf go, Gavin?"

Gavin motioned to his cabin down the trail. "He said if we wanted his help, to come get him. He was up a lot last night and went back to the cabin to take a nap."

"Let's go. Weapon reloaded?"

Gavin nodded. "When I was listening to Trevor. I wanted him to know that I was armed and dangerous if he was on the wrong side of the law."

That's when Cameron wondered if Kintail knew yet about Gavin shooting Hilson. He set the mugs in the dry sink and poured water into them. "I'll wash them when we return." He pulled on his parka while Faith got hers on.

Gavin looked again at Cameron's sleeve. "Faith, the wolf, wouldn't have had anything to do with the way your sleeve looks, would she have?"

"No," Faith said, walking out ahead of the men. "She's the one that saved Cameron's butt."

Cameron shrugged at Gavin. "Actually, you're looking right at her. Faith, the woman, clobbered the wolf with a healthy swing of a snow shovel. That little lady is not someone you ever want to piss off."

Gavin chuckled. "Sounds like you've met more than your match." He climbed onto his snowmobile and turned to Cameron. "So what's the real story about David and Owen?"

Kintail had barely returned Hilson to his own lodge when six of his people hurried to greet him, everyone of them looking like he was going to beat them within an inch of their life. "What's happened?" But he suspected it had to do with David and Owen and that they hadn't recaptured them.

Well, that was one bargaining chip he'd lost. Although he hadn't intended to give them up, ever. They were much better off with him since he knew the ropes and could keep his people safe. Normally. The *lupus garou* killers were another story though.

"Lila's gone. They came through the kitchen. You can smell their scents," Whitson said, limping around in a walking cast, one eye blackened, but at least Cameron hadn't killed him.

"Wait, what? Some damned human came here and Lila went with him?"

"No," Whitson said, his expression more than concerned. "From the smell of them, it appears there were three of them, all male. One of them was the same we smelled in your offices in Millinocket where Sutter died. Lila was alone while the rest of our people were trying to track down David and Owen when these men took her. And Elizabeth went with David and Owen, if you didn't get word."

Kintail stared at Whitson, shook his head, and stormed down the hall to the kitchen. He walked into it, lifted his nose, and smelled. The humans' scents were unmistakable, sweaty with fear, doused with heavy spicy colognes, mixed with the lingering aroma of roast and gravy still clinging to the air.

His voice fierce, he growled, "Where'd they take Lila?" He stalked back into the great room where Hilson was sitting on one of the couches, still looking pretty beat up from the gunshot wounds.

Whitson shook his head as he hurried after him. "We're not sure. A couple of our men think maybe they grabbed Cameron's partners and Elizabeth also. They saw some snowmobilers, not any of our own people. So our people backed off when they saw these guys had guns. Immediately they worried they might be the killers and if they were, their bullets would be silver. Since the wolves they were after weren't part of the original pack, and Elizabeth chose to go with them, they didn't feel any need to go getting themselves killed over them."

Kintail swore under his breath and gave the men gathered a steely eyed glower. "We're a damned pack. So act like one. One for all and all for one. Whether we have new men or women, or we were born that way. Hell." He stared out the window. "Did you see any bodies afterward?"

"No bodies," one of his men said. "After they left, we searched the area and found where the wolves had lain in the snow. We think they carried the bodies away this time. Maybe thinking they have proof we're werewolves? The tracks led toward Millinocket. We didn't want to get too close. We heard gunshots, three of them, and figured the men and Elizabeth were dead. They shouldn't have run off."

Unable to shake loose of the misery he felt, Kintail said, "It wouldn't have mattered, it seems. They took Lila."

"Because they ran off, we were out looking for them. That's how they got Lila."

Kintail didn't think it would matter to him one way or another as detached as she'd been toward him ever since he'd brought her into the pack. He knew she'd had difficulties from where she was from, but she'd never discuss it with him, and he'd never wanted to pry. But after what Trevor had told him, he was rethinking her plight and now, he couldn't help worrying about her. She didn't deserve to die at the hands of these lunatics. She was a member of his pack, to protect always, even if she didn't want to be his mate. "Where did they take her?"

"The snowmobiles reached the trailhead, then the tracks disappeared. We really think they're somewhere in Millinocket."

"Gather all our men. Send word to Cameron and his partner, Gavin, whoever's doing the killings has either taken his men hostage or killed them. And make sure they know they've got Lila and another of my females, too, that they're probably alive and hostages for now."

Hilson held his side where Gavin managed to shoot him all four times. "I'm going."

"Like hell you are. Just stay here and recuperate."

"You can't have her, Kintail," his brother growled.

"What? You never changed her, never mated with her. It's too late for you to have her."

Hilson gave him a sour look. But Kintail knew his brother well. If he really had wanted her, he would have taken her. Which meant the woman was up for grabs. Although, he was seriously considering giving her to one of his other bachelor males, any of whom would be eager to have the woman. "You shouldn't have gone after Cameron against my orders."

"I couldn't let him have her. But damn it, someone had already turned her."

Kintail suspected Cameron had done it, but of his own free will, or by accident?

Whitson limped over to the couch. "What do you want me to do?"

Kintail shook his head. "Babysit my brother. The two of you are a pair." He stalked out of the house, hoping to hell he could end this nightmare once and for all in short order, and Lila would be so grateful, she'd have a change of heart concerning him.

---※---

Owen woke from the worst nightmare he'd ever had about being pursued by wolves on snowmobiles, to a nightmare he was still living as he realized he, David, and Elizabeth were caged and locked in a basement. Not Kintail's either. He poked his snout at David, who looked up sleepily at him. Then they both considered where they were, a large cage in a moldy wet basement. David hurried to nose Elizabeth's face, trying to wake her.

And Lila?

Eyes widening, Owen stared at her. How the hell did *she* get here?

Sitting on the bottom step of the stairs leading out of the basement, she leaned against the wall, her eyes closed. It looked as though she was every bit as much a hostage as they were. Which was probably good. Kintail would want her back, even though they seemed to share a lot of animosity. Still, she was his pack member, and he seemed really protective and possessive of everyone in the pack.

Everything was dark in the room, but they could see as if it was a cloudy day. Traffic noises could be heard, not a lot, but a horn blew, and cars speeding up at a traffic light, slushing through melting snow on the roadways rushed nearby. They were in town. Maybe Millinocket? It wasn't far from the cabin resorts, maybe an hour and a half at most.

What they needed was a window. Well, that and a crowbar. Too bad their pursuers had taken only Lila hostage. She had some wicked teeth when she was in her wolf form, but they needed a couple of more guys with muscle instead.

Owen stood, stretched the kinks out of his wolf's body, then walked over to the padlock on the cage. Looked like an old one, slightly rusted, and… it was a combination lock. Like an old school lock. If he could shapeshift, although he was rather reluctant in the event he couldn't shift back before the killers returned, he figured he could decipher the combination. But if they caught him in his human form, he'd have proved their theory if they had any doubts. But also, he'd be naked and freezing.

He made a little woof sound. Lila didn't stir. He did it again. David and Elizabeth joined him and looked at the padlock.

Lila's eyes snapped open. "Jeez, it's about time you three woke up."

Owen poked at the padlock. She stared at him, then the lock. "I can't open it. I tried."

He poked his nose at the lock again and looked at her. "All right, but it won't work."

She crossed the floor and lifted the lock, then twisted the knob around real slowly. As soon as he heard the telltale click of the tumbler being in place, he nudged her hand with his nose.

She smiled, then twisted it in the opposite direction for the next number. Closer this time. He nudged her hand again. "Good boy," she said.

He growled and she chuckled. She turned the knob in the same direction as the first time. When he heard the click, he pushed her hand, but he was afraid either he'd moved too slowly or she was a little too enthusiastic and moved too quickly this time, not allowing him time to react.

She paused and looked at him. He shook his head, but she pulled on the lock anyway. Nothing.

"It's okay, I've got the first two numbers down, and the third was just a couple before that I think." She tried again, but twisted the knob even slower on the third number.

He bumped her and this time when she pulled, the lock opened, and she jerked it off the cage. He wanted to howl! Howl. That's how they could get word to the others. If anyone heard them it would most likely be Kintail's people, but only if any of them were nearby and could hear a wolf howling from a basement without windows. If the men who took them prisoner heard them? Either they'd shoot them with tranquilizers or shoot them with silver bullets. Neither a good scenario.

She pulled the cage door open and motioned for them to come out. "I haven't really been a good pack member as far as the two of you are concerned, but believe me right about now, all of you are the closest thing to a dream come true." She gave each of them a hug, and they licked her cheeks in response.

One thing about wolf pack members is they make up easily enough, and since she was the one with the human hands, Owen felt pretty good that she was in the same boat with them. Well, served her right for being one of the ones who kept them in captivity, too. Now she knew what it felt like.

"Except to bring you here after they dumped me here, I haven't seen any of them. I don't even want to think about what they plan to do with us."

Kill them, if what the murderers did with the others was any indication. But Owen didn't plan to die anytime soon. And he doubted David, Elizabeth, or Lila felt that way either.

But what to do now?

"Someone's walking around up there. Someone's making gingerbread. Otherwise, I haven't heard a soul talking. I think we're in Millinocket. We've been here about an hour. I'm hoping Kintail will be sending the cavalry soon."

But to where? Unless Lila had left a trail of wolf tracks, Owen doubted Kintail would ever find them. Or if he did, it would be too late.

———

As soon as Faith, Cameron, and Gavin reached Leidolf's cabin, he hurried outside, but before they explored the renovated cabins for evidence the hot tub guys had been there, she wanted to speak with Leidolf, *alone*.

"I have to talk to you." She grabbed his arm and led him back inside his place. She glanced at Cameron and his expression said he understood and would stay with Gavin while she had her little discussion.

Her heart was beating so hard with concern over her father, she was sure Leidolf could hear it. She closed the door and moved across the sitting area to the other side of the cabin to ensure that Gavin would not hear their conversation.

Sure of himself as usual, Leidolf crossed the floor to join her. "If this is about your father…"

She scowled. "It is."

Leidolf shrugged. "He should've kept the *lupus garou* secret until the day he died, Faith. As a sociologist, he should have been aware of how important keeping our identity hidden is to us. He should have realized we couldn't have allowed him to publish his research or give a lecture on it."

The blood drained from her face as her eyes watered and her stomach hit the wood floor.

"He's not dead. I didn't mean that. But he is in my jurisdiction, and I couldn't allow him to threaten our kind with exposure. He was working on the speech again after you left, still hoping you'd get the flash drive back to him because he was afraid he might have omitted some important details."

"So… what are you going to do? About my father?" Her voice sounded ghostly faint, as if she hadn't the strength to fight him on this.

"It's done, Faith. He was a loose cannon. Now he's one of us."

It took a minute or more for that particular news to soak in. "A red?" she squeaked. "You made my father a red wolf?"

Leidolf smiled in his arrogant way. "It's the best kind of wolf there is."

Her head swam with the notion as she tried to gather her wits and recall previous conversations with her father. "But I talked with him. He seemed himself."

"I gave the order once you arrived here. Once I realized you were still in pursuit of the flash drive. That was the reason you wanted to see Hilson. I tried to warn you he wasn't in a good mood. I wanted to prevent you from seeing him, afraid he'd turn you. But as it was, he'd already left the area for the time being."

She didn't give a damn about Hilson. Her father was who meant the world to her. "Where is my father?"

"One of my older females is staying with him, taking his classes at Portland Community College, a devoted listener. He's really quite all right with it."

Faith leaned against the wall, not comprehending any of it. Her father. A werewolf. A red werewolf. And she was an Arctic wolf? And on top of that he had a girlfriend? Who really served as a guard to keep him in line?

"She genuinely cares for him, Faith. And he adores her. Who wouldn't when a woman acts like the ground the male walks on should be worshipped?"

"But it's all a lie."

"Catherine lost her mate ten years ago. None of the males in my pack have impressed her in all the years she's been with the group, according to others. I haven't been in charge all that long. But she truly cares about your father. She has one of those nurturing personalities and she needs to feel needed. So they're perfect for each other. He's worried about you, though, knowing now that Hilson was an Arctic wolf, who had stolen his research. Catherine's reassured him I'm looking after you."

"You could have told me, damn it. You could have let me know what you'd done."

"You weren't a *lupus garou* at first, although I suspected Cameron would soon change that. Not on purpose. That's why we don't like to have newly turned *lupus garous* running around on their own. Too unpredictable. They make dangerous mistakes."

"My father's a red werewolf," she said, her voice soft and rife with disbelief.

Leidolf touched her arm. "He's going to be just fine. Better than fine. He's giving a speech on the observations of a group in search of Bigfoot in the wilds of Maine instead. And he's really happy, although he wants to hear that you're all right."

Faith glowered at him, then headed for the door. "You could have let me turn him. Then he would have been an Arctic *lupus garou* like me. What's he going to think when he learns I'm a white wolf when the urge swamps me?"

"I'm sure he'll love you just the same."

She growled and paused at the door. "If he's disappointed in me…"

"If it's any consolation, he talks nonstop about you to Catherine. And she's dying to meet you."

"But your kind don't mix. You said so."

"We'll make an exception just this once."

Faith watched Leidolf's expression for any hint he was lying to her. "He really is all right?"

Leidolf smiled. "He's fine."

She frowned again and grabbed the door handle. "He should have been an Arctic wolf." Because then he would have joined Cameron and her newly formed pack. Now he was going to be in Leidolf's pack? She told herself if he was happy, she was happy, but it wasn't really sinking in. Until she realized what the matter was. She always took care of him. He'd expected it of her ever since her mother left him. And now Faith had been replaced by another woman.

Faith looked back at Leidolf. "I'm not needed anymore."

"I'd say someone else needs you more now." Leidolf shrugged. "It's just the way of things."

"He'd better be as happy as you say." Then she yanked the door open and when Cameron and Gavin saw her scowl, she figured she'd better let them know everything was all right in a hurry, and smiled. "Ready to find the killers?"

But both Gavin and Cameron looked like they'd missed one hell of a conversation, and she knew Cameron would be dying to find out what she learned once Gavin wasn't listening in.

When they reached the first of the cabins under renovation, the party climbed onto the porch where the windows were all boarded up.

"Charles said they'd had some vandals come in and break the windows and tear up the cabins, which is the reason for the renovations." Leidolf peered through a couple of slats.

"Ah, there," Faith excitedly said as Cameron lifted her high enough that she could peek between the upper slats of wood covering one of the picture windows. "There's all kinds of stuff in there."

"Renovation materials," Leidolf said.

"No, there." She poked her finger at the window. "See on the floor next to the sofa. An empty package of chips."

"I don't see anything from this angle. And besides, the workmen could have left it," Leidolf said.

Faith didn't believe it. Well, Leidolf could be right, but she didn't want to believe him. "Let's find a way in."

Before Cameron could put Faith down and use his lock picks on the door, Leidolf pulled out a set of his own.

"Standard keyset?" Cameron asked.

Leidolf gave him a warning look, then opened the door.

Both Cameron and Gavin pulled guns. Leidolf and Gavin entered first while Cameron stayed with Faith on the deck. Then Gavin shouted, "All clear."

Faith entered with Cameron, but before she checked out the potato chip bag, she smelled something else. The redhead, named Chris. She turned to Cameron, but the look on his face said the same thing. But not only him, the other two men, and the woman, and the smell of gingerbread.

"Sense anything?" Leidolf asked.

"They've been here," Faith said, barely breathing, thankful now that she hadn't gone looking for these men alone.

"How long ago?" Gavin asked.

"Not today. Maybe yesterday." Cameron looked under the cabinets.

Faith smelled gingerbread next to the couch. She looked under the couch. Nothing but dust balls. She pulled out the cushions. The second one hit pay dirt. A empty package of gingerbread cookies from Specialty Cookies, Millinocket.

"Is this a processing plant in Millinocket? Or a small business? Maybe a family-run business?"

"It might just be sold at the grocery stores. Anyone could buy it," Leidolf said.

Faith cast him a frown. "Let's ask George Roux. Maybe he'd know."

But first, they explored the other cabins under renovation. Every one of them had evidence that someone had been eating in the places. Maybe sleeping here. Watching the comings and goings of the guests and owners?

Suspecting that maybe Charles and his family were in with the werewolf culture? And that brought something else to mind. "When Charles was injured at his campsite, we thought it was Kintail or his men. What if it was Chris and his thugs instead? Maybe because he does business with Kintail and Chris and his Dark Angels believe that he's in on the werewolf business."

Gavin shook his head. "I've heard some crazy things in the police business and in our private eye concerns, but this really takes the show for the most bizarre."

Leidolf exchanged looks with Cameron as if he was warning him the trouble he could be in with keeping his friend on the mission.

They mounted their snowmobiles and headed back in the direction of the lodge, but when they reached Cameron's place, Trevor drove toward them, waving for them to stop. He seemed so agitated, she knew the news couldn't be good. And because he was here to tell them, she figured it had to do with David and Owen. Cameron's whole body went rigid. She imagined Gavin's did, too.

"They've got them," Trevor hurriedly said. "They've got David and Owen and Lila, too. And one more of our females."

She didn't have to ask who had taken them. She felt light-headed as if the knowledge Cameron's partners were at death's door delivered a blow to her brain. Instantly, her thoughts switched to the day the little neighbor girl ended up missing. About how hard they tried to find her before she was murdered. About how they were too late.

She broke the silence first. "Are they in Millinocket?"

Trevor's eyes teared up and he wiped his nose with his gloved hand. "We think so. We think they're not dead yet. But every second they're gone…"

"Let's go," Cameron said. "We'll tear the town apart."

"Wait." The men all turned to hear what Faith had to say. "Is there a place called Specialty Cookies in Millinocket?"

"Near the library. Yes," Trevor said.

"All right. We'll check the place out while we're at it."

Cameron waited for her to speak further, and she could have hugged him for believing in her. "Let's go," she said, and reached out to squeeze his hand.

His grip was gentle, but hers was not. She wanted him to know she was in this for whatever it took, damn the consequences. And he seemed to understand.

Then the five of them took off for the trailhead, first dropping by the location where she'd left her snowmobile when she'd had the urge to shapeshift—and she hoped the hell she wouldn't do that again anytime soon.

From the snowmobile rental shop, they could pick up her SUV and Cameron's rental car. Although her SUV fit five, the backseat was awfully small for three adults, so she figured they would divide up and a couple of the men would take Cameron's vehicle.

And then like Cameron said, tear the town apart.

Chapter 20

EVEN THOUGH KINTAIL AND HIS MEN WERE SCOURING Millinocket, he hoped the hell Trevor had gotten word to Cameron and the others since they were more equipped to handle investigations. Kintail, although normally in control and never rattled, felt like the proverbial chicken with its head cut off as he searched down every side street, drove past every home, but there wasn't anything to say, "Here's the house where your werewolves are being kept hostage," and he didn't feel he was getting anywhere—totally useless, at a complete loss as to what to do. But more than anything, he couldn't help worrying about Lila. She'd really gotten under his skin.

He pulled his gray pickup off to the side of the road. Even though he'd intended to leave Hilson and Whitson safely behind at the lodge, they both had insisted they come along to be part of the pack despite their injuries. Since he'd arrived in town, even Adams, suffering from his concussion, called him on his cell phone from the hospital, wanting to join in the search.

Kintail said no to that, but if Adams acted anything like Hilson and Whitson, Kintail doubted he had any control over his pack members, all of whom wanted to help save Lila and the others, and all who knew in his present state of mind, no meant maybe and that's all they needed to hear.

His phone buzzed and Kintail saw it was Trevor. Thank God. "Yes."

"We just made it to town. We're on our way first to Specialty Cookies. Faith thinks it might be a lead."

"We're on our way there now." He hoped to God the woman was right, and they found Lila and the others before it was too late.

———❦———

"There it is," Faith said, pointing out the window while Cameron drove her SUV. They'd meant to split up the passengers, two in Cameron's rental, and the rest in Faith's because the seat was really crowded for three men to squish in back there.

But everyone, Leidolf, Gavin, and Trevor did just that, squished together in the backseat, because Cameron wouldn't let Faith ride with them in the back instead of one of the men, and the men all wanted to stick with the woman who seemed to be in the know.

"I know it's a real long shot." Faith didn't want them to think she knew for sure, but she was used to following dead-end leads in her work, and she figured both Cameron and Gavin would realize that. But Trevor and Leidolf might not.

"It's the best shot we have right now," Cameron said, his voice attempting reassurance, but an edginess was evident.

But all that kept going through her mind was a little girl with dark curls and dark eyes and a winning smile who drew pictures on the sidewalk in colored chalk across the street from her parents' home, annoying the eighty-year-old next-door neighbor who claimed it was graffiti and hosed it down every chance he got.

The day of her disappearance, he hosed down the last memory of her, and that was the last Faith remembered of the smiling little girl. Faith stared out the SUV's window and fought the tears. She thought she'd gotten over the memories so long ago. But every time she had a case like this where the victim was still possibly alive, she felt the same cloud of doom, feared the same ending.

And all she was left finding was the killer on the loose, the victim sacrificed for yet another meaningless cause.

"Faith?" Cameron said, touching her shoulder.

She clenched her teeth and looked at him.

"We're here."

"Right." She grabbed for her door handle, but Gavin was already opening the door for her. And then she saw the quaint little house with the gingerbread trimmings like lilac lace and the rest of the house painted in garish pink, reminding her of Hansel and Gretel and the witch who lived inside with her big oven and children made into gingerbread ornaments in the front yard. Here a white picket fence enclosed the small front yard, and a sign hanging between white porch columns said: SPECIALTY COOKIES, OPEN MON-WED, 1-5 PM.

It was Thursday, so no problem there. Cameron led Faith up to the front door, but none of them bothered to knock. Leidolf whipped out his lock picks and opened the door as if he were a master thief, quietly, without making a sound. Thankfully, there wasn't any kind of an alarm to let the occupants know someone had come in through the front door. But Gavin gave Cameron a look and Faith assumed he wanted to know what business Leidolf was in where he carried lock picks wherever he went. That made her curious, too.

The entryway had a quaint little parlor filled with two antique love seats, curved mahogany legs and seat backs, and bright yellow floral fabric. A counter with an old-time cash register sat nearby. And a plastic display contained chocolate fudge of various kinds— vanilla, with nuts, without, chocolate, next to it, the aroma mouthwatering. But deeper inside the house, the fragrance of gingerbread filled a kitchen, which was decorated in yellow, bright and cheerful. Antique platters and plates and paintings gave the place an old-world feel, but the splash of constant color made it more Alice in Wonderland in appearance, when ironically Faith thought it could be a front for a bunch of "Dark Angel" lunatics bent on killing werewolves.

While Faith investigated each room thoroughly, Gavin, Trevor, and Leidolf hurriedly explored every room throughout the two-story house and the basement also, looking for any sign of hostages or hostage takers.

Cameron stayed with Faith, his gun ready, protecting her while she looked in every kitchen cabinet, in every drawer for some kind of clue.

Just cooking supplies and cooking utensils, nothing else. But then she found a drawer full of receipts. Again, for cooking supplies, shipping orders, nothing that would indicate whoever owned this place was involved in hunting werewolves. She moved on to the basement, but she didn't smell any of the men who had visited them at the hot tub.

"You don't smell them here, do you?" Cameron asked. She shook her head.

She walked to the second floor up the creaky wooden stairs covered in an old worn tapestry muffling her foot-falls and examined the two bedrooms and bath when she got there. All were very feminine with frilly curtains, frilly bedspreads, frilly lace pillows, in frilly pink and purple colors. She looked in the drawers. In one, the folded sweaters were big and bright. In another, she found underwear, all white. In another, she noticed a bright, neon pink strap of bathing suit fabric beneath a pair of denim shorts. She reached for the strap and pulled the bathing suit out and stared at it. The woman in the hot tub. The woman who had seen Bigfoot. Mary.

In the other room, the chest of drawers was completely devoid of clothing. Downstairs in her office, they didn't find anything but her billings to customers and to grocery stores in the area.

"I'll…" Trevor started to say when the front door swung open and Gavin and Cameron pointed their weapons at the entrance.

Kintail held up his hands in surrender, his amber eyes darkening, narrowed. "Just me. Find anything?" he asked Faith, looking at her as if she was the only hope he had in the world.

"A swimsuit," Trevor eagerly said. "She's one of them. A woman."

"Older, gray-haired, heavy-set, Mary McNichol's her name," Cameron said, holding up an invoice.

"And the men?" Kintail asked.

"It appears they've never been here. We couldn't find any trace of their scents." Faith looked back at the kitchen.

"But there was an empty bag with her cookie company's name on it at one of Charles's cabins that's under renovation. We smelled all of them there. So they work together, only the men must avoid her house for some reason."

"Do you have another clue?" Kintail asked.

"No, but if we split forces, we could ask various business owners, like these grocers," Faith said, pointing to a list of the places Mary sold to wholesale, "if they know Mary and have any idea about a redheaded Chris and a dark-haired Matt. It's worth a try. Surely someone's seen the woman with the men, and they'll know last names and an address."

"I'll go to the grocery store here," Trevor said.

Kintail waited for Faith to say where she planned to go. "I'll be checking out the lodge where Cameron and I first stayed. A clerk I talked to knew a lot about you and your wolves. Maybe she knows something about Mary and her friends," Faith said.

Kintail looked like he wanted to go with her, but she handed him a list, thwarting him. "You might want to have your people check out these other businesses that dealt with her. Before long, everything will be closing. So we need to hurry."

Almost in panic, Kintail immediately began snapping orders to his men, while Cameron escorted Faith back to the SUV, with Gavin and Leidolf joining them.

"If we make Faith one of our partners," Gavin said, walking with them back to her SUV rental, not leaving Faith and Cameron's side for an instant, "we could sit back and watch her work and she could solve all our cases for us. Of course we'd provide her with protection. Think that could work?"

Cameron opened her door for her and shook his head at Gavin.

"I don't know," Gavin said, smiling, "I really think she's worth taking a chance on."

But she wondered if he'd think so if he knew what she and Cameron had become. She climbed into the front passenger seat and watched as Leidolf came around to the left side of the car and climbed in. She thought he was going to go sleuthing on his own. He'd been so quiet all along, she wondered what he was thinking.

But when they got to the hotel, she saw just what he intended to do. After getting a room so he could use the Internet and one of the lodge's guest computers, he sat down at one in the lobby and began searching through websites, looking for the Dark Angels. Gavin remained with him while Faith and Cameron got a room for the night.

Unfortunately, the clerk who'd been on the desk the evening they had arrived wasn't here tonight. But when Faith described her to the man at the desk, he said, "Sissy? Yeah, she knows everybody's business. We learned a long time ago if we wanted a rumor spread, tell Sissy. If you don't want the world to know, mum's the word around her."

"But she'll be on duty here in the morning, right?"

"First thing, six in the morning."

"Good, that's my kind of time." She took Cameron's hand and led him to Leidolf's table as he surfed the Net, barely pausing to see what she wanted. "We'll be in Room 213. What's your room number, Leidolf?"

"It's 442. Gavin can stay with me."

"If you find anything, let us know, okay? We're going up to the room to discuss plans."

A small smile lifted Gavin's lips, but he didn't say anything. Leidolf glanced up from the computer screen and frowned at Cameron. "Remember what I said, Cameron. We do things differently. Once you reach a certain point, there's no turning back. Not for us."

"I'll keep it in mind, Leidolf. Thanks for the advice." But Cameron sounded like he was peeved that Leidolf would mention it.

But she understood. Being a pack leader, Leidolf was used to taking charge of a situation. He probably didn't trust Cameron and her to follow the rules of their society, yet. And he was probably right not to trust them. At least, she figured some of the rules might need to be broken.

Cameron walked back out to the vehicle to get a single bag for each of them, then he led her to the elevator. "You really were talking about discussing plans to locate David and Owen, right?"

"Absolutely. I have to assimilate what I've seen. I kind of categorize everything in my mind, run over it mentally, back and forth, until I come up with another idea. There's no one way to do this. Something triggers something, and then that triggers something else. And then we've got our man, or woman."

"Or three men and a woman."

As they walked to their room, Faith said quietly, "Or more."

Once they were settled in the room, Faith pulled off her parka, hat and gloves, kicked off her snow boots, and climbed onto the bed. "Want to order some room service?" She leaned against the pillow and closed her eyes.

"You're going to go to sleep?"

She didn't open her eyes. "This is how I think, Cameron. Really. I have to have absolute quiet, shut down everything but my mind, so I can think."

"What do you want to eat?"

"Salmon. If they have any."

"What did Leidolf say to you?"

Faith opened her eyes and narrowed her gaze at Cameron. "My dad's a red wolf, damn it, and he has a red wolf girlfriend. And he's happy with everything that's transpired." She snapped her eyes shut.

Cameron moved in close to the bed and kissed the frown on Faith's forehead. "He's alive and well, and that's all that's important, Faith, honey. That's all that matters."

Afraid that her father might have been eliminated, or would be soon, Cameron was damned relieved her father was fine.

She quit frowning. "You're right." And then she didn't say anything more.

He watched her, worried that she was going to fall asleep on him when every minute that passed meant his partners were at risk. Then he gave up and ordered the salmon dinners. Every officer, every investigator had their own methods to work things out. Some looked over evidence a million times, some had to visit the crime scene to visualize what might have occurred, everyone did something a little bit differently. Combing through the physical evidence was more his style, so just thinking about random happenings didn't work for him.

For a while, he stared out the window at the parking lot, trying to figure out where they could look next, hoping that Kintail's people would pick up another lead, or that Leidolf would. He glanced at Faith. Her breathing seemed shallow. Hell, she *had* fallen asleep.

He kicked off his boots and joined her in bed, pulling her against his body, her head resting on his shoulder, her hand planted on his stomach, her inner thigh pressed against his thigh. Breathing in her subtle lavender fragrance, he felt the shaft of desire slamming into him. Every sense on higher alert—the sound of her soft intake as she took a deep breath, her fingers spread across his belly in a tantalizing touch, her leg draped over his as if screaming *I'm yours, take me*—keenly affected him. Ever since he'd felt he'd nearly lost her when she was in her wolf form, he'd been forced to realize how much the woman was already part of his life. How much it would kill him if she no longer was.

He stroked her hair, his other arm wrapped around her, holding her close, enjoying the moment of silence, of peace, wishing he didn't have to worry about his friends being in trouble at a time like this, when there was a knock at the door.

"Room service," a man cheerfully called out.

Cameron slipped out from under Faith and headed for the door. When he opened it, the man rolled in the cart, the same one who had brought him the steak the first night Cameron had been here. The man glanced at Faith, and Cameron expected him to smile at the sight of her sleeping on the bed, figuring he'd have remembered her slipping on her boots while Cameron was wearing only a towel, and that the lady was more or less a permanent guest of his, when Cameron noted a tattoo on the man's hand.

The words *Dark Angel* in small print stood out as if the letters were as visible as a billboard on a high speed highway.

Faith opened her eyes and took a deep breath. "The food's here."

The man was already edging toward the door, his eyes wide. Something clued him in about who Cameron and Faith were, or maybe just Faith, but he wasn't waiting for his tip and that confirmed Cameron's suspicions.

The man turned to bolt. Cameron tackled him to the floor. The guy was wiry, flailing with arms and legs, trying to connect with anything that might help him break free, but with his stomach pressed against the floor, he didn't have much leverage. If Cameron hadn't needed him to be coherent, he would have just as soon knocked him out.

"Who is he?" Faith asked, as she hurried to get Cameron's gun from his holster on the bedside table.

"One of them."

The man's green eyes widened even more when he saw Faith pointing the gun at him. "Where are they?" she asked, in a voice that bordered on dangerous.

He grew very still.

Someone knocked on the door, and Faith called out, "Yes?"

"It's me, Gavin."

Cameron nodded, still pinning their Dark Angel conspirator to the floor. Faith went to the door, but had the gun poised just in case Gavin wasn't alone.

She might not be a police officer, but she sure knew what she was doing.

Gavin said, "Leidolf found their website and—" That's when he stared at the gun Faith was wielding, although she lowered it quickly, and then he saw Cameron sitting on the Dark Angel. "Holy hell, who's he?"

"Brought our meals, but he gave us the wrong brand of tartar sauce," Cameron said, sarcastically, pointing at the man's hand bearing the tattoo. "He recognized us, started to book before he had his tip. Now the question is, what kind of torture should we use on him to get him to reveal our partners' location?"

Gavin closed the door, stalked into the room, and stood with his boots pressed against the top of the man's head. "We're werewolves, right? So why don't we turn into wolves and start eating body parts? Slowly."

The man began to tremble. He might think he's a killer, but he wasn't anything more than a scared pup, probably talking big when he was with his *gang*. Without them as moral support, egging each other on? He was nothing.

Faith crouched next to him. "Gavin's teasing. He's got an *insanely* sinister sense of humor. Werewolves don't exist. But their partners' lives are at stake, and right now, I doubt I can keep them from torturing you so they can learn their location. If you don't think they'll do it, believe me, they've used some techniques even I can't stand to watch. And I've seen some pretty hideous stuff, being a forensic scientist."

Gavin raised his brows at Cameron. Cameron gave him a small smile back. The woman was worth her weight in diamonds.

"We've seen you change," the man bit out, his words muffled with the way Cameron was pressing him against the hotel's carpeted floor.

"Me?" she asked and Cameron detected a hint of alarm.

"Not you, specifically. But some of the others."

Cameron figured Gavin wouldn't believe any of it, so he assumed the best way to get the truth out of the guy was to play along with it. "My partners?"

"They're wolves right now. The bastards are in a cage nice and safe and sound—for the moment."

Hell, didn't sound good. Did they have the shape-shifting trick down pat? Or would they inadvertently shift at the wrong time?

Gavin grunted. "Hell, you've got some of Kintail's wolves and think they're David and Owen?"

"We saw them shift, damn it. Them and some woman they had with them. They buried their clothes and shapeshifted near where Kintail's lodge was. Surprised the shit out of us. We were watching the lodge, ready to get any of his men who ventured out of the place alone, when these three ran for the barn like the devil was after them. Then in a few minutes, they headed for the woods as others from the house shouted they'd escaped. At first we assumed the three of them were prisoners, and we thought to rescue them from Kintail's people. Then we'd solicit them to join our group."

He squirmed a little, but Cameron tightened his hold on him.

The man groaned and quit resisting. "After they started tossing their clothes, we changed our minds. You sure as hell turn fast. One minute a man or woman, the next a wolf. If I'd looked away for a second or two, I would have missed the whole episode. But it wasn't the first time we'd seen it happen. When we were on that trip with the hunter guide, Trevor Hodges, looking for Bigfoot? We got separated from him, and then we saw Kintail's woman shapeshift. We wanted to tell Trevor and Kenneth O'Malley, the weird dude who kept taking notes. But then we thought they wouldn't believe us. So we kept them out of the loop and changed our focus from hunting Bigfoot to werewolves. For a long time, we just watched Kintail and his wolves. And then we decided to act. Why should they pretend to be normal people like us? So we killed them with silver and it worked."

"Anyone can die from a lethal injection of silver. Even anyone as stupid as you," Faith said.

The man's eyes widened, then narrowed. "Says you."

"If you're so well read up on stuff, you could easily find out that what I'm saying is true. In fact, we could run to the health food store tonight and get some silver supplements to feed you. See how long you live. Hell, how do we know *you're* not a werewolf?"

He scowled at her. "We wanted you to join our team. We thought you'd understand us. But it seems you're one of them now. Either that or just clueless." He didn't say anything for a few seconds, then took up with his story again. "So here are your friends running as wolves through the forest in the direction of Charles's resort. We figure he's either a wolf, too, or a friend of theirs. The next thing we knew, Kintail's men were in hot pursuit of your partners and that woman. At first, we just observed them, not sure what to do. Then we figured, what the hell. We have what it takes to show who's superior. Who shouldn't exist. And we showed off our guns, and that made their pursuers run away like scared little rabbits. So much for them being bad ass wolves. Didn't take long for us to run your partners and the woman down and dope them up. We got Kintail's main squeeze, too."

"Where are they?" Cameron growled.

"If I tell you, you'll kill me."

"Quickly, mostly painlessly," Gavin said. "Believe me, you don't want a wolf eating at your organs while you're still alive. That's got to hurt, *lots*."

"I don't know where they are, exactly. They took them to one house, but Chris said he'd moved them to another later. Just in case anyone might have tracked us."

"Why not kill them like you did the other men?" Cameron asked, still puzzled about why they'd keep them alive this time.

"Hell, we could just kill all your sorry asses. But we'd have to do it secretly, and someone would eventually try to arrest us for mass murders. So we have to prove you're werewolves. And then, we can become famous for finding the first real werewolves. Fame, fortune, we'd be able to make public appearances on all the talk shows, maybe even get honorary degrees. If we were in England, the queen would even knight us."

"Lead us to the house Chris had taken them to," Cameron said.

"Change into a wolf. You're not going to shoot me with that gun. And you can't scare me like this. Shapeshift, growl at me, bare those wicked teeth. Then I'll take you there. But I can't guarantee they'll be there."

"Sorry, we're all newly turned. We can't just shape-shift any time we want to," Faith said shrugging.

"But I can shift anytime I want to," Leidolf said, and everyone turned around to see him standing in the doorway, his amber eyes lethal.

Chapter 21

HOW IN THE HELL HAD LEIDOLF UNLOCKED THE DOOR? Cameron's lock picks wouldn't work on key card slots. And how long had he been standing in the room listening? The guy moved like a phantom.

But he got the Dark Angel's attention.

"Do it, tough guy," the man sassed back as if he didn't really have the faintest idea how dangerous Leidolf could be.

Maybe it was Cameron's heightened senses that clued him in, besides the threatening tone Leidolf used, or the look of aggression on Leidolf's darkened face. But a scent of a coming battle hung in the air. Of murderous intent. An alpha who would show the beta he wasn't one to be messed with.

"Gavin's not one of us," Leidolf smoothly said, his voice still deep and dark, his fierce gaze locked on the man's eyes. "Can't do it in front of him."

The man studied Gavin, who was looking every bit as menacing. "He said he was one."

Leidolf smiled, but the look was pure evil. "He might wish he was, but he isn't. Trust me."

"Whatever. Have the dude leave then."

"You won't like what you see when I shift."

"It's the only way I'll feel intimidated enough to tell you where they are."

"Fine." Leidolf glanced Gavin's way. "Leave, before it's too late." The way Leidolf said it wasn't as much of an order, as more of a challenge.

"Sorry, I'm staying for the show."

Hoping to encourage him to leave before his partner lived to regret it, Cameron said, "Gavin."

Gavin shook his head. "We're all on the same team, no matter the circumstances."

Cameron knew his friend would not believe this one iota, but Leidolf wasn't waiting, wasn't about to try to talk any sense into him, and began stripping out of his clothes. Faith looked like she was going to be sick. She caught Cameron's eye. He knew what she was thinking. If Leidolf went through with this, Gavin had to be changed. And the man who tried to sound so brave, would die once they located the house where their partners were being held hostage.

She left to put on her boots, not bothering to watch Leidolf get naked and shift.

Cameron watched the man, saw the stupid smirk on his face. Gavin observed the Dark Angel's expression, too, probably wondering how Leidolf's stripping out of his clothes was going to force this man to reveal anything to them.

But as soon as Leidolf growled, baring his teeth, his nose and face wrinkling, his eyes narrowed with dangerous contempt, and his hackles raised as a highly pissed-off red wolf, he garnered everyone's attention. For a moment. Cameron quickly glanced at Gavin to see his take. Faith was watching him, too. But Gavin was still observing the man's posture, seeing if Leidolf's threats were working, as if he didn't need to see what Leidolf had become. As if he already knew.

The man had quit smiling, and he was trembling again, but even so, Cameron didn't feel as though he was ready to spill his secrets. That's when he released his hold on him. That's when the man started to sit up, and that's when Leidolf lunged at him with a fierce snarl that made Cameron both respectful and proud to be one of them.

Faith quickly turned on the television to help drown out the sounds in the room.

The so-called Dark Angel threw up his hands to instinctively block his face. Leidolf clamped down on one of his hands, and the man screamed out in pain.

He looked like he was about ready to faint, his skin turning ashen, his eyes rolling into the back of his head. Leidolf quickly released him, then stepped aside, shifted, and dressed. "He's one of us now," he said with menacing conviction. He glanced at Gavin. "You should have left the room when you had the chance."

"I wouldn't have dreamed of being left out of this little adventure."

That's when Cameron suspected Gavin had seen Faith shapeshift on the trail. So his partner had truly already known.

Leidolf gave Gavin an evil smile. "He'll make a good pack member." Then he turned his attention to the Dark Angel passed out on the floor. His hand was bleeding, but Leidolf hadn't crushed the bone like he could have.

"Are you sure he's one of us now?" Faith asked, pausing to pull on her parka. "What if he isn't?"

"He's one of *my* kind, I should say," Leidolf said in that arrogant way of his. "Which means I'll either have to eliminate his sorry ass if he causes me any grief, or take him back with me and make him part of my pack. Although there is a slight chance I didn't change him.

He still won't be sure either way. So he's ours, pliable once we revive him."

"I'll get some ice," Faith said, but Gavin stopped her.

"I'll get it."

Faith looked at Cameron as if she feared Gavin was getting ready to run. But Cameron knew his partner better than that. He handed him the ice bucket. "Fill it to the top."

Kintail knew they were getting closer to finding Lila, Elizabeth, and Cameron's partners. He smiled at Trevor, unable to hide his own deviousness. He still had it in mind that Faith would be his if Lila wouldn't change her tune and David and Owen would remain with the pack, although he couldn't stop thinking about Lila and how his taking Faith would affect her. Some distant niggling kept warning him he couldn't do it to her, that he had to give Lila more time.

But as far as Leidolf went, he didn't believe the red would interfere in his plans, being that this wasn't his territory, he was a red, and he wouldn't want to mess in Kintail's pack business.

Cameron and Gavin were another story. He didn't believe he could let them live if he wanted to keep Faith and their partners.

"So we've found six leads, but this looks like the best one yet?" Kintail asked Trevor, raising the list of leads he'd scratched off.

"Yeah. Just waiting for your go ahead."

"Let's go."

"What about letting Cameron and the others know?"

Kintail smiled again and Trevor shook his head.

"Kenneth O'Malley saw Lila shift, didn't he?" Kintail asked Trevor for the hundredth time.

"At the time, I didn't think he had."

Finally, his pack member was being honest with him. "That's just what I thought."

They climbed into his truck, and Kintail glanced into the backseat of the King Cab. Hilson was sound asleep. Whitson was dozing and snapped his head up. "We got a lead?"

"Yeah, this time, it's got to be the right place." But how to kill the bastards without the residents of Millinocket believing Kintail's wolves had done the deed?

—◊◊◊—

Owen figured if they could maintain their wolf form, he and David would be a hell of a lot more intimidating than as naked humans if the men tried to come into the basement. Armed with guns though, the werewolf killers would be a hell of a lot more menacing. Still, they had to chance rushing them, if nothing else. Somehow, they had to get upstairs and out of this place. Once they did, he figured they could hightail it back to Charles's cabin resort, meet up with Cameron and Gavin, and take it from there.

Lila was standing at the top of the steps, her ear to the door again listening. She looked back at them and shook her head. "But Kintail will be here soon to rescue us," she said, her voice hushed and more hopeful than trusting.

For the first time, she seemed vulnerable, and Owen thought a little bit frightened. He knew this could all go badly for them in a split second. He didn't have any illusions. The werewolf killers were trigger-happy nutcases and if he and David didn't do what they needed to do to make the outcome right... they could all be dead.

"Someone's coming," she whispered, her voice half excited, half worried.

Showtime.

Sarge, so named because he'd been in the army before he had been dishonorably discharged for illegal drug use, held his injured hand, now wrapped in a hotel hand towel, the blood spotting the white terrycloth. His face wore a scowl, but he was trembling hard as he climbed into the SUV seat between Leidolf and Gavin.

"You didn't have to bite me, damn it," Sarge said to Leidolf. "You were only supposed to growl."

"I growled, and you weren't talking," Leidolf said, his voice darkly amused.

"Yeah, but hell, now I'm one of you."

"Yeah, you are. So now your buddies will want you dead," Gavin said. "So start talking. Where'd they take them?"

"If I tell you, they'll kill me."

"You're alive with us, so far. It's the only chance you've got," Cameron said, glowering at him from the front seat. "Either start talking, or Leidolf will bite you again."

Sarge looked at Leidolf, probably figuring he wouldn't dare change in the vehicle.

"Windows are darkly tinted, Sarge. Better do as everyone says," Faith warned.

Sarge tightened his wounded hand against his chest. "Two-hundred East Dover. I can't guarantee that they're there. I told you that already. Chris said they'd move them after a time."

"Which way?" Cameron asked.

"Take a right at the next light. Head straight for six blocks, then turn right on Amy."

Cameron roared off, then made the six blocks in record time. Faith wanted to tell him to slow down or they'd get picked up by the cops, and then what? But they reached Amy without incident and after turning right on the street of little brick homes, Sarge said, "Next street is East Dover. Seventh house on the right."

"Whose home is it?" Faith asked.

"Matt's. He lives with his girlfriend, but she's working late at a hamburger joint tonight."

They pulled up six houses down from the brown brick house. Then, with Sarge in tow, although Cameron wanted Gavin to wait in the vehicle with Faith—she opted to stick with the group—and they headed for the house. Gavin had a gun, and they might need all the firepower they could get. She didn't need to be protected in the SUV.

Cameron didn't argue with her, although he didn't seem to like it that she'd go along. Gavin did argue with her, but he wanted Cameron to stay and protect her. Leidolf didn't say a word. And Sarge started to say something about staying behind with her, but all three men cut him a glare and he shut up.

Cameron and Faith went around the back where birdbaths were covered in ice, and bird feeders filled with snow were hanging in a number of trees. Gavin went to one side of the house. Leidolf took Sarge to the front door and knocked.

The place looked dark and quiet. No lights, no chimney smoke, no movement, nothing.

Faith was pretty sure no one was home. Which meant that either Sarge was lying, or Chris had moved their hostages like Sarge said he would.

Within minutes, Leidolf was opening the door to the backyard. "No one here. Why don't you come in and see if you can get a clue."

Faith, Cameron, and Gavin hurried into the house and began searching the place. In the basement, she and Cameron got a whiff of Chris and his companions. And they smelled wolves. But since Faith and Cameron had not smelled David and Owen since they'd been changed, they couldn't tell for sure that it was them. Although they suspected it was.

"Wolves have been here," Faith said, lifting a couple of white hairs off the cement floor.

"Where to now?" Cameron asked Sarge, glowering at him as if he was ready to change into the wolf himself and bite him somewhere new.

"I told you—"

"Where!" Cameron snapped.

"We can check Chris's house. It's on the other side of town," Sarge rattled off really quickly.

"Let's go." Cameron grabbed Faith's arm and hurried her up the stairs.

Barely able to keep up with his long stride, she said, "Might be easier if you just tossed me over your shoulder and hauled me to the car."

Gavin chuckled.

In a deviously sexual way, Cameron smiled at Faith. "If you're asking me to do it, I'd be happy to oblige."

"No, it was a subtle way for me to say, 'Slow down,' so I could keep up."

But he didn't slow down, and she had to run to keep up, although she couldn't blame him. She didn't want him telling her she should have stayed in the vehicle.

Suddenly, the headlights of the SUV flicked on and the vehicle drove in their direction. When it stopped, she wondered how in the world Leidolf had gotten to the rental vehicle that quickly. Then she recalled he had already left the basement before Cameron began dragging her up the stairs.

"Where is Chris's house?" Cameron growled.

Sarge hesitated only a second before he began giving the directions in a hurry.

The door swung open into the basement, and at that instant, David and Owen jumped from the top steps where they were waiting in rabid anticipation and knocked down the blond-headed man who was in their direct path. He didn't have time to squeal or shout, his blue eyes round with shock when Lila came out of the opening and swung a cane at him, striking him in the head, either knocking him out cold or killing him. Owen didn't have time to check him out or even care. David made sure Elizabeth stayed behind him, protecting her as if she were his mate already.

Freedom loomed in front of them, the door to the outside just down the long hall that opened onto a living room. Before Owen could navigate it, a redheaded man stepped in front of the door, wielding a damned gun.

Owen didn't hesitate. Kill or be killed, and he leapt, farther than he ever thought he could manage. Only leaping and dodging bullets was another thing. The weapon discharged and Owen felt the damned projectile lodge in his chest at the same time he slammed into the redhead. At least Red couldn't shoot David or Elizabeth or Lila.

He grabbed the man's raised arm and bit before his mind faded into darkness, his last thought, he saved them. He'd saved his friend and the two women. Then his thoughts dissolved into oblivion.

Kintail looked at the damn list again, his blood boiling with fury that Cameron and Faith had already been here in this house, already searched every inch of it, and without sending him word. "Where the hell are they?"

Trevor jumped in the truck. "They've been at this house. All of them. That Gavin, Leidolf, Cameron, Faith, and some other man I've never smelled before. Do you think it's one of the Dark Angels? Do you think he's guiding them to the members' houses?"

"Hell, yeah. And from the blood we smelled, I'd say that one of the *lupus garous* resorted to pressure to convince the guy of making the right choice."

They drove off down the street and headed west. Trevor looked over the list. "Here's a house we haven't checked yet. It's on the other side of town. Supposed to be Mary's nephew's place. Maybe check there?"

Kintail drove in the direction Trevor gave him. The moon was waning, lights in the town winking out for the night, but the aurora borealis lit up the dark sky in a flashy display of greens and mauve almost as an omen. The wolves would win tonight.

———

"Chris's house," Sarge said, pointing at a white clapboard that blended in with the snow.

As it grew darker, the aurora borealis flowed across the sky in an unbelievable array of colors from a blending of mauves and greens, dizzying and magnificent. Faith felt as though she was witnessing a dreamlike light display, as if she had fallen into a fantasy world where the sky was full of shifting, flowing, colorful lights and the ground a palette of ice-white frozen whipped cream. A world where men and women could turn into wolves. That's when she realized that she had changed when the moon was waning. So the tales of how werewolves could only shift during the full moon wasn't true. What of when the new moon was present? Or did they never get a break from the threat of shifting?

"He'll be well armed," Sarge warned, breaking into her thoughts. "He'll kill every one of you."

"He can try," Cameron said, jerking his door open. He glanced at Faith, but she was already getting out of the vehicle.

"No, Cameron. I'm not staying behind." She hurried with Leidolf and Gavin, who wedged Sarge between them in case he tried to bolt.

Cameron slipped his arm around Faith's shoulders and held her close, his touch protective and caring. "You can't blame me for wanting to keep you safe."

She smiled up at him. "I'd worry if you didn't."

That's when gunfire rang out inside the house, and Faith's blood chilled. Before anyone had time to react, a green all-terrain vehicle barreled out of the driveway and sped down the road. Cameron released Faith and rushed for the door with Gavin and Leidolf, his hand firmly on Sarge, as she caught the license plate number. Their guns drawn, Cameron and Gavin kicked the front door open, then rushed inside with Leidolf and Sarge.

But a gray pickup rumbling toward her caught Faith's attention. *Kintail*. She frantically waved at him to follow the green ATV, and Kintail gunned the engine and tore off after him.

Seeing Chris's fuzzy red hair sticking out the front entryway where he must have fallen, Faith hurried up the front steps. Inside, she saw Lila hiding behind a grandfather clock, a cane readied in her hands while she watched down the hall where Gavin, Cameron, and the others must have run.

A white wolf was lying motionless next to Chris, who appeared to have passed out, but was coming to. That's when Faith saw the gun lying on the floor next to Chris's injured arm.

She bolted for it, but not before he grabbed the weapon and pointed it at her, his green eyes on fire. "You're one of them, aren't you? We thought you could be one of us." He scooted himself up to a sitting position against the wall, but he was losing a lot of blood. "You're my ticket out of here."

She froze only a couple feet away from him. If he shot her, she'd be dead. He couldn't miss at this distance.

"Out the back way," Cameron shouted to the others from deeper inside the house, oblivious to her plight. The door slammed open and banged against a wall.

But she figured Lila saw what was going on with her. Lila could have helped. But then again, maybe not. She only had a cane, and from where she was standing, she couldn't easily reach the lunatic. "If you shoot me, you won't have any leverage," Faith reasoned.

He dragged himself up the wall, leaving a streak of blood in a wide stripe on the rose wallpaper. "If I don't take you hostage, I'll never make it out of here alive. Come closer."

She didn't move an inch in his direction. He seemed so wobbly she didn't think he could walk, he was having such a difficult time even standing against the wall.

"Come here!" he snapped.

But she wasn't going anywhere with him, no matter how much he commanded her. And then without warning, a wolf snarled and snapped behind her. Where Lila had been, only the cane and her clothes were left behind and a wolf now stood, with light brown almond-shaped eyes narrowed in contempt. At Faith.

But then she realized what the woman, wolf, wanted. Faith moved out of the path of Chris's gun, and Lila leapt. The bastard got a shot off and Lila yelped, but she still managed to tear at his throat. Chris slid to the floor and let out his last breath. Her heart pummeling her ribs, Faith closed her eyes. What would they do now? Wolves would be accused of killing a man. Even if in self-defense. And Lila and the other wolf were dead—which one was he? David or Owen?

Then she saw the first wolf stir. He wasn't dead? She rushed to him and ran her hand over his body, leaned over and listened to his heartbeat, steady, tired, but he wasn't dead. She searched the wolf's body again and found a dart. A tranquilizer dart. Thank God.

She reached over and ran her hand over Lila's head. "Thank you, Lila." The wolf that was Lila stared at her for a moment, closed her eyes, and growled sleepily.

Then the gray pickup roared back in front of the house, its front grille crumpled some. Had the werewolf killer gotten away? Kintail stalked out of the truck, up the walk, and into the house, while Trevor rushed to keep up with him.

"Lila," Faith said, stroking the wolf's head, although after she said who the wolf was, she figured Kintail would have already known and thought she was an idiot for telling him. But hell, most of the wolves all still looked the same to her.

Kintail's hard face looked sick with grief, but Faith quickly explained, "They've been shot with tranquilizers."

"Owen, too?" Kintail said, crouching down to lift Lila into his arms, and Faith thought his tenderness toward the woman indicated he'd had a change of heart concerning taking Faith into the pack. "That's Owen?" Somehow she figured he'd have been bigger, taller. Less furry. She wondered what Gavin's take would be on all this, when she suddenly realized there was no sign of David or the other woman who was supposed to have been taken hostage.

"Where are Elizabeth and David?" Kintail asked.

"Cameron and our friends are with them." She hoped.

Kintail grunted, then he headed out to the truck with Lila. Trevor opened the truck's door for Kintail. But then Faith worried that Kintail may just still try to take both her and Owen with them. She slammed the front door closed and locked it. Kintail glanced back at the house, his look treacherous.

He could look mad all he wanted, but she wasn't going to go with him while Cameron and the others were chasing down the killers. Still, she wanted to see if David was all right. Then Kintail stormed up the walk, his expression still furious, and she figured he'd huff and puff and threaten to blow the house down.

"Open… up… Faith," Kintail growled, and he sounded as if he could knock the house down with his fierceness.

Chapter 22

HER HEART RACING, FAITH HOLLERED TO KINTAIL THROUGH Chris's locked door, "Cameron's hunting down the other killers. You've got Lila back. You can take care of how to deal with the cleanup/cover-up, whatever you want to call it. But Cameron and his partners are all returning to the Northwest, and I'm going with them. So like it or not, that's what's going to happen." She wasn't sure about the woman he called Elizabeth, so she left her out of the equation on purpose.

She halfway expected Kintail to act civilized. To let them alone. But when the cedar chair that was sitting on the front porch crashed through the picture window, she realized he didn't mean to play by her rules at all. She considered the cane. If she swung it just right, she might be able to knock him out. But then again, what if he was expecting her to do something like that? Not like when she hit the wolf with the snow shovel the last time. He hadn't expected it. Kintail most likely would.

She glanced at Chris's gun. As soon as she lunged for it, Kintail jumped through the window frame as a wolf. She screamed, but grabbed the gun and didn't hesitate to shoot him, at the same time as she heard footsteps at the back of the house. Kintail knocked her down, the dart not putting him out like she'd hoped. But she didn't dare shoot him again and risk killing him with too much tranquilizer.

Kintail's front paws pinned her chest down, his weight suffocating, but she couldn't see who was running down the hall. What if it was a Dark Angel?

Kintail looked back.

Cameron swore under his breath. "My bullets might not be silver, but they're like Gavin's. They can give you some heartburn. So move away from Faith, and I'll pretend this didn't happen."

She swore Kintail almost smiled. Maybe because Cameron didn't take any crap off him? She wasn't sure. But he did step away.

Afraid he still might leap at Cameron, she held her breath. Would Cameron shoot him? She suspected he would.

"You've got to take care of Lila and your pack. Take care of this mess so your wolves aren't blamed for it," Cameron said.

Kintail looked back at Chris. And then he turned and jumped out the window, stumbled outside and landed on his belly, the drug finally taking effect. Hilson and Whitson hurried out of the pickup and with Trevor, the three of them managed to carry their wolf pack leader out to the truck.

"You all right, Faith?" Cameron asked, his long stride eating up the floor to get to her.

"I'm fine. Where's David and the other woman?"

Cameron pulled Faith off the floor and into his arms. "He runs faster than we do. He chased Matt down and dropped him. The woman stayed with him. Think he's found someone to call his own. The blond guy? He took off in the ATV."

"What will we do with Matt?"

"Turn him over to the police."

"Adams and Whitson? But they're Kintail's people."

"Officer Adams is out back. He's willing to turn Matt in to take the blame for the killings, saying that they were fanatics who murdered some of Kintail's men. None of them can prove werewolves exist, and the police department needs to resolve the crimes."

"What about Chris?"

"Kintail can say his wolves were protecting him. Lila okay?"

"Sleeping like Owen… and Kintail."

Gavin hurried into the house with David and Elizabeth, Faith guessed, still in wolf form, and Leidolf and Sarge. "Owen all right?"

"Sleeping," Cameron said. "Let's get him into the SUV. Leidolf?"

"I'm staying a while longer to ensure there are no more of them." He patted Sarge on the shoulder. "He's going to help me."

Sarge looked as though he was going to be terminated at any minute. She wondered, given Leidolf's expression, if he recognized the man hadn't been turned. If so, he'd be up on murder charges also.

"Gavin?" Cameron asked.

"I'm ready to get back to Seattle and the job. Think we could rent a bigger SUV and travel that way instead of by plane?"

Faith wrapped her arm around Cameron. "As far as I'm concerned, that's the only way we should travel, considering."

"A woman after my own heart," Gavin said.

"Only she's got mine," Cameron said, giving her a comforting squeeze. "Help me lift Owen, and let's head back to the lodge. You can make the reservation for a full-sized SUV for our return trip. Leidolf, we'll see you around?"

"Find a pack to join, Cameron. You can't do this on your own as newly turned *lupus garous*."

"I guess this means you owe me a diamond ring and marriage license, Cameron, if we're going to make this official," Faith said.

"No jewelry, no weddings," Leidolf said, his voice slightly amused. "We can't wear jewelry. It's too difficult to shift quickly if we're wearing rings and the like. And we don't marry, we mate. That's why you need to be with an established pack, so you can learn our rules."

Faith glanced at Sarge. "What about Mary?"

"Mary McNichol? Chris's aunt? She's harmless, a big believer in Bigfoot and that's why she was running around with our gang. But she never was one of the Dark Angels, didn't believe in werewolves, no matter how many times we tried to convince her they were real. That's why we never let her in on the killings. She would have turned us in. She just wanted to be with us in case we spotted Bigfoot. And Chris, especially, hoped she'd change her mind."

Faith sighed, glad to hear the older woman hadn't taken part in the murders. "Why did you do it, Sarge? Why kill them?"

"We thought we were doing the world a good deed. That's what we thought. Then we figured if we could get money, it would be even more of a good thing. We didn't think we'd get caught."

"What about the trees cut down on the trails?" Faith asked.

Sarge shrugged. "We were trying to create a mess for Kintail's people. Harassing maneuvers."

"And Charles?"

"Hell," Sarge said, scowling, "he's either one of Kintail's people, or he helps them conceal who they are. So he *is* one of them, no matter what. We just wanted to give him a wake-up message. Watch out who your friends are. Could be dangerous for your health."

Faith hoped the bastard didn't turn, and he was tried for murder. Someone as evil as that didn't deserve to be in Leidolf's pack, or anyone else's.

Leidolf's expression was revealing though. The more he listened to Sarge bury himself with the deeds they'd done, the darker Leidolf's face became. Then he turned to Cameron and said, "I told Gavin he could have my room for the night, share it with David and Owen. I'll be sticking with Sarge until I'm assured we've finished with business here. And, Faith? You're one of us, even though you'll be with an Arctic pack. But anytime you visit your father, you're part of my extended pack."

Faith pulled Cameron close. "And Cameron and his partners?"

Leidolf gave them an elusive smile. "Sure, as long as no one plans to stay long. Only one alpha leader per pack. Anything else would cause real problems."

Faith wondered how that would work with Cameron and his partners. Owen and Gavin both seemed to have real leadership tendencies. She wasn't sure about David, but he might be more the emergent kind of leader when the others weren't around to take charge, he'd step right in. None of them seemed very beta to her.

"I'll see you again soon then," Faith said with promise, because she had every intention of seeing the woman her father had hooked up with and making sure he really was all right. Although as soon as they returned to the lodge, she was calling him.

"Let's go then," Cameron said, and he carried Owen out to the SUV as David and Elizabeth trotted next to him, and Gavin got the door.

Faith slipped into the driver's seat and Cameron looked at her, his eyes a little rounded.

"My rental SUV, and last time you drove, you were speeding. I thought you were an Eagle Scout and always obeyed the laws." She started the engine.

He smiled and buckled his seat belt. "Always. So no diamonds, and no marriage license, I guess. Uncomplicates things and makes for a cheaper union."

She hmpfed. "We're getting married. I can see Leidolf's point about the jewelry. I suppose in a few years if we've got the shapeshifting business under control, you can get me a ring then. But there's no reason we *can't* get married." She drove back to the lodge, at the correct speed.

Cameron chuckled. "I told my partners I'd never get married. *Ever*. Not after all the girlfriend problems I've had. I really thought I'd be keeping my promise."

"There won't be an engagement if that will help."

He leaned against his seat and smiled.

Gavin said, "I was wrong, Cameron. First time ever. If I had a woman like that, I wouldn't hesitate to make her mine."

The horrible notion slipped into Faith's brain that they had an outsider in the vehicle who had to be changed. "What are we going to do about Gavin?"

"I'm not biting him," Cameron said. "He'll just have to live with us and pretend everything's the way it was."

Gavin shook his head. "Faith can bite me, as long as she's gentle."

Cameron pressed his hand on Faith's thigh. "She wouldn't do any such thing."

Gavin folded his arms across his chest. "I guess I'll just have to keep the secret then."

He sounded a shade disappointed. Faith figured either Leidolf or one of his people would turn him, but it was probably better if they were all the same kind of wolf, in case they tried to do what Kintail had done in Maine, pretend the wolves were his pets, one big happy family.

"Leidolf won't like it," Faith warned. "When he learns none of us ever turned Gavin, he'll probably do it."

"Then Gavin will stay home when we visit your father."

That seemed to be the end of the matter, but Faith suspected it wouldn't be. "What if there's already a pack in Seattle?"

"I thought of that. We'll just have to open a business in Tacoma, or somewhere else. Maybe move to the coast of Oregon. I always liked the beaches down there when I visited. Leidolf said it was a nice place and might be just our kind of area to relocate. We'll just have to see what happens."

"And hope that we don't run into major problems," a deep male voice that she didn't recognize said from the backseat.

Faith glanced in her rearview mirror. David had shifted. The blond, bearded man with vivid blue eyes reminded her of a Norseman as Gavin quickly pulled off his parka and gave it to him.

Yep, their little band of werewolves was going to have fun with this shapeshifting business. She could see it now—all five of them vying to get into the washrooms on a plane home when they all had an uncontrollable urge to shift. Good thing they were driving home.

Kintail woke to find himself naked in bed with a nude Lila curled up against him, sound asleep. He brushed his hand through her golden hair, breathed in her special fragrance, assumed that whatever trauma she had experienced in the past, she was ready to deal with. But he'd take it slow and easy with her in any event.

"Kintail," she whispered to him, her eyes still tired.

"Sleep the drug off, Lila. We'll talk later when you're more awake."

"I'm sorry," she murmured, her hand on his chest, and he could have sworn her touch was possessive, but the tranquilizer kept her from having the force she might have used. Her eyes drifted closed. "You're mine." Even though her voice had a sleepy, drugged quality, her announcement pleased him.

He leaned her back and kissed her forehead. She lifted her lips as if asking for a kiss there. Chuckling darkly, he pressed his lips against hers, but she wasn't awake enough to respond. "Later," he promised, then slipped off the mattress, pulled on a pair of black denims, and

headed downstairs to the great room where he heard
Trevor talking to Whitson and Adams.

"Evening," Kintail said as he reached the bottom step.

His men nodded in greeting, but no one said anything.
Probably trying to figure out if they had an alpha female
pack leader now.

Both Whitson and Adams's bruises had faded to
mere shadows of what they'd been. Hilson was chowing
down at the kitchen table, having a midnight snack, so
he seemed to be feeling better also.

"What's happening with the investigation?" Kintail
asked, stalking into the sitting area, while a fire roared
in the fireplace, and the wind stirred the snow in little
eddies outside.

Adams spoke first. "Matt's in custody and will be
charged with first-degree murder in the cases of Sutter
and Larson. The blond dude we chased in the ATV,
survived the accident and he's up on charges also.
Apparently," Adams smiled a little as he spoke, "the
group was heavily into drugs. Anyway, there's tons of
evidence to prove they were and now it's their word
against ours that they were tripping out when they
spied the werewolves. A woman, Mary McNichol,
never believed in werewolves, according to Sarge. I
questioned her, but she seems sincere, so for now she's
off the hook. But we'll keep a close eye on her. Sarge
is staying with Leidolf until he turns into a red wolf.
So far Leidolf hasn't seen any evidence of a change.
Probably too soon. Leidolf said he'll take him into his
pack. Although if he gets out of hand, Leidolf said he'll
either take care of the matter personally, or hand him
over to you for disposition."

Kintail gave a small smile. "He didn't mean it."

"No. He was trying to emphasize the importance of the guy obeying him while he spoke to me in front of him. He might kill him, that much was evident. But he wouldn't turn the responsibility of the job over to you."

"Leidolf's too much of an alpha for that," Kintail said. "What about Gavin?"

"Leidolf said he'd be turned."

"All right. And Kenneth O'Malley?"

"Already changed, so no more problems with him giving lectures on werewolves, unless he uses old mythologies in his talks."

"Good. Chris's body will have to disappear."

"Done. By the time the spring thaw comes, he'll be nothing but worm food. Matt didn't see what had happened to him. We cleaned up all the evidence that anyone had been killed in the house. We'll be sure to concoct a good story about how Chris went out on one of his crazy werewolf hunts, without his partners, got lost, froze to death, and the animals in the wild found his body a delicious smorgasbord of sorts. Sarge will go along with it, since he was one of his best friends. Believe me, about now the guy is willing to say or do anything to keep on breathing."

"Any other loose ends?"

"Leidolf's making sure there aren't any, and we've got a couple of men with him to help watch his back. But other than that…"

A silky feminine voice called from upstairs. "Kintail."

Everyone turned their attention to the stairs.

Maybe Lila didn't need any more time to get over her past. "Good job, men," Kintail said. "Keep me informed." But the way he said it, he was certain his people got his meaning. Don't disturb him unless the building was on fire.

Then he headed for the stairs, ready to take a mate. For the first time in years, he felt lighthearted and ready to conquer the world.

━━━━

Thankfully, Cameron, Faith, and Gavin were able to sneak David into Leidolf's room at the lodge without anyone seeing him half naked, only wearing Gavin's parka, his legs and feet bare, while Elizabeth ran beside David in her wolf form. And Cameron carried a still-knocked-out Owen, in wolf form, inside.

"Have any trouble, you know our room number," Cameron said to David and Gavin.

"I can see now why Lila was pissed that Kintail was interested in Faith." David smiled at Faith in a congenial way, sitting down on the bed, still looking a bit wiped out. Although even so, he managed to take down Matt just fine.

Elizabeth was sitting next to him still in her wolf form while he stroked her back.

"I'll get Elizabeth a change of clothes in a minute. I don't think Kintail was too happy with me once I shot him with a tranquilizer dart." Faith smiled and wrapped her arm around Cameron. "There's only one wolfish guy for me."

"You should see what she did to Cameron's snowmobile. The rental people weren't too happy about it," Gavin said, "but Cameron, being the big sport he is, said it was his fault when he was trying to stop the guys who stole the machines."

Faith chuckled. "Yeah, Cameron was just afraid what the clerk would think if they knew he had such a violent girlfriend."

Cameron headed for the door with his arm around her waist. "Which is just the way I like you. I get into a fix again, you can rescue me."

David and Gavin laughed. "And us," Gavin added. "Wouldn't hurt my feelings none to have you save my butt."

"I'd say she's been approved as one of the partners." Cameron opened the door. "When Owen wakes, let him know."

"He'll be agreeable," David said. "We're just glad to be kicking for another adventure." He glanced at Gavin. "What are we supposed to do about you?"

"He won't talk," Cameron said.

Gavin shrugged. "I told Faith she could bite me, but she didn't want the job."

David laughed. "The lady's got selective taste." He rose from the bed. "I'll go with the two of you so you don't have to make another trip down here with clothes for Elizabeth."

"Night all," Cameron said to the others, then closed the door. The situation with Gavin could be resolved another day, or left the way it was. All he cared about was being alone with Faith and getting on with the really important business that awaited them.

As soon as Cameron, David, and Faith headed down the stairs, Cameron said, "You know the rules about mating for life, right, David?"

"You're talking about Elizabeth and me?" David shook his head. "We've hardly gotten to know each other. We'll take our time." He raised his brows at Faith as if intimating that Cameron might want to do the same with her.

"It's a done deal where we're concerned," he said, although officially it wouldn't be until Cameron got rid of David. Not wanting to delay the inevitable a moment longer, Cameron hurried Faith to their room.

Their room. Not his or hers any longer, but *theirs*.

Inside the room, Faith fished through her bag until she pulled out a pair of jeans and a sweater. "Will these fit Elizabeth all right?"

"She's about your size," David said. "It should be fine. And welcome to the team."

"Thanks, I look forward to helping you guys out. Guess I need to give notice in Portland. Tell Elizabeth I'm thrilled she's with us. She can teach us what we need to know."

Cameron hadn't considered that, but he agreed the woman could be a real asset to the group.

David said his good nights and with the door bolted, Cameron eyed Faith. She smiled at him knowingly. Ever since he'd seen the angel who had ended up in his room while he was taking his shower after he'd first arrived in Millinocket, he'd known what he wanted to do. Now, he was ready to actually act on that urge. He shoved the cart of cold salmon out in the hall, too late to order anything else.

"I'm going to take a shower, Faith." He wanted to wash the night's activities out of his mind and get a fresh start. Although he hoped Faith might join him.

She nodded and stared out the window at the Northern Lights, their spectacular display still lighting up the sky. He thought about what Charles had said about the magical wolves coming down from the streams of lights. Charles was right. They were magical, and despite being newly turned and not able to keep the shifting perfectly under control, he felt as though he'd always been this way, and he wouldn't give it up for anything.

He took his shower, longer than usual, hoping Faith would walk into the steamy room any minute, but she never did. Finally, he shut off the water, toweled dried his body, then began working on his hair and stepped out of the bathroom.

Just hanging up the phone, Faith had removed her boots and coat and turned to smile at him. "I called my father while you were in the shower. He's fine." He noted she'd been lying on the bed, the covers pulled aside, an open invitation to join her there. She motioned to the ice bucket filled to the rim, a couple of sodas, and two packages of chips. "Dinner. No room service interruptions this time," she said, her gaze taking in every bit of his body, and she looked hungry. He definitely was hungry, and for a hell of a lot more than paltry snacks from a vending machine.

She stood against the windows now where she'd left the curtains open, the aurora borealis still providing a brilliant blending of lights as a backdrop, their room dark otherwise, although he could see with his nocturnal vision as if the lights were on in the room. "Beautiful, isn't it?" she said.

"Beautiful." But he wasn't talking about the lights. He stalked toward Faith just as if he was a wolf on the prowl. Only she wasn't some meek little prey. She was every bit the predator he was: just as clever, just as undaunted in her craving to come out on top. And she was all his.

Her eyes and lips smiled, but before he could pull her sweater off, she was jerking it over her head. He slid his hands around her back, lower to her sweet ass, but didn't feel any panty lines underneath the skintight ski pants. He raised his brows and smiled a little. Worked for him.

He slipped his hands under the elastic waistband, no zippers or belts or buttons to thwart him, and cupped her bare buttocks in his hands. Her sweet flesh was soft and malleable in his greedy grasp. Already, he was hard with need, just the smell of her, the willingness, the way she touched him in return, her fingers tracing his hard back, her body pressed against his. He pulled his hands free and slipped her shirt over her head, revealing a lacy peach bra, her nipples hardened to stiff peaks. Moving a little as if to tease him with her sexy body, her lace-covered nipples brushed against his bare chest, her belly gently rubbing his arousal.

She was his, not Kintail's or Hilson's or anyone else who'd ever had the notion to be with the vision. And she *was* a vision—from her sparkling green eyes clouded with lust, her peach skin soft and sensuous to touch, her golden curls sweeping her shoulders, and the sweet fragrance of her desire for him, soliciting his further attention.

He lowered his mouth to hers as she ran her fingers over his back, her head tilted up, her lips readied for his kiss. And she kissed him back just as rabidly, and licked, and softly bit, then speared him with her tongue like he wanted to do with his cock between her legs. His hands molded to her lace-covered breasts, his fingers tweaking her nipples, her breath coming faster, her heart beating harder, and his own at virtually the same frantic rhythm. Then her hands slipped down his back. Lower, until she was squeezing his ass, and when she did, he unfastened her bra, dragged the straps down her arms and covered her nipple with his mouth. God in heaven, she was perfect.

As soon as his lips tugged at her nipple, she groaned and arched against him. That's when he released her and pulled her ski pants down to her knees, slipped his hand between her legs, and felt her drenched curls, every bit of her eager for him.

"Ready," he said as he reached down to pull her pants off the rest of the way, not willing to let another second go by without getting her to the bed. Then he lifted her under her buttocks, her legs wrapped around him, hugging him tight, her mouth opened to his. He kissed her again, his tongue spearing her mouth this time, and she moaned with pleasure. Her eyes closed and her hands gripped his back as if she was afraid he'd let her go.

But he didn't. Not even when he had her on her back on the mattress. He was between her legs now, her knees raised, her hands stretching out to him as her eyes watched him in anticipation. Her pink feminine lips had flushed to red, her center moist, and swollen with need. He knew she was ready.

Faith was all that mattered now. The feel of her satiny skin beneath him. The fragrance that was hers and only hers. The way she hmmed, and stroked his needs, and cared about him and no one else as he lathed his tongue over one extended nipple and then the other, her breasts swollen with arousal.

She spread her legs farther, inviting him in. And he obliged, filled her wet heat with his thickened shaft, stretched her and pushed and thrust as she gasped and moaned and stroked his back.

He kissed her mouth, felt her smile slightly beneath his lips, as he paused to thrust deep inside her again. And then she shifted a bit, raised her legs over his back, dug her bare heels into his ass, and welcomed him deeper.

Her face was flushed with pleasure as he dove deeper, her heart beating out of control. He shifted a bit to help her climax, inserted his fingers in her wetness and stroked her swollen nub. He wanted the bliss to last forever, but she suddenly gripped his shoulders and stifled a cry, her pelvis muscles throbbing. He watched her sigh and smile, and then entered her again. With wild abandon, he thrust deep inside her, nearing his own climax until he couldn't hold back any longer. He spilled his seed, once again without a condom. A tinge of panic sneaked up on him—what would happen if Faith got pregnant?

Gavin's comment about wolf pups came to mind.

He groaned as her own muscles contracted around his arousal, milking him for every bit of him, but Faith seemed perfectly content. Still connected, he rolled off her and pulled her onto his stomach, then stroked her back. He wasn't willing to join an established pack. But he did think maybe, just maybe, he ought to learn a little bit more from someone like Leidolf, who would give him one of those smirks. Yeah, the newbie *lupus garous* were clueless again. Then again, perhaps Elizabeth could be their resident adviser in all things werewolf.

Cameron held Faith close and stroked her back, feeling himself harden again as she licked his nipple and spread her legs wider over his, inviting his touch. "You know," he said, his voice still raspy, his hands sweeping lower to the tip of her spine, "we can live a very long time."

She rested her chin on his chest and looked at him with those luminous eyes of hers that said she was ready to eat him all up all over again. "Is that a promise, or a threat?"

He laughed. "A promise, this is only the beginning, Faith, honey. Just the beginning."

And Faith knew she'd done the right thing to come here to rescue her father's research from Hilson, even if nothing worked out as planned. She just didn't know that the man she'd wished were part of the amenities in the hotel room when she first found him would truly end up hers after all.

She licked his other nipple, and his hands drifted lower down her backside, his lips and eyes smiling. Yeah, he knew she didn't plan on letting him get any rest tonight. Maybe not for several nights. Maybe not for years. There was something that had changed about her. She still wanted to get up early, but now… she loved the night…

And she wondered how it would be running with Cameron through the woods as wolves, playing and cavorting as they explored them together.

"Good," he said as if reading her mind. "It'll be good."

"Better than good." She cupped his face in her hands as if he was the most precious person alive, and he was. She kissed his mouth, emphasizing how much she wanted him all over again. "Much better than good," she repeated, her voice taking on a silky quality. "It will be magical."

Epilogue

CAMERON'S WOLF PACK WAS OFF TO A BAD START. NOT THAT he expected everything to go smoothly, but hell, he'd hoped some things wouldn't be a pain right away.

He glanced at Faith as she slept in the front passenger's seat of the Suburban, his sleeping bag draped over her body, her parka an impromptu pillow against her window as he drove the long drive back to Seattle. His mate was the only one who hadn't given him any trouble. He smiled, unless keeping him up all night was a bad thing. He yawned.

Yeah, he wouldn't be able to last at this much longer. But damn, he thought someone else could take a turn driving. Owen and David were willing, but both had complained of feeling the shift coming on. Faith couldn't keep her eyes open, and *she* was the morning person!

On top of that, Gavin had shifted twice in the four hours they'd been driving. Twice! They made him stay in the farthest backseat he was so restless, pacing back and forth as a wolf, then occasionally he'd fall asleep, and then shift again. Cameron glowered again at David who grinned like an idiot.

David shrugged as he snuggled with Elizabeth, who slept soundly in his arms. "You know Gavin would have been hell to live with if we ran off in the woods together and left him home alone."

"You could have waited to bite him when we got home. If you had to do the deed at all."

"Owen bit Gavin, not me. And it was all because Owen was sleeping so long and Gavin got worried. He touched his chest to feel his heartbeat, and well, you know the rest. But from what Faith said, she went to tend to your wound and you bit her. So it seems the two of them were in the same boat. What's done is done, in any case."

Same old David. Perfectly laid back. Never any problems. Especially now that he might have found his mate.

Owen scratched his head. "Are you sure we got all the Dark Angels? Are you sure that woman who was Chris's aunt wasn't guilty of complicity?"

"Kintail's men will watch her. And Leidolf said Sarge turned during the night, and he wished he had let me change the guy instead—then we could have had him in our little pack." Cameron smiled at the notion, glad they didn't have to deal with someone like Sarge. But that was the call Leidolf had made to Cameron last night. Leidolf should have known Cameron would have been too busy to answer the damned phone. That time, or the other three times he'd called. What difference did it make that Cameron know anyway? Leidolf was the one who would be responsible for the guy.

"What about the others? What if they say Sarge helped you to locate us because Leidolf bit him?" Owen asked.

"Nah. One of Kintail's wolves bit him when they thought he was going to hurt Lila. That's the story. Lila and the pack will be creditable enough witnesses.

With all of them involved in illegal drug use, Chris and Matt will have a tough time proving they're not lying." Cameron saw hotel signs at the next exit and pulled off.

Owen perked up. "Are we getting something to eat?"

"I don't know about the rest of you guys, but I've got to get some sleep." Cameron looked at Faith. She was now smiling at him with one of those I-need-some-more-loving kind of looks, and he was sure sleeping wasn't what she had in mind.

"Hell," Owen grouched, "I've got to get me a mate."

David chuckled. "You thought you had a rough time finding the right girl for you before, mainly because you were too damned choosey. Now look at what it's going to have to take."

Cameron smiled. No matter how much trouble running a pack of *lupus garous* was going to be, he couldn't do without his partners in crime-fighting. And Faith was the reason to make everything all right again. He pulled into the Mountain View Hotel and figured they could drive later tonight instead.

Unless Faith changed his mind.

The smile on her face said she might just do that.

At this rate, they'd never reach Seattle.

The End

Acknowledgments

I want to thank my family for always being there for me while I dive into my adventures, help me brainstorm when I need them to, and encourage me always. To my fans who continue to write heartfelt letters about how much they love the worlds and the characters I create. To my editor, who loved the tag I'd created for *Legend of the White Wolf* from the very outset, and is a dream to work with. To my publicist, who helps me market my books to the nth degree and no matter how harried she probably is, never lets on. To the art department that makes the most beautiful covers, art any author would be proud of. And to my Rebel Romance Writers who are always there for me through all the worst dilemmas! Thank you!

About the Author

Award-winning author of urban fantasy and medieval historicals, **Terry Spear** also writes true stories for adult and young adult audiences. She's a retired lieutenant colonel in the U.S. Army Reserves, a Distinguished Military Graduate of West Texas A&M, and has an MBA from Monmouth University. Originally from the West Coast, she has lived in nine states and now resides in the heart of Texas. She is the author of *Heart of the Wolf*, a *Publishers Weekly* Best Book of the Year, *Destiny of the Wolf*, *To Tempt the Wolf*, *The Accidental Highland Hero*, and *Deadly Liaisons*.

Heart of the Wolf

BY TERRY SPEAR

A *Publisher's Weekly* Best Book of the Year

"A fast-paced, sexy read with lots of twists and turns!" —Nicole North, author of *Devil in a Kilt*

"Red werewolf Bella flees her adoptive pack of gray werewolves when the alpha male Volan tries forcibly to claim her as his mate. Her real love, beta male Devlyn, is willing to fight Volan to the death to claim her. That problem pales, however, as a pack of red werewolves takes to killing human females in a crazed quest to claim Bella for their own. Bella and Devlyn must defeat the rogue wolves before Devlyn's final confrontation with Volan. The vulpine couple's chemistry crackles off the page, but the real strength of the book lies in Spear's depiction of pack power dynamics...her wolf world feels at once palpable and even plausible."

—*Publisher's Weekly*

978-1-4022-1157-7 • $6.99 U.S. / $8.99 CAN

DESTINY

of the WOLF

BY TERRY SPEAR

Praise for Terry Spear's *Heart of the Wolf:*

"The chemistry crackles off the page."
—*Publisher's Weekly*

"The characters are well drawn and believable, which makes the contemporary plotline of love and life among the lupus garou seem, well, realistic." —*Romantic Times*

"Full of action, adventure, suspense, and romance... one of the best werewolf stories I've read!" —*Fallen Angel Reviews*

ALL SHE WANTS IS THE TRUTH

Lelandi is determined to discover the truth about her beloved sister's mysterious death. But everyone thinks she's making a bid for her sister's widowed mate...

HE'S A PACK LEADER TORMENTED BY MEMORIES

Darien finds himself bewitched by Lelandi, and when someone attempts to silence her, he realizes that protecting the beautiful stranger may be the only way to protect his pack...and himself...

978-1-4022-1668-8 • $6.99 U.S. / $7.99 CAN

To TEMPT the WOLF

BY TERRY SPEAR

"This dark, sexy alpha hero will capture you—body, mind and soul." —Nicole North, author *Devil in a Kilt*

HE'S VOWED TO PROTECT HER—ESPECIALLY FROM HIMSELF

Tessa Anderson is obsessed with wolves, but she doesn't understand why wolves seem to be fascinated by her, and she certainly doesn't know that werewolves exist. Now she's being stalked—but is her stalker wolf or man? And who is the gorgeous stranger whose life she saved, who now swears he'll protect her?

Hunter Greymore is an Alpha without a pack, facing a deadly enemy. When he encounters Tessa, he's alone and injured, but in his attempts to shield her from harm, Hunter discovers that Tessa entices him beyond endurance—and it's only a matter of time before his wild nature can no longer be restrained.

"*Terry Spear weaves paranormal, suspense, and romance together in one non-stop rollercoaster of passion and adventure.*" —LOVE ROMANCE PASSION

"*Enchanting romance with a unique twist!... The characters were so well developed and the writing so superior that it felt real to me, my reactions were as if I was a part of the story.*" —THE ROMANCE STUDIO

"*A fast-moving read with a sizzling romance and danger-filled action that keeps readers engaged to the end.*" —DARQUE REVIEWS

978-1-4022-1904-7 • $6.99 U.S. / $8.99 CAN / £3.99 UK

To Officer Raymond Hawkins, thanks for the ride and the great insight.

To United States Attorneys Jeffrey Taylor and Glenn Kirschner, for your courtroom knowledge and expertise of how the D.C. criminal system works.

To Tom and Bob, for financial brainstorming.

To Dr. Monica Smiddy, who makes my forensics look so good.

To Dr. Alli Guleria, as always, for your help.

To Bob Schule, for your advice and political expertise.

To Tanmoy Mukherjee, M.D., for your medical expertise.

To the charity auction "name" winners. Don, I "hope" I did the name justice. To Julie, Mandy, and Kelly of Hamilton, Petrocelli & Sprissler, I hope you liked your page time.

To Lynette and Deborah, for doing what you do so damn well.

ACKNOWLEDGMENTS

To Michelle, the primary reason I write about strong, independent women.

To Mitch Hoffman, for good counsel, excellent critiques, and well-placed cheers.

To David Young, Jamie Raab, Emi Battaglia, Jennifer Romanello, Tom Maciag, Martha Otis, Anthony Goff, Kim Hoffman, and all at Grand Central Publishing, for helping me every step of the way.

To Aaron and Arleen Priest, Lucy Childs, Lisa Erbach Vance, Nicole Kenealy, Frances Jalet-Miller, and John Richmond, for being so supportive.

To Maria Rejt and Katie James at Pan Macmillan, for all your great work.

To Grace McQuade and Lynn Goldberg, for keeping my name out there.

To D.C. Police Chief Cathy Lanier, for allowing me to see a terrific slice of the job.

To Lt. Morgan Kane, for coordinating everything and being patient and professional.

To Officer Rob Calligaro, thanks for the education and the boat ride.